Meet Me Where the Stars Fall

Lucky and Dee

Summer Lake Silver
Book Ten

By SJ McCoy

A Sweet n Steamy Romance

Published by Xenion, Inc

Published by Xenion, Inc.

First paperback edition May 2023

www.sjmccoy.com

Cover Design by Dana Lamothe of Designs by Dana
Editor: Kellie Montgomery

Cover Model: Sean Rae
Cover Photography: Golden Czermak at FuriousFotog.com

ISBN: 978-1- 960017-05-5

Dedication

This one is for Sean.

I am so thrilled to have your image grace the cover of Lucky and Dee's story. I have no doubt that you will have a long and illustrious career in the modelling world, and I'm honored that this is your first cover.

I also want to thank you for your input to Lucky's character; you gave him a little something extra – and made him a better man for it.

Life knocks us all down sometimes. It's what we choose to do when we're down that defines us.

Fall seven times; rise eight.

With love
J

Chapter One

Lucky placed his elbows on the table and held his head between his hands as he stared down into his coffee. He felt like shit. Maybe this move was a bad idea. Then again, maybe it was just that this morning his mood was like his coffee – dark and bitter.

It had been a rough night. He'd thought – hoped – that he was finally getting past the nightmares, but they seemed to come back with a vengeance whenever he changed his routine. Moving here to Summer Lake was definitely a change.

So far, it had been a change for the better in most respects. Except the nightmares.

Echo came and rested her chin on his lap, staring up at him with those big brown eyes of hers. He didn't know how he'd do anything if it weren't for her. She looked out for him in a way that no human ever had. She woke him every time his demons had him in their grip – she'd had a busy time for the last few nights.

He ran his hand over her head. "Sorry, lady. I'll get it together. I'll get my ass into gear, and we'll go."

She licked his hand and trotted to the hallway, returning with her leash between her teeth.

Lucky blew out a sigh. "I hate putting that thing on you."

Echo sat and put her paw up on his knee. He knew that she hated it, too, but it felt like she was telling him it was okay.

"How about we leave it off today? It's still early; I bet we can get our run and get home before there are any two-leggeds around."

Echo's tail swished across the floor behind her. Lucky took his coffee and dumped it out in the sink. He didn't need it – water and a run would do him more good than sitting around here trying to fix his mood with caffeine.

He let Echo out the front door, and she waited for him at the gate. He hesitated when he reached it, checking up and down the road to make sure that there wasn't anyone around. He wasn't worried about Echo – she wouldn't harm anyone. She wasn't big on people in general, but she was more into avoidance than aggression. Even if someone approached her, she'd come back to Lucky before she engaged with them; she obeyed his every command. But he was also aware that some people were afraid of dogs, and it just wasn't worth the hassle if someone saw her off leash and complained about it.

He'd been right; they didn't need to worry about it this morning. It was still early, and being a week day, he doubted they'd see a single soul down on the beach.

Echo smiled up at him when he nodded and opened the gate. She waited while he closed it behind him and then they crossed the road and jogged along the sidewalk until they reached the steps that led down to the beach.

Once they were down there, Echo ran around him in circles, her gaze never leaving his. He knew what she wanted. She loved the water. It was a pain in his ass to have to give her a bath when they got home, but she was worth it.

"You want to?"

She came to him and sat down at his feet. She sat as still as a statue, except her ears, which pricked forward, quivering as if trying to reach him.

He smiled. "Go swim!"

She let out an excited-sounding little yip as she took off toward the water. Lucky felt some of the tension leave his shoulders as he watched her. She deserved this. She'd earned her retirement as much as he had – as much as any of their team had. She wasn't just a dog; she was a teammate. She'd lived through life-and-death situations with him and the rest of the guys – and saved all of their lives more than once.

He watched her swim. She moved powerfully through the water – but then again, as a former Navy SEAL, that was only to be expected. He walked along the shoreline, keeping pace with her as she swam. Perhaps when the weather warmed up a bit more, he'd swim with her. That thought made him smile. He used to have to swim in water a damn sight colder than Summer Lake, but these days he was retired – he didn't have to, so, he wasn't going to.

Echo swam parallel to the shore as he walked. It was a habit that she'd gotten into whenever he let her go in the lake. She seemed to enjoy it, and it suited him just fine. They'd already covered quite a distance, and he looked up at the larger houses that lined the beach.

The houses and the yards got bigger the farther away from town he walked. He was already familiar with them – he and Echo had been out on the beach every morning since they arrived. He'd never thought that a big fancy house would appeal to him – he had no need for one; there was only Echo and him. But he wouldn't mind a place with a pool. The trouble was, the lots with the best views and enough space for a pool sold for the most money. It made sense that the people who bought them also wanted a big house.

Echo came out of the water and shook herself off before running over to him. He crouched down in front of her and ran his hand over her head.

"You enjoy that, did you, lady?"

She shook herself again, spraying him with water. He had to laugh; he'd swear she did that on purpose – the smile on her face when she did it gave her away.

"Come here." He took her special little towel out of his pocket, and she came closer. He carefully dried her ears, and when he was done, she butted her head against his chest as a thank you.

He got back to his feet. "You're welcome. Are you ready to run?"

She gave a short, sharp bark and started to run in circles around him again.

"Don't rub it in. I know you're faster than me, and you've still got way more energy, even after your swim."

Echo just barked again and set off up the beach ahead of him. Lucky lengthened his stride to catch up with her. After just a few minutes, he was grateful that he hadn't decided to skip their run this morning. He'd wanted to while he was staring into his coffee, but getting out here like this was so much better for him – and there was no question that it was better for Echo.

As they ran on, the distance between the houses that lined the shore grew. These were the big-bucks places. Most of them were set back in the trees, as if they cared more about their privacy than about the view of the water.

He looked up to check how far they were from the house that marked his usual turnaround point. If the other houses cared about their privacy, then this one cared about being noticed. To Lucky, it was an eyesore. It was built on a headland, its terraced grounds leading down toward the water.

The one thing that he did like about the place was that on the lower level there was a big terrace complete with stone balustrade, surrounding a huge pool. He'd never seen anyone there – it was probably just a summer house for some rich city folks – but whoever they were, it looked like they knew how to enjoy their pool time. There was a pool house, an outdoor kitchen with a big, stone fireplace, and a gazebo for shade. It was a great setup.

He slowed his stride when he realized that, for the first time, there were loungers set out around the pool. Maybe the city folks were here to visit? And what did it matter to him? He whistled to Echo, who'd gotten out way in front of him while he'd been lost in his head.

She turned around and came straight back at the sound, falling in beside him and matching his stride as they ran on.

"Sorry about that, lady."

She looked up at him but, not surprisingly, didn't reply. The rest of the guys used to joke with him that she was his ideal woman. She could keep up with him – physically and mentally – she listened to everything he had to say, and rarely said much– although she made her feelings clear when she felt it necessary.

They had a point. He got along with her way better than he ever had with any woman, and it wasn't as though that was going to change now.

As they neared the headland, he kept glancing up at the pool terrace. The house might not appeal to him, but he'd love to be able to swim in that pool every day.

Just as he was about to turn around to head back, he spotted movement up there. Instead of turning, he watched as a woman wandered slowly past the pool, carrying a mug. She was wearing a robe, which made him wonder if she was going to swim. He wouldn't mind waiting around to see her take the robe off if she were. And where the hell had that thought come from?

Echo looked up as if she was surprised at him, too. It wasn't like him to pay much attention to a woman – in any respect. He'd been married when he was in his twenties, but that was half a lifetime ago now. His career had always been more important to him, and since Echo had come into his life, he joked that she was the only female he needed.

He should probably drag his gaze away from the woman and turn around to head back, but there was just something about her. He didn't even know what it was. She wasn't some sexy young thing – he guessed that she was around his age. As he got closer, he realized that she looked as though she'd just woken up. The way she sipped her coffee made him smile. Yep, that was definitely her first caffeine of the day, he could tell by the way she closed her eyes and savored it. Her hair was piled up in some kind of knot on top of her head, but it was messy – another indication that she'd just gotten out of bed.

And what the hell? His dick twitched at the thought of her in bed – *his bed* to be precise. It had been a long time since any woman had caught his interest in that way.

Echo looked up at him again and followed his gaze. When she spotted the woman, she let out a short, sharp bark. Shit! The woman turned at the sound, and her eyes widened in surprise when she saw Lucky.

Lucky met her gaze and gave her a brief chin lift. He didn't know what it was about her, but just looking at her made him smile. A shiver ran down his spine when she acknowledged him with a nod. Damn! She wasn't exactly beautiful but then, beautiful women had never really appealed to him. They tended to be high maintenance in his experience and had a whole different set of values than he did. No, the woman standing on the terrace might not be beautiful in the traditional sense, but there was something about her that was incredibly attractive.

Whatever that something was, it became even more powerful when she gave him a small smile and lifted her hand by her hip – as though she'd been about to wave but thought better of it. It made him smile, and he nodded. She gave him a real smile, but then Echo barked, not wanting to be left out of the interaction.

When the woman's gaze landed on Echo, she paled and gripped her mug tighter before turning and hurrying back toward the house.

Lucky's smile faded as he watched her go. Dammit. He doubted that he'd ever speak to the woman, but he'd already been thinking that she might be a highlight on his morning runs in the future. But if she was afraid of Echo, then she just wasn't his kind of woman – no matter how attractive she might be.

He turned abruptly and picked up his pace, sprinting back in the direction from which they'd come. Echo kept up easily, staying by his side the whole time. She was all he needed.

Dee shuddered when she reached the pool house and slid the glass door closed behind her. Her hands were shaking so hard that she dropped her mug.

"Crap!"

She closed her eyes and drew in a deep, shaky breath. Well, wasn't she a fool? That man down on the beach was gorgeous! Swoon-worthy. Panty-dropping hot. There were dozens of ways to describe a man like that – she should know, she had to come up with new ways in every book she wrote. But the men she wrote about were fictional. The one down there on the beach? Good Lord above! He was about as real as it got.

And he'd seen her, smiled at her even. If she wasn't mistaken, he might have shown a hint of interest – but she probably was mistaken because, *come on*, a man like that would never be interested in her. He probably wouldn't have been interested in her twenty years ago, let alone now that she was in her mid-fifties. And that wasn't her being down on herself. Oh no, that was her simply being realistic.

As unfair as it might seem, men in their fifties often became a hot commodity – at least, they did if they kept themselves in shape like runner-guy on the beach. But women? Even former supermodels who kept themselves in great shape didn't receive the same kind of admiration from men – young or old. Even when they were described as beautiful, it was usually tempered by the addition of phrases like *for her age*.

Dee stared down at the broken mug and puddle of coffee. She needed to get her act together. She needed to get out of her head and into the real world. Any normal human being would be too concerned about the mess they'd just made to be standing here lost in their thoughts.

She spent far too much time lost in her thoughts. But this morning, for once, it wasn't because she was thinking about the story she was writing. So that was something. She smiled to herself. Runner-guy on the beach was something, all right.

His smile! That was one hell of a smile. But then his dog barked. She shuddered again. And what had she done? She'd turned and fled like the coward she was. Not that it mattered. It didn't matter at all. So, she'd made a fool of herself in front of a man she'd never seen before and would no doubt never see again. Big deal, right?

She sighed as she made her way to the sink in the kitchenette that took up one wall of the pool house. There had to be a dishcloth or something she could use to clean up the mess.

If she wanted to find a bright side, at least she hadn't turned and fled from social interaction – tiny as that interaction had been – just because she was afraid of making a fool of herself. This time, she had a legitimate reason for running away. Some people might see it as an excuse, but in Dee's mind it was a valid reason.

That dog! All the little hairs on her arms stood up as she collected the roll of paper towels and went back to start mopping up the spilled coffee. She wasn't afraid of dogs – not dogs in general. Just German Shepherds. Alsatians. Whatever they were called. Just killer dogs like that one down on the beach.

She carefully picked up the broken pieces of mug and collected them in a wad of coffee-sodden paper towels. The sound of her phone ringing startled her so badly that she gripped the broken ceramic in her hand so tightly that she cut herself.

"Shit!" she exclaimed as she dropped it. That was all she needed. She didn't imagine that finger cuts were a big deal to most people, but for a woman who made a living writing, a woman who was currently writing to a deadline, a cut finger was a huge deal.

She grabbed a fresh sheet of paper towel and wrapped it around her finger, hoping that it was just a nick. The speed with which the paper towel turned crimson dashed that hope.

Her phone stopped ringing, and she gave an evil glare in the direction of her pocket when it started up again. Whoever it was would just have to wait. She wasn't going to blame them for cutting her finger – it was her own damn fault – but she didn't particularly want to talk to them, either.

She peeled the paper towel back, prepared for the worst. Then, she let out a little laugh. It really was just a nick. She was overreacting – that seemed to be the theme of the day so far.

Pulling her phone out of the pocket of her robe, she checked the screen and smiled.

"Hey, Emma, sweetie. What's up?"

"Hi, Dee. I hope I'm not disturbing you, am I? It's not too early, is it?"

"No. It's fine. I'm up and about. In fact, I'm out in the pool house already."

Emma laughed. "You are? How come?"

"What do you mean how come? I could be drying off after my morning swim for all you know."

"You could, but we both know that's highly unlikely. What are you up to?"

"You know me too well. To tell you the truth, I brought my first cup of coffee out here, thinking that I'd enjoy the early morning peace and quiet." She frowned at the mess on the floor in front of her. She really needed a coffee.

"But...?" Emma prompted.

"But it didn't quite work out that way. I saw..." She stopped herself. Emma didn't need to hear the story – that wasn't what she was calling for. And Dee really did need a fresh coffee. "Let's just say that things didn't quite go the way I thought. And now, I need to head back up to the house in search of caffeine."

"And do you plan to start work as soon as you're fully caffeinated?"

"Why? Do you want to come over?"

"I wondered if you wanted me to. Jack's mom has Isabel and Daniel this morning. So, if you want some company, I can come over there. But feel free to say no if you don't want me. If anyone understands that you don't need intrusions when you're writing, I do."

Dee thought about it as she let herself out of the pool house and started on the trek back up to the house. If she didn't see

Emma today, who knew how many days would go by before she came back to the real world for long enough to meet up with the younger woman?

"Come on over. Whenever you like. You know that you'll have to take me as you find me. I'd love to see you. I just need to get myself a cup of coffee before you arrive."

Emma laughed. "I'll pick you one up from the bakery on my way through town. How are you drinking it these days?"

Dee closed her eyes and smiled, almost tasting the words as she said them. "If you bring me a bucket of vanilla mocha, I'll be forever in your debt."

"Done. I'll be there in about half an hour, if that works?"

"That'll be perfect. Thanks."

"Okay, see you soon."

Chapter Two

Dee settled back into her chair and closed her eyes as she savored the first sip of the vanilla mocha that Emma had brought her. It was heavenly.

She opened her eyes when Emma laughed.

"You're welcome."

Dee chuckled. "You've always been high up on my list of favorite people, but I think this might put you right at the top. There's a coffee shop right here in town that brews this magical potion?"

"It's not a coffee shop exactly, it's the bakery."

Dee rolled her eyes. "Oh no! Are you telling me that in order to get my coffee, I'll have to face a display case full of pastries, too?"

"I'm afraid so. And I should probably warn you that everything they make is amazing." She got a faraway look in her eyes, and a little smile played on her lips when she said, "I love the donuts; sometimes we go really early in the morning for them when they're fresh. And Missy, you remember Missy, right?"

"I do. I remember her coming to visit you. I forgot that she lives here."

"Yes, she's lived here all her life. And if you were to ask her about the bakery, she'd tell you that the chocolate croissants are the absolute best. But I'm afraid to say that you're pretty much guaranteed to get addicted to whatever you buy in there."

Dee shrugged. "Oh well, I just have to accept my fate, then. Give me a couple of months and I'll be even rounder than I already am."

"Oh, stop it! You're gorgeous."

"Thanks. But what else are you going to say? You're my friend. I know what I am, and I'm good with it. By the time you get to my age, you learn to be okay with the way you look. I'm not bad for an old bird." She laughed and patted her thigh. "Even if I do come with a little extra stuffing."

Emma just shook her head. "I'm not getting into that one with you. I told you what I think – you're gorgeous, inside and out."

"Then, all I'll say is thank you. I appreciate the compliment. But come on, you didn't come over here to talk about pastries and build up my ego. Tell me what's going on with you. How are the babies? I can't believe that you're a mother of two. When you were still in LA, married to the asshole who shall not be named, I used to worry about you having kids with him. Now look at you; you're living out your perfect life with your gorgeous, wonderful hubby and two little ones, who get to grow up in this wonderful place with the two of you for their parents."

Happiness shone in Emma's eyes as she smiled. "I still can't believe how lucky I am. Sometimes, it feels like I'm living a dream. I just don't ever want to wake up from it."

"And what about work? Have you had any interesting projects lately?"

Emma shrugged. "I haven't been doing much lately, no. I've been too busy with the children. You know what it's like as far as screenwriting goes – once you're out of LA, you cease to exist. Not that I really mind."

"Did you ever finish your book?"

Emma gave her a shamefaced smile.

"What?" Dee asked. "What's that look for? What does it mean?"

"It means that I've finished three of them – and I'm half way through the fourth."

Dee frowned. "You have? Why don't I know about this? Who are you working with?"

"You don't know because I haven't said anything. If you want to know the truth, I'm not working with anyone. I didn't want to go the whole route of getting an agent and trying to get a traditional publisher interested. My original plan was to self-publish. But when it came down to it, life kind of got in the way."

Dee gave her a stern look. "We're going to put them out while I'm here, right?"

Emma turned away to look out at the lake.

Dee just waited. She knew that there was a lot more to self-publishing than most people understood. She could understand why Emma hadn't gone ahead with it when she had two small children to take care of. At the same time, she was disappointed that Emma hadn't gotten in touch before to ask for her help.

"I didn't like to ask. We haven't seen much of each other since I left LA. I didn't want to be one of those friends who only got in touch when they wanted something."

Dee reached across and patted the younger woman's hand. "Didn't we used to say we were family?"

Emma nodded.

"Well then."

"I just … I didn't want to pester you. And I knew you had enough on your plate."

Dee set her, now empty, mug down on the table. "I haven't had much on my plate for the last couple years. The divorce was final not long after you moved up here. The only thing I've had going on since then is writing my own books."

That wasn't quite the truth – she'd also had plenty of wreckage from her old life to try to navigate. But she would have had all the time in the world to help Emma if she'd reached out.

"I'm sorry."

That made Dee laugh. "Don't go apologizing. It's all okay. I just want to help out. And now that I'm here, I'll be able to."

"Aren't you writing yourself?"

Dee laughed. "I'm always writing. You know that. But I can fit plenty of life in around the edges – especially if it means helping a friend."

"Okay then, thank you. Now that you're here, I will make the most of you." Emma looked around. "How long have you rented this place for?"

"For the summer. Do you like it?"

Emma laughed. "What's not to like? It's right on the water. You have fabulous views of the lake." She gestured with her arm, taking in the pool and terrace. "This is wonderful. And you even have a dock, don't you? Down on the other side?"

"Yes, there's a dock. But can you see me using it? Don't get me wrong, I like boats, but I wouldn't know how to drive one. And even if I did, I wouldn't trust myself not to crash it into the dock."

"I'm sure you'd get the hang of it. They rent out boats at the marina in the resort. You should give it a try; see how you like it."

"I might just do that." Dee did like the idea of being able to walk down the little path to the dock and hop on her own boat to take it for a spin around the lake. She loved the water, and the weather was already warming up.

Emma waggled her eyebrows. "Although, if you really can't handle it by yourself, we could find someone to captain your vessel for you."

Dee burst out laughing. "Why does that sound so incredibly dirty?"

Emma laughed with her. "You tell me."

Dee looked away. She wasn't sure that she wanted to admit to Emma that she heard sexual innuendo where it wasn't intended far too often these days. Well, she wouldn't mind admitting that she kept hearing it – it was the reason why she did that was embarrassing.

Emma gave her a puzzled look. "What's wrong? You went all serious."

Dee rolled her eyes. "I'm not serious. I'm embarrassed. I'm embarrassed that I'm going through what might be the longest dry spell of my life and – even at fifty-five – I miss it. So, when you talk about finding a guy to captain my ship … " She burst out laughing. "My little mind is coming up with letting him dock in my port, hoping he'll bring his rod and let me use it, and we're not even going to start talking about him being a man of the sea."

Emma chuckled. "You know, if you're in need of a man, you came to the right place. It seems that everyone who comes here meets someone, falls in love, and settles down and lives happily-ever-after with them."

"I know that's how it worked for you and Jack, and for a whole bunch of your friends. And I'm happy for you. It's a different story for me though, isn't it?"

Emma shook her head adamantly. "No. It really isn't. You don't understand. It's the same for the older couples, too. You know about Jack's mom, right? And her sister, Marianne. There's a whole bunch of them. I don't know, maybe eight or nine couples who are all around your age."

"I wasn't even talking about my age. I know fifty-five might seem old to you, but they say – and I believe them, whoever *they* may be – that sixty is the new forty. I'm not saying that I'm over the hill. I'm saying that, for me, happily-ever-afters are what I write – not something that I'm looking for in my own life."

"Why not?"

"Emma! You know more about me than most people do. Why do you think?"

Emma shrugged. "I've been married before, too."

"Once. Everyone's allowed one mistake. You got out, you learned your lesson, and you chose very wisely indeed the second time. I, on the other hand, did not. I didn't make a better decision the second time – in fact, if anything, it was worse. No way on earth do I want to be that woman who's on husband number three. I tried marriage. I suck at it. I went back a second time to test the theory and proved that it was true."

Emma made a face at her. "Okay. I'll drop it if you want me to. But I'm not giving up."

"That's sweet of you, but let's move on."

"Okay. Are you going to tell me what you're working on?"

Dee smiled, and the tension she'd been feeling started to fade away as she told Emma about her latest book. No matter what was going on in the real world, she could always lose herself in her stories. And luckily for her, over the years, she'd gathered a large tribe of readers who enjoyed getting lost in them, too.

~ ~ ~

"Well, hello hello! I've been waiting to see you in here. You're Lucky, right? Dalton's friend?"

Lucky eyed the bartender warily. Dalton had warned him about her. Kenzie – that was her name. He'd seen her when he'd come into The Boathouse with the guys after work. He hadn't talked to her, though. He didn't want to now.

"That's me." His reply sounded terse, even to him.

It didn't put her off. In fact, she smiled and rested her elbows on the bar as she leaned toward him.

"Taryn was right, then? You're going to take a bit of warming up, aren't you? Well, just hang in with me, and I'll fill you in on a few things okay, sugar?"

Lucky just stared at her. That really wasn't okay. Whatever she had to say, he didn't want to hear it – he wasn't interested in friendly advice or local gossip or anything else she might have to say. If he wasn't waiting for his takeout order, he'd turn around and leave without a second thought. But he'd come in to pick up his steak – and Ben, who owned the place, had promised that he'd make sure there was an uncooked steak bone with his order.

Kenzie cocked an eyebrow at him. "I know what you're thinking. You're wishing that I'd shut the fuck up, and go get your order so that you can get out of here, right?"

"Right." He wasn't going to deny it.

She laughed. "You'll get used to me. I stick my nose in where I'm not wanted." Her expression softened. "I know better than most that just because I'm not wanted doesn't mean that I'm not needed. I think we're more alike than you would ever want to admit."

"Alike? You and me?"

"Oh, yeah buddy." She winked at him. "You're proud, and you're smart, and you're strong, right? You don't need anyone. You can do it all for yourself and by yourself."

"Yeah." It was true. That was how he saw himself. It'd been different when he was still with his team. They worked as one. They needed each other, relied on each other – trusted their lives to each other every minute they were deployed. But that life was over now. He wasn't going to explain that to the girl behind the bar, any more than he would tell her that proud, smart, and strong as he might be, he didn't know if he'd make it through the night without Echo.

Kenzie blew out a sigh, apparently – hopefully – getting the message that whatever she had to say, he wasn't interested.

"You're going to be a tougher nut to crack than the rest of 'em. I can tell."

He nodded.

"Well, don't think that means I'm going to give up. If you found your way here to Summer Lake, there's a reason for it. And I'm going to help you figure out what that reason is."

"Why?" He wanted to kick himself. He didn't want to engage in conversation – didn't want to encourage her.

She smiled and reached across the bar to pat his arm. "Because, as I was saying, we're alike, you and me. I know where you're coming from – I'm not claiming to know all the details, and don't worry, I don't want to – but I can see it; I remember it.

"You think that you're all on your own. That you have to fight your battles by yourself. That being strong means you can't accept help – and being proud means you sure as hell won't ask for it. I was the same when I first came here to visit my sister. My life was a mess. I was a mess. But I still thought I had to go back there. I didn't deserve to be here. This place was for happy people who had their shit together. That wasn't who I was – and it's not who you are, is it?"

She held his gaze, but he just waited.

She shrugged. "You don't have to tell me a damn thing. I'm not asking for that. All I'm asking is that you keep an open mind, okay?"

"About what?"

"About the possibility that you're wrong. See, it's not that this place is for happy people who have their shit together – it's that being here somehow helps you get your shit together and find ways to be happy. I don't really know how it works. A lot of it is down to the people – they're awesome, but they can't help if you don't let them in." She chuckled. "Ask me how I know. But there's more than that, too. Maybe there's something in the water. Maybe it's some kind of magic – and I wouldn't normally buy into that shit, but there's something. Something that will get to you – if you let it."

Lucky nodded.

She pushed back from the bar and shook her head at him as she straightened up.

"You're not buying it, are you?"

He gave her a rueful smile. "For what it's worth, I appreciate you trying."

"Fair enough. I can't blame you. I was the same in the beginning. I didn't want to hear it, either." She turned when a guy came out from the back, carrying a takeout bag.

Kenzie took it and looked inside before handing it over. "Ben said to make sure there was a raw bone in there. Is that right? Shouldn't it be cooked?"

"No. Cooked bones splinter more easily – she could choke on it, or it could tear up her insides. Raw bones aren't brittle – and they have way more nutrients."

"Wow. I stand corrected. I'll know in the future. Is it a special treat or can she have one every time?"

"Maybe not every time."

Kenzie laughed. "That's the first genuine smile on your face since you came in here. You love her – her name's Echo, right?"

"Yeah."

"Okay. I'll let you get on home to her. But remember what I said." She winked at him as she rang up his order in the cash register. "I don't mean remember that the chick behind the bar is a pain in the ass. I mean, remember that you don't have to do it all by yourself – and that you can figure your shit out and be happy here – if you give yourself the chance."

"Thanks." Lucky took his change and shoved a twenty into the tip jar.

Kenzie grinned. "If that's hush money to make me shut up, it's not going to work – but I'm still taking it. Thanks."

He had to laugh. "No. It was a thank you – for meaning well, if nothing else."

"You're welcome. Now go on. Scoot. Get yourself home to your steak and your dog. I'll see you soon, I'm sure."

"See ya."

Lucky hurried out through the bar and across the parking lot, relieved to be away from her. She might mean well but … He opened the door to his Hummer and placed the bag carefully on the passenger seat. Maybe she had a point? Nah. Or if she did have a point, it was that he should get his ass home to Echo so that they could enjoy their dinner.

Chapter Three

Dee closed her laptop with a smile and got up from her desk, shrugging her shoulders as she went. It had been a long day, but a productive one. She was pleased with what she'd written. The book was coming along nicely, and she was even ahead of schedule. She pressed her lips together, wishing that she could take that thought back. She didn't allow herself to go there – it was like tempting fate. Whenever she got ahead of schedule, something would come up that slowed her down.

She walked across the office to stand in front of the windows that looked out at the lake. It was later than she'd realized; the sun was setting. It was such a beautiful sight, she wanted to make the most of it. She hurried into the kitchen to pour herself a glass of wine. Instead of going back to look out through the windows, or even out onto the balcony, she let herself outside and trotted down the steps to the pool terrace, gripping her glass tightly as she went. She was already two coffee mugs and one dinner plate down thanks to her clumsiness. She really didn't want to add a wine glass to the list of items she'd need to replace. And more importantly than that, she really wanted to enjoy her glass of wine while she watched the sun go down.

She reached the seating area outside the pool house without mishap, and gratefully sank into the cushions on the big wicker sofa. This was the life! She took a sip of her wine and gazed out at the lake. There was no wind, and the water was calm. The surface moved with gentle ripples that reflected the soft colors of the sunset.

She loved the sunset. She liked to think that the sunset was a reward for a good day – like life was saying, *You did well today. Here – have something pretty.* That would probably sound stupid to some people, but it felt right to Dee.

From where she was sitting, she couldn't see the sun itself – she'd need to be on the other side of the lake for that. But the sky put on a beautiful show of its own. In the short time that she'd been here, she'd come to think of Summer Lake sunsets as being crimson and gold. This evening was different – the pale pinks, yellows, and light blues were less dramatic, but no less beautiful. They were a fitting reflection of her day. There hadn't been anything dramatic going on – in her world or in the story she was writing. In the story, everything was flowing.

She took another sip of her wine. And in her life? That wiped the smile off her face. There wasn't anything dramatic going on – not at the moment. But her life was hardly flowing. She was kind of stuck. Coming here to Summer Lake had been an attempt to get unstuck.

She'd thought that a change of scenery would do her good. And even though she'd been here less than a week, it seemed to be working in that respect. But she was fully aware that she wasn't putting her life back in motion. Perhaps that was okay? Perhaps after the turmoil of the last few years – of her divorce and all the crap that came after it, and then immersing herself in her work, and keeping herself so busy that she didn't have time to worry about anything else — perhaps this was what she needed.

Whether she was doing what she needed for herself and enjoying a little respite from life before she launched into whatever would come next, or she was fooling herself and hiding out while she remained stuck, would no doubt become apparent over the course of the summer. Whichever it was, she wasn't going to stress out about it. She had a beautiful house to hang out in, a beautiful lake to look at — and possibly enjoy from a boat if she got the nerve up — and plenty of work to keep herself busy.

She took another sip of her wine. She was hoping that the boys might come out to visit. She planned to tempt them with photos of the pool and the lake. She was sure that photos of a new boat would go a long way toward convincing them that they needed to come and see her, too. Emma had only been saying the other day that she would love to see them again.

She smiled as she thought of Emma. She'd thought the world of that girl since they first met in LA. Dee didn't even want to try and figure out how many years ago that was. It'd been a long time, that was for sure. Emma had made a big name for herself in the industry back then, adapting novels into screenplays.

They'd first met when Emma was working on one of Dee's books. At the time, Emma was married to a real asshole, Rob Rivera. Dee couldn't stand him, and she couldn't for the life of her figure out how such a sweet girl as Emma had gotten involved with him, let alone married him.

With time, as their friendship had grown, she'd come to understand that Emma was not only sweet, but a little naïve, too. Dee was almost old enough to be Emma's mom, and that whole situation with Rob had brought out her mama bear instincts with a vengeance.

Rob had taken an intense dislike to Dee, and as a director, he'd done his best to make sure that it would be difficult for her to work in LA again. Emma had felt terrible about that, but it hadn't worried Dee. The movie industry wasn't for her. Sure, she wanted her stories to reach a wider audience around the world, but not at the cost of her sanity.

She preferred hiding away and writing to schmoozing with execs in Hollywood. As far as she was concerned, being pretty much blackballed as a writer whom anyone in LA would work with was a small price to pay for helping her young friend escape her horrible marriage and survive her divorce.

She made a face and took a big slug of wine. She'd been an expert on divorce even back then – she already had the first one under her belt.

The colors in the sky faded as she sat there musing about her life. She might not have been able to make a marriage work, but she was a good friend, a good mom to her boys – even if only one of them was biologically her boy. The other one, her former stepson, was a child of her heart.

The next time she looked out at the lake, she had to laugh at herself when she couldn't see it – it had gone dark. She had no clue what time it was. Her stomach rumbled, indicating that it was after dinner time. She looked up at the inky blue sky. Stars twinkled back at her, making her smile. She needed to check with the website that her son, Max, had told her about, but she was fairly certain that there was a big meteor shower coming up soon. Max would be able to tell her, but she liked to figure it out for herself. When she asked, he acted like she was being a pain in his ass, but if she showed interest and talked about what she'd learned for herself, he was thrilled to chat for ages and tell her so much more.

She'd better go up to the house to eat but perhaps afterwards, she'd come back out here with a fresh glass of wine – and a sweatshirt; it was getting chilly, she realized. She wanted to ring the boys, but there probably wasn't much point in doing that on a Saturday night. They'd be out, enjoying their lives.

A thought flashed across her mind that perhaps she should be doing something along those lines herself – enjoying her life. But she chased the thought away. She was enjoying her life; she was just doing it in a different way. She enjoyed sitting in solitude, taking in the beauty of her surroundings, and letting her mind wander – to the stories she wrote, and the ones she made up about life.

~ ~ ~

Lucky kept Echo on the leash while they crossed the road on Sunday morning. He was hoping that it was still early enough that there would be no one down on the beach. But until they got there, he didn't want to risk it.

She looked up at him eagerly when they reached the bottom of the steps. He checked in both directions, but there wasn't a soul around. Slipping the leash off over her head, he smiled.

"The first sign of any two-leggeds and you come straight back to me, okay?"

She barked her agreement as her tail swished across the sand.

"You want to swim?"

She got to her feet and pranced in place, waiting for him to give her the go. He checked up and down the beach again, but it was all clear.

"Go swim!"

He smiled as he watched her bound away, not even slowing as she entered the water. She turned to swim parallel to the shore as he started walking. He'd run soon – once he was awake. It'd been another rough night. He was hoping that he would adjust soon. If change was what brought the nightmares back, with a bit of luck, they should subside once he'd been here for a while.

He watched Echo as he walked. It was warm out this morning; when spring turned into summer, he'd be out of excuses for not swimming with her. Then again, he wouldn't want excuses once the warmer weather arrived. He'd be as eager to get in the water as she was.

He took his eyes off her and looked ahead. He guessed that the rest of the town was probably still in bed. He imagined that most people in a place like this, whether they were tourists or locals, made the most of their Saturday nights. As for his own Saturday night, Dalton had invited him to go over to his lady, Taryn's, new restaurant. Dan Benson, who he was working for, had invited him to go to The Boathouse with the rest of the team, but Lucky had chosen to stay home with Echo – that was his idea of a good time.

Perhaps next weekend he'd make an effort. He was using the excuse that he was still getting settled in. He wasn't against getting involved in life here, he just wanted to have a better handle on himself – and on the nightmares – before he tried.

He laughed when a shower of water droplets hit him, and Echo barked.

"Sorry, lady. I deserved that, didn't I?"

He hadn't even noticed her come out of the water; he'd been so caught up in his thoughts.

She sat down and waited for him to dry her ears. It was a habit that they'd gotten into years ago when she'd suffered an ear infection after they and the rest of the team had spent an entire night in a stagnant pond waiting to make a move on their target. And people thought the life of a Navy SEAL was glamorous!

When her ears were dry, he tucked her towel back into his pocket. "Ready to run?"

She let out a little yip and set out at a trot ahead of him. When he caught up, she picked up the pace and he laughed, chasing after her. He didn't know yet what else his time in Summer Lake would hold for him, but his twice daily visits to the beach with Echo were already making life more enjoyable.

Dee drained the last of her coffee and set the mug down on the table. She didn't think of herself as a hugely outdoorsy kind of person, but she was enjoying this. Last night, she'd watched the sun go down from out here on the pool terrace. This morning, she'd been treated to the most amazing sunrise. She wasn't a huge fan of the East Coast, having grown up and spent most of her life in the Pacific Northwest, but watching the sun rise out of the water here at the lake, had made her wonder about taking a trip. Sunrise at the ocean was something that she now wanted to see.

She got to her feet; her ass was starting to go numb she'd been sitting out here for so long. She reached for the mug, then had second thoughts. She could either go up to the house in search of more caffeine, or she could, if she were feeling brave, go down to the beach. She'd already been down to the dock a couple of times. She felt comfortable there since that was in a more private spot – it wasn't accessible from anywhere except the house and the water. The beach was a different matter. She hadn't seen many people down there, but there had been a few.

She smiled when she remembered runner-guy from the other day. She hadn't minded seeing him down there. Well, she hadn't until she'd seen that big, vicious dog of his. Just the thought of it wiped the smile off her face.

Dogs were the reason that she was afraid of the beach. But if she wanted to be realistic about it, she could decide to just get over it, once and for all. It was just a memory – a memory from almost fifty years ago! Hmm. She'd never thought about it like that before but now that she did, it made her feel pretty silly. Something that happened all that time ago – and that didn't even happen to her – shouldn't still affect how she lived her life.

She looked down at herself. She'd shed her robe, but she was decent enough in a pair of shorts and cami top, and of course a bra – she rarely left her bedroom without a bra. Even if she did run into anyone down there, they wouldn't suspect that her outfit was actually her pajamas.

She looked at her mug again, wishing she still had some coffee to take with her – to give her fortitude. But she knew full well that if she went up to the house for a refill, she wouldn't make it back down to the beach. She could get another cup as her reward afterward instead.

With that thought, she opened the gate at the top of the steps that led down to the beach. That was one thing she loved about this house – everything that needed a lock was operated by a keypad. She'd never been great at remembering to carry keys around with her, but she did have a knack for remembering numbers.

She hesitated half way down the steps. Was this a bad idea? No. It really wasn't. The thought that it might be was just old fears raising their ugly heads. She'd never get past them if she never faced them.

The steps were cut into the headland. Before she reached the bottom, there was a little stretch where she was walking down a path cut through the slope of the land. It was almost claustrophobic, but she focused on the narrow view of the beach and lake ahead of her.

It was silly to get spooked like that, but she couldn't help it. She picked up speed until she was running down the last few steps. Then, she was out on the beach. She put her hand over her thumping heart and laughed at herself.

Then she heard a bark, and when she turned to look, her heart raced even faster. It was like she was reliving her worst memory. She knew it wasn't a flashback; the dog running toward her right now was different. It wasn't the same as the ones that had… In fact, even in her panic, she recognized it. It was runner-guy's dog.

She was so terrified that she stood rooted to the spot. So much for fight or flight; she wasn't capable of either – she froze. The dog had almost reached her, and all Dee could think was to wish that she'd called the boys one last time.

When the dog was maybe ten yards away, she closed her eyes, her hands coming up to cover her face as she prepared to meet her fate.

A piercing whistle cut through the air, and then a shout, "Echo! Return!"

Dee registered the sounds, but they didn't drag her attention away from the dread that she was about to feel vicious fangs sink into her flesh. That dog was about to tear her apart – that was what they did.

Except … It should have happened by now. Why…? She slowly lowered her hands from her face and opened her eyes. The dog was sitting stock still no more than five feet in front of her. It wasn't barking, wasn't snarling, or growling. In fact, the expression on its face looked a lot like a smile. She wasn't going to let that fool her. It was probably smiling because there was enough meat on her to make a decent meal.

"Hey. Sorry about that. You're fine. She's fine. She won't harm you; I promise."

Dee slowly dragged her gaze away from the vicious animal. Runner-guy was standing beside it – smiling! How the hell could he smile when he'd just witnessed her close encounter with death?

She met his gaze but didn't speak. She couldn't. She was shaking like a leaf, and the dog was still watching her closely. Runner-guy looked concerned.

"Are you okay?"

She shook her head rapidly and slid her gaze toward the dog.

"You're scared of her? There's no need to be – I promise."

Dee swallowed.

Runner-guy ran his hand over the dog's head. "Echo, wave hello to the nice lady."

Dee inhaled sharply, silently cursing him for redirecting the dog's attention toward her.

However, rather than snarling and lunging for her as she'd expected, the dog sat up on its hind legs, and waved one paw at her. Dee just stared.

Runner-guy gave her a puzzled look. "Shit! I'm sorry. You're not just scared – you're terrified, aren't you?"

She nodded rapidly. Finally finding her voice she asked, "Can you hang onto it while I slowly back away? If you give me a couple of minutes, I can make it back up the steps and behind my gate."

Runner-guy frowned. "I promise you that she won't hurt you."

Dee let out a small, strangled sounding little laugh. "Forgive me if I'd rather not take your word for it."

He frowned. "You're forgiven. I apologize. We're leaving" He slipped a leash over the dog's head. "Come on, Echo."

He started to lead it away, but to Dee's surprise, it looked back over its shoulder and made a sorrowful, whining noise. And its eyes – the look in its eyes hit her straight in the heart. It was a look she recognized – a look full of love and longing.

"Wait!"

They turned around, and there it was again – that damn dog actually was smiling at her!

"What?"

She gave an embarrassed little shrug. "I… I don't really even know. I guess I feel like I need to apologize. Your dog didn't do anything wrong."

"Echo."

"Excuse me?"

"Echo. That's her name. And no, she didn't do anything wrong. And she wouldn't."

"I can see that now. I get that I might have overreacted."

He cocked an eyebrow, making his opinion on that clear.

"Jeez! Give me a break, would you? I said I'm sorry. I can see that she's important to you. But if you understood what my deal was, you might be a little more understanding." Here she went. Why did she always do this? Why couldn't she just let it go? He didn't need to know – wouldn't want to know. But she felt like she needed to explain herself.

"What is your deal?"

"This is my first time down on the beach. I don't go on the beach because I'm scared. I'm afraid of the beach because I'm afraid of dogs." She sucked in a deep breath. "When I was a little kid, I was playing on the beach by myself. My parents were only a short distance away – they were buying ice cream."

Even as she said it, the scene filled her mind. She could feel herself back there. She straightened her shoulders. She wasn't back there. She wasn't a little kid anymore. She was a fully grown woman, and it was way past time that she got over this.

"Two of those dogs – Alsatians – came running over the sand. I was excited – I thought they were coming to play with me. But at the last moment, a little boy, just a baby really, he was younger than me and I was only five. He started squealing and waving his arms at them when he saw them. They changed direction; instead of coming toward me they went for him. And they literally did *go* for him."

She shuddered and turned away. The therapist she'd worked with a few years ago had taught her not to relive the worst parts of the memory.

"It wasn't pretty. The boy didn't make it."

Runner-guy closed his eyes and shook his head slowly. "I'm sorry."

Dee pulled herself together. "There's no need. I just wanted you to understand." Now, she sounded like a complete idiot! There was no reason for him to understand. All he really needed to do was go on his way – and take his dog with him.

She risked a look down at the dog – Echo, apparently – it, no *she*, still had that same look in her eyes. Love and longing – it was a feeling that Dee was all-too-familiar with.

"If it helps at all, she's not an Alsatian."

"German Shepherd then."

"Nope. Not even that, she's a Belgian Malinois."

"A what?"

Runner-guy smiled, and suddenly Dee remembered that he was one good-looking guy.

"A Belgian Malinois," he repeated. "She's also a veteran of the United States Navy. A former Navy SEAL, to be exact."

Dee looked down at the dog again, and then back up at him. What was she supposed to say to that?

He gave her a rueful smile. "Anyway, we'll get out of your hair and let you enjoy the beach for the first time. And don't worry – we'll run somewhere else in the future."

"You live here?" She wanted to clap her hands over her mouth as soon as the question was out.

"We do. We can find another route to run while you're here."

That hit her wrong for some reason. How did he know that she was just visiting? "I live here, too," she said impulsively.

"You do? Sorry. We're new in town. I just assumed…" He looked up at the house. "I thought it was probably a vacation place."

She relaxed – not knowing why she'd gotten defensive in the first place. "It is. I just rented it. I …"

She managed to stop herself before she started chatting at him – she'd be telling him how long she was here for, and how she knew Emma, and a dozen other irrelevant details, if she got started. Amazingly enough, she was no longer terrified by the presence of the dog – Echo. But that didn't mean that she should start over-sharing with him. The poor guy was probably desperate to get away.

"I'm going to go back up now. But please, don't change your route because of me. I doubt I'll venture down here again. And even if I do –" she shot a look at the dog "– I won't overreact next time. Thank you, Echo."

The dog made a small whining noise, and her tail swished in the sand behind her. To her surprise, it made Dee smile. She gave runner-guy an embarrassed little shrug before turning and hurrying back up the stairs. She risked one look back over her shoulder. He was still there, watching her go. He raised his hand and smiled before turning away. Echo looked up at her with what Dee could only describe as a smile on her face. She held Dee's gaze for a few moments before giving a short, sharp bark and following him.

Well, damn! She didn't feel any fear anymore – if anything, Echo struck her as a real character – not a killer. And runner-guy? Wow! He was … sexy as hell! He was too rugged looking to be described as handsome. He looked as though he'd seen too much of the dark side of life. There was a slightly dangerous air to him. No, not dangerous. She hadn't felt threatened by him in any way. But he wasn't the kind of guy who anyone would want to mess with. It was obvious that he could take care of himself.

She reached the gate at the top of the steps and let herself back in. She really needed that second cup of coffee now. She didn't regret going down there, though. She wasn't sure that she was over her fear of dogs, but she was no longer afraid of Echo. Although maybe she wouldn't see them again – maybe they would change their route and run somewhere else. It was ridiculous to feel disappointed about that – but she did.

Echo was a dog with a story – no question about it. He'd said that she used to be a Navy SEAL dog. Did that mean he'd been a SEAL, too? She'd love to talk to him some more – learn more about both of them. But that probably wasn't going to happen. She huffed her way back up the steps to the house. She didn't need to go getting any ideas about tracking him down and talking to him – she loved to learn people's stories, it helped with her writing. But runner-guy didn't look like the type to open up. And besides, she hadn't even asked his name. If they didn't run by the house again, she wouldn't even know how to track him down.

She smiled. Of course, she would! He was the guy who owned Echo! People would know who she meant if she asked about him. But no. She needed to focus on the story she was writing and not on whatever one man and his dog's story might be.

Chapter Four

Lucky hung back as he followed the other guys across the parking lot to The Boathouse. He didn't know them that well yet, but they were his kind of men. Cal, Manny, and Ryan were former law enforcement and intelligence. He'd worked with enough men like them in his life to know what he was dealing with. They were good people.

Dalton looked back over his shoulder when he realized that Lucky wasn't with them. He stopped and folded his arms across his chest as he waited. Dalton was the one guy here whom he did know. Dalton had been on his team. They knew each other inside out.

"Were you planning on peeling off and heading home?"

Lucky shrugged. "No. I said that I'd come for a beer, but I'm not staying. I want to get home to Echo."

Dalton smiled. "I know. I wasn't going to try and nag you into coming. I just wanted to check in with you before you disappear. We've hardly had the chance to talk. With work finally starting to pick up, you being out of the office most of the time, and me spending all my evenings over at the restaurant with Taryn, I haven't seen much of you."

Lucky smiled. "Let me guess; that's what Taryn said to you – pretty much verbatim – either last night or this morning. You know better than to worry about me; she's the one who's concerned about how I'm settling in, right?"

Dalton laughed. "Yep. And you probably also realize that she expects me to report back in later. So, I can tell her that I talked to you, and that you're finding your feet and settling in just fine, yeah?"

"You sure can."

Dalton's eyebrows drew together. "And will I be telling her the truth when I say that?"

"Sure."

"But?"

"But nothing."

Dalton held his gaze for a moment. "You getting much sleep?"

Dalton knew his deal, but it wasn't something that they talked about. There was no point.

"Echo's helping."

"I'm sure. What are you doing this weekend?"

Lucky hesitated. He knew that Dalton's lady, Taryn, wanted him to go over to her restaurant on the other side of the lake. He wouldn't mind, he liked Taryn. He liked seeing his friend happy. But he wasn't all that enthused about spending an evening in a social setting. He preferred to spend his time with Echo.

Dalton gave him a knowing smile. "I'm not about to suggest that you come over to the restaurant – I get it, but I won't be able to run interference with Taryn for you for much longer, either. What I was going to say is that I need to get some more work done on Adam's house. I've almost finished it now, and it'd get done a lot faster if I had another pair of hands."

"In that case, count me in."

"How do you think Echo will feel about babysitting Star while we work?"

"They'll be fine." Lucky couldn't help smiling, he knew that Echo would enjoy spending some time with Dalton and Taryn's puppy. Although how much work he and Dalton would get done with the dogs there, he wasn't sure.

"We can figure out the details tomorrow. But at least now I can put Taryn's mind at ease."

"Tell her I said hello." Lucky lifted his chin in the direction of the restaurant. The others had already disappeared inside. "We'd better get in there. I'm not staying for long."

"I know." Dalton smiled. "You already said. And like I said, I wanted to check in with you."

"Appreciate it."

Dalton grasped his shoulder. "Don't give me that shit. It's what we do, right?"

"Yeah." He had a point. The two of them, along with the other four guys on their team and Echo, had lived and worked together in life-and-death situations for so long that they had formed bonds that were closer and stronger than most people would ever understand.

That thought hit him hard. He missed the rest of the team. He missed the guys they'd lost over the years. He closed his eyes briefly in an attempt to shut out images that had no place here – not here in this small town, and not here in the present day.

When he opened his eyes again, Dalton was watching him closely. "Are you sure you want to do this?"

"No. I'm going home. Can you make some excuse for me?"

"Always. One condition, though."

"What's that?"

"You call me if it gets bad."

"Will do." Lucky just wanted to go home.

"And I'm going to stop by and see you before I head home later. Okay?"

"There's no need. I'll be fine. I just don't want to be here. I want to go see Echo."

"I know. I'll see you later."

"Okay." Lucky wasn't going to hang around to argue about it. If Dalton wanted to stop by to check on him, he didn't have a problem with that. "Later," he said before he turned around and headed back to his Hummer.

When he reached it, he sat behind the wheel for a minute, just breathing – waiting for the noise in his head to quiet. When it started to subside, he pulled out and noticed that Dalton was still standing in the doorway to the restaurant, watching him with a concerned look on his face.

Lucky raised his hand as he drove past him. Dalton was just going to have to get over it. He'd be fine soon. He just needed to get settled in.

~ ~ ~

Dee was shocked when she looked up from her computer and saw the time. The afternoon had gotten away from her – and the evening, too. Her stomach rumbled right on cue. She really should stop work and find something to eat. If she could ever figure out a schedule – and stick to it – she'd probably manage to get some weight off. But as it was, she wrote without concern for – or even awareness of – the time or often even the day. She stopped to eat when she remembered or when her stomach protested loudly enough that she noticed.

She saved her files and shut the computer down. It had been a productive day. Looking out at the lake, she smiled. It was still beautiful outside. The weather was warming up, and she was loving it. Soon, she'd be able to swim in the pool after she finished working. She loved to swim, and the pool had been the detail that had convinced her to rent this place. The house itself wasn't exactly her style. The interior was comfortable and stylish, she didn't have a problem with that, but the way the place sat up on the headland as if it were trying to show off and lord it over the other, less intrusive, properties made her a little uncomfortable.

She got up from the desk and rotated her shoulders as she headed for the kitchen. It was too late to start making anything substantial. Instead, she foraged through the fridge and the cabinets in search of something quick and easy.

After she'd eaten, she poured herself a glass of wine and carried it down to the pool terrace. She loved that the days were getting longer, and even though she'd worked much later than she'd intended, she was still in time to catch the sunset.

She looked down at her phone when it beeped with an incoming text. A big smile spread across her face when she saw her son's name on the display.

Max: If you're still writing, stop!

She laughed. He knew her too well. And bless his heart, he did his best to look out for her.

Dee: Ha! I already stopped for the day. And I've eaten! Aren't you proud of me?

Max: You think I should be proud of you for behaving like a functioning adult for once?

Dee: Yes! You should know by now that your mother responds well to positive reinforcement.

Max: True. How about... Well done! Aren't you a good girl?

She had to laugh.

Dee: Why yes. Yes, I am. Thank you!

Max: But now it feels more like I'm training a dog than chatting with my mom.

Dee: Thanks a lot!

Max: You know it's true.

Dee: Maybe so, but never mind all that. How are you?

Max: I'm good. Just checking in. I haven't heard from you for a few days. I figured you were probably lost in your book. How's it going?

Dee: It's going great. How about you? What are you up to?

Max: I've been busy in the lab. But I'm taking the night off tonight. I'm going to the observatory with some of the guys. I wanted to let you know that tonight's the first night.

Dee: Of the meteor shower?

Max: Yeah. It won't peak until sometime next week. You should make some plans to get out and watch one night if you want to see it. I thought the more notice I give you, the more likely it is that you'll both remember, and make the time.

Dee: Thanks. You'd be surprised, but I've been spending my evenings outside watching the sunset. In fact, that's what I'm doing right now. This place is beautiful, and I feel safe. There are blankets in the pool house, so I think I'll snuggle up on one of the loungers later and see what I can see.

Max: There's a pool house?

Dee: Yes. I told you that. And there's a big outdoor fireplace that I think can cook pizzas. And a dock too.

Max: Does it come with a boat?

Dee had to smile. She'd known that would get his interest.

Dee: No, but I saw Emma the other day and she told me that they rent boats at the resort. I thought I might give it a try.

Max: ???

Dee: What does that mean?

Max: Give what a try?

Dee: Renting a boat.

Max: By yourself?

She made a face at her phone.

Dee: Unless you want to come and join me?

Max: I'll come soon. I promise.

Dee: You know I'd love that. I wasn't trying to guilt you into it though.

Max: I know. But I want to come see you. See what the place is like. Make sure you're ok.

Dee: Aww!

Max: I talked to Pax. He said that he might be going soon.

Dee loved that her boys were still so close. Max was the only child she'd given birth to, but Pax – Paxton – had come into their lives when she met her second husband. Officially, he'd become her stepson. But it went way deeper than that; she'd come to see him as her other boy. He and Max had become brothers – and best friends. Although the marriage hadn't lasted – hadn't been great – she would never regret it any more than she regretted her first disaster of a marriage. Her first husband had given her Max, and her second had given her Pax – if not in the same way.

She hadn't heard a peep out of either of the men she'd been married to in years. But she and her boys were close. Max lived in Tucson where he worked at the university – and spent most of his time studying the dark, night skies of the desert. Pax had moved to Chicago, and he worked for Dee. He ran the online side of her business and took care of all the online marketing details that made her brain curl up around the edges.

She looked back down at her phone; she knew she was fine to get caught up in her thoughts. Max didn't expect a text conversation to go back and forth like a tennis match. She liked to communicate that way though. If she took too long before replying he'd get distracted doing something else, and who knew when she'd get to chat with him again.

Dee: Yep. We talked about getting him out here in a few weeks. We need to have one of our catch ups and set our goals for the next few months. Do you want to come when he's here?

She watched the screen and was pleased to see the three little dots start bouncing up and down, indicating that he was replying.

Max: That's what I was thinking. Can you let me know the dates?

Dee: We can make the dates fit whatever works for you. Just let me know.

Max: K. Will do. I need to go in a minute. You sure you're okay?

Dee: Promise. You?

Max: I'm good. Don't forget to keep an eye on the sky the next few nights.

Dee: I will, you know I love to see the stars fall.

She laughed when he replied with a little smiley face that was rolling its eyes. It was bigger and more detailed than an emoji. He'd somehow made his own version – and some of them were much more expressive than regular emojis. She found the one that was covering its mouth with its hand while it giggled and sent that back.

Max: Love you, Mom. Talk soon.

Dee: Love you more. I'll send you some dates.

Max. Thx. You going to send the plane for me too?

Dee: You bet.

She watched the screen until it faded to black. She used to keep asking one more question – anything to keep him a little longer, but she'd learned over the years, that just irritated him. It wasn't fair. He had his own life that he was getting on with. She should just be grateful for whatever time he gave freely – and she was.

She set the phone down and took a sip of her wine. She'd have to talk to Pax tomorrow and figure out when she could get them both out here. Pax had worked remotely for her since before remote working had become as common as it was.

They didn't really need to meet up in person, but Dee made sure she set up quarterly sessions – it was good for the business side of things, but more importantly it meant that she got to see her boys regularly. Max didn't always join them, but more often than not he made it.

She blew out a sigh. That was still a few weeks away. She was going to have to make an effort to get out and about and discover what life in Summer Lake was like before then. She knew damn well that if she didn't make a conscious effort, she'd probably never leave the house. She'd felt a mixture of disappointment and relief when Emma had told her that there was no delivery service in town – not a one! The grocery store didn't deliver, The Boathouse didn't. Oh, wait. Emma had said that there was an Italian restaurant – Giuseppe's? – and they delivered. But only in town.

She made a mental note to find the place and stop in the next time she went to town. Emma seemed to think that this house probably wouldn't be classed as *in town*. Dee was hoping that she was wrong about that.

She looked out at the lake. She hadn't paid attention to the sunset while she'd been texting with Max. The sky was quickly fading to gray. She got to her feet. If she was going to hang around down here to see if she could spot any falling stars – *Meteors,* she mentally corrected herself on Max's behalf – she was going to need to bring some blankets out. And another glass of wine.

She turned when a noise caught her attention. It sounded like someone was coming up the steps from the beach – and coming fast. Her heart started to pound. But she was safe. The gate was locked, and it was tall and sturdy. It wasn't as though anyone would be able to break it down. She eyed the gate warily. It was solid wood panels – more of a door than a gate really. It spanned the gap in the wall that surrounded the property and was set into a frame that was maybe seven feet tall. She started to back away as the sound grew louder. If who – or what! – ever was out there was capable of climbing over the gate, there'd be no point whatsoever in her trying to make a run for it. If they could scale the gate, they were in a damn sight better shape than she could ever hope to be. They …

She heard a thud, then spotted movement on top of the wall – the dusk had fallen now, and she couldn't make out the details of the dark shape – she started backing away more quickly. She should probably turn and run, but she couldn't take her eyes away from the shape that became clearer as it leaped down from the wall.

"No!" This could not be happening.

Chapter Five

Lucky sprinted up the steps after Echo. He couldn't believe this!

"Echo, return!"

All he saw was her rear end flying through the air as she leapt up onto the wall beside the gate. He had no idea what had gotten into her. They'd been walking down on the beach, not even out for a run tonight. He'd just brought her out to play after dinner. He'd thought that it would do them both good to relax.

She'd been weird ever since they hit the beach. They hadn't run in this direction since their encounter with that woman. Echo always set out to come this way, but he'd been able to persuade her that they should go toward the resort instead. Until tonight, that was.

She'd been determined to come this way. Even when he'd thrown her ball toward the resort, she'd ignored it and started heading down here. By the time Lucky had collected the ball, she was a good way ahead of him and had refused to come back.

He hadn't thought much of it. Sometimes, she got an idea in her head, and he didn't like to override her. Her instincts had saved their team on more than one occasion. They might not face life-and-death situations together anymore, but he trusted her.

As he watched the tip of her tail disappear over the wall, he didn't even question whether that trust was misplaced. He simply ran at the wall and jumped, getting a foothold from which he managed to boost himself up.

He almost tumbled over the other side when he heard the woman scream. She sounded terrified.

"Echo! Return!" he shouted as he swung his legs over and dropped down on the other side. He could see what was coming, but there was nothing he could do to stop it. Echo kept bounding toward the woman, and she kept backing away.

"Stop!"

The woman didn't tear her gaze away from Echo, she just kept going backward until the inevitable happened. She stumbled and fell back into the pool.

Echo showed no hesitation in leaping in after her, and Lucky wasn't far behind. He had no idea if the woman could swim – she probably could if she had a pool. But there was no doubt in his mind that she was going to panic when she resurfaced and realized that Echo was in the water with her.

Coolness and air bubbles rushed past his face when he dived in. It wasn't the time to be thinking it, but he realized how badly he'd missed the water. When his head broke the surface, he reached the woman in two powerful strokes. Her arms were flailing, and she was gasping as she tried to get away from Echo.

"It's okay. She's trying to help. Hold on to me." He gave her a moment, waiting to see how she would react. Some people would do their best to drown another in their attempts to save themselves.

He was relieved when this woman turned out to not be one of those. She simply turned and stared at him.

"I've got you," he reassured her as he positioned himself behind her, wrapping his arm around her waist.

He was stunned by his own reaction when he felt her relax against him. His heart felt as though it swelled in his chest with a rush of warmth and... something else. Pride. He didn't understand it, but there was no denying it. He felt prouder than he maybe ever had that this woman – this stranger – trusted him enough to relax, even though she was terrified of Echo.

She grasped his forearm, clinging to him, but not so tightly that it felt like desperation. Another rush of emotion hit him when he realized that not only was she trusting him, but in that moment, she was depending on him.

He wished that he could see her face. Since he couldn't, he needed to hear her voice.

"Are you okay?"

She turned her head so that she could look at him. "I... I... Oh my God! What the hell is happening? Echo. She came out of nowhere." She clung tighter to his arm, the action belying her words. "It's okay. I can swim. Where is she? Where's Echo?"

"It's okay. She won't come after you."

He'd reached the shallow end of the pool all too soon. He set his feet down and reluctantly let go of her when she did the same. She took a step, and when she seemed unsteady, he was quick to wrap his arm back around her.

"I've got you."

They walked up the shallow steps, until they were out of the water.

The woman looked around. "Where is she?" she asked again.

Lucky looked around. "Over there."

Echo was sitting beside the table watching them intently. He scowled at her. He had no idea what had gotten into her.

She didn't look ashamed of herself, which was what she usually did whenever he frowned – he didn't do it often, and never without reason. Instead, she smiled at him and let out a happy sounding little yip.

"What the hell, lady?"

"Excuse me?"

He turned back to the woman. "Shit! Sorry. I didn't mean you. I meant her. She's never done anything like this before. I don't know what her deal is. I'm sorry. Are you okay?"

The woman looked over at Echo, and when she looked back at him, he realized that he still had his arm around her, and she wasn't making any move to get away from him.

"I'm okay." She glanced over at Echo again. "She scared the living daylights out of me."

"I'm so sorry…"

All his breath caught in his chest when she chuckled and patted his arm.

"No, really. It's okay. I don't know what her deal is. But she's obviously not here to eat me, is she? She didn't come in the water after me to kill me – she was trying to rescue me, wasn't she? I could feel it. Before you arrived, she was trying to help."

"Yeah. If I hadn't arrived, she probably could've gotten you out of there."

The woman shook her head and looked over at Echo again. "The other day… you know when I was so scared of her, and then I spilled my guts to you? Told you about what happened with those dogs when I was a kid?"

Lucky nodded. He was surprised to hear her put it that way. In his experience, women talked too much without any awareness that they were doing so.

"When I ran back up the steps because I'd embarrassed myself, and you left, she didn't go straight after you. She waited a moment – and this is going to sound stupid, I know it is, but I swear it's what happened, she smiled at me before she followed you."

Lucky had to smile himself. "It doesn't sound stupid. Not to me. She is a smiler." He cocked his head to the side. "Although, I don't think I've ever known her to smile at a stranger before."

When he thought about it, he realized that wasn't true. Dalton had told him that Echo took a shine to Taryn from the very first time she met her – and she smiled at her, too. He realized that he was still holding the woman and quickly let her go.

Just because Echo had helped Dalton to find himself a woman, that didn't mean that Lucky wanted her to do the same for him.

He let both arms fall to his sides. "I apologize again."

The woman gave him a puzzled look. "I'm fine. Honestly." Then, she did the last thing he would've expected her to do. She held her hand out to him and said, "I regretted not catching your name last time. I'm Dee. It's nice to meet you."

He looked down at her hand, caught off guard by the gesture. He would have expected her to be hysterical either with fear or anger. Yet, here she was introducing herself as though they'd just bumped into each other on the street.

When he realized that the moment was dragging out long enough to become awkward, he reached for her hand and shook it. Even wet, her skin felt warm and soft. The feel of it sent a current zapping down his spine, and he let go too quickly.

"And you are?"

Shit! He was so thrown by the whole situation that he was probably coming across as… He didn't know what.

"Lucky."

She gave him a puzzled little smile. "I'm very happy for you. Do you have a name, too?"

There was something about her that made him relax. He let out a short laugh. "Yeah. That is my name. Lucky. That's what everyone calls me."

Her eyes shone with amusement. "Does that mean you don't want to tell me what your name is? It's totally fair if you don't. I only gave you my first name."

"I don't mind telling you my name."

"Go on, then. I'll tell you mine if you tell me yours."

For some reason, that sent another shiver down his spine. He smiled through pursed lips and held his hand out again. "I'm Evan, Evan Penny. Nice to meet you."

She laughed as she shook hands with him again. If he wasn't mistaken, she liked holding his hand. He couldn't know for sure, but he wanted to think that might be true, so he didn't let go as he asked, "And you?"

She smiled, but a look of trepidation crossed her face before she answered. He'd guess that she feared that he might recognize her name.

"Like I told you, I'm Dee."

He cocked an eyebrow and waited.

She let out a short laugh. "Okay! A deal's a deal. I'm DeeDee Patterson."

It sounded vaguely familiar, but Lucky couldn't place it. Knowing that she was uncomfortable about giving her full name for some reason, he opted to let it go.

"Nice to meet you, DeeDee. But you go by Dee?"

She nodded. "It's just easier."

"And Lucky?" She chuckled. "Oh no, wait! Let me guess lucky penny?"

He smiled through pursed lips.

She gave him a puzzled look. "You don't like it?"

He shook his head slowly. He'd tell her if he needed to, but he had a feeling that she'd figure it out for herself. He knew he was right when her eyes grew wide, and she pointed at him.

"No! I get it! You're a tough guy! You said that Echo is an ex-Navy SEAL – I bet you are, too. You wanted a tougher sounding name, right?" She looked around at the night sky, as if the answer might be written up there somewhere. Then she laughed and looked back at him. "You didn't expect people to call you Bad, did you? That's all I can think of. Bad penny. Lucky penny, bad penny, what else? What other kind of penny? I can't think."

He gave her a rueful smile. "You got me. Most of the guys ended up with nicknames that make them sound like people you wouldn't want to mess with. Me? I'm just lucky."

The way she smiled did something to his insides. He wasn't used to reacting to a woman like this. But he couldn't say that he disliked it.

"*Just* lucky? I'd say that lucky is one of the best things a person could be. You don't need a nickname to tell people that you're a tough guy. You don't need any words for that." She looked him up and down, and he felt himself stand a little straighter under her gaze, even as he hoped that the stirring inside his soaked pants wouldn't lead to anything down there standing up straight.

A flush spread over her cheeks, and she looked away. "Don't mind me. Sorry. I wasn't ogling you – at least, I didn't mean to. I just meant that … Well, it's obvious that you …" She let out an embarrassed laugh. "I should probably just shut up now, right?"

He reached out and touched her arm. "You're okay. It's fine. If you want to know the truth… I can't remember the last time that anyone looked at me in the way that you just did, but I can tell you that it's been even longer since I enjoyed it."

Once the words were out, he clamped his jaw shut. Where the hell had that come from?

~ ~ ~

Dee couldn't believe that she'd just said that! She'd just looked him over like he was a juicy steak, and she was a starving dog. That thought made her glance over at Echo. That dog really did smile and right now, Dee would swear that was a knowing smile on her face. Oh well, Echo might be a different species, but she was a fellow female. Dee closed her eyes in an attempt to stop from thinking of herself as a bitch in heat.

She opened her eyes in a hurry when Lucky cleared his throat. The sound brought her back to the moment. She had to get with the program! She might have embarrassed herself by looking at him in a way that probably gave him the impression that she was planning to push him down onto one of the loungers and have her way with him, but he hadn't run away screaming.

She forced her mind to focus on the words that he'd said … She slowly lifted her gaze to meet his.

He looked embarrassed. "I'm sorry. I shouldn't have said that."

His words took her by surprise. "Hey! Don't go apologizing. I was the one who was out of line." She risked a smile. "Hearing that you didn't mind me ogling you like that let me off the hook."

As he held her gaze, a small smile played on his lips. "I didn't say that I didn't mind it."

"Oh." Crap! She should let it go while she was ahead. "Then I should be the one apologizing."

He reached out – not that he had to reach far, they were still standing close. "No. You shouldn't. What I said was that I liked it."

A shiver ran down her spine, and she wondered if he could feel the goosebumps as they broke out on her arms. She didn't dare look down. She'd shortened her name from DeeDee to Dee in high school – but it was too late to prevent other kids from teasing her about having her name inside her bra. The size of her breasts had been both an advantage and a burden at different times in her life. The one thing about them that had always been a real pain was the fact that there was no hiding when she was aroused – her nipples gave her away every time.

She could feel that they were drawn tight, no doubt pointing straight at Lucky. No way did she want to draw his attention to them.

He tilted his head to the side, as if he was getting impatient for an answer. Although he hadn't actually asked a question, so she raised her eyebrows as she shrugged.

"Well, I think I made it quite plain that I liked looking, too."

A gorgeous smile flashed across his face before fading quickly. Dee had to wonder what that was all about; and then it hit her. He was probably married. He was a guy, and in her experience, all guys liked to hear that women found them attractive. But she'd guess that his smile disappeared when he remembered that he shouldn't feel that way. She looked down at his left hand.

"Not married. No significant other. There hasn't even been an insignificant other in a long time."

Dee's gaze flew back up to meet his. She felt guilty as hell that he'd caught her. At least he didn't look mad about it. In fact, he looked slightly amused – but only slightly. If she had to describe the look on his face, she'd be more likely to choose the word confused. Though what he was confused about, she had no idea, and she had even less idea what to say.

They both turned when Echo barked. It wasn't an aggressive sound, but Dee still jumped. She didn't even know why. Even though she should probably be more terrified now than she had been before – given that Echo had proved that she could scale the wall and get in any time she wanted – Dee wasn't even scared of her.

Lucky didn't know that, though. He moved in closer and wrapped his arm around her, to reassure her.

"It's okay. I promise you she won't hurt you."

Dee reacted instinctively; she wrapped her arms around Lucky's waist and leaned in close.

His arm tightened around her shoulders. "It's okay. I've got you."

She felt so bad. What would he think if he knew that she wasn't even scared anymore? He'd be running back up the beach as fast as he could go if he knew that she was just a desperate woman who was making the most of some physical contact with a male body.

That thought was so ridiculous that she couldn't stop herself from chuckling.

He looked down into her eyes without letting go of her. "Are you okay?"

That just made her laugh harder. The poor man! "I'm sorry. I'm fine. I'm not hysterical, honestly. It just struck me as funny."

He cocked an eyebrow.

She started to unwrap her arms from around his waist. "I have to tell you the truth. I'm really not afraid of her anymore. When she barked, it startled me, but that's all. And you went all big, strong, protective hero, and I grabbed onto you." She let her arms fall to her sides and gave him a shamefaced smile. "I'm sorry."

She made to step away from him, but he held her gaze. His eyes were a beautiful, deep brown. She could get lost in them if she wasn't careful. Then she realized, it wasn't that he'd pinned her there with his gaze; he still had his arm wrapped around her shoulders.

When he smiled, she could feel it reflected on her own face. "I think I already told you that you don't need to apologize. I don't know about the hero part, but I have no complaints about you grabbing on to me."

Wow! She didn't know what to say to that, so she replied in a way that she knew would make her feelings clear. She wrapped her arms back around his waist. "Well, in that case... Don't mind me. I'll just be down here hanging onto my knight in soggy armor."

He chuckled. "I'm not worried about that. You're soaked as well, though." He finally let go of her, and she stepped back, immediately missing his warmth. "We should let you go inside and get dried and changed." He glanced over at Echo. "All I can say is that I'm sorry. I don't know what got into her. We've taken up enough of your time. We should go."

Echo let out a long, low whine, and Dee echoed the sentiment. She didn't want him to leave. But she could hardly say so. She liked to think that she was a good judge of character. But as a woman alone, it didn't matter that she already knew in her bones that Lucky was a good guy. There was no way she should invite him and his *killer* dog into the house. She smiled as a thought struck her – at least, not until she knew them better.

"Yes. I should let you go." She turned to watch Echo trot around the pool toward them.

When she reached them, she sat down beside Lucky and leaned against his leg.

"Are you okay with her?"

"I am." It surprised the hell out of her, but Dee wasn't afraid of Echo in the slightest.

"She won't hurt you," he said as Echo leaned forward to sniff Dee's hand.

"I know." She looked down. "It was wrong of me to judge you, and I'm sorry."

When Echo looked up at her, Dee realized that she had the same big brown eyes as Lucky. She imagined that between them they stole a lot of hearts.

"Will the two of you run this way again tomorrow?" She probably shouldn't be so forthright about it, but she had to ask.

Echo let out a happy sounding little yip, and Lucky chuckled. "I don't know. We're probably better off steering clear of your part of the beach – as this lady apparently can't be trusted."

Dee had to laugh when Echo looked at him and made a low growling sound.

Lucky just made a face at her. "You pushed it too far tonight, lady. We're both lucky that Dee's being so cool about it. She could be suing us."

To Dee's surprise, Echo shuffled across the space between them, and leaned against her leg.

"It's okay. I'm glad you came."

"Glad?" Lucky looked skeptical.

What the hell? If she didn't go for it, she'd regret it. "Yes. I am. I've wondered about the two of you since the last time I saw you. We're both new in town, and I don't know about you, but I could do with making some new friends – maybe even going on a date. So, how about we meet up for coffee sometime soon?"

Lucky didn't hide his shock very well, but just as she started to feel foolish for even asking, he smiled.

"Sure. I'd like that." Echo barked, and he chuckled. "She says that she would, too. But don't worry, I'll leave her home."

Echo barked louder this time.

"That's okay," said Dee. "We can get the coffee to go, if you like and take it down to the beach." She smiled down at Echo. "That way, you can come along."

"Want to give me your number and I'll call you?"

He sounded kind of abrupt, but Dee realized that they were both still standing there, soaking wet, and he probably just wanted to get home.

"That sounds like a plan, but how about we exchange numbers in the car?"

"The car?"

"Yes. I can't let you walk back down the beach in wet clothes like that. I'll give you both a ride."

He threw his head back and laughed, and she felt stupid without knowing why until he explained. "Former Navy SEALs, remember?"

"Oh! Of course. But you're retired now, and you're not wet because you're on some mission to save the world. So, do you want that ride?"

Echo's swishing tail and happy little bark made her opinion clear. Lucky shrugged and gave Dee a rueful smile. "Since you're offering, it'd be rude to refuse."

Chapter Six

When he pulled up in the parking lot at work the next morning, Lucky turned to Echo, who was sitting in the passenger seat.

"You pushed your luck last night, lady. You'd better be on your best behavior today."

She put her paws up on the console and leaned across to lick his cheek, making him chuckle.

"Okay, okay! I agree, it worked out okay." He gave her a stern look. "But don't get into the habit of pulling shit like that, okay?"

She just panted at him in a way that didn't reassure Lucky at all.

"I mean it!"

She got back down into her own seat and pawed at the door handle. Lucky was about to tell her that he wasn't finished yet, but Dan Benson appeared by the passenger door and smiled in at them. He pointed at the handle and Lucky nodded.

"Best behavior," he murmured to Echo before Dan opened the door.

Of course, she completely ignored him and greeted Dan by offering her paw to shake.

Dan shook it with a smile. "Good morning, Echo. I'm happy to see you."

"I promise you she won't be any trouble."

Dan met his gaze. "That's okay. I know she won't. I told you from the beginning that I'm happy for her to come into the office whenever you want to bring her. To be honest, I've been looking forward to it."

Lucky rolled his eyes when Echo looked back over her shoulder at him with a smile.

"I'm glad I caught you," Dan said. "How are you settling in? You've been out and about most of the time, and it seems that we usually miss each other in the office."

"I'm doing well. Liking the work." He met Dan's gaze. "Is everything okay?"

Dan gave him a puzzled look. "What kind of everything?"

"The work. Are you happy with what I'm doing?"

"Happy? I'm thrilled. I'm surprised you even need to ask. We've needed someone to cover the investigative side of things since the contracts started coming in. You're the ideal guy. Are *you* happy? Is it enough for you?"

"Hell yeah, I'm happy. This suits me just fine. I just wanted to make sure that ..." Lucky wasn't even aware what he wanted to make sure of. He just needed to know that Dan was happy with his performance. In the years since he'd retired from the service, he'd only worked on freelance contracts. This was the first time he'd had someone he considered to be a boss. His only frame of reference was his chain of command in the Navy. Dan's style of management didn't exactly fit with that.

"As far as I'm concerned, you're exactly what the team needed. I'm glad you're here," Dan said. "You know my story – I don't have the kind of background that you guys do. If you need something different from me – something more – just let me know. My approach is more laid back and I trust all of you guys to do your thing your way."

Lucky felt some of the tension leave his shoulders. "Sorry. I knew that. Dalton explained it all to me before I came, and you did when I first arrived. I'll find my feet."

Dan opened his mouth to speak, but Echo cut him off when she barked. She'd spotted Dalton, who'd just parked across the way from them. She looked back at Lucky again, and he knew what she wanted.

"You might want to stand aside a second, Dan." Once he'd moved out of the way, Lucky nodded at Echo. "Go time."

He chuckled at the expression on Dan's face as Echo sailed through the air past him, then took off to greet Dalton as he climbed out of his SUV.

"She's amazing," said Dan.

Lucky nodded happily. She really was.

"I'd better get inside," Dan said. "I've got a meeting with Leanne first thing, and I don't know how well you know her yet, but I don't want to be late."

Lucky smiled as he watched him go. He didn't know Leanne very well yet, but he knew enough to understand what Dan meant – she was a tough cookie, and you didn't want to mess with her. From what he understood, she and Dan had been friends since their college days at Berkeley. It struck him as an unlikely friendship, but there was no missing the fact that they were close and that they worked well together.

He climbed out of his Hummer and made his way over to Dalton and Echo, who were still fawning over each other as if this were their first time catching up in years.

Dalton straightened up when he reached them and folded his arms across his chest.

"Did you forget that I was stopping by last night?"

Shit! Lucky had forgotten all about it. "Sorry."

Dalton nodded slowly. "Where'd you go?"

Lucky held his gaze for a moment. "For a run on the beach." It wasn't a lie.

"And?"

Lucky didn't bother asking *and what?* There was no point. He knew Dalton too well; he was onto him.

"Why don't you tell me?"

"I don't know what else you did; all I know is that some woman brought you home afterward."

"Yeah."

"That's all I get? Yeah?"

"What else do you want?"

Dalton looked down at Echo. "I swear to God, you're more talkative than he is most of the time."

Echo barked happily.

Lucky shrugged. "It's a long story."

Dalton grasped his shoulder. "I've got the time. You're in the office today. You can hang out with me and tell me this story. We can get coffee, bring it to your office, and you can tell me all about it."

Lucky blew out a sigh. There was no point in arguing. It wasn't that he didn't want to tell Dalton. It was just that there wasn't much to say. Well, there was the whole deal about Echo taking off like that – he knew that would surprise Dalton. He wasn't sure what to say about Dee, though.

Dalton was already steering him toward the door. Once they were inside, he kept hold of Lucky's shoulder and pointed him in the direction of the coffee room.

Once they had their coffees and were settled in Lucky's office – Dalton had decided that they were less likely to be disturbed in there – Dalton raised an eyebrow at him.

"Go on, you'd better get started on telling me this story if it's so long. We don't have all day."

Lucky leaned back in his chair and gave his old friend a dark look.

"Come on! I need to know!"

That made Lucky laugh. "It's not like you to beg."

Dalton laughed with him. "What can I tell you? I'm intrigued. Who is she? How did you meet her? I mean, it's not like you, is it?" He glanced at Echo, who had curled up on the floor, next to the big fluffy dog bed that someone – Lucky really should find out who – had thought to provide for her when they set up his office. "And what does *she* think about it? She's used to being your one and only."

Lucky shook his head with a smile. "You always say that you wish she could talk; so do I. She owes me an explanation."

Echo lifted her head to look at him.

"Dee, that's her name, is staying in one of the big houses on the water farther down the beach. We've seen her a couple of times when we've been out on our run."

He told Dalton about their encounters with Dee prior to last night and about how they'd taken to running toward the resort so that Echo wouldn't frighten her again.

Dalton held his hands out to Echo, and she went to sit between his knees. He had a great big smile on his face as he fondled her ears. "You are one smart lady."

Lucky cocked an eyebrow. "How so?"

Dalton laughed. "She's picked this Dee out for you. Let me guess, you took her on the beach last night and she was determined to go to her house?"

Lucky pursed his lips. "Not just go to her house."

He scowled at Echo, but she ignored him as she pressed her nose into Dalton's hand.

"She took off down the beach, even though I said we weren't going that way. Then, when we got there, she went right up to the house. It's that big house on the headland. There's a path with steps leading up from the beach. At the top, there's a gate and a wall – like, a seven-foot wall. But she didn't let that stop her."

Dalton looked down at Echo. "That's just a *little* wall, isn't it, lady?"

Echo yipped happily.

Lucky couldn't help but chuckle. "It was nothing – to her."

"I bet you didn't have any problem hauling your ass up there after her, did you? That's what happened, right? Echo here went in search of Dee, and you went right on after her?"

"Yeah. And if that wasn't bad enough, the gate leads to the pool terrace. Dee was out there, and Echo scared the life out of her. So much so that she fell in the pool."

Dalton laughed. "That's awesome!"

"Awesome?"

"Yep. I mean, you had to dive in and rescue her, right – be the hero?"

"Yeah." Lucky felt something tingling in his chest as he remembered what she'd said – that he'd gone all *big, strong, protective hero.*

He straightened up when he realized that Dalton was watching him closely. "What do you think? Should we try to get you a date?"

Lucky cocked an eyebrow at his friend. He wasn't offended. Dalton wasn't asking if he needed his help. It was more a case of him asking permission to help with something that he and the other guys had been telling Lucky for years that he needed to do.

"Too late."

Dalton's smile disappeared. "Oh, shit! Do we need to do any damage control?"

Lucky had to laugh. "No! I don't mean I already blew it. I mean, we already set up a date."

Dalton looked down at Echo again. "You're a little miracle worker, aren't you, lady?"

"You should know," said Lucky. "She's the one who found Taryn for you."

"She didn't exactly find her. Taryn and I had been bumping heads for months until Echo came along. It's fairer to say that Echo brokered a peace treaty between us."

"It is."

"So, when is this date? What's the deal?"

Lucky shrugged. "It's not exactly a date. Not really."

"Why not? Where did you ask her to go?"

"I didn't ask her. She asked me. She said we could go for coffee sometime."

"Just some time? You haven't set anything up?"

Lucky pursed his lips. Dee had given him her number, and he'd said that he'd call. She'd also told him that she'd be in the bakery on Saturday morning, if he wanted to join her for coffee.

"Lucky?" Dalton's eyebrows were pinched together.

"What?"

"Did you set anything up?"

"She talked about going to the bakery for coffee on Saturday morning."

"Are you going to back out?"

He shrugged. "Probably. What's the point?"

Dalton scowled at him. "Echo seems to think there's a point."

They both looked up at the sound of a knock. "Come on in," Lucky called.

Cal stuck his head around the door and smiled at them. "Am I disturbing you guys?"

"No," said Lucky. "Come on in; what can I do for you?"

"Terry wanted me to ask if you'll have dinner with us all at The Boathouse tomorrow night. I've been putting her off ever since you arrived." Cal smiled. "I've done my best, but she's sociable like that. I told her that you probably wouldn't want to, and she should wait until you decide of your own accord that you want to come out. But the options she gave me this morning were either I ask you, or she'd come by here on her break today and ask you herself."

"She would, too," said Dalton. "Terry's a lot like Taryn. If you don't come out with us soon, I reckon the two of them will drag you out."

Lucky looked down at Echo. He really did prefer to spend his time with her. He knew from the look in her eyes that if she could talk, she'd be telling him to go.

"Okay, I'll be there. I won't make a night of it, but I'll have dinner with you guys."

"Great," said Cal. "I'll tell her."

Dalton raised an eyebrow at Lucky.

"What?"

"Nothing."

Cal laughed. "I'll leave you guys to some teammate talk, huh? Catch you later."

"What?" Lucky asked again after Cal had gone.

"I was thinking that maybe you could take this Dee out instead of coming to dinner with everyone."

"We talked about coffee, not dinner."

"Exactly. You should go. It's only coffee."

Lucky rolled his eyes at him. "I'll see. I have her number."

"And you know that she'll be at the bakery on Saturday morning."

Lucky nodded. He'd like to see her again; he was attracted to her, there was no question about that. But it wasn't that simple.

"Don't overthink it. Just do it."

"Maybe."

"What's the harm in it?"

"There's no harm in having coffee with her. It's just…"

"It's just where it goes after the coffee?"

He nodded. "She's new in town; she said she could do with making some friends. If it were just friendship … I'd be okay with that. I could do that."

Dalton got to his feet. "I'm not going to push you. You know I won't. Maybe all she wants is a friend. Maybe friendship is all you can handle." He pulled the door open. "But Echo thinks there's something more than that there, and so do I."

He closed the door behind him as he left, and Lucky stared at it for a few moments. He didn't know what to do about Dee. He knew he had a lot of busy work to catch up on, though. He fired up his computer and made a face at Echo when she whined at him.

"I didn't say I *wasn't* going, did I?"

~ ~ ~

Dee closed her eyes and lifted her face to the sun. This felt so good! She'd forced herself out of the house today because she needed to go in search of groceries. Despite her good intentions, she hadn't ventured out in days. Now, she was wondering why.

When she'd parked in the square at the resort and seen people sitting out on the deck over the water, she decided to treat herself to lunch. That had been over an hour ago, and she was still sitting here, enjoying the sunshine, the view of the water, and the ebb and flow of people. Some of them were obviously tourists, others she'd guess were locals. In the time that she'd been sitting here, there had been a steady stream of them. Some were here to eat, others were just enjoying a drink and the beautiful surroundings.

She looked around. Actually, most of them were enjoying each other's company. That thought wiped the smile off her face. She hadn't had much company since she'd come to the lake. Emma had been over to the house a couple of times. But other than that, the only person she'd spoken to face to face was Lucky.

Just the thought of him brought her smile back again. He was a good guy. No question about it. He was guarded, there was no missing that. She hoped that he would show up in the bakery on Saturday morning, but she wasn't going to hold her breath. He'd said that he would call her, but she didn't expect him to. And that was fine.

She'd asked him if he wanted to meet up with her in a social setting. She'd love to think that he might become a friend. Of course, she'd love it if he wanted to go on a date or three, but she wasn't really expecting him to. There was an attraction between them, but that didn't need to mean anything.

Just because two people felt the spark of attraction, it didn't have to go anywhere. She'd been married twice and dated her fair share of men. If she'd ever been a hopeful romantic – and she wasn't sure that she ever had – she was beyond all of that now.

"Ms. Patterson?"

She shaded her eyes as she looked up. She recognized the guy standing before her, but she couldn't place him.

He smiled. "I'm Ben. Emma's friend. We met in LA a couple of times."

"Oh, of course! Ben! I'm sorry, it took me a moment."

"No problem. It's been a long time. How are you? Emma told me that you're here for the summer?"

"I am. And so far, I'm loving it." She looked around, remembering that it was Ben's family who owned the resort. "Your folks must be proud of this place. It's wonderful."

Ben was still smiling, but she could tell that it was forced now. "I'm sure they are."

They both turned when Emma appeared beside him. "I wish the two of you knew each other better. I consider you both to be amongst my very best friends. So, I'll wade in and say it like it is. Ben's folks were never interested in the resort. He's been running this place by himself since we were kids."

"Not really. Joe…"

Dee watched with interest as Emma nodded. "Yes, Joe held the place together until you were old enough. But it's always been you, Ben." She turned to Dee. "Joe is Ben's grandpa. He's awesome. You'll meet him while you're here, I'm sure."

Ben nodded. "And how's your stay going so far? Are you settling in okay? Can we do anything to help?"

Dee remembered him as being a kind, wonderful young man. When he'd come to visit Emma in LA, she'd hoped that the two of them might get together. But Emma had explained that he was like a brother to her. Dee could see it now.

"That's sweet of you. But I'm doing just fine, thank you. Although, I did want to ask you about renting a boat." She laughed. "That sounded wrong. Don't worry, I'm not going to ask you to personally set up an hour's rental for me. Since I'm here for the whole summer, I'm wondering if you might rent me one for the season – if we can find someone who'll teach me how to drive it first."

Ben looked thoughtful. "Let me think about it? It's not something we've done before. But considering that you're staying at the Reynolds place, it'd be a shame to let that dock go to waste for the summer."

"Thanks. And don't feel obliged just because I'm Emma's friend. If it's not something that works for you – if you need all your boats for your hourly business with the tourists – just say no. I'll understand."

"I'll let you know. I'll have to look into the insurance issues."

"Okay. Thanks. I'm good with whatever exorbitant premium they come up with."

Ben chuckled. "That's what I'm afraid of – that it will be exorbitant. And I don't know if you'll need to take some kind of class in order to be considered competent."

Dee laughed out loud at that. "If that's the case, we can probably forget it. My boys are already concerned that I might sink it and drown myself."

"Oh, shush!" said Emma. "You're not that bad."

"I guess we'll find out, won't we?"

Emma made a face at her. "You'll do fine with a boat. And just think, when you get the hang of it, you can come up to North Cove to visit us. Jack loves getting to show off the dock that he built for us. Anyway, I can't stop. I was surprised when I spotted you out here. I was planning to call you to ask if you want to come out with us tomorrow night. We're all coming over here to listen to the band."

Dee hesitated. She knew that Emma meant well, but she wasn't sure how she felt about hanging out with the younger woman and all her friends.

Ben smiled at her. "I hope you'll come. I should have some news for you by then on how we can handle renting you a boat."

"Okay."

"Great," said Emma. "I'll call you later, Dee. We can come and pick you up on our way in if you like."

"It's fine. I can get myself over here."

Emma narrowed her eyes at her. "I know that you *can*, I'm just not sure that you *will*."

Dee had to laugh. "I'll most likely come, okay?"

"Hey, Ben, sorry to interrupt."

They all turned to see a woman giving Ben an apologetic smile. Dee guessed that she was around her age.

The woman smiled at her and Emma. "I'm sorry. I just need a quick word with him."

"That's okay, I was just leaving," said Emma. "I'll call you later," she told Dee.

Dee smiled at the woman. "You're fine, he's probably glad to escape me."

"No. I'm glad to catch up with you. I thought I would have seen you around before now." His smile faded. "And I'm sorry, I should introduce the two of you. Dee, this is Taryn. She owns the restaurant in the Lodge over at Four Mile Creek. Taryn, meet Dee, she's …"

Dee waited, wondering how he would introduce her. It wouldn't be a problem if he announced that she was DD Patterson. Not everyone knew who she was. Not everyone was a reader, but sometimes it got a bit awkward when people realized that she was a so-called famous author. Mostly she managed to fly under the radar, but it seemed that a lot of people remembered the movie adaptations of some of her earlier thrillers.

She needn't have worried. Ben continued, "She's an old friend of Emma's from LA. She's here for the summer."

A flash of recognition registered on Taryn's face, but she hid it quickly and stepped forward with her hand extended as she smiled.

"It's a pleasure to meet you. Do you have family here in town?"

"No. As Ben said, just Emma – she's an old friend."

Ben smiled. "I'd like to think that I am, too."

Dee smiled back at him. "Of course." She didn't know him all that well, but she knew enough to know that he was the sort to make everyone feel welcome and to go out of his way to help.

There was a strange gleam in Taryn's eye as she said, "Well, if you feel like getting to know a whole bunch of people, there's a crowd of us going out for dinner tomorrow night."

She smiled at Ben. "And no offense to this guy or to Emma, but you might have more fun with us than with the youngsters."

"Thanks." Dee wouldn't mind getting to know some more people, but there was something about the way Taryn was smiling that made her a little uneasy. "It's kind of you to offer, but I just told Emma that I would see her."

"Oh, okay." Taryn looked more disappointed than Dee felt the situation warranted. "Maybe some other time?"

"Maybe so." Dee got to her feet. "For now, I need to be going. It was lovely to meet you, Taryn. I'll talk to you soon, Ben."

She was probably being rude, but she wasn't too worried. Taryn seemed like a nice enough person, but there was an undeniable undercurrent. Maybe she recognized Dee and … And Dee didn't know what. All she knew was that she didn't want to stick around to find out.

She made her way inside the restaurant and went to the bar to pay her tab.

The girl behind the bar grinned at her. "Hey, you're Dee, right?"

She nodded. All of a sudden, she wanted nothing more than to get out of here. "That's right, but I'm sorry, I can't stop to chat. I'm in a bit of a rush." She set her check down on the bar with more than enough money to cover it and a generous tip, and turned to hurry away before the girl could say anything else.

Chapter Seven

"Are you sure you don't mind her coming in with me?" Lucky looked around the gym from where he stood just inside the door. There were only a couple of guys in there and Russ, who owned the place, had told him enough times already that he didn't mind Echo coming in, but this was the first time he'd brought her.

It was early on Saturday morning, and he'd had a rough night. Echo had woken him just after midnight. He'd been bathed in sweat, and his heart was pounding – which was hardly surprising considering that in his nightmares he'd been running as fast as he could. He'd only slept fitfully since then.

He came back to the moment when Russ answered him. "I don't know how many ways I can say it before you believe me. But honestly, she's fine. I enjoy her being in here. She's a good girl, aren't you?"

Echo wagged her tail as she looked up at him.

"She used to come in with Dalton all the time when she was staying with him. People have been asking about her since they know that she's back in town."

Lucky looked down at her. "Will you sit on the mats and behave?"

She let out a short sharp bark of agreement.

"Okay. Thanks, Russ." He led Echo inside. He'd planned to run on the beach this morning, but she'd refused to go. Well, she would have been happy to go down the beach – in the direction of Dee's place, but she'd literally dug her heels into the sand when he tried to get her to go in the opposite direction. In the end, he'd put her leash on, and they'd walked the streets until they arrived at the gym.

He was dressed for a workout, and since he wasn't going to get his run this morning, he figured he could at least lift weights. He heard the door open behind them and turned to follow Echo's gaze when her ears pricked forward. He half expected to see Dalton there, given her reaction, but he didn't recognize the man who'd just come in. Well, Lucky knew that he'd seen him somewhere before, he just couldn't place where. And they hadn't spoken, he would have remembered that. They could have passed each other in the grocery store for all Lucky knew.

Russ greeted the guy with a chin lift. "Damon. To what do we owe the honor? It's not like you to be in this early."

The guy – Damon, apparently – chuckled. "I'm not here of my own free will, believe me. With the hours I'm working over at the restaurant, I'd forgotten that there were two six o'clocks in the day. It's just… Last night was not a great night."

Russ nodded and glanced back at Lucky. For one paranoid moment, Lucky got the impression that Russ was about to introduce him as someone else who had trouble making it through the night. Of course, he didn't do that. Even if he knew – if he'd guessed – Russ wasn't the type to talk about anyone's business. That was one of the many things that Lucky liked about him.

"Have you two met before?" Russ asked.

Lucky and Damon both shook their heads as Damon approached. Russ grinned.

"Lucky is a former SEAL – and this here, is Echo, another former SEAL. Damon is an old friend. A fellow former Marine."

Echo's tail swished across the floor behind her. Lucky knew he was going to like the guy by the way that he addressed her first.

"It's an honor to meet you, Echo." He looked up at Lucky. "Is it okay if I say hi?"

"It is."

Damon got down on his knees in front of Echo and held his hand out to her. Lucky had to laugh when she shook hands with him and then sat back on her hind legs and waved at him with one paw.

"I think it's safe to say that she likes you."

Damon grinned up at him. "It's safe to say that it's mutual. She's a Belgian Mal, right?"

"That's right."

"I have so much respect for these dogs." He turned his attention back to Echo. "Thank you for your service, ma'am. I might not know you personally, but I know you saved a lot of lives out there, didn't you?"

Lucky nodded silently. She had – his own and their teams included. But he'd come out this morning, come into the gym, to get away from thoughts about their past life.

As if he sensed Lucky's discomfort, Damon got back to his feet. "It's a pleasure to meet you both. Are you coming over to the restaurant with the rest of the gang tonight?"

Lucky nodded slowly. He'd told Cal and Dalton that he would go out with them all, but the closer the time got, the less he wanted to go.

Russ chuckled. "I hate to tell you this, but if you don't at least show your face, Terry and Nina may well come and hunt you down."

Lucky frowned, not so much at the threat of his friends' women trying to force him to join in, more because he didn't understand the connection. Terry was with Cal, Nina was with Manny; he didn't get why Russ was talking about the two women as if he knew them so well.

"I can tell them not to if it's that much of a problem." Russ looked concerned.

Lucky realized too late that his face must be giving him away. "No. It's not that. It's just... It sounds like you're close with them – with the women."

Russ laughed. "Oh! Sorry, I forget that you don't know everyone yet. Terry, Nina, and Tino – I don't know if you've met Tino; he owns Giuseppe's – we all grew up here together. We've been friends since kindergarten. If it sounds like I'm too familiar with your friends' women, it's only because I see them as my sisters."

"Right. Sorry. It's just taking me a while to get the hang of the dynamics of the group."

Damon smiled at him. "The women will catch you up all too quickly if you come over to the restaurant with them tonight."

He nodded slowly. He still wasn't sure that he wanted to go, but he didn't see the point in spelling that out.

He obviously didn't need to. Damon smiled at him, then at Echo. "But I'll look forward to seeing you both around." He walked over to one of the treadmills, and Echo watched him go.

"I get the impression that the two of you might have some things in common," said Russ.

"Yeah." Lucky did too.

~ ~ ~

Dee managed to snag a booth by the window when she got to the bakery. She felt a little guilty taking up a whole booth where a bunch of people could sit when she was by herself, but she was hoping that she wouldn't be by herself for long. It was probably a forlorn hope; she didn't really expect Lucky to come. She hadn't given up hope completely. If she had, she would've stayed home this morning. But the last thing she wanted was for him to show up and to think that she'd stood him up.

She didn't mind if he stood her up – of course, she'd be disappointed, but not too surprised, and she could certainly handle it. As strange as it may seem, she felt as though she was the more robust of the two of them – in that sense, at least. Lucky didn't strike her as the kind of guy to go out of his way to be sociable. If he did make the effort, she'd hate for him to feel as though it had been a mistake.

She took a sip of her vanilla mocha and stared out the window. This was why she'd wanted to sit here; she got to watch the world go by. Summer Lake had struck her as a sleepy little place when she first arrived, but it was proving her wrong this morning. It seemed that she'd come to town at the very beginning of the tourist season. In just a couple of weeks, the weather had warmed up, the sun had come out, and it had brought the people with it.

Main Street was bustling this morning. It was fun to watch the people and try to determine whether they were locals or tourists. In some cases, it was easy to guess. Tourists behaved like tourists the world over.

Whoever they were, and whatever their business, Dee had always enjoyed people watching. Sometimes, people's actions sparked the seed of a story in her mind. Other times, she noted interesting quirks and characteristics that would later shape the people who populated the pages of her books.

This morning, she wasn't as attentive as usual; she was more interested in looking out for a certain tall, guarded, watchful man and his dog. After she'd been sitting there for half an hour, she accepted that he wasn't coming. Yes, she was disappointed – but not surprised.

"Can I get you anything else?"

She smiled at the younger woman, who'd come to clear the table. "No. I'm going now, thanks. And I'm sorry I hogged the booth for so long."

"That's fine. That's what they're here for. I'm not trying to rush you out. I just noticed that you'd finished, so, I thought I'd come and say hi and see if you needed anything else. I'm April by the way. You're not a tourist, are you?"

"I'm not. At least, I'm not a weekend visitor. I'm here for the summer – maybe for longer. It's nice to meet you, April. I'm Dee."

"Oh, you're Emma's friend, right? You're a writer, aren't you? She said that you might be coming out with everyone tonight – to listen to the band. My fiancé, Eddie, is in the band. I hope you'll come. I mean, I know everyone gets all excited when Clay's going to sing with them, and it's just Eddie and Chase tonight. But they're good."

Dee loved the way she smiled as she talked about her fiancé.

"I'm sure they are. I look forward to hearing them play. And if I don't show up tonight, it won't be because I don't want to hear them. It's more because you youngsters don't need me hanging around."

April laughed. "You don't have the hang of Summer Lake yet, do you? After you've been here for a while, you'll realize that the generations all party together – always have, always will. I thought that was kind of strange myself when I first came to live here. But it's true. Eddie's dad, Ted, and his lady, Audrey, come out with us all often enough. And so does my son, Marcus. It's just how things are. Do you mind if I ask you something?"

"Go ahead," said Dee.

"It's just… I'm not being nosy – well, I am, but not for the sake of being nosy. Are you here by yourself?"

"I am. But that's nothing unusual for me." She gave April a reassuring smile. "I'm not lost and all alone. If you're worried about me, I appreciate it, but there's no need."

April chuckled. "You didn't strike me as someone I needed to worry about. I was just going to suggest that if you're not comfortable coming out with all of us, you need to get to know Ted and Audrey and the rest of them. They're good people – and they have a lot of fun."

"Thanks. I'm sure I'll bump into people around town while I'm here."

April finished wiping down the table and stood back. "I'm sure you will. Everyone's friendly here. And if ever you want anything – a coffee, a pastry, someone to chat to – I'm here most days. And even when I'm not, Renée is." She tilted her head in the direction of the counter, where a redheaded young woman was serving. "She owns the place. She's awesome."

"Thanks."

Dee was trying to keep her attention on the sweet young woman in front of her, but she couldn't help looking at the door when it opened. It was silly, and she knew it. If Lucky was going to come, he would've shown up a while ago. It was even sillier to feel disappointed when it wasn't him who came in.

April opened her mouth as if to ask a question, but then she closed it – apparently thinking better of whatever she'd been about to say.

"Well, it was lovely to meet you, April. I'm sure I'll see you again soon."

"I'll look forward to it. Sorry for being nosy, but were you supposed to be meeting someone here?"

Dee was surprised to feel a touch of heat in her cheeks. "Is it that obvious that I've been stood up?"

April shook her head rapidly. "No! I'm sorry. I didn't mean that. I..."

"Sorry," said Dee. "I didn't mean to embarrass you – or myself. I suppose I'm just feeling a little self-conscious. I haven't exactly been stood up. I'd just thought that I might meet up with someone."

April nodded, clearly not knowing what to say.

Dee rolled her eyes at her. "On that note, I'll go. It was lovely chatting with you, April. I'll look forward to seeing you again."

Once she was outside, she looked back in through the window. April was back at the counter, and she was chatting with that woman Ben had introduced Dee to the other day. Taryn? She turned away hurriedly when they both looked out through the window at her. She felt a little uncomfortable – as if they were talking about her.

She shrugged the feeling off as she walked down Main Street away from the bakery and back to the square where she'd parked her car. It had been a good morning. She'd enjoyed getting out, enjoyed meeting April. If she and Taryn were talking about her, it was hardly surprising; she was a new face in a small town. There was no point in thinking that there might be anything more to it than that. There was no point in being disappointed that Lucky hadn't shown up, either. She'd expected that. So, why did she feel so down?

She blew out a sigh as she unlocked the car and climbed in. She knew better than to base even the tiniest part of her happiness on a man. It was no big deal. She started the engine with a smile. The day was getting warmer, it was the weekend, and she was going to treat herself to an afternoon off. She could swim in the pool and sit out in the sun. That sounded perfect.

~ ~ ~

Dalton grabbed two bottles of water from the fridge and threw one to Lucky. He caught it and took a long drink before wiping his arm over his forehead.

"Thanks."

"If there's any thanking to be done, it should be me thanking you. But we don't need that, do we?"

Lucky shook his head. He knew what Dalton meant; they were teammates. They helped each other out. It used to be that they helped each other to take down their targets and stay alive in the process. These days, he might be helping Dalton to finish renovating Adam's house, and Dalton might be giving him a cold drink of water, but the principle was still the same – no thanks were required.

They'd spent the afternoon working in the yard. Dalton had finished most of the interior work already. There were only a few jobs still to do before the house would be finished. Adam had let Dalton stay here rent free when he first came to town, and in exchange Dalton had promised that he would finish renovating the place for him.

Dalton had moved to a new place across the lake with Taryn before Lucky arrived, but there was no way that he would not keep his word to Adam. Lucky was happy to help him out. And it wasn't as though he had far to go. He was staying in the house that Taryn had been living in. It was another rental, and it backed up to Adam's place.

He looked around for Echo and Star, and smiled when he spotted them curled up together at the top of the steps that led to the back door. He tilted his head in their direction and said to Dalton, "It's good to see the two of them together."

"It is," Dalton agreed. "I know that Echo gets all the human affection and attention a dog could need from you – and the same goes for Star with Taryn and me, but I think it does them good to have another dog to hang out with."

"Yeah." When Lucky had finally received the papers giving him ownership of Echo after they retired, it had been suggested that he should get another dog to keep her company. He hadn't wanted to – as far as he was concerned, they had each other and that was enough. But seeing her with Star was making him question that decision.

"I take it you didn't go for coffee."

Lucky shook his head slowly.

"Why not?"

"What's the point?"

"Echo's not the only one who would benefit from making more friends."

"Yeah."

Dalton blew out a sigh. "So, we're not going to talk about it?"

"No."

"Okay. Are you still coming out tonight?"

"I don't want to."

"I know that. You haven't wanted to all along. But you said you would."

Lucky took another drink of his water before making a face at his friend. "I know I should make the effort."

"You're right, you should. I…" The sound of Dalton's phone ringing cut him off. He pulled it out of his back pocket and checked the screen. When he smiled and said, "Sorry, I need to take this," Lucky guessed that it was Taryn.

"Hey, where are you? We're almost done over here."

Lucky wandered away from him toward the dogs. He didn't need to stand there listening in their conversation.

"Hang on a minute. Lucky?"

He turned around. "What's up?"

Dalton held his phone out. "She wants a word."

Lucky tried to hide his frown as he took the phone.

Dalton laughed. "Sorry. I do what I can, but if it's a case of pissing Taryn off, I'm going to throw you under the bus every time, buddy."

"Hey, Taryn. What's up?"

"Lucky! What happened to you this morning?"

He straightened up. How the hell did she even know? Dalton had only asked him a few minutes ago.

"What do you mean?" he hedged.

Taryn laughed. "Don't give me that shit. You know exactly what I mean."

"Why don't you tell me, just so that we know we're on the same page?"

"Were you supposed to meet Dee at the bakery this morning?"

His heart started to pound in his chest. See, that was why he didn't bother with women. Yes, he was attracted to Dee, he'd even thought that she might be his kind of person, but if she went around bitching to her friends that he'd stood her up – especially when he hadn't committed to anything, then…

"Shit! I'm sorry! I'm talking to you the same way I do to Dalton. He's used to it – just ask him, he'll tell you. I'm a piece of work. I apologize for getting all up in your business, but I won't apologize for being who I am. And before you go thinking that she's running around telling people that you let her down, she didn't say a word – not to me or to anyone else.

"I just happened to see her in there, and when I asked about her after she left, April told me that she'd been hoping to meet someone, but they hadn't managed to show up."

Lucky nodded at the phone. It wasn't as though she'd be able to hear that, but he didn't know what else to say.

"Don't be mad at me?"

"I'm not mad. I just don't know what to tell you."

Taryn laughed. "You could tell me that you're going to call her and ask her to come over to the restaurant with everyone when you come tonight – because you *are* still coming, aren't you? You wouldn't want to disappoint me twice in one day, would you?"

He smiled through pursed lips. He'd never say it, but she really was a piece of work. "I hate to disappoint you, but I'm not going to ask her."

"Why not?" It was easy to hear the disappointment in her voice.

"Well, for starters, I already stood her up once today. I don't think she'd be thrilled to hear from me at this point."

"You won't know that unless you try, will you? Call her."

Lucky glanced over at Dalton. He wanted to shut Taryn down, but he didn't want to risk offending her – or his friend.

Dalton gave him a wry smile and spoke in a voice loud enough that Taryn would be able to hear him. "It's okay, Lucky. You can tell her to back off; she probably won't listen, but you can try."

Taryn's laughter rang out of the phone. "Okay, I'll leave it. But I had to try."

Lucky went to hand the phone back to Dalton, but he shook his head.

As he brought it back up to his ear, he heard Taryn say, "Sorry, Lucky. Dalton has warned me – repeatedly – not to interfere. I just… I want to see you happy. That's all."

"Thanks."

She laughed again. "Thanks, but no thanks, right?"

He had to laugh with her. "Something like that, yeah."

"Okay, I'll drop it – for now. But you do realize you have to come out tonight – if you don't, I'll think that I upset you and that you're avoiding me."

"No! It's fine. We're fine. I just don't want to…"

"Please come?"

He closed his eyes. How could he say no to that? "Okay. But just for dinner. I'll drive myself over there. I'm not hanging out with everyone afterward. I'll drive myself home as soon as I'm ready."

"Fair enough," said Taryn. "I'll see you later."

The call ended, and Lucky handed Dalton his phone back.

His friend shrugged as he put the phone back in his pocket. "You okay?"

"Yeah."

"I can't apologize for her – I won't. For one thing, in this case, I happen to agree with her." He chuckled. "And for another, it's not as though I could stop her, anyway. She's a law unto herself, I'm just along for the ride."

Lucky had to laugh at that. It was true. Dalton had always been the guy on their team who people backed down from. He was a big guy, imposing – intimidating was probably a better word. People tended to get out of his way, or to go along with whatever he wanted. Taryn was the first woman who Lucky had known to be able to keep up with him – and she didn't just keep up, she got out in front of him most of the time.

"It's okay, but like I told her, I'm just going to eat and run."

"And that's great. That's all you need to do. I think you've noticed by now that it's probably better to do enough to keep them off your back – you'll get more peace that way."

Lucky was starting to see that he was right – that was probably the best way to go.

Chapter Eight

Dee stood out on the pool terrace. She'd enjoyed her afternoon, but now it was time to make up her mind about the evening. Emma had called a little while ago and offered again to pick her up when she and Jack were on their way to The Boathouse. Dee had refused and had tried to talk her way out of going. Emma was so sweet – she'd said that she would understand if Dee didn't show, but Dee knew that she would be disappointed.

She'd probably end up having a good time if she went. She did know some of Emma's friends – Ben was lovely, and Emma had told her all about his wife, Charlotte. Dee was eager to meet her – she wanted to pick her brain. Charlotte was English, and Dee had an English character coming up in her next book. She was hoping that Charlotte might be able to help her with some British English slang.

There was Missy, as well. Dee adored Missy. She'd met her a few times when she'd come down to LA to visit Emma. Back then, she'd been a struggling single mom, but she was a fighter, a survivor. Dee had been happy to hear that she'd married the perfect guy for her. On paper, he didn't sound like a great match for Missy at all. Missy was down to earth, she was a practical soul who liked to talk, and knew how to have a good time. Her husband, by all accounts, was a mild-mannered techie – a geek, if you wanted to call it that. But from what Emma had told her, Missy and... Dan, that was his name, couldn't be happier together.

Dee blew out a sigh. She no doubt would have fun with Emma and her friends if she went, but she also knew that she would feel like the mom amongst them. Emma was a little older than Max and Pax, but Dee had always played a motherly role in their friendship.

She could always stay here and hang out to watch the stars fall. She could make her excuses to Emma the next time they talked. She turned around and started back up the steps to the house. Maybe she'd get dressed and plan to go. She could decide when she was ready whether she would see it through.

As she put the final touches to her makeup, she'd almost convinced herself that she really should go. It was terrible, but the one thing that was pushing her on was that she might possibly see Lucky there.

She probably wouldn't. But just that tiny hint of possibility was enough to make her get her ass out the door and into the car. She didn't even know what she'd do if he was there. He hadn't shown any interest in a friendship with her. He hadn't shown up at the bakery this morning, and he hadn't called. She should probably just take the hint. If he was there tonight, she should leave the poor man alone.

She was surprised that the square at the resort was already packed. There wasn't a parking spot to be found. She wanted to take that as her sign that she should go back home. But she'd come this far, so she decided that if she found a space in the first street that she tried, she'd still go in.

She was a little disappointed that there was an empty spot just twenty yards down the first street that she turned into. But she'd made a deal with herself. So, she parked the car and got out. She hadn't realized that this street ran parallel to the beach. In fact, there were steps leading down there.

She looked back at The Boathouse. She could hear the music from here and see the light spilling out onto the water from the open deck. She turned back toward the steps. She didn't really want to go into the crowded bar, but she wouldn't mind listening to the music and soaking up the atmosphere from a distance.

It was a crazy thought, but she was tempted to go down onto the beach. She'd thought that she was afraid of the beach – but that was all tied up with being afraid of dogs. She couldn't claim that she was afraid of dogs anymore – Echo had proved that.

She locked the car and walked over to the steps. She didn't have to stay. She could just go down there and see. It wasn't even dark yet. She trotted down the steps before giving herself the chance to overthink it.

She slipped off her sandals and wiggled her toes in the cool sand. This wasn't so bad. She could see the deck of the restaurant more clearly from here. She could also see that there was a set of steps that led up to it from the beach. Perhaps she would go and join Emma and her friends, after all.

She set off in that direction, dangling her sandals from her fingers.

"Hey, lady! You missed me, huh? I missed you, too."

Lucky made a fuss over Echo the second he got through the front door. She was as eager to see him as always, and he was even more eager than usual to see her. Dinner had been fine. Taryn's restaurant was a great place. And as soon as he'd walked in, he realized why Damon had looked so familiar – he worked behind the bar. That made Lucky think it might not be so bad to go over there and hang out sometimes.

He liked all the guys from work. He'd known that he wouldn't mind spending an evening in their company. They were good people – his kind of people. Their women were cool, too.

He had a sneaking suspicion that one of the guys – or perhaps all of them – had warned the women not to get on his case about being more sociable. They'd all been welcoming, all encouraged him to come out with them more often, but they hadn't pushed when all he'd offered were noncommittal noises of agreement.

He was just relieved that he'd done it. He'd gotten it over with, and now he was home with Echo. He squatted down in front of her in the hallway, and she butted her head against his chest.

"What do you think, lady? Want to watch a movie?"

She sat back on her haunches and gave him what appeared to be a stern look.

"No? What's up?"

To his surprise, she turned around and went to the shelf at the end of the hall. She took her leash between her teeth and brought it to him.

"You want to go for a walk?"

She sat back down and panted at him.

"Mind if I get changed first?"

She let out a low growl.

"Come on. It'll only take me a minute. There's no need to be like that."

She let out an angry sounding bark.

"For fuck's sake. Give me a minute, would you?" He caught her face between his hands and pressed a kiss to her nose to soften his words. "Let me get back into my jeans, then we can play on the beach, okay?"

She set the leash down on the floor and lay down beside it, resting her chin on her paws as she heaved a huge sigh of resignation.

Lucky laughed as he jogged up the stairs. "There's no need to be so dramatic about it. I'll be back in a minute."

Five minutes later, he was opening the front gate to let them out. Echo was on the leash. He wanted to let her off, but he figured that they should probably check out the beach first. It was Saturday night – and there were a lot more tourists in town than he'd seen up until now.

When they reached the sand, he checked up and down both ways. He could see people in the distance between here and the resort. Looking the other way, his heart rate picked up a little but at the same time a heavy weight settled in his chest. He felt bad that he hadn't gone to the bakery today. It wasn't that he didn't like Dee – the problem was that he liked her a little too much. He didn't know what to do about it, so he'd opted for his time-honored tradition when it came to women – and done nothing.

He looked down at Echo and then back in the direction of Dee's place. Perhaps if they went that way, he might …

Echo started pulling on the leash. Instead of dragging him toward Dee's, which he would've expected, she was straining to head toward the resort. He glanced the other way again. It was better not to head down there. Even if she were around, what would he say – what could he say? If he wanted to talk to her, wanted to see her, he had her number – she'd given it to him willingly. No. That whole deal was better left alone. He might be attracted to her, might be interested in getting to know her, but it wouldn't be right. Even if it were only as a friend, she didn't need the kind of complications that he came with.

Jesus, he couldn't even make it through the night without his dog and a night-light. No woman would want a man like that.

He let Echo lead him in the direction of the resort. When she looked back over her shoulder and waited for him to catch up, he gave her an apologetic smile.

"We can go this way, but I think you need to stay on the leash."

She barked in what seemed to be agreement and fell in beside him. She wasn't up for a leisurely walk, though. She stuck close to his side, but she pranced, as if she wanted to take off.

He looked down at her. "Do you want to run? Is that it?"

He broke into a jog, and she did the same. They passed a few different groups of people. He'd guess that most of them had spilled out from the resort. Some of them were loud – drunk already. The sunset had faded to gray, and the dark was descending. The lights from The Boathouse shone out onto the water, and the strains of music from the band grew louder the closer they got.

Movement off to his left made Lucky's head snap around. Adrenaline flooded his system as he prepared to fight off an assailant hidden in the rocks. But of course, there was no assailant. It was a couple making out in the shadows. He sucked in a deep breath in an attempt to calm himself as he and Echo jogged on.

A few minutes later, he slowed as he tried to assess a situation that was playing out ahead of them. A figure was hurrying toward the steps; it appeared to be a woman. Two larger figures were closing in on her as she went. All the hairs on the back of Lucky's neck stood up as they caught up to her and one of them grabbed her arm, stopping her.

He lengthened his stride and looked down at Echo. She'd seen the same thing that he had, and she let out a low growl. The next thing he knew, she lunged forward, tearing the leash right out of his hand.

"Echo!" he yelled as he sprinted after her.

He assured people all the time that she wouldn't hurt anyone, but right now, he wasn't so sure about that. She'd never witnessed violence in a civilian situation before. She was trained to attack, disarm, and if necessary, disable an attacker.

His lungs and his legs burned as he powered after her, hoping to reach the woman before the guys hurt her – or Echo hurt them.

Dee had dropped her shoes a little while ago. She wasn't worried about them right now. She was sure that Jimmy Choo would forgive her for abandoning her pumps in the sand, considering that she was faced with what felt like mortal danger.

When she'd gotten down onto the beach, she'd discovered that she was absolutely fine. She hadn't felt any fear – no fear at all. In fact, she'd been enjoying the feel of the sand between her toes as she listened to the music that drifted down the beach toward her. She'd gone and done what she always did and gotten lost inside her head.

She'd been thinking about Emma and her friends, thinking about Max and Pax and getting them out here for their visit. She'd even been comfortable enough to think that she should hang around until it went dark – she might get to see some stars fall. As usual, her attention had been all over the place – everywhere except in the here and now.

She'd realized too late that she was walking straight toward two guys who were obviously a little worse for wear. They were laughing and staggering, slurring their words – and it seemed that every other word was a cuss word. She'd quickly doubled back, hoping that they hadn't spotted her or paid any attention if they had.

Those hopes were dashed when she heard one of them say to the other, "Did you see the tits on that?"

She hurried forward, ducking her head and hunching forward, as if that might somehow disguise the fact that she was the one he was referring to. Damn double Ds!

The sand that had felt so cool and silky before seemed to hold dozens of sharp stones that tore at her feet as she hurried back toward the steps. It was no use; they were following her – she could hear them. And they were getting louder and closer with every step she took.

She'd almost made it to the steps when a hand grabbed her arm. She tried to pull away but let out a little yelp when the fingers dug in hard.

"Where do you think you're going, sweetheart? Me and Andy want to talk to you."

She sucked in a deep breath in an attempt to calm herself. It didn't work. She tried to pull her arm away again, but he just gripped it tighter.

The sneering smile disappeared from his face, and he gave her a shake. "I asked you a question."

His friend appeared beside him. They were both drunk. "You wanna party, gorgeous?"

The second guy – Andy, apparently – leered at her. Then, he squinted and leaned in closer. Dee wrinkled her nose when the fumes that were his breath hit her face.

"She's old!"

For a second, Dee felt offended. But if her being old was enough to deter them from whatever they were planning on doing, then she was on board with it. Hell, they could call her ugly, too.

"I know, but dude, look at the tits on it. I'm going to get me some of them, I could…"

Dee started to shake – she really didn't want to hear what he could see himself doing. As it turned out, he didn't get the chance to say.

All Dee knew was that one second, he was reaching out, about to touch her, and the next, all hell broke loose. What appeared to be a ball of brown fur went flying through the air. One guy fell, and the other shouted. Dee backed hurriedly away, unable to figure out what was going on, and the next thing she knew, someone else had hold of her from behind. There must've been a third guy, but she hadn't seen him.

She opened her mouth to scream, but the sound died in her throat when lips moved against her ear and warm breath fanned her neck.

"It's okay. It's me. I've got you."

She spun around. "Lucky!"

"Are you okay?"

She nodded but couldn't form words. At least, she couldn't until she remembered… She spun back around. "Echo!"

Echo had both men down on the ground. It didn't look like she'd bitten them, but they were obviously terrified of her. And Dee could see why. They were sitting, huddled together in the sand. Echo was circling them, snarling and snapping whenever either of them moved.

Lucky was still standing behind Dee, and he tightened his arm around her waist. "Are you okay?" he asked again.

She closed her eyes and relaxed back against him. Now that the danger was over, her mind was having trouble catching up. She didn't know what to say – what to tell him about what had happened or what to ask him about where the hell he and Echo had come from. All she knew was that she was safe.

"Are you okay to stay here with us while we take care of this?"

She turned to look up at him. "Take care of it? What are you going to do to them?"

He pursed his lips. "Not what I'd like to do, and certainly not what Echo would like to do. When I said take care of it, I meant call the police."

Dee's heart sank. "Do we really need to do that?"

Lucky met her gaze, his brown eyes full of concern. "We don't *have* to, no. Not if you really don't want to. But before you make your decision, tell me this – are you happy to let them get away with it…"

"I just want it to be over, to put it behind me."

To her surprise, he reached up and touched her cheek. "I know that. But you didn't let me finish the question. What I was asking was, are you happy to let them get away with it and let them think that they can do it again without repercussion – to someone else, someone who won't have Echo and me looking out for them?"

Dee stared back into his eyes. After a few moments she let out a short, humorless laugh. "Well, since you put it like that… I think you know what my answer is, don't you?"

"I hope so." He pulled his phone out of his back pocket. "I'll call it in."

"Okay."

When he ended the call – which he'd made without letting go of her – he gave her a wry smile. "I knew I should've come to the bakery today."

"Why's that?"

"Because there's something here." He waved his fingers between the two of them. "I don't know what to do with it.

So, I was trying to avoid it." He met her gaze. "Maybe we're meant to be friends or something – but even as I say that, I know it's an excuse. It's more than that. I just don't know what to do with it."

"Maybe you're just feeling protective again because you saw me in trouble… again."

To her surprise, he tucked his fingers under her chin and made her look up into his eyes. When he had her full attention, he shook his head slowly. "No. I spent my whole career protecting people, rescuing them from trouble and from situations far worse than the one you just found yourself in. And I have never – and I mean *never* – felt the way I did when I realized that it was you who these assholes were harassing."

She stared up into his eyes, not knowing what to say.

"When we're done here, I'll take you home. We need to talk. You good with that?"

Dee nodded. She *was* good with that. She didn't know what he'd have to say for himself. But considering that having his arm around her was enough to make her forget that two guys had just tried to attack her – and that the last time she'd seen him, his arm around her had made her forget that his dog had just scaled her wall, leading to her falling in the pool, then he was probably right – they might well need to talk.

If he thought that there was something between them, she'd be happy to investigate what it might be.

Chapter Nine

Lucky ran his hand through his hair as he watched the deputy drive away with the two drunken assholes in the back of his vehicle. He knew that they'd most likely get nothing more than a night in jail and a slap on the wrist. That pissed him off, but it wasn't his place to do anything about it. It was a good thing that they were tourists and had claimed that they were planning to leave town tomorrow anyway.

He looked down at Dee when he felt her shiver, realizing as he did that he'd felt it because he still had his arm around her. He didn't know what his deal was with that, but it seemed he couldn't help himself. On the bright side, she didn't mind. She snuggled closer in to his side. He liked the feel of her there; she didn't cling, even though it would have been understandable if she did.

He usually got claustrophobic around women, especially when they hung onto him. Dee's arm had been around his waist pretty much the entire time since he'd reached her, but it just rested there, lightly. It wasn't that he didn't feel he could get away from her – more like he didn't want to.

"Did you walk here?"

"No. I parked over there." She pointed to her Mercedes SUV that was parked not far from the steps.

"Do you still want to have that talk? Or would you rather I just let you go home?"

Her eyes looked huge in her face as she met his gaze. "I'm curious to hear what you have to say, but you've already gone above and beyond tonight." She gave him a rueful smile. "If you prefer, we could meet up tomorrow and have that talk over coffee?"

He chuckled. "If that's what you want, we can do that. But I *will* show up this time. However, if you're just saying that to try and let me off the hook, there's no need."

She gave him a puzzled look.

"I'm already well and truly hooked." He gave her an apologetic shrug. "I can't claim to know what I'm doing. I can't even tell you that I'm happy about it. But there's just something about you…" He didn't know what else to say, because he didn't know what the hell he was doing. What the hell he was even thinking. Then again, he wasn't thinking.

This woman had him acting on his instincts, just like Echo. There was no denying the fact that Echo had a special sense for anything and everything to do with Dee. Now, he was questioning whether he was picking up on what Echo felt – or whether, perhaps, she'd picked up on what he felt even before he had.

Dee tightened her arm around his waist just enough to give him a quick squeeze before stepping away from him.

"I don't know about anything else, but I can tell you that I could really use a drink right now. Do you want to come back to the house with me?"

"Yeah. If you're comfortable with us being there." He looked down at Echo. "If you like, I could drop her at home first."

Dee let out a short laugh. "If you're worried that I'm still afraid of her, there's no need." She looked down at Echo, who came to sit right beside her and leaned against her legs.

A strange, tingling feeling filled Lucky's chest as he watched Dee stroke Echo's head.

"How could I be scared of you anymore, lady?" she asked. "You've saved me twice, now."

"She saved you tonight. But last time, she only saved you from a situation that she created."

Echo whined and licked Dee's hand.

Dee laughed. "She's already apologized for that; it was just a misunderstanding." Her expression sobered as she looked back at Lucky. "Honestly, I couldn't be more surprised myself, but it turns out that after half a century of being terrified of dogs that look like her, Echo managed to get me past it in just a few brief meetings. You don't need to take her home on my account. Though, I understand if you'd rather I just drop you both off."

Lucky shook his head rapidly. He still hadn't figured out what had possessed him to tell her that they needed to talk in the first place. But since he'd said it, he wasn't going to back out of it. He knew himself too well; if he did that, he'd then have to avoid her. That would be pretty hard to do in a town as small as Summer Lake, and more importantly – he didn't want to.

"No. We'll both come with you. I want to make sure that you get home safe."

When they reached her vehicle, she opened the back door and Echo jumped in and settled down as if this was her regular ride. Lucky cringed at the sight of her sandy paws on the cream leather. Dee had been cool about it the last time she'd given the two of them a ride, even though they'd both been wet from their dip in her pool.

He climbed into the passenger seat, and she turned to him when she got behind the wheel.

"You can change your mind, you know."

"I don't want to. I just don't want to make you uncomfortable."

She chuckled. "You're the one who looks uncomfortable."

"If I do, it's because my dog has her dirty paws and her hairy ass all over your back seat – again."

Dee threw her head back and laughed. "I told you last time, I'm not one of those prissy women who's going to get all bent out of shape if my car gets dirty. I've raised two boys, I'm sure they've done worse things in the back of my vehicle than Echo would ever dream of doing – especially when they were teenagers."

Lucky nodded. She had reassured him last time – and she certainly didn't strike him as the kind of woman who got stressed out about a little sand. Perhaps it was just that he felt out of place in her vehicle – he didn't know too much about Mercedes, but he had seen the AMG badge. That meant this thing had probably come with a sticker price somewhere north of a hundred grand.

Dee's place was a little outside of town, but it still only took a few minutes to get there. That made him wonder why she'd been parked where she was, and why she was down on the beach at all – given that she'd told him she was afraid.

When she pulled up in front of the automatic gate at the house, she looked over at him. "You can ask me anything."

He turned and gave her a puzzled look.

"You have a question – it's written all over your face."

"It is?"

She nodded. "Let me guess, you're not used to people being able to read you, are you?"

"No. I'm not. In fact, I've been told in the past that I am the proverbial closed book."

"I imagine that you are – to most people."

The way her lips quivered with a small smile sent a shiver down Lucky's spine. He liked the idea that she might be able to read him – able to understand him – in a way that most couldn't.

As she pulled the vehicle forward, she said, "But go on… What was your question?"

"It wasn't a question as such. Or maybe it was. I was wondering about who you are."

She raised an eyebrow as she swung the SUV around the circular driveway to park in front of the house.

"How do you mean?"

There was something about the way that she asked that made him feel that she might have something to hide.

"I just meant… I don't really know what I meant. If you want to know the truth, I started out worrying about Echo making a mess of your seats. That went to thinking that this thing probably cost you a pretty penny. You're living here, by yourself, renting this big ass house… I don't know." He really didn't know. And it was becoming apparent to him the more he spoke that he really didn't know how to talk to a woman.

She cut the engine and turned in her seat to face him. "Well, if we're going to be friends – and I hope that we are. Then, I imagine that we'll get to know more about each other as time goes by. But for starters, I can tell you – because I don't believe I did the other night – I'm a writer. I'm also my own publisher. I do pretty well for myself – and that's probably an understatement in most people's eyes. I do very well for myself. You're right, this *thing*…" She laughed and patted the steering wheel "… Did cost me a pretty penny, but that's okay because I'm worth it. I really don't care if Echo gets it dirty back there. I don't care if she scratches up the leather."

She laughed. "I wouldn't be too thrilled if she decided to take a poop back there, but I think she's more of a lady than that. My point is that, to me, *things* aren't as important as people. And I'm aware that it's much easier to say that when you can afford to replace things. That hasn't always been the case for me, but even when I didn't have two pennies to rub together – and I had plenty of times like that earlier in my life – I still valued people more than I did money and the things it can buy."

"Yeah. I can see that about you." And he could. She might be the rich lady – and there was no question that she was a lady – who lived in the big house on the headland, and who drove the fancy Merc, but she was down to earth. She was good people – his kind of people.

She smiled and reached for the door handle. "Do you want to continue this conversation inside? I really could use a drink."

Lucky got out and opened the back door for Echo, who jumped down and trotted around to Dee's side. He followed them up the pathway to the front door.

"What made you choose this place?" he asked.

She opened the door and gestured for him to go in ahead of her before she answered. "Mostly the pool. I mean, it's way more house than I need for just me. Although, it is nice inside. Oh, wait! If you're judging me by the house, then you'll definitely get the wrong impression."

"I wasn't judging."

She laughed. "It wasn't an accusation! It's just that I can imagine how you see this place."

"How?" He was curious to see what she would say.

"Well, maybe I'm just projecting, but I imagine that you probably see it the same way that I do. Seeing it from the beach – seeing it from where you did when you were running – only emphasized the way I already felt about it. It's… Ostentatious? I don't know, I tend to think of houses as having personalities. Seeing it from the outside, I'm not sure that I like this one's personality. It looks like it's lording over the neighbors. I mean, all the houses around here are very nice, but most of them sit back amongst the trees, minding their own business. This one sits up on the headland, almost as if it's shouting, *look at me!*"

Lucky grinned. "You're not projecting. That's exactly the way I saw it." He looked around. The interior was nothing like the exterior. It was nicely done, with obviously high-end design and furnishings but it felt warm … homely. "But there's a lot more to it when you see the inside."

She gave him a look that he couldn't fathom before nodding and gesturing for him to follow her. She led him straight to the kitchen, where he was surprised to see her pour herself a generous glass of Jack Daniels before she even looked up at him.

"Sorry, I really do need this. What can I get you?"

"I'm good with the same, thanks."

She poured one for him and slid the glass along the counter toward him.

He chuckled. "Were you a bartender in an old saloon in a former life?"

She laughed with him. "Possibly. I've written a few books set in the old West. I like to think I would have survived as a pioneer."

"I'd say you would have done well." He took a sip of the whiskey, suddenly feeling uncomfortable – like he shouldn't have come. What had he been thinking earlier? Perhaps she was right. Perhaps he'd just gotten swept up in the moment. Perhaps it was just adrenaline that had made him tell her that they needed to talk.

He took another slug, and the burn down his throat set him straight. The danger that she'd been in, his urge to protect her, might have brought things to a head, but he hadn't been lying when he said that there was something between them.

When he risked a glance at her, she was giving him a puzzled look. "Are you okay?"

"Yeah. I'm good." He made himself smile, and it became genuine when she smiled back. "I'm a bit out of my depth here, but I meant what I said earlier."

He was relieved when she didn't make him spell it out.

"I know." She took a sip of her whiskey before raising her gaze to meet his. "I agree. There's a spark." She smiled. "I'm too old, and I've been around the block too many times to want to play games. So, I'll just come out and say it. I find you attractive. I'd like to get to know you. Whether that leads us to friendship, or to something else, or to nothing at all, remains to be seen. But I'd like to investigate – if you would."

All the tension left his shoulders as he leaned back against the counter and smiled. "I'd like that a lot. Although, I should warn you now that I'm not a great bet."

Echo leaned against his leg and looked up at him as she let out a short bark.

~ ~ ~

Dee had to laugh. It had been obvious from the first time she saw them that Echo adored Lucky. Dee loved to see her sticking up for him, even when she was defending him against his own words.

"She disagrees with you there. And I have to tell you that so far, so do I."

She wished that she'd kept her mouth shut when he straightened up and frowned. The smile that he'd just given her was the most relaxed that she'd seen him, and somehow – she didn't know how – her words had set him on edge again.

He pursed his lips. "I'm serious, Dee. I'm not just being self-deprecating. When I tell you that I'm not a great bet, I mean it. I'm trying to warn you."

She reached out and touched his arm, wishing that she could soothe the tension in him.

"Do you want to sit down and explain what you mean?"

He cocked an eyebrow. "That's it?"

"That's what?"

"You just want to sit down and talk about it? You're not going to insist that I'm wrong – or run screaming because I might be right?"

She rolled her eyes at him. "I'm going to guess that you haven't had great experiences with women in your life – you seem to expect the worst. To be fair, I haven't done that great with relationships, either. But, Lucky, I'm fifty-five years old – I'm too old for all the games that men and women get into. I've played them all before and I'm not interested in playing them again. I'm a straight shooter, and it strikes me that you are, too. If you're trying to warn me off you, I'm going to take that at face value. There are things that you think I should know – so I asked if you want to sit down while we talk about it. That's all."

She gave him a rueful smile. "And if we're being completely honest – which I plan to be – my legs are still a bit shaky after what happened out on the beach."

His expression gentled. "Sorry. Let's get you sat down before anything else." He looked around and then lifted his chin in the direction of the family room. "In there?"

"How about down by the pool?"

She could tell by the way he looked down at Echo that he thought she'd rather have them outside the house.

She gave him a stern look. "I suggested that because it's a beautiful evening and I love sitting out there. If I didn't want Echo in the house, I'd say so. Straight shooter, remember?"

He chuckled. "I'll try to in the future. How about that?"

"Fair enough."

Echo trotted ahead of them, down the steps to the pool terrace. Lucky stuck close to Dee's side. She couldn't figure him out for the life of her. He was closed off, guarded, and as she'd said, he seemed to expect the worst of women. At the same time, he was attentive and protective. He made her feel something that she'd rarely felt in her life – he made her feel safe.

When he set their drinks down on the table, she felt bad that Echo didn't have one.

"I'll just get her a bowl of water."

Lucky frowned. "She'll be fine. There's no need to go back up there."

"That's okay. I don't need to." She pointed to the pool house. "There's a kitchenette in there."

When she let herself inside, Echo followed and waited at the door, looking around the interior curiously. Dee filled a bowl of water and when she turned back, Lucky was standing beside Echo.

"This is handy."

"Isn't it? When I first saw the pictures of this place, I loved that it had a pool, but I wasn't too thrilled that it was down all those steps from the house. The pool house makes it perfect. I can hang out down here for the afternoon and not go back up to the house to …" She managed to stop herself before she talked about needing to go to the bathroom. He didn't need to know that. "To get a drink, or a snack, or anything. And I've been coming to sit down here in the evenings, too. I've been watching the sunsets from here – it's so beautiful. And when it's dark, there's so little light pollution that I get to see the stars fall." She was rambling and she knew it, but she couldn't stop it.

She was grateful to him when the puzzled look on his face gave her reason to pause. "What? I talk too much. If we're going to be friends, you should get used to it. I can apologize for it, but I can't stop it."

His whole demeanor changed when he chuckled. It was a deep rumbling sound that did funny things to her insides. She didn't want to risk looking down and bringing attention to them, but she knew her traitorous nipples had to be pointing at him.

"I don't have a problem with it. If we are going to be friends, it's probably better that you talk too much – I don't talk enough."

She smiled. "I bet I can get you talking."

She'd thought that he was handsome from the first time that she saw him. Perhaps not classically handsome; other than his full lips, his features were harsh. But he was unquestionably attractive. The smile on his face right now took him to another level – he was gorgeous.

"What's so funny? she asked.

He shook his head. "Nothing."

"No, go on. Tell me."

"I guess just the fact that I already know that you probably will get me talking. It surprises me – but it doesn't make me want to turn around and leave."

"And that's your go-to, right? If in doubt, run away?"

He laughed again. "You make me sound like a coward."

She shook her head rapidly. "I don't mean it that way."

"What other way is there?"

"In my mind, that's not cowardly, it's smart. *You* wouldn't turn around and run away because you were afraid. And removing yourself from situations and people that you don't want to have to deal with is a sign of self-awareness – not cowardice – in my book."

"Thanks."

"Not thank youable, just true."

She carried the bowl of water back out, and Lucky stepped aside to let her through the door. When they were settled at the table again with their drinks, and Echo was enjoying hers, Lucky raised an eyebrow at Dee.

"Mind if I ask you something?"

She sat back in her seat, pleased that he was relaxed enough to want to ask her a question. She'd feared that he might treat this more like an interview and wait for her to do all the asking.

"Fire away. I'm an open book."

He smiled. "And if you don't mind, I'll get around to asking about your books soon. First, I'm just curious about something you said earlier."

"What's that?"

"You said you sit out here to watch the stars fall; what does that mean?"

She chuckled. "Sorry. I forget. I'm so used to saying that to my son. There's a meteor shower this week. Oh, you should probably know that he's a researcher at the Asteroids Laboratory in Tucson. He's been fascinated with the stars since he was tiny. It's just a standing joke between us. He could tell you all the scientific data behind what's really happening up there, and I like to play dumb and just say that I think it's pretty when the stars fall."

He held her gaze as he took a sip of his drink.

"What?" she asked, feeling self-conscious.

He chuckled. "Just trying to figure you out. You hit the nail on the head earlier when you said that I haven't had great experiences with women. Normally, I'd think that was how you really saw it – that you thought the stars were falling out of the sky. But you're not dumb. Not by a long shot. My guess is that you used to say stuff like that to him when he was small. You played dumb in order to give him the chance to explain it, right? You did it to put him in the position of … Perhaps not authority, but definitely autonomy."

She smiled. "Yeah. He was quiet and shy. I looked for every opportunity I could find to help him build his confidence – and yes, authority. That's not a bad thing to have."

Lucky nodded. "You're a good mom."

She liked the way he said that; he didn't mean it as a compliment. It was more like he was stating a fact that he had observed. And for some reason, that meant more.

"Thanks. I'm going to guess that you don't have kids?"

He shook his head slowly. "Nope. I was married when I was younger. Not for long, thankfully, for her sake, my sake, and that of any children who might have come along. But kids weren't really an option. I was too focused on my career, and she was too…"

The silence dragged on for so long that Dee had to bite down on her tongue to stop herself from prompting him to go on.

"… She didn't want kids. She didn't have the time for them."

"A career woman?" Dee ventured.

He threw back his head and laughed.

Dee was pleased that there was no bitterness in the sound.

He shook his head with a smile. "If she aspired to a career, it was that of a trophy wife. She started out thinking that I was a catch because I was a SEAL. We were young – neither of us knew any better." He shrugged. "Reality set in soon enough.

Between my deployments, and the mess that I was when I came home ..." He shrugged again. "No. No kids."

From there, the conversation flowed more easily. Dee was aware that she was doing most of the talking, but she wasn't worried. He'd been right – they complemented each other in that respect. He didn't have too much to say, but when he did, he made his words count. He made her think and made her laugh. It had been a long time since anyone had done that – let alone a man.

Echo lay between them, occasionally looking up. When she got to her feet, and rested her chin on Lucky's knee, he checked his watch.

"Shit! I'm sorry."

"For what?"

"That it got so late. You should've said something. We'd better get going."

Dee looked down at her own watch and was surprised to see that it was almost one in the morning. "Wow! I had no idea."

He smiled at her. "Thank you. I enjoyed this."

"I did, too. I'll give you a ride home."

"No. We're good. It's not far down the beach, and we're good with a walk, right, lady?"

Echo let out a small bark before coming to press her nose into Dee's hand.

"She's saying thank you and that she had a good time."

Dee stroked her head. "Thank you for saving me."

"Are you sure you're good? Do you want us to walk you back up to the house before we go?"

"No. I'm fine, thanks. I'd rather give you both a ride home, but if you want to leave from here, I'm not going to let you walk up the steps with me only to come back down again."

She followed them toward the gate and pressed in the number to unlock it.

"Thanks. Echo had no problem going over the wall, but I prefer this way."

She had to laugh. "Happy to help."

Echo went out through the gate, and Lucky followed her. Just as Dee was about to close it behind them, he startled her when he spun back around.

"Are you busy tomorrow?"

She smiled. "No."

"Want to hang out again?"

"Yes."

"What time do you get up?"

She shrugged, aware that it was already one o'clock in the morning. "I can't say for sure, but if you come for your run this way and I'm up and about, you'll be welcome to join me for coffee."

He smiled. "Okay." He took a step away and then turned back again. "And if we don't see you on our run, I'll give you a call a bit later."

"I hope so."

He stepped in so quickly that it was over before she knew it had happened. He pressed a quick kiss to her cheek, and then he was gone, jogging away down the steps. Half way down, he stopped and looked back over his shoulder. "See you tomorrow."

Dee knew that she had a silly smile on her face as she walked back up to the house, touching her cheek the whole way.

Chapter Ten

The darkness seemed to pulse with oppressive silence. Lucky's pounding heartbeat seemed to echo in the void. He was burning up. Between the heat that seared his skin and the impenetrable blackness all around, it'd be easy to believe that he'd already reached hell.

He rolled over, seeking the only comfort that he'd discovered since he'd been held here. The floor of his cell was cool, smooth stone. When he pressed his forehead against it, he found a few moments of blessed relief – usually.

That wasn't the case right now. He could hear the footsteps approaching; they were coming back for him. For a moment, he hoped that this time would be the last – that they'd finally kill him and put him out of his misery. But even in his current state – wracked with fever, already half beaten, and half starved to death – his mind refused to let that thought take root. He'd survive. He wasn't destined to die out here in a cave. He was stronger than that; better than that. The only easy day was yesterday. He would not let those fuckers win; they might take his life in the end, but they would never break his will.

The footsteps drew closer. His body began to shake involuntarily. He tried to burrow deeper inside his mind – to withdraw from this place, from *this hell, and go to the place where he and Echo got to live in peace – a beach somewhere with a backdrop of mountains. He tried to picture her beautiful, furry face. She was his strongest motivation to survive.*

He had to believe that she'd survived. She was the last thing he'd seen before he lost consciousness as his captors dragged him away. She was fighting to get him, but Tiny – the only guy on their team big and strong enough to hold her against her will – had her pinned to the ground underneath him. And Lucky loved him for it.

There was no visible movement in the blackness that surrounded him, but the squeaking of the door as it swung open made him curl up into a ball. He knew what was coming. He tried once more to press his forehead against the coolness of the stone underneath him, seeking one last moment of reprieve.

But there was no relief to be had. Instead of stone, there was something soft, yielding. There was no coolness, only warm, sweat-soaked … fabric?

He didn't understand. He curled up tighter when one of the bastards touched his shoulder. Against his will, a scream tore from his lungs. He knew what was coming.

Except, it didn't.

Instead of the heavy boots kicking his back and ribs as the fuckers yelled at him to get to his feet, all he felt was warm wetness on his face. He tried to brush it away – dreading to think what they were doing to him.

Instead of cruel laughter, he heard a low whine. Everything started to shift. He was drifting away from the scene. He wasn't there anymore.

A warm tongue licked his ear. He slowly relaxed from the ball that he'd been curled into. He reached one hand out, and his fingers sank into Echo's fur.

He opened his eyes and lay there panting, waiting for the horror to recede, and for his pounding heart rate to return to normal. Echo lay down beside him and rested her chin on his chest, her big brown eyes staring into his. He stroked her head gratefully.

"Thanks, lady. I'm sorry."

She whined.

"I know you say that I'm not supposed to apologize, but I need to. Okay?"

She lifted her head and licked his cheek.

He wrapped both his arms around her and hugged her close. "You got over it. Why can't I?"

He didn't know how many times he'd asked her that question over the years. He wasn't surprised that she still didn't have an answer.

He looked around the room. Everything was the same as it had been last night. He didn't know why but he always checked after he woke from a nightmare – checked to see if anything in the outside world had changed.

One of the therapists who he'd spoken to early on had told him that it was good to have an *anchor*, a solid frame of reference in the here and now.

He hadn't taken on board much of what any of the therapists had said – how the hell could they know? Many of the guys he'd served with couldn't fully understand – how would some woman whose only knowledge came from books and lectures? But that thing about having an anchor; he kind of liked that. He used his night light. In his mind, it was the light that led him back out of the darkness.

If therapists knew anything, they'd use a different word. An anchor – especially to guys who'd served in the Navy – was something that held you in place; worse than that, it was something that tethered you to the dark depths.

He blinked his eyes a few times rapidly – focusing on the night light as he did. That was just something that he'd made up for himself – and it seemed to work.

Echo sat up; she'd learned to recognize his blinking as his cue – she was the best therapist he'd ever known – and the only one he trusted.

He pushed himself up to sit beside her, leaning back against the headboard. She leaned against him, and he wrapped his arm around her.

"Thanks, lady. We made it through another one, huh?"

She licked his cheek, and her tail swished back and forth across the covers.

"I think I need a drink of water. Do you want one?"

She gave her answer by jumping down from the bed and waiting for him in the doorway.

In the kitchen, Lucky filled her bowl with cold water from the fridge. To Echo, chilled water was a special kind of treat – after their time in the desert, Lucky understood it. She did so much for him; that was the very least that he could do for her.

He drank a tall glass of water himself before looking down at her.

"What do you reckon, are we going to get any more sleep?"

She trotted to the shelf in the hallway and took the leash between her teeth. She brought it to him and dropped it at his feet.

He chuckled. "Okay. We'll go. And you don't need that."

She wasn't just smarter than the therapists – she was smarter than he was, too, and he didn't mind admitting it. There was a time when he would have tried to go back to bed and back to sleep, but that was just a waste of time.

Echo had trained him that it was better to get outside, get some fresh air and some exercise – even if it was three-thirty in the morning.

~ ~ ~

Dee smiled to herself as she sipped her coffee. The sunrise cast the lake in beautiful pinks and golds. She hadn't expected to be up this early – not after last night. But here she was.

She felt great, too. She wasn't tired and bleary-eyed. She chuckled at the thought that instead, she was bright eyed and bushy tailed. She'd slept well – she could claim a deep, if not dreamless, sleep. And those dreams? Hoo boy! But she wasn't worried – Lucky didn't need to know what her horny little mind had been up to.

She turned to look up the beach in the direction of his house. She hoped that he would come this morning, but even if he did, it was too early yet.

A smile spread across her face as she reached up and touched her cheek. He was such a sweet guy! She would never have guessed it. Sure, it was obvious that he wasn't exactly comfortable around women. But she would have guessed that he would be the type who, when he decided to go for it, would haul a girl in for a deep kiss – tongues and all – that he controlled.

Instead, Lucky had given her the most surprising kiss on the cheek that she'd ever received. It hadn't been a friendly kiss, certainly not a superficial meaningless peck. It had been quick, over all too soon, but there had been feelings there.

Or, was she just fooling herself? As she thought about it, a shiver ran down her spine. No, she wasn't fooling herself. No way. Just the feel of him standing that close had done strange things to her insides. And it wasn't just her, either. When she'd realized what he was doing and had leaned in toward him when his lips met her cheek, his fingers had tightened on her arm. He felt it too – she knew he did.

She took another sip of her coffee. Unfortunately, she wouldn't be surprised if he'd scared himself off again. He was like a wild creature. He was powerful, could be dangerous if he chose to – she had no doubt about that – but he relied on his wits to survive.

He'd stepped outside his comfort zone to kiss her cheek the way he had. She knew that instinctively. What she didn't know was if he would now retreat. Her odd little mind conjured up an image of a sleek, black panther approaching a stream to drink. He'd tasted the water and fled – and she had no idea whether he would be back to drink his fill.

She laughed out loud as she looked down into her empty coffee mug. "Where do you come up with this shit, Dee?" she asked out loud.

She looked around feeling a little self-conscious. If she were inside the house, she'd answer herself. Out here, even though it was highly unlikely, there was the possibility that someone might overhear.

So, instead of voicing the thought that she didn't know, and it didn't matter – being able to come up with that kind of imagery helped with writing her books, if not with figuring out her life – she got up and took her mug back up to the house for a refill.

She'd told herself that she should probably stay up there for a while, but it was a beautiful morning and she wanted to make the most of it. Of course, if Lucky and Echo did come by, she wanted to be out there to spot them.

Armed with fresh coffee, her phone, and a magazine, she settled back down at the table by the gazebo. The day was already warming up, and she was tempted to take a swim. But no way was she going to do that this morning.

It wasn't that she was ashamed of her body; she had nothing to be ashamed of. She'd never been svelte, she was more on the chunky side, but she was good with that. One benefit of the double D's was that the rest of her looked smaller by comparison. Still, she wouldn't want Lucky to think that she was parading for him.

That thought made her chuckle. It was ridiculous. If he even noticed that she was in a swimsuit …

She blew out a sigh. She needed to stop this. He probably wouldn't come. So, last night, he rescued her from those assholes on the beach. She sat up straight. See, that was how caught up on him she'd been. Since the moment that he and Echo had come to her rescue, all her thoughts had been focused on him – on what a great guy he was, on how sexy he was, on what might possibly happen or not happen between them. That was messed up!

She knew that she wasn't that big on living in the real world, but when the real world presented the kind of danger that it had last night, surely she should pay more attention to it.

But no, not her! She'd completely glossed over the terror that might have happened and instead, only focused on the good stuff that might happen with Lucky.

She blew out a sigh. What she should probably do was get out of her head and back into the real world. She checked her watch. It was eight thirty. She should make that the wake-up call that she needed.

Whenever she'd seen Lucky and Echo on the beach it had been before seven thirty. She might as well just face the fact that they weren't coming.

She picked up her phone, but the only people she really wanted to call – Max and Pax – would both still be in bed at this time on a Sunday morning. She might as well just face the fact that it was time to get on with her day – her day right here in the real world. She didn't have any people here to share the day with, so she worked her way down to her next priority in life.

For her, writing usually came first. On Sundays, that wasn't allowed. So, people came first. In the absence of people, food came next. She got to her feet. This called for a breakfast banquet. Cooking kept her busy, and eating made her feel better.

It might not be the healthiest way to deal but, for today, it was all she had, so she might as well go with it.

Echo pulled at the leash as they jogged down the steps to the beach. Lucky felt bad, but he was more cautious about letting her roam free on the weekends because there were more people around. He still trusted her. She might have taken off after those guys last night, but she hadn't harmed them – even though he wouldn't have blamed her if she had.

When they reached the sand, she surprised him by straining hard against the leash. He gave her a stern look.

"Can we, please, not make a new habit of you taking off on me?"

She came straight back to his side and stood up on her back legs. Placing her front paws at his waist, she barked sharply.

He cocked an eyebrow. "What? What's the problem? You remember that we were down here for half the night, right? I thought you might be up for a leisurely stroll this morning."

She barked again before bounding away from him. He understood what she was up to when she started heading down the beach – toward Dee's place.

"Okay, all right! Have a little faith, would you? We're going to her place!"

As he started to follow, she gave him one of her smiles.

"Don't get too excited about it, lady. Last night was good, I'm glad that we got to hang out with her. But…"

Echo looked up at him.

"Where can it go? If you think about it, it can't go anywhere. I mean, sure, maybe we could be friends … And I'd like that. But…" He blew out a sigh. "I'd like to explore more than that – and she's already said that she would, too. How the hell am I supposed to do that?"

As they walked on in silence, he wished that Echo could answer him. As it was, the look she gave him spoke volumes.

"You know why! Last night was the perfect example. The way I see it, I have two choices; I can either tell her that I can't make it through the night without you and a night light." He ran his hand through his hair. "What woman would want to be with a guy who's afraid of the dark?"

Echo let out a low woof that made him smile.

"I mean woman of the human variety. I know you love me." Hearing his own words felt like a punch in the gut. Nobody was talking about love. He sure as hell wasn't!

"If I don't tell her about the nightmares, about… the rest of it, then what? If we're talking about more than friendship, then there's going to come a point where we want to spend the night together. Two choices again – either I don't warn her, and we both know that all hell will probably break loose in the middle of the night, or I make excuses as to why I have to leave."

He shook his head. "No way I could do that. I already have too much respect for her, and besides, she wouldn't let me get away with it. She's already said – not that she needed to – that she's not into playing games. If she thinks that's what I'm doing, she'll call me out on it, I have no doubt."

Lucky had to smile when Echo let out a low woof that apparently expressed her agreement.

"See? You're the one who took a shine to her – even though we don't really know her yet, we both know what kind of person she is."

He slowed his stride when he looked up and realized that they were almost there. There was no sign of Dee out on the pool terrace. He'd been hoping that she'd be there and would spot them.

Echo looked up at him.

"What do you reckon?"

She gave her answer by tugging at the leash, dragging him toward the steps that led up to the gate.

"No. No way are we letting ourselves in again. Echo, wait."

She froze at his command and sat down in the sand beside him.

For a moment he hesitated. For all the reasons that he'd laid out for Echo, they should probably just turn around and go back home. But, to his surprise, he didn't want to. Instead, he pulled his phone out of his back pocket. It was finally time to do what he'd said he would and give Dee a call.

Chapter Eleven

Dee set her phone down on the kitchen counter. She really hadn't expected Lucky to call. While she'd been cooking breakfast, she'd made herself face the fact that he'd changed his mind. So, hearing that he and Echo were down on the beach had come as a pleasant surprise.

She stopped in front of the mirror as she hurried outside. She had to laugh. She was a mess! But what the hell? He'd sounded strained on the phone. She had a feeling that he was going to tell her that he wasn't interested in being anything more than friends. And that was fine. Was she disappointed? Absolutely. But that was the way things went.

She ran her fingers through her hair as she trotted down the steps to the pool terrace to let him in. She stumbled and almost fell, and that brought her back to her senses. There was no rush. He and Echo were just out for a walk on the beach. They were stopping by to see her because she was a new friend. That was all. Friends didn't worry about the way they looked for each other – and they sure as hell didn't go breaking their necks because they were in too much of a hurry to see each other.

She took a deep breath before she carried on down. It would be nice to see them both. Hell, she'd made a breakfast banquet that would feed at least half a dozen people. She'd be grateful to them if they helped her to eat it. If they did, and they hung around to chat for a while, that would brighten up her Sunday. That was all this needed to be.

Still, no matter how much she tried to talk some sense into herself, butterflies took to flight in her stomach as she tapped in the code to open the gate. When she pulled it open, the sight of him standing there took her breath away. He was gorgeous! And when he smiled, he only grew more so.

"Hey. I'm sorry we didn't get here earlier."

"That's okay. I'm glad you came." She looked down when Echo pressed her nose into her hand. "And hello to you, too. It's nice to see you again."

Echo looked up and smiled. It made Dee laugh.

"Well, let's not stand here at the gate. Come on in. Do you want to come up to the house?"

"Thanks." He smiled. "We'll both wipe our paws on the way in."

Dee rolled her eyes at him. "If that makes you feel better, then have at it. But honestly, it's fine by me. Although, I should probably wipe mine too since I'm not the one who will be cleaning." She gave him a shamefaced smile. "That's one of my little luxuries in life. I can hardly be described as domesticated, and I prefer to work to my strengths. So, no matter where I'm living, I always have a cleaner come in a couple of times a week."

He grinned. "I get it; believe me, I do. Housework isn't near the top of my list of favorite things, either." He looked down at Echo. "And keeping a place nice with this lady around isn't easy." His smile faded. "I don't have a cleaner, though."

Dee felt as though she'd messed up. Was he highlighting the fact that paying for a cleaner was outside of his budget? She hoped not. She hadn't intended to imply that she saw herself as being above doing household chores. That wasn't the case, at all.

He turned to her when they reached the top of the steps. "Sorry. I didn't mean anything by that. It makes sense for you to have a cleaner. I'm sure that you make way more in an hour than you pay someone else to clean your house. It wouldn't make sense – economically – for you to spend your hours cleaning, would it?"

She smiled. "No. It wouldn't. And I'm glad that you see it that way. I didn't exactly grow up wealthy, and what you just said is how I usually justify it – to myself and to other people, not that anybody else really cares."

She felt herself relax when he smiled. "You don't need to justify yourself to anyone – whether they care or not. Who gives a shit what people say – or what they think?"

She chuckled. "My boys are going to love you. Apparently, I give a shit, even though I know I shouldn't. And they're always reminding me that I shouldn't."

She pressed her lips tightly shut when she realized what she'd said. Her boys were going to love him? That was a bit presumptuous of her.

She slowly raised her gaze to his, afraid that he might be ready to take off.

He didn't exactly smile, but his eyes twinkled. "I look forward to meeting them."

"Come on in." She let him into the kitchen. "Do you want a coffee?"

He shook his head slowly. "I'd love one, but I already had one this morning. I'll take a glass of water."

She raised her eyebrows. "You have *one* cup of coffee a day?" she asked incredulously.

He chuckled. "These days, yeah, I do. I used to live on the stuff, but…"

Dee was fascinated by the way his expression changed. One moment he was chuckling. The next, it was as if the clouds rolled in. His smile was gone, replaced by a troubled look. She wanted to ask what that was all about but didn't feel as though she had the right.

Instead, she filled a glass with ice and water from the fridge for him. Then, she fetched a bowl and did the same for Echo. Whatever Lucky's problem was, she figured that he might need a moment to recover without her attention on him.

When she straightened up from setting the bowl in front of Echo, he gave her a grateful nod.

"Thanks. Although, don't be surprised if she comes flying over your wall again soon."

"Why's that?"

"Iced water." He nodded to where Echo was alternately lapping at the water and crunching ice cubes. "I give her chilled water, but ice cubes? That never occurred to me."

"It didn't occur to me to do anything different for her than I did for you. You said that she thinks chilled water is a treat. Maybe I'm trying to win her over by going one step further."

He gave her a puzzled look, and Dee's heart sank. Why did she keep going and saying stupid stuff? She wasn't some desperate woman who was trying to reel him in. She really would be happy if he just wanted to be friends. Yet, within the space of a few minutes, she'd talked about her boys approving of him, and said that she was trying to win his dog over.

She turned back to the fridge to give herself a moment to recover from her embarrassment.

"Have you eaten?" she asked without turning around.

Shivers ran down her spine when she felt him move closer. He didn't stand inappropriately close but, apparently, she was attuned to him – she sensed his presence acutely.

"We're fine."

She turned back around. Whatever they were doing here, she didn't want either of them to feel as though they had to tiptoe around each other. "Are you saying that to be polite, or because you just ate a huge breakfast before you came out?"

"Honestly? To be polite."

She laughed. "Then, how would you feel about setting a ground rule for… *This* …" She waved two fingers between them in the same way that he had on the beach last night when he'd said that they needed to talk.

"Whatever this turns out to be – friends, acquaintances, enemies, or …" She managed to stop herself before she said lovers, but she could tell by the look on his face that he'd filled in the blank for himself.

"How about we just go with being honest over being polite?"

He surprised her by holding his hand out. She looked down at it for a moment before she understood what he meant.

"That would suit me just fine," he said. "In fact, it'll make things a lot easier for me – that's my standard MO."

She nodded as she shook hands with him. "I thought as much. I can't say that it's my standard, but it's definitely my preferred way to operate."

He met her gaze and held it; she could get lost in those eyes if she wasn't careful. Especially when he smiled – and he was smiling now. It dawned on her that he was still holding her hand, too.

"What?" she asked when the moment felt like it had dragged out for too long.

"If we're going with honest over polite, I'm wondering if there's a third option."

"What kind of option?"

He pursed his lips. "The kind where I don't have to be completely honest straightaway."

That wiped the smile off her face in a hurry. She started to withdraw her hand, but he held on to it.

"Shit! That came out wrong."

"It did. Want to try again?"

He blew out a sigh. "Want to? Yeah. Know how to? Probably not."

This time, he was the one who tried to pull his hand back, and she hung on to it. She already knew that he wasn't the kind of man who would deliberately withhold the truth for nefarious reasons. He was more likely thinking about protecting himself until he knew her better.

"Tell me, Lucky, are you an honorable man?" It felt like a strange question – because it was. And she already knew the answer.

He stood a little straighter. "I am. I swear."

"And whatever it is that you want to hide from me, do you have my best interests at heart?"

The way he frowned didn't bode well, but she felt a little better when he spoke. "I believe I do – although I am prepared to be honest enough to tell you that it's more about protecting myself. I... I'm... Shit! *Afraid* is the honest word, the word that I don't want to use, but I will. I'm afraid that when you know more about me you won't ..."

Dee had to clamp her jaw shut in order not to prompt him to go on. Whatever he had to say, he needed to come up with his own words in his own time.

He scrubbed his hand over his face before meeting her gaze and holding it. "You ever heard of PTSD?"

"Yes."

He shrugged and looked as though he was waiting for her to say more.

She couldn't resist. "Are you telling me that's something that you struggle with?"

She didn't miss the way that his hands went into his pockets, and his gaze went to the floor. "Not in any over the top kind of way."

Dee was starting to understand. "Well, I don't know if this will address what you mean, but don't you dare go thinking – even for a minute – that I would think any less of you for that. I have no idea what you went through. I'm just glad that, whatever it was, you lived through it. And if that's something that you don't want to be completely honest about straightaway, I understand."

She smiled, hoping to get him to do the same.

Echo had come to sit beside him and was leaning against his leg. He was stroking her head as she stared adoringly up at him.

Dee caught hold of his other hand again and gave it a squeeze.

"I'm good with that being part of our deal."

When he finally lifted his gaze to meet hers, she couldn't read his expression.

He didn't leave her wondering for long. He tugged on her hand, drawing her closer. His other arm came around her waist, and before she understood what was happening, she was pressed up against his chest.

When she looked up into his eyes, they were filled with an intensity that surprised her.

A small smile played on his lips. "There's something else that I'd like to make part of our deal, too," he said.

"What's that?" Her words came out as barely more than a whisper.

"This," he breathed.

Then, his lips met hers. It was just a brief touch, but it held so much promise. She slipped her arm around his waist and was surprised when he lifted his head.

"Is that going to be okay with you?"

"A peck on the lips like that? Yeah, I think I can live with that."

He shook his head at her with a smile. "I think I need to make myself a little clearer."

He ducked his head, and this time, there was nothing brief about it. He nipped her lips as his arm tightened around her. He finally let go of her hand and reached up to cup her cheek. Dee felt as though she melted against him.

He demanded that she open up for him, and when she did, he kissed her deeply. She clung to him to keep herself upright. She was no starstruck girl – but damn! Her knees actually buckled beneath her – and despite having been married twice, she'd honestly believed that was nothing more than a phrase that romance authors used.

Holy crap, had she been wrong!

When he finally lifted his head, her breath was coming fast, and she was relieved to see that his was, too.

~ ~ ~

Lucky cocked an eyebrow. He was shocked at himself. But he couldn't say that he regretted it. He just hoped that he hadn't overstepped.

"Was that okay?" he had to ask when Dee didn't immediately say anything.

He might not know her all that well yet, but he knew that – good or bad – she wasn't afraid to speak her mind.

That weird, tingly feeling filled his chest when she beamed up at him. "Hell no! That was not okay. That was amazing!"

He loved the way her arms tightened around his waist. He loved the way she felt against him. She was soft and yielding. He bit the inside of his cheek. It had been a long time, and this was *so* not the moment to go thinking about her yielding to him.

He met her gaze when she reached up and touched his cheek. "Are you okay?"

He cupped his hand around the back of her neck and pressed a kiss to her forehead. "Way more than okay. Thank you."

He rolled his eyes when she laughed and said, "*Thank you?* Seriously?"

"Sorry. I'm out of practice with this kind of thing. I…" He started to feel stupid but, as if she noticed that, she cut him off.

"If this is you *out* of practice, then I'm signing up to help you get back *in* practice." She waggled her eyebrows.

He had to laugh and as he did, he couldn't even remember what he'd felt stupid about.

"It's mighty kind of you to offer. And I'd be happy to take you up on it. Thank you."

She grinned. "No thank yous, remember?"

He smiled through pursed lips. "Okay. If I'm not allowed to say thank you in words, I'll just have to think of other ways, won't I?"

"Ooh! I like the sound of that. Want to tell me what you have in mind?"

"Nah. Well, maybe I'll tell you later. For now, I'd rather show you."

He lowered his head again, and loved the way that she rolled up on her tiptoes to meet him. Everything about her felt welcoming. Her soft, warm body felt so good against his own. Her arms wrapped around his waist felt more like she was supporting him than anything else. And the way she kissed him? Holy shit! She was warm, and wet, and welcoming, and he was already thinking of all the ways that he'd like to thank her without words.

He had no idea how much time passed before they finally stopped making out in the kitchen like a pair of kids. Something about her made him feel like they were kids. Whenever he'd been in a relationship before, he didn't know whether it was him, or the women that he'd chosen, but he was more used to feeling cynical – both in and about relationships. Dee was open and fun, but she wasn't naïve or clingy.

Her eyes sparkled as they looked up into his. Yeah, he wanted to get to know this woman.

That feeling only got stronger when she laughed and said, "You're welcome."

He ran his fingers down her cheek. "I have no idea what might happen between us, but this is me telling you, that I'd like for us to become more than friends."

She chuckled. "I think you just made that abundantly clear with your thank you. And…" Her expression grew more serious "… Just so that we're both clear; I'd like that, too. It strikes me that I might need to spell things out for you so that…" She frowned at him as her words trailed off. "Well, I don't even know why. That's just the impression that I get. Am I wrong? Is it going to be annoying for you if I go around stating the obvious about how I see things and how I'm feeling?"

"No. You're not wrong. I already told you that I'm not a great bet. I didn't mean that I don't want to be, I meant that I'm not sure that I know how. I don't want to let you down, but I can't promise that I won't withdraw when I don't understand."

"Fair enough. All I ask is that you tell me now – I don't like not knowing – when you withdraw, is it because you want me to come after you or because you want me to leave you alone?"

His heart sank. She wasn't going to like his answer. But this was something that he could be honest about – and he knew that he had to be. He cleared his throat before he said the words that he knew could end this thing before it even started.

"Leave me alone."

She didn't look shocked, in fact, she gave him an understanding smile. "That's what I thought."

"Is that okay?"

"I can live with it. I'm just glad that I asked, and that you told me." She laughed. "But who knows where this is going, anyway? You haven't even tasted my cooking yet. I vote that we have breakfast, we can eat out by the pool if you like. All of this stuff that we're talking about might not matter in a few hours anyway."

"What can I help with?" Lucky was grateful that she was so easy going – and she was right. They didn't know each other yet. But, as he helped her remove dishes from the fridge, he couldn't help hoping that today would be just the first of many that they spent together.

Chapter Twelve

"Are the two of you okay to hang out for a while?" Dee asked.

She was enjoying Lucky's company – and Echo's, for that matter – and she was hoping that they might stick around now that they'd eaten.

Her heart sank when he pushed his chair back from the table where they were sitting.

"We'd love to," he said with a smile. "And even if you weren't going to invite us to, I wasn't planning on leaving until I've cleaned up the kitchen for you, anyway."

She got to her feet and waved a hand at him. "Oh, shush! Don't worry about it. I'll take care of it later."

He chuckled. "What, because you're so domesticated and you enjoy doing it?"

She stuck her tongue out at him. "No, because I was thinking that we could go and sit down by the pool instead of hanging out here in the kitchen." She looked down at Echo. "You'd rather be outside, wouldn't you, lady?"

Echo's tail swished across the floor behind her. Then, as if she understood every word that Dee had said, she trotted to the back door.

Dee laughed out loud when she looked back over her shoulder at Lucky before reaching her paw up to pull the handle down and open the door.

Lucky gave her a stern look, but she just sat there panting at him.

"So, this is how it's going to go, is it?" he asked with a smile. "I'm going to have the two of you ganging up on me?"

"No –" Dee began, wanting to reassure him, but Echo cut her off. She let out a happy sounding little yip as she came back to Lucky.

Dee was amazed to see her take Lucky's finger between her teeth and gently tug on it. Lucky just rolled his eyes at Dee as he let Echo lead him toward the door.

"Don't worry, I'm not blaming you," he said with a smile. "This lady usually ends up getting her own way."

A shiver ran down Dee's spine when he added, "And I can already tell that you will, too."

She wanted to reassure him that she wasn't the kind of person who always expected to get her own way, but she figured that they'd already had as much deep and meaningful talk as he could handle this morning.

So instead, she gave him a playful smile. "I'm hoping that you'll get things your way just as much as we do."

She was tempted to say that he could have his way with her whenever he wanted. But that was a bit too forward, even for her. She didn't want to go making things awkward between them before they knew each other well enough to joke like that. It was strange; she wouldn't normally hold back, but she had the impression that Lucky wasn't the kind of guy who would be comfortable with that kind of innuendo.

When they got down to the pool terrace, she and Lucky took seats at the table under the gazebo. If she were by herself, Dee would have opted for one of the loungers, but she doubted that Lucky would be able to relax enough to lounge.

She looked down when she felt Echo rest her chin on her lap.

"Hello, lovely. What can I do for you?" She stroked Echo's silky ears before she even remembered that not so long ago, she'd been terrified of her.

Lucky laughed when Echo trotted over to the pool house and pawed at the door.

Dee gave him a puzzled look. "What's so funny? What does she want?"

"I hate to tell you, but I think you might have created a monster."

"What kind of monster? What does she want?"

"She knows that there's a source of cold water in there. Remember how she went in there with you last night?"

Dee had to laugh. "Of course!" She got to her feet. "I'm sorry, I'm not a very good hostess, am I? Let's get you a drink."

"Thanks," said Lucky. "Although, I'd say that she's the one who is not a very good guest. You have better manners than that, lady," he added in a stern voice directed at Echo.

Dee had to laugh when Echo turned her back to him and sat down, facing the door. She laughed harder at the sound of Lucky grumbling behind her as she went to get Echo a drink.

When she came back out and sat down beside him, he gave her a rueful smile.

"Thanks. But don't feel that you have to pander to her. If you don't mind me going in there, I can do it in the future."

Dee liked the sound of that. She liked the idea of the two of them spending time over here with her. "I don't mind doing it, and I don't mind you doing it, either." She met his gaze. "I hope that you'll make yourself at home here."

Her heart sank when he got that shuttered look again.

"Sorry. I only meant that I hope you'll feel comfortable."

He nodded but didn't meet her gaze. Instead, he looked around the terrace and smiled when he spotted a row of bushes over by the wall. "I hope you'll feel comfortable when she starts watering those – and she will; just look at the way she's guzzling down that water."

Dee relaxed. "They could probably use it. And I'm glad that you mentioned it. When I rented this place, the guy at the property management office, Austin, told me that there's no yard service included. Apparently, the owners' son used to do it, but he's just moved away. Austin offered to set something up for me, but I foolishly said that I'd do it myself. I don't know what I was thinking. But I need to get on it soon."

Lucky gave her a strange look.

"What's that supposed to mean?" she asked with a laugh.

"Sorry. If ever I get a weird look on my face – which I'm guessing that I just did – it's not about anything that you said or did. It's because I'm considering my words, considering whether I should say what I'm about to say. The guys used to give me shit about it. Apparently, it's a bad habit of mine."

"Noted," she said with a smile. "And thank you, knowing that will probably save me a bit of worry."

He frowned. "I don't want you to worry."

She waved a hand at him. "I will, but not in any big way. But go on, what was it that you weren't sure that you should say?"

Deep wrinkles furrowed his brow as he considered his words for a few more moments. "I was going to offer my services."

She choked back a laugh. "Your services?" Her voice was high and squeaky, and there was no hiding the humor in it.

He smiled through pursed lips. "My landscaping services."

"Oh, no! Thanks, but no. There's no need. I…"

The look on his face made her stop. She pressed her lips together to stop herself from going on – it was obvious that he had more to say.

"I was thinking of a trade."

She so could not let her mind go near the thought of trading landscaping services for sexual favors.

The smile that played on his lips told her that he knew exactly what she was thinking about.

"Dee Patterson!" he said in a mock stern voice. "I would never proposition a lady in that way."

"Damn, that's a shame!" She laughed out loud at the shocked look on his face. "Joking! I'm going to give you the benefit of the doubt – I'm going to believe that you're shocked because you just don't know me and my sense of humor that well yet."

He chuckled. "Thanks. I admit that you took me by surprise. You're going to keep me on my toes, aren't you?"

She nodded happily. "More than likely. I'm glad we're starting to understand each other."

"Well, since we are, do you want to hear me out?"

"Ooh! You're getting the hang of this, aren't you? You were trying to say something, and I took us off on seven tangents. Sorry. Go ahead."

"Hey! If I'm not allowed to say thank you, you're not allowed to say sorry."

"I'll do my best. But I'll tell you now that if I feel like I've screwed up, I will always say sorry."

"Good to know. I will, too. But anyway, back to my proposition." He shook his head with a smile. "I'm talking about an exchange of landscaping service for pool use."

Dee sat back in her chair. "You can use the pool any time. You don't need to trade for it." In her mind, that went without saying.

"I didn't mean to offend you."

"You didn't. I'm not offended, just surprised. I don't like thinking that you feel you need to trade for something that – to me – is just something that friends do naturally. I mean, I have a pool. You like to swim or at least, I imagine that you do. I can't imagine an ex-SEAL not enjoying swimming –"

"Former."

She gave him a puzzled look.

"Sorry. I didn't mean to interrupt you, but it's not *ex*, it's *former* Navy SEAL."

"Oh. Sorry. Why? What's the difference?"

"Ex implies *no longer*." He gave her a wry smile. "Like ex-wife or ex-husband. That's not the case with team guys. We don't cease to be SEALs, we're just no longer active, or we're retired."

Dee nodded slowly as she pondered that information.

"I'm not saying that explanation would necessarily hold up if you went to the dictionary and looked up the meanings, but that's just how it is to us."

"No. I get it. Semantics – different words can mean different things to different people. That's something that I have to bear in mind when I write. It can mess with your mind if you try to please all the people all the time – you can't. So, I go with using words in the context that my characters would use them – and trusting my readers to understand where they're coming from." She smiled. "Sorry. I don't mean to go on about myself, I just find it interesting. In this case – about former Navy SEALs – the interpretation that matters, the one we should go with is the point of the view of the people involved – you and Echo, and your other teammates, right?"

"Yeah."

"And you said team guys – that didn't sound like it meant just the guys on your team?"

"No. That's how we refer to each other. I'm sure you've heard talk about SEAL teams?"

She nodded.

"That's how things are structured." He shrugged, and Dee didn't want to push. She knew that a lot of information about Special Forces was public, but there was an element of secrecy, too. She didn't want to be too intrusive – even if she was fascinated.

~ ~ ~

Lucky chuckled; he could tell that Dee had questions but was holding back from asking. Usually, it pissed him off when people bombarded him with their curiosity. In her case, he'd be happy to answer what he could.

She opened her mouth to speak, but the sound of her cellphone ringing cut her off.

She laughed as she took it out of her pocket. "It looks like the bell saved both of us! Me from asking dumb questions, and you from having to answer them."

She looked down at the screen. "I'm sorry. I should take this. I won't be a minute."

He nodded and started to get to his feet; she might need privacy.

She waved for him to sit back down as she answered.

"Hi, Emma."

Lucky looked around the yard, trying not to listen.

"Oh! Okay. Yeah. I'm up. You know the code. We're down by the pool." She glanced at him and smiled.

"That's okay. It's my friend, Lucky, and his dog, Echo." When she laughed, Lucky wondered what her friend had said about them being here.

"No, it's fine. Come on down."

She ended the call and met his gaze. "Sorry about that. That was my friend Emma – she's the reason I came here. We knew each other in LA years ago and …"

He started to get to his feet. "We can get out of your hair. I …"

He sat back down when she put her hand on his arm. "You don't have to." She pulled her hand back. "I mean. Of course, go if you're not comfortable… I just meant …"

The look of disappointment on her face made his decision for him. He wasn't big on socializing, and he wasn't thrilled at the prospect of being subjected to her friend's curiosity. But no way would he walk away and leave her with that disappointed look on her face.

He smiled. "I'll stay."

"Good. She won't be here for long. She picked me up some pastries from the bakery this morning. She's been trying to get me to go out to breakfast or dinner with her and all her friends, but I keep refusing – so she keeps bringing me baked goods instead."

Lucky didn't see the connection. "As a consolation prize?"

He loved the way she threw back her head and laughed. In his experience, women didn't usually laugh like that. Dee wasn't like other women he'd known – she was so caught up in enjoying the moment that she didn't seem to care how she came across.

"No! She knows that if I keep sitting around here on my ass eating pastries, I'll get bigger than I already am. It's her way of trying to make me go out with them. If I go, I can eat a salad and take a walk afterward."

Lucky couldn't help letting his gaze travel over her. He'd tried to avoid letting himself get too caught up on her looks; *she was perfect!* He didn't just see it – he'd felt it the couple of times that he'd held her against him – she was soft and welcoming and …

Shit! And she'd caught him looking her over.

Her smile disappeared, and she patted her thigh self-consciously. "I know, right? I *so* should not be eating pastries. I'm on the chunky side as it is." She lifted her chin and nodded. "But I'm okay with me."

He reached over and grabbed her hand. "I probably shouldn't say this, but you are …" He couldn't help it, he looked her over from head to toe again "… you're fucking *perfect!*"

She swallowed visibly, and her fingers tightened around his.

"Sorry to put it so bluntly, but if I tried to figure out a polite way to say it, I'd come across as insincere."

She chuckled. "I prefer blunt. Especially when –"

"Hello?"

They both turned. A blonde woman, who was maybe in her late thirties was waving at them as she trotted down the steps. The first thing that Lucky noted was that she was much younger than he'd expected. He'd thought that Dee's friend would be around the same age as she was. He was also surprised that she wasn't alone. The tall, dark-haired guy at her side had to be her husband. And for some reason, he looked familiar.

He and Dee both got to their feet to greet them. He looked over at Echo. She was watching attentively, and he could tell from her reaction that they were good people. He hadn't expected them to pose any kind of threat – if he had he would have called her over. But more than that, she was watching them eagerly, her tail twitching behind her.

"Sorry to intrude on your morning," Emma told Dee as she hugged her.

Lucky had to hide a smile as the younger woman eyed him curiously.

The guy held his hand out. "Nice to meet you. I'm Jack, Jack Benson."

"Ah! That's why you look familiar, you must be Dan's brother?" Lucky said as he shook hands with him. "I'm Lucky."

Jack nodded. "You work with Dan, right?"

"Yeah." Lucky liked the way that people around here referred to it that way. The guys didn't work *for* Dan – they worked with him.

"How are you liking life here so far?"

"It's good, thanks." He looked down when he felt Echo lean against his leg. "Are you okay with dogs?"

Emma turned to smile at them. "Okay? You'll have to watch yourself or we may kidnap her! Hello, Echo beautiful. I was so sad when you left town." She looked up at Lucky. "And so glad that you came back with her."

"Thanks."

"Is it okay if I say hi?" asked Jack.

"Sure."

Jack got down on his knees in front of Echo and held up his hand. Lucky laughed when she high-fived him. "I take it the two of you know each other?"

"We do. I had the honor of getting to know Echo when Dalton used to bring her into the gym." Jack looked up at him. "I haven't seen either of you in there."

"I've only taken her in there early in the morning. I haven't figured it out yet."

Jack seemed to understand what he was talking about. "Well, if part of figuring it out means that you're not sure that you should bring her in when it's busy, I can tell you that everyone's hoping that she'll start coming again."

"Good to know. Thanks."

"Anyway," said Emma. "We won't intrude on your day. I just wanted to drop off your pastries." She gave Dee a meaningful look. "Since you turned down the breakfast invite *again*."

Dee laughed. "Thanks."

"Oh, and the other thing I wanted to ask is if you know when Max is coming yet. You know Missy's son, Scot? I was telling him about the lab where Max works. I'd love to get them together if we can while Max is here."

"Of course. Is he choosing colleges?"

Emma laughed. "No! He's about to graduate. He's been offered some job that I don't understand – he does all this advanced math stuff," she explained to Lucky. "Dan suggested that he should talk to as many people, in as many different careers as he can before he commits himself to academia. I thought about Max."

"Of course. And I'll ask him if he can think of anyone else who might be a contact for Scot to talk to. There are some NASA guys in the lab, and physicists and ..." she shrugged. "The kind of people who Scot might enjoy talking to."

"Awesome. Thanks." Emma smiled at them. "Okay. We'll see ourselves out. It was lovely to meet you, Lucky. I hope we'll see you again soon. In fact, maybe you can help me to get Dee out and socializing. Everyone's going to The Boathouse next Saturday night – you should both come."

Lucky nodded. Maybe it was time to start making an effort to be more sociable – and if he and Dee could do that together, it sounded more appealing.

After they'd gone, Dee cocked an eyebrow at him. "*You're* signing *me* up to be more sociable and go out with everyone?"

He laughed. "Sorry, I didn't mean to throw you under the bus."

She laughed with him. "Not a problem – as long as you're going with me."

"That's the plan."

She searched his face, and he stepped closer, sliding an arm around her waist.

"I like the sound of this plan," she breathed in the moment before his lips came down on hers.

He didn't know what had gotten into him – hauling her close and kissing her like this. But she wasn't complaining – and he sure as hell wasn't.

Chapter Thirteen

After Dee closed the gate behind Lucky, she looked down at Echo.

"Well, do you want to come up to the house with me while I get changed?"

Echo let out the happy sounding little yip that Dee had already learned was her way of saying yes.

"You know, lady," she addressed Echo as they made their way up the steps to the house, "I don't know who was more surprised about this turn of events. I'm shocked at myself that I'm so comfortable having you here with me – and I'd say that your man is just as shocked, if not more so. I mean, he can't believe that I'm okay with you staying here and I think he's just surprised at himself for being comfortable leaving you."

She stopped when they reached the patio outside the kitchen.

"I think you're the only one who isn't shocked by any of it. What are you up to?"

Echo sat down and cocked her head to the side as if she was listening intently.

Dee laughed. "Do you think that I might be good for him?"

She felt foolish when she realized that she was hoping for an answer.

"Well, I don't mind telling you that's what I'm hoping. Is that okay with you?"

Echo let out a short sharp bark.

"Come on. You might as well come upstairs with me while I get changed; if we stand around here talking, he'll be back before we're done."

They'd had a lovely day so far, and the weather was perfect. The pool looked so inviting, and Lucky had already talked about wanting to use it, so Dee had suggested that they should swim.

Of course, she hadn't thought about swimsuits.

As tempted as she'd been to suggest they should go skinny-dipping, she got the impression that he wouldn't be comfortable with that. Instead, she'd said that it would take her so long to go upstairs and change, that he'd have plenty of time to go home and do the same.

She'd offered him her car keys – it seemed logical to her that he should take the car, but he'd refused. He'd insisted that he could run down the beach in less time than it would take to drive, but she could tell that it was more about him being uncomfortable borrowing her vehicle.

It didn't matter. All that mattered was that they were going to spend the afternoon and hopefully the evening together. As she pulled open the dresser drawers, looking for a swimsuit, she realized that it also mattered to her how she looked.

A shiver ran down her spine when she remembered the way he looked at her earlier – and what he'd said. He looked at her like he was a starving man, and she was a juicy steak. She didn't think that she'd ever forget the look in his eyes when he'd said, *you're fucking perfect.*

She looked down at Echo, feeling a little embarrassed.

"I don't think that you can read my mind. But just in case you can, I apologize. I know he's your man, and I would never try to take him away from you. But damn, girl! I can tell you that I wouldn't mind sharing him with you." She laughed. "It's okay, though. I want him for very different things than you do."

To her surprise, Echo jumped up on the bed. She held Dee's gaze as if she was listening to every word.

"Is that your way of having some honest girl-talk with me and letting me know that we don't have to tell him *everything*? You know he said that you wouldn't go on the furniture, right? I'm not saying that I mind you being up there – I don't."

Echo let out a short sharp bark.

"So, let me get this straight. You're telling me that just like he has no clue about the non-PG rated thoughts going through my mind, he has no clue that you like to climb on the furniture?"

She had to laugh when Echo lay down, resting her head on the pillow.

"Not just climb on the furniture, then? You like to be comfortable?"

She ran her hand over Echo's head. "I bet you had it tough working with all those men, didn't you? I know you're a soldier and everything – oops, sorry, sailor? That doesn't sound right either. But you know what I mean. You're a highly trained, Special Forces… whatever you are, but you're still a girl, right? You still need some pampering and some girly time?"

Echo let out a big sigh.

"What's that? Relief that someone finally understands you?"

Even though Echo couldn't use words to explain, Dee felt as though she had it right.

"How about we stick together, you and me? I'll take care of you with chilled water and ice cubes, and a fluffy bed and…"

Echo's bark sounded different this time.

"No? No to which bit? I know that you like chilled water and ice cubes, so are you telling me that you don't want a fluffy bed?"

Echo barked again.

"Okay. So, you like my bed. You like my pillow. But you don't want a fluffy bed of your own?"

She ran her hand over Echo's head again, and then it hit her.

"Is fluffy too hot? That's it, isn't it? You want a nice soft bed, but not a fluffy one."

When Echo panted at her, she felt as though she'd landed on the right answer.

"Okay. I'll do some research online and see if I can find you a nice soft bed of your very own with a cover that isn't fluffy."

She pushed up off the bed. "But for now, I need to get myself into a swimsuit and we need to get back down by the pool so that we'll be there when he comes back."

She hadn't hesitated for even a moment before giving Lucky the code to open the back gate to let himself in when he returned. She thought about that as she hurriedly changed into her favorite one-piece swimsuit. She considered herself to be... sensible, if not hypervigilant, about her safety.

She wondered if the boys would give her a hard time over trusting Lucky so much so quickly. She shrugged. They wouldn't if they got to know him; she was sure of that. She just hoped that they would get the chance to. She really needed to get their travel plans set up and get them out here.

Once she had her swimsuit on, she went and grabbed a cover-up wrap from the closet and put that on, too. A quick twirl in front of the mirror reassured her that she would do.

"Are you ready?" she asked Echo.

~ ~ ~

Lucky checked his watch as he jogged back down the steps to the beach. He'd gotten back to the house and changed in record time. He didn't even really understand why he was in such a hurry.

If he had to explain himself to anyone, he'd say that he was concerned about Dee with Echo. He knew damn well that Echo would take good care of her, and it seemed that Dee's fear of her had evaporated. But he wasn't convinced that a lifetime's fear – especially not a fear caused by the kind of story that she'd told him – wouldn't come back out of the blue when she was left alone with Echo.

When he hit the beach, he broke into a jog. He wasn't going to lie to himself and claim that it was good exercise. He was jogging because he was too damn impatient to walk.

He scowled when his cell phone rang in his pocket. Whoever it was, they could wait. He could call them back some other time. He kept telling himself that as he listened to it ring, but he couldn't do it.

He slowed to a walk and took his phone out just as it stopped ringing. He made a face when he saw Dalton's name on the screen. Hopefully, he'd take the hint. They'd see each other at work tomorrow, anyway.

Just as he was about to put the phone back into his pocket, it started ringing again.

"Dalton. What's up?"

Dalton laughed. He did that a lot these days. It suited him – even if Lucky couldn't remember him laughing much at all in the old days.

"I thought I was supposed to be the grouch."

"I'm not being grouchy. I'm just in a hurry." Lucky squeezed his eyes shut. Why in the hell had he said that?

"What kind of hurry? Where are you going?"

Lucky pursed his lips.

"The woman?" Dalton asked after a few moments of silence.

"Her name is Dee."

He wanted to kick himself when Dalton laughed again. "I know! I just wanted to return the favor. I remember how I reacted when you called Taryn *the woman*."

"This isn't the same."

"The same as what?"

"Stop trying to be a smartass. You know what I mean."

"I'm not sure that I do. I am hopeful, though. So, why don't you tell me what's going on?"

"Because like I told you, I'm in a hurry."

"Are you going to see her?"

"Yeah."

"The first time?"

Lucky blew out a sigh. "Yes and no."

"What does that mean?"

"I ran into her last night. I was over there this morning. I'm headed back there now."

"Damn! You didn't waste any time."

"What do you mean?"

"You ran into her last night, and you were still there this morning?"

"No! I ran into her last night. Then, I went home. She invited us to go over and hang out today. We went and had breakfast with her. I've just been home, and now I'm on my way back. Is that enough detail for you?"

He could hear the smile in Dalton's voice when he said, "No. I need a little more clarification. You said that *we* had breakfast with her, but then you said *I've* just been home."

"Jesus! Pick me up on every little detail, why don't you?"

Dalton laughed. "What can I say? You left the threads dangling; I just pulled them."

"Okay. So, Echo stayed there with her."

"She's good people, then."

"Yeah. She is." Lucky looked up at the house when he realized that he was back there already. There was no sign of Dee and Echo out on the pool terrace, though. "Anyway, did you call for anything in particular?"

"You're back at her place?"

"Yeah." He climbed the steps up to the back gate.

"Okay, I'll let you go. Before I do, though, tell me something?"

"What's that?"

"What do you like about her?"

Lucky stopped at the top of the steps. He'd just raised his hand to tap the code into the keypad on the gate, but he let his arm fall back down to his side as he thought about Dalton's question.

"She's real. She's not… pretentious. I don't even think that's the right word. But you know how women pretend? They try to be what they think you want them to be? She's not like that. She's … herself." He smiled as he thought about it. "And she's not afraid to call me out. I don't know, Dalton. There's just … There's no bullshit."

"It sounds like she'll be a good friend, then."

Lucky felt himself stand up straighter. "What's that supposed to mean?"

"Just that the things that you like about her make it sound as though you see her as a friend."

Lucky scowled. "Then try this. I see her as a whole lot more than just a friend. Maybe I was just giving you the abridged version. Maybe I didn't want to say out loud that I'm fascinated by her. That I love the way her mind works – she's really smart, and she's funny, too. Maybe I didn't want to tell you that she's so goddamn beautiful that it makes something inside me ache – and there's no way in hell I would ever tell you what else aches when I get near her. Maybe…"

Shit!

Two things happened at once. Dalton started laughing, and that was bad enough. But worse still, the gate in front of him swung open, and Dee stood there with a stunned look on her face.

"You still there?" Dalton asked.

All Lucky could do was stare into Dee's wide, shocked eyes.

"I have to go."

"What's up? Are you okay?"

"Yeah. I'll see you tomorrow."

"Don't you dare hang up on me, Penny. What the fuck is wrong?"

"I'm back at Dee's. She's here."

Dalton chuckled. "And she heard everything that you just said?"

Lucky's heart was pounding, and he couldn't tear his gaze away from Dee's. "Yeah." He gripped the phone tighter as he made his decision. "Dee heard everything that I just said. I have to go now, because I need to make sure that she understands that I meant it."

"Nice," said Dalton. "I'll see you tomorrow. Or call me."

Lucky hit the button to end the call, then let his arms fall to his sides.

"Sorry."

A rush of warmth filled his chest when she smiled.

"Sorry? What for? I hope you're not going to apologize to me for just having told your friend that I'm smart, funny, and beautiful?"

When she put it like that, he had to laugh. "I guess it would be pretty dumb to apologize for that, huh?"

"I wouldn't call it dumb, but I hope that you won't do it."

"Then I won't."

She pulled the gate open wider. "Are you coming in?"

He followed her through the gate. He had to ask. "How much did you hear?"

"Enough to know that you see me as more than a friend." She smiled and came back to him, lifting her hand up to stroke her fingers down his cheek. "Enough to know that I can relax a little, and feel safe when I tell you that I, too, hope that we'll become more than friends."

He caught her hand and held it against his cheek. "So, you're saying that, instead of screwing up, I just saved us a bunch of time?"

She laughed. "It looks that way, doesn't it?"

"It does. And tomorrow I'll tell Dalton that he has you to thank for me not kicking his ass."

"While you're at it, please tell him that I said thank you."

Lucky raised an eyebrow at her.

"He's the friend who pushes you, isn't he?"

Lucky nodded slowly. "Yeah, I guess he is."

~ ~ ~

"Are you sure you don't want to take a shower?" Dee asked when she came back downstairs.

The day had flown by, and it was only when she'd started to get a little chilly that she'd realized how late it was. She'd asked if they wanted to stick around for dinner and had been pleasantly surprised when Lucky had said yes.

She'd told him that he was welcome to use the shower in the guest suite on the main floor, but he'd refused. His swim shorts had long since dried in the afternoon sun.

"Unless you're trying to tell me that I stink, I'm good."

She rolled her eyes at him. "You don't stink. And what do you think, should we order something from Giuseppe's for dinner – they deliver. I could make us something – probably just salad and a sandwich, or I have frozen pizza. Or…"

"Or we could order something from The Boathouse and go pick it up." He looked down at Echo. "That way I could pick up her dinner on the way back."

"That works. But only if we both go."

"Why's that?"

"Well, you refused to take my car earlier – so I don't imagine that you would take it this time. And no way am I going to let you jog home just to get your car."

"Fair enough. You can drop me off at my place to collect Echo's dinner, and I'll follow you back over here."

"I don't mind driving you home again later."

He gave her a wry smile. "You might not mind, but I do."

She cocked an eyebrow at him.

"I wouldn't feel comfortable making you drive back here by yourself."

When he held her gaze, she could see that there was no point in arguing.

"Okay. So, the plan is, we'll order something from The Boathouse, then stop at your place on the way back."

"Yeah. But don't look at me like that. I'm not saying that I just want you to drop me off there. You can come inside with me; I'll show you around the place, if you like. I've got nothing to hide."

"That hadn't even occurred to me. But since you're offering…" she added with a smile.

He shrugged. "It occurred to me that it might sound as though I didn't want you to come to my place. That's not the case at all. It's nothing fancy, but it's a nice place – and it looks out on the lake."

"Well, alrighty then. I'll look forward to seeing it. But here …" She opened the drawer and handed him a menu from The

Boathouse. "First things first; we need to figure out what we're ordering."

As they entered The Boathouse, Dee hung back when she saw the way that the girl behind the bar was eyeing Lucky. He turned when he realized that she wasn't beside him.

He gave her a puzzled look, but the way that he reached for her hand and tugged her along with him reassured her. For a moment there, it had hit her that she had no idea what kind of history he had with other women.

The blonde girl behind the bar gave her a friendly smile as she came to greet them.

"It's good to see you again, sugar. I was starting to worry about you. But..." She grinned and looked pointedly at the way he was gripping Dee's hand. "I can see that I don't need to." She looked at Dee. "I'm Kenzie, it's nice to meet you. You're Emma's friend, aren't you?"

"That's me. It's nice to meet you, too."

"What can I do for you guys? Are you here for a drink? Dinner?"

"Just to pick up a takeout order."

Dee glanced at Lucky, surprised that he sounded less than friendly – almost hostile.

Kenzie winked at her. "It's okay. He's a bit wary of me, that's all. I tend to dish out advice, and your man here doesn't want to hear it."

Dee couldn't help smiling. She could tell that she was going to like Kenzie, but she could also see that she might be a bit much for Lucky.

She looked at him, and he surprised her with a smile as he slid his arm around her waist. "Kenzie's right. She was trying to give me a few home truths the last time I was in here." He gave Kenzie a pointed look. "But you got it right, you don't need to worry about me."

Kenzie laughed. "I'm glad to hear it. But just remember – I'm here if you need me. And that goes for both of you." She looked at Dee. "Are you new in town or just a summer visitor?"

Dee tensed when Lucky's arm tightened around her, and he gave her a puzzled look. She had told him that she lived here.

"I think I'm going to stay. I've been looking for a new place to settle." She smiled at Lucky. "And so far, this place is great."

She frowned when her phone started to ring in her purse. Kenzie took that as her cue to go and collect their order, and Lucky stepped away from her.

"Go ahead. Take it," he said. "We'll probably be here waiting for a few minutes, anyway."

By the time she got her phone out of her purse, it had stopped ringing. She frowned when she saw Max's name on the display. She hated to miss a call from him. She was about to call him back when the phone beeped with a text.

Max: No need to call me back. Just wanted to let you know that the meteor shower peaks on Tuesday night. It should be a good show. And I talked to Pax, he'll talk to you about dates.

Dee: Okay. I'll call you tomorrow.

Max: K.

She knew from his one letter answer that she wouldn't get any more out of him tonight, even if she tried.

"Everything okay?" Lucky asked when she looked up.

"Yes. It was my son."

"Is he okay?"

"He's great. He was just letting me know that the meteor shower peaks on Tuesday night."

Lucky smiled. "Want to make it a date?"

She nodded happily. "I'd love to. We can sit out by the pool and …"

"I think I can come up with something better than that."

"You can?"

He grinned. "Do you trust me?"

"I do."

"Then, I'll surprise you. Okay?"

"Damn girl!" Kenzie had reappeared and set the bag on the bar. "If this guy's smiling at you like that, and offering to surprise you, I'd say you've got it made!"

Dee tried to hide her smile, but she couldn't. Kenzie's laugh was infectious, and Lucky looked so uncomfortable, it was adorable.

Kenzie held her hand up over the bar, and Dee high-fived her.

"I can see that we're going to get along just great. You better bring your ass out with the girls, soon. Okay?"

"Okay. I'll look forward to it. But for now…" Dee shot Lucky an apologetic smile. "We'd probably better get home for dinner."

Lucky just rolled his eyes. "Remind me to stay out of the way when the two of you get together."

Kenzie laughed out loud at that, and Dee took hold of his hand as they made their way back outside.

Chapter Fourteen

Lucky glanced over at where he'd left Echo sitting on the pile of mats. It seemed that Russ was right, and he didn't need to worry about her. She was lying flat on her side, looking totally relaxed. Only her eyes gave her away – she was tracking his every move.

She turned to look over her shoulder when Russ came out of the office. It was still early, and there was no one else in the gym yet.

"How are you settling in?" Russ asked. "I thought you'd become one of my regulars. I'm surprised how little we've seen of you."

Lucky set down the free weights that he'd just picked up and walked over to Russ.

"I'm finding my feet. And I do expect to become a regular, it's just..." He turned to look over at Echo again.

Russ laughed. "I don't know what it'll take to convince you. I've told you every time that you've come in – she's more than welcome. If you want to know the truth, people have been asking about both of you. Everyone fell in love with her when she was staying with Dalton. He used to bring her in most days."

Lucky nodded. "Sorry. I guess it's just different for me. I'm not used to to…" He didn't know how to explain himself. He knew that Echo was fine around people, and Russ wasn't the only one who'd told him that she was more than welcome in the gym. It was just…

Russ grasped his shoulder. "Okay. You don't need to explain. I'm guessing that it's different for you because you and Echo are used to having each other's backs. She's the only one you really trust, right?"

Lucky blew out a sigh. "And doesn't that make me sound like a loser?"

"Hell no! To me, it makes you sound lucky." He laughed. "Is that where you got the name from?"

Lucky just shook his head.

"I'm not trying to force you into anything. I just wanted to make sure that you know that you're both welcome here anytime." Russ checked his watch. "The guys will no doubt start trickling in in the next few minutes. I'm surprised that Cal isn't here already. He and Damon are usually the first in on Monday mornings. Oh, and Davin's back in town this week. I don't know if you've met him, but he and Echo became buddies. So, all I'm saying is, don't feel that you need to rush out of here when they start coming in."

"Yeah." That had been Lucky's plan, but perhaps Russ was right. Perhaps he should stick around. He had plenty of time before he needed to get to work. And after last night, he needed a decent work out.

The front door opened, and Damon came in, greeting them with a smile.

"Morning. I thought I'd be the first."

"Lucky and Echo beat you to it today," said Russ.

Echo had sat up, and her tail swished back and forth behind her.

Damon raised an eyebrow at Lucky. "Is it okay if I go and say hi?"

"Absolutely."

Russ chuckled as they watched Damon sit beside Echo on the mats. She held her paw out to shake with him, and he grinned over at them.

"She's awesome!"

"She is," Lucky agreed.

They all turned when something outside the front window caught Echo's attention, and she started to whine.

"What can you see, girl?" Damon asked.

"I'd put money on Dalton being out there," said Lucky.

He was proved right a few moments later when the door opened, and Dalton walked in. He grinned when he saw Echo, and they both looked over at Lucky.

He grinned. "Go time. Bring me a Dalton."

Echo leaped from the mats, covering half the distance to the door before she hit the ground. She ran to Dalton, looking as though she was about to collide with him and knock him over but in her usual style, she stopped on a dime just in front of him.

Russ and Damon both laughed when she gently took Dalton's finger between her teeth and started leading him toward Lucky.

"Thank you," said Lucky.

When she let go of his finger, Dalton stroked her head. "It is good to see you, lady. And you," he added to Lucky. "I take it that you being in here this morning means that you weren't somewhere else last night?"

Lucky scowled at him. For one thing, it was none of his business. And for another, even if Lucky wanted to talk about it, there was no way that he would mention Dee in front of the other guys.

Russ picked up on the undercurrent between them, and slapped Lucky on the back. "I need to get back in the office. I'm glad you're here. I hope we see you again soon."

"What?" Dalton asked. Lucky was still scowling at him as Russ walked away.

"It's none of your business where I was last night."

Dalton chuckled. "I know. But I also know that I won't get anything out of you if I don't keep poking you."

Lucky rolled his eyes at him. "You could just go ahead and ask."

Dalton looked down at Echo. "Is he trying to say that he's capable of normal and open conversation?"

Lucky blew out a sigh. "Don't bother answering that, lady."

"So, how are things with Dee? I take it that you didn't stay at her place last night?"

Lucky glanced over at Damon. "Things are good, and no I didn't."

"You working your way up to that?"

Lucky pursed his lips. "I'm taking my time."

Dalton narrowed his eyes at him. "You still not making it through the night?"

Lucky turned away and walked back over to the free weights.

Undeterred, Dalton followed him. "Well?"

Lucky spoke without turning around. "No." He glanced over at Damon again.

Damon met his gaze and gave him an apologetic look. "I can leave if you like. But with just us here, and since Russ hasn't put the damn music on yet, I can hear everything you're saying. I know it's none of my business – but if it's any consolation, I'm in the same boat. It's not as bad as it used to be, but it's rare that I get through a whole week without the nightmares coming back."

Lucky was tempted to call for Echo and leave. He didn't want to talk about it. He hated what he deemed as weakness. How could anyone call it anything else? He was a grown freaking man, and he couldn't get through the night without a night light and Echo.

What the hell was he even thinking when it came to Dee? When it came to being *more than friends* there was a whole set of expectations between a man and a woman – expectations that he didn't see how he could live up to. On the physical side, he'd like to think that he could keep her happy. But how happy would any woman be with a man who insisted that he had to go home afterward?

Dalton's hand on his shoulder jolted him out of his thoughts.

"Let it go. Get your workout. You're thinking so hard right now that steam's going to start coming out of your ears. I'm pushing you for your own good – not because I enjoy it. Believe me, I don't. But until you get out of your head, until you start letting me – and maybe others – help you, nothing's going to change."

Lucky couldn't bring himself to look his friend in the eye. He couldn't avoid Damon's gaze, though.

"He's right, you know. I don't know you well enough to say much. All I'll tell you is that if you want to talk to someone who has some insight, you know where to find me."

Lucky stared at him. "I don't."

"I'm usually in here during the day – I work with a few personal training clients. And in the evenings, you'll find me over at Taryn's restaurant, behind the bar."

"That's right," said Dalton. "And you really need to get your ass over there soon. Even if only to save me some earache. Taryn wants to see you."

"Okay." Lucky didn't even know what he was saying okay to; he just wanted the conversation to be over.

"You should bring Dee for a drink one night," said Dalton.

"Maybe."

~ ~ ~

Dee scooted her ass across the booth, trying to keep her head down as she did. She'd come out to get groceries this morning and had decided to treat herself to coffee and pastry at the bakery before she went home to start work.

It was quieter in here than she'd expected – but then again, it was Tuesday morning. As busy as the resort had been over the weekend, it seemed that tourist season wasn't in full swing yet.

Once she was as far across the seat as she could go, she angled herself to look out the window. She was hoping that woman wouldn't notice her. Taryn. That was her name.

Dee was sure that she was nice enough, but she felt a little uncomfortable with her. That probably wasn't fair. Taryn had tried to be friendly; she'd invited Dee out with a bunch of her friends. But there had definitely been an undercurrent of... Dee didn't know what, but there had been something there.

She closed her eyes when she sensed someone approaching the table – it was Taryn, she just knew it was.

"Hey, it's Dee, isn't it?"

She plastered a smile on her face before she turned around. "Hello again. That's right. I'm Dee. And you're… Taryn?"

"Yep. Mind if I sit?"

She didn't get the chance to decide if she could bring herself to be rude enough to say no. Apparently, it was only a rhetorical question. Taryn was already sliding into the seat opposite her.

"How's Echo?"

Dee gave her a puzzled look. That was the last thing she'd expected Taryn to ask.

"Oh, shoot! You don't know, do you?"

Dee's heart started to pound. Once again, she was reminded that she knew nothing about Lucky's dating history. Taryn might be an ex who had a vested interest in Echo's well-being.

"Oh my God! I'm making this worse by the minute, aren't I? Can we rewind to hello, and I'll start again?"

"That might not be a bad idea."

Taryn laughed. "I'm sorry! I bet that I've weirded you out since the first time we laid eyes on each other, haven't I?"

It was the truth, but Dee wasn't sure that she should admit it yet.

Taryn rolled her eyes. "Shoot! I'm still doing it, aren't I? I really can be an asshole!"

That was such an unexpected declaration that Dee couldn't help laughing.

Taryn shook her head. "Let me start at the beginning. Has Lucky ever mentioned Dalton?"

"He has."

"Okay then. Dalton is my man. And we got together thanks to Echo."

That piqued Dee's interest. "She introduced the two of you?"

Taryn laughed. "No. We'd known each other for months already when she came to stay with him. But to say that we didn't get along is probably an understatement. It took Echo to make us see that we were both being a bit... Stubborn." She laughed again. "To tell you the truth, we're both difficult people. So difficult, that instead of calling each other honey or sweetie, I call him a pain in the ass, and he calls me a piece of work."

Her expression grew more serious. "And I apologize again, at this point, you probably agree with him. And I admit, I can be a real piece of work. And I know that I'm messing this up. All that I really wanted to do was to check in with you and make sure that you're okay.

"I don't know Lucky that well, but I have a lot of respect for him. To Dalton, he's like a brother – probably closer than that. And Echo owns a piece of all our hearts. So, since I've heard that you and Lucky have been hanging out, I wanted to make sure that you know that I'm around if you want someone to talk to."

Taryn pursed her lips. "I'm not making this any better, am I?"

Dee had to smile. "Not really. But I appreciate the effort."

"Just tell me that I haven't put you off? Dalton will be so mad at me if I've gone and put my foot in it. And like I said, I don't really know Lucky all that well, but I do know that he's a good man and that he deserves to be happy."

"Don't worry. You haven't put your foot in it. Like I said, I appreciate the effort."

Taryn's shoulders sagged. "You appreciate it, but you'd rather I left now, right?"

Dee thought about that for a moment, and Taryn watched her.

"It's tempting to say yes." Dee smiled to soften her words. "I'm not big on opening up to people I don't know."

Taryn nodded. "I'm sorry…"

Dee held her hand up to stop her. "I only said that it's tempting. But if I'm going to be living here, I don't want to start out on the wrong foot. I mean, what kind of bitch would I be if I sent you packing when all you were doing was trying to help?"

Taryn smiled. "You wouldn't be a bitch. It'd be perfectly understandable. But since you're giving me an inch, I'm going to try and take a mile. How about you give me half an hour? We both have coffee to drink anyway." She checked her watch. "If you've had enough of me by ten-twenty, just say, *thanks, this was great.* And I'll get up and leave. You never know, we might find out that we're getting along well by then. And if that's the case, we can maybe arrange to do something together sometime. How does that sound?"

"It sounds fair." Dee still wasn't sure what to make of the other woman, but she appreciated her straightforwardness if nothing else.

Taryn took a sip of her coffee before setting her mug down. "Okay. I'll go first. I moved here to Summer Lake to follow my friend, Evie. She was hiding from the Russian mob."

Dee almost choked on her coffee.

Taryn laughed. "I'm not bullshitting you. It's true. Evie was on the run from the mob. The asshole she was running from had my restaurant burned down. Then they came here and tried to kidnap her." She rolled her eyes. "Evie met and fell in love with a great guy named Adam – I'm sure you'll meet them both soon. And I met and started up a love-hate relationship with Dalton. He was actually the one who brought me down here after they burned my restaurant down."

Dee shook her head. "And I thought this was just a nice, quiet little town."

"It is ... Mostly." Taryn gave her a shamefaced smile. "I think if you talked to anyone else around here – and there's a whole bunch of couples around our age who you need to meet – their stories would be more in line with what you might expect. You know, second chances at love, finding romance later in life and all that good stuff?" She chuckled. "I think I'm the only one who antagonized my man into bed."

Dee laughed out loud. "With Echo's help, no less?"

Taryn nodded happily. "Yeah. Has Lucky told you about Star?"

"Star?"

"When Dalton and I first got together, Echo was living with him – or at least, staying with him while Lucky was away working. I was heartbroken when Lucky came back, and she went home to him. Lucky helped Dalton to find us a puppy – Star. She's a Belgian Mal, like Echo. She was even in training to become a SEAL dog, but she didn't make it through the program.

"Anyway, sorry. I guess my mind is racing because I'm trying to think of things to say that might make you like me."

Dee sat back in her seat. "You don't strike me as someone who needs people to like her."

"You're right; I don't need it." She met Dee's gaze. "But I'd like it if we could become friends. Dalton and Lucky are close. Echo loves Star – the guys get them together so that they can play whenever they can. And... And I was going to say that because of that it would make sense, you know, be convenient, for us to be friends. And that *is* true, but if I'm being honest, I'd like it just for me. I told you that I followed my friend, Evie, here. Right from the beginning, I've felt as though I was muscling in on her new life. It's not like that – she doesn't see it that way, but I can't help feeling..."

Dee watched with interest as the other woman pulled herself together. She could tell that Taryn was about to brush off what she'd just said.

"I don't want to wait till ten twenty."

"You want to leave now?" Taryn asked.

"Relax. I'm saying that I'd like for us to be friends, too."

"Awesome! And I thought I'd just blown it!"

Dee had to laugh. "You were trying your hardest!"

Taryn laughed. "I figured if we're going to be friends, you should probably know what you're in for from the beginning."

"You should probably do the same. All you know about me is that I've been hanging out with Lucky. I could be boring or bitchy or anything."

"Nope. I might not know Lucky all that well, but I do know that he wouldn't put up with you if you weren't his kind of people. And I know that his kind of people are my kind of people."

Dee held up her coffee cup, and Taryn clinked hers against it.

"Cheers."

"Cheers. Now, when are you going to come over to the other side of the lake? You should come to the restaurant for lunch."

"I'll have to see about that. I don't usually venture out during the day, I'm usually working."

"Okay. Let's exchange numbers, then. Maybe the next time Dalton and Lucky are working on Adam's house, we can take the dogs for a walk or something."

Dee didn't know Adam or anything about his house, but she happily gave Taryn her number. She just hoped that Lucky wouldn't feel as though she was trying to muscle her way into his life.

Chapter Fifteen

Lucky tugged at the collar of his shirt as he drove up the long driveway to Dee's house on Tuesday night. It was only a polo shirt – he hadn't gone all out and worn a button-down. He was second-guessing himself about that. He was second-guessing himself about everything to do with this evening – right down to whether he should have suggested it in the first place. It was too late to back out now, though.

When Dee had mentioned that tonight was the peak night of the meteor shower, he'd spoken before he thought about it. She'd suggested that they could watch them from her house, but he'd had what, at the time, seemed like a great idea.

It still was a great idea, he told himself as he brought his truck to a stop in front of the house. He didn't know much about meteors, he wasn't sure that Dee did, either. But he'd noticed the way her eyes lit up when she talked about it. He didn't know if that was because it was something that was important to her son, or if she genuinely enjoyed watching – he smiled through pursed lips – watching the stars fall as she insisted on calling it.

His idea had been to drive her out to a spot that he and Echo had found on the road that led up out of town. There was a pullout and a viewing area just over the crest of one of the hills – folks around here called them mountains, but he'd grown up in Montana, and these weren't mountains.

Dee's place had a good view of the open sky over the lake but to his mind, there was way too much light pollution. He and Echo had been up to the spot that he had in mind a few times. When they first arrived in town, he took her up there to walk before he was convinced that people wouldn't mind her being on the beach. They'd spent more than a few nights there, too – when the nightmares woke him, and he couldn't get back to sleep.

Cutting the engine, he looked up at Dee's fancy house. What had he been thinking? She would probably be more comfortable here, sitting by her pool outside her pool house, than sitting in the back of his truck with him in the ass end of nowhere just off the side of the road.

He sucked in a deep breath and ran his sweaty palm over his thigh. Looking across at the passenger seat, he wished that he'd brought Echo. He should have brought her. Dee wouldn't mind.

He looked up when light flooded the circular driveway around him. The front door was open, and Dee stood there, looking out. The sight of her, silhouetted in the light from the big chandelier in the hallway shining behind her, made him smile. For all that he might be messing up and overthinking it, he knew damn well that he was living up to his name when it came to her.

Lucky was the only word for it. How and why a woman like her would even give him a second glance was beyond him. He needed to get his act together and not give her cause to change her mind.

He climbed out of the truck and when he saw her smile, he felt himself smile back. He didn't make a conscious effort to do it – it seemed that was just his natural reaction to her.

He tried to ignore another natural reaction that stirred as he looked her over. What had she called herself? Chunky? Hell no! *His* description of her had been spot on – she really was fucking perfect. And no; no way could he afford to let his mind go anywhere near the thoughts those words conjured up. He shoved his hands in his pockets as he started up the stairs toward her.

"I'm ready if you just want to go." She peered over at his truck. "Or if you want to come in, you should bring Echo."

His smile faded. "She's not with me."

"Oh. Okay. I didn't think. I mean… I thought." That was the first time that he'd seen her flustered.

He reached the top of the stairs and didn't stop until he was directly in front of her. "Is that okay? Or is she the main attraction?"

That weird, tingly feeling bubbled up and filled his chest when she smiled at him. "If we're talking about attraction, it's definitely you."

He stepped in closer before he even knew what he was doing. "Nope. That'd be *you*," He slid his arms around her waist, and she looped hers up around his neck.

"Hi." Her eyes shone with amusement as she looked up at him.

"Hello there." He ducked his head and brushed his lips over hers. Her lips were plump and soft – just like the rest of her. He shifted his hips away, not wanting her to notice the effect she was having on him.

To his surprise, she pressed herself against him. Not just her chest – which so far, he'd managed to not pay too much attention to, but damn! She leaned the full length of her body against him so that they were touching from their knees to their chests. There was no hiding what she was doing to him, but it was evident that she didn't have a problem with it.

She cupped her hands around the back of his neck and rolled up on her tiptoes to press a peck to his lips. The feel of her luscious body moving against his like that made him groan – there wasn't a damn thing he could do to stop himself.

She waggled her eyebrows at him. "I'm very happy to see you, too."

He chuckled. "And I thought that I needed to be careful."

"Careful? Why?"

He didn't know if she genuinely didn't understand or if she was toying with him. Either way, he needed to make himself clear. He slid one hand down and closed it around her ass, holding her closer so that there was no way she could misunderstand what he meant.

"I didn't know what you'd think about that."

He had to close his eyes when she rocked her hips against his.

"What do I think about it? I like it. I like it a lot. In fact, I like it so much that I don't mind if you want to skip the meteors – I know you're only doing that to humor me."

That brought him back to his senses. She'd taken him by surprise in a good way, but this was moving faster than he knew how to handle. The last thing he wanted was for her to feel like he was rejecting her, but he just couldn't ...

He felt bad when a flush crept over her cheeks. "I am so sorry!"

He removed his hand from her ass and brought it up to stroke her cheek instead. "No. No way do you get to say sorry. Please. I ... I want to go there with you, Dee. I do. I just... Not right now, okay?"

She nodded rapidly. "Okay. And just for the record, I wasn't saying that I was sorry for suggesting it." A rush of relief swept over him when she gave him a sassy smile and added, "I'm glad that I brought it up."

He rolled his eyes, and she laughed.

"Forgive the pun. What I meant was that I'm glad that I brought the subject up. We both talked about wanting to be more than friends. To me, that means that I'd like to take our relationship to a physical level. But the last thing I want to do is rush you."

This was way outside his comfort zone, but he was grateful that she was taking the conversation there – he wouldn't have known how to. At the same time, he didn't feel great that she was the one leading.

"I've been out of the dating game for a long time. But back in my day, it was usually the guy who was rushing the girl. I want to ask if I'm taking too long about it – but we haven't known each other that long."

She smiled through pursed lips. "Well, it seems to me that these days, the girl is just as likely to rush the guy. I think you've already noticed that I'm not some shy, retiring little violet. I'm the kind of person who knows what she wants in life and isn't afraid to go after it. However, I think that perhaps I was being a little too forward. That's what I was apologizing for – not for letting you know that I'm looking forward to taking you to bed, just for saying it before the time is right."

"Okay." He felt like he should say something more than that – the trouble was, he didn't know what.

~ ~ ~

"Hey." Dee caught hold of his chin and made him look at her. "If I'm too much, you can say so." He looked so damn uncomfortable, and she hated that, but she knew from bitter experience that they needed to be honest with each other. She'd learned the hard way that if she tried to fit herself into a box – tried to be who and what she thought a man wanted her to be – it just made things worse.

She was hoping that Lucky liked her just the way she was. But if he didn't, it'd be better for both of them if he just admitted that now.

His big brown eyes were full of concern when they met hers. "You're not too much. You're..." He gave her a wry smile. "Last time I said it I was talking about the way you look." His arms tightened around her. "This time, when I tell you that you're fucking perfect, what I mean is that ..."

She stepped back in surprise when he let go of her and ran his hand through his hair. "You're too good for me, Dee. I'm a mess."

He walked a few steps away and stood with his back to her; she could sense the tension rolling off him. She waited, wanting to give him a chance to gather his thoughts – and to see if he was going to elaborate.

The moments dragged on, and when she sensed that he was only working himself up more, she went to him, and rested her hand in the middle of his back.

She wasn't sure if it was the right move. Relief swept over her when she felt his taut muscles start to relax. He still didn't turn around, though.

"If you don't want to talk about it, that's okay by me."

He didn't say anything.

"Mind if I ask you a question?"

"Go ahead."

"You saying that you're a mess – does that have anything to do with the things that you didn't want to tell me about straightaway?"

His shoulders slumped. "Yeah."

She rubbed her hand up and down his back. "You don't seriously believe that I'm too good for you, do you?"

He finally turned around and sighed. "Yeah. I do. I mean, look at you. You're a gorgeous, successful, down to earth, smart, funny, gorgeous woman."

"You said gorgeous twice."

She was relieved when he finally smiled. "That wasn't a mistake. I'll say it again because you are – you're gorgeous." His smile faded. "But you're so much more than that. You're amazing. And me?" He shrugged. "I wasn't lying when I told you that I'm not a great bet."

"I wish Echo was here to back me up. You know that she'd argue with you about that. And I don't want to argue, but I will tell you that you're a good man. I know you are, Lucky. I think you're hard on yourself. And I know that you have more issues that you don't want to tell me about. I'm guessing that's to do with the PTSD."

He got that shuttered look again, and she reached up to touch his cheek.

"Like I said, you're hard on yourself. I'm not going to go pretending that I know how you feel or what you go through. All I will say is that I think *you're* the amazing one. I want to get to know you better. I'd like to think that maybe I could even help you – if you wanted me to. But that's up to you," she added hurriedly.

He leaned in toward her, and she lifted her chin, but instead of kissing her, he rested his forehead against hers and looked deep into her eyes. "You're a good woman, Dee."

"And you're a good man. I know that without a doubt. And I meant what I said. I'd like to be able to help you – whether that means listening if you want to talk or accepting that you don't want to talk. Whatever you need."

His hand closed around the back of her neck, and he pressed a kiss into her hair. He rested his chin on top of her head before he spoke again.

"I don't know how to talk about it. I ... I don't think that I'm being hard on myself. I should just... I should be better... Stronger."

Dee desperately wanted to ask him to explain. Instead, she waited and was rewarded when he went on.

"I should have figured it out by now. Should have worked my way through it and be on the other side. As it is, I still struggle."

She wanted to ask him what exactly it was that he struggled with – he might be guarded, but at no time had she felt that he was struggling. Perhaps he just hid it well?

"Can I ask another question?"

"Go ahead."

"Do you struggle when we're together?"

He leaned back so that he could look down into her eyes. "No. Being with you is…" She loved the way that his smile lit up his face. "It's easy. When I'm with you, I relax."

She cocked an eyebrow at him.

He chuckled. "You haven't seen me when I'm not relaxed. I mean, I guess being around you pushes me outside my comfort zone – but in a good way."

"Okay. So, I'm not making things worse for you?"

"No. You make things better."

"Well then, can we agree that I'm not too good for you – that in fact, we're both pretty amazing people – and that since we enjoy each other's company, we should keep hanging out and see how things go?"

"I'd like to …"

"But?" she prompted.

"No. There is no but. But shit! I feel like – for your sake – we should call it quits now."

She was surprised how hard his words hit her.

It must have shown on her face.

"Hey." He ran his fingers down her cheek. "I feel like I should say that, but I don't want to. It might make me a selfish bastard, but I'm not going to. I want to keep spending time together. There's some shit that will no doubt come up at some point. I should probably tell you about that now…"

She could tell that he was thinking about it, but she already knew he wasn't ready to spill his secrets. What surprised her was that she didn't mind. It wasn't that he was hiding something from her. It was that he was wrestling with his demons. She knew all about that. She'd gone more than a few rounds with demons of her own over the years. She wanted to help him. She'd love to be able to, but even though she'd offered, she knew it didn't work that way. The most that she could hope for was that he'd allow her to support him while he fought his own battles.

"… Is that okay with you? I want to tell you before we run into any of my shit. But I don't want to tell you right now."

"However you want to handle it is okay with me. I trust you, Lucky."

"Thanks."

"How come you didn't bring Echo?"

He chuckled. "Not a very subtle change of subject."

She laughed with him. "I didn't think subtlety was required. I figured that you might appreciate a swift change of direction."

He pressed another kiss to her forehead. "I do. Thanks. And the honest answer to your question, is that I didn't know if I should bring her."

"Why, where are we going?"

"To watch the stars fall, remember?"

"Duh. I remember that. But you never told me where."

"To a place where the sky is a bit darker."

"Ooh! Max will be impressed with you. But that doesn't explain why Echo can't come."

"I wondered… And we don't have to if you don't want to… I don't even know if it'd be a good idea…"

She laughed. "Just spit it out, man."

He surprised the hell out of her when he straightened up and put his hands on his hips. Standing like that, he was quite an imposing figure – and she loved it.

He gave her the same stern look that she'd seen him give Echo, but she could see the humor shining in his eyes.

"I might be acting like a pussy, but don't go bossing me around, lady."

She had to laugh. "Ooh! Why? What are you going to do about it?"

He chuckled as he grabbed her hips and pulled her closer. "I'm going to kiss you to shut you up."

"I'm not ready to shut up. I ..."

He cut her words off when his lips came down on hers. It was the perfect way to bring an end to the serious conversation that they'd gotten caught up in. That had been her hope, when she told him to spit it out, but she hadn't expected it would turn out this well.

She shivered when his hand ran down her back and closed around her ass. He might think that it was too soon, but his body – if not his words – made clear that he was as eager as she was.

~ ~ ~

Lucky wrapped his arm around Dee's shoulders as they lay back, looking up at the stars. He'd thought that he'd blown it earlier. No way would he have believed that less than an hour after the conversation he'd dragged them into, they'd be lying in the bed of his truck, looking up at the night sky.

Echo lay between them. Dee had asked if they could stop to get her on their way through town. He'd been happy to. For the last ten minutes, Echo had been alternately resting her chin on his chest and Dee's stomach.

He stole a quick glance. Yeah, there was no way that Echo would be able to rest her chin on Dee's chest – she'd have to sit up to do that. He swallowed. He wouldn't mind resting his own chin there.

When he looked back up, she was watching him with a little smirk on her face. It was obvious that she'd caught him.

"What can I say?"

She laughed. "You can say whatever you like."

He laughed with her when she cupped her breasts in her hands and jiggled them.

"Over the last forty years or so, I've gotten used to the way guys react to these things."

He bit down on his bottom lip and curled his hand into a fist at his side. She was only joking around, but he would love to be able to get his hands where hers were.

"I wasn't sure about you at first," she continued. "I thought maybe you were an ass man."

He burst out laughing. "What makes you say that?"

She rolled her eyes. "What do you think? The vast majority of guys are either ass men or tits men. I have plenty of experience with men who talk to my chest instead of to my face. You've never done that, not even once. At first, you didn't even look."

He cocked an eyebrow.

She laughed. "At least, I never caught you looking."

"I was looking all right. I take it you don't mind?"

"I don't. Since I've had to heft them around all these years, it's nice to know that you appreciate them."

He held her gaze, as he shifted his hips. He didn't think that he'd ever talked to a woman about her breasts like this before. It felt strange to chat about it instead of act on it, but there was no denying that he was aroused.

His voice sounded deeper than usual when he spoke. "I appreciate them."

She waggled her eyebrows. "You can appreciate them any time you like. I'm not pushing – we already covered that. I'm just saying that whatever else you have to figure out in your mind, you don't need to worry about me. I'm happy to go there whenever you are."

He reached across Echo and took hold of Dee's hand. "You're not like other women, are you?"

"I don't know, but I doubt it. If I had to guess, I'd say that we women – just like you men – are all individuals. We all have our own quirks and flaws, and we do our best to work with them."

She turned on her side to face him, and he did the same. When they were looking into each other's eyes, she smiled.

"I'm guessing that what you really mean is that I'm not like the women you've known in the past. I'm happy to tell you that you're nothing like the men I've known in the past, either. So, here we are, with a clean slate if we want it."

"Yeah. I like the sound of that."

He leaned closer, and she leaned in to meet him. Just as their lips met, Echo sat up and barked. Lucky and Dee both scrambled up to see what her problem was.

Lucky had to laugh when he realized that rather than looking around, she was looking up at the sky. Dee followed Echo's gaze and pointed up with a laugh.

"That's right, lady. You spotted them, didn't you?"

Lucky watched in awe as one meteor after another streaked across the sky. "Wow!"

"Right?" said Dee. "Isn't it amazing?"

He could only smile as he watched her wrap her arm around Echo, both of them smiling up at the sky.

She turned to him. "Does it hold any appeal for you? Are you just waiting for this to be over? We don't have to stay too long if you don't want to."

He shook his head. "I love it. I can't say that I've ever gone out of my way to watch a meteor shower before." He winked at her. "But I can tell you that I will never forget this — I'll never forget the first time I watched the stars fall."

Chapter Sixteen

Dee looked up from her screen and had to squint when the bright sunlight shining in through the windows hit her eyes. She checked the clock on the wall and was surprised to see that it was eleven-thirty. That meant that she'd been writing for six hours already.

She got up from the desk and stretched. The time had flown by, but her body was all too aware of just how long she'd been sitting. She rolled her shoulders as she went to the kitchen for a glass of water. She really wanted a soda, but she only allowed herself one a day, and if she had it now, she'd feel deprived later.

She stood in the kitchen, guzzling the water and staring out at the lake. She'd like to think that she might see Lucky later, but she didn't know if that was going to happen. She hadn't seen him since Tuesday night.

That had been a great time – the meteor shower had been spectacular. She'd wondered if it just seemed more intense because she was so in the moment – because she was enjoying Lucky and Echo's company so much. He'd been right – sitting out in the back of his truck under the dark sky in the middle of nowhere was way better than sitting out on the pool terrace would have been.

Max had set her straight when he called yesterday. He'd informed her that there had been more meteors per hour than usual. The average for the Lyrids was around ten meteors per hour, and this year had seen a rare surge of up to ninety per hour.

She chuckled to herself. She still liked her version – that the show had been even more special than usual because she was with Lucky.

She set the glass down on the counter with a sigh. Lucky had been so sweet when he told her that he'd never forget the first time he got to watch the stars fall. He might be a big, tough guy, but he was incredibly sweet when he let his guard down.

He'd certainly let his guard down when he dropped her back at home afterward. They'd made out in his truck like a pair of teenagers! She'd been so turned on. And she knew that he was as well. When they came up for air for what must have been the fourth or fifth time, she'd finally caved and asked him to come inside with her.

She blew out another sigh. He'd refused. He'd been as caught up in the moment as she was – she knew it. But he'd gone cold on her. He'd made some excuse about getting Echo home. Dee had even forgotten that Echo was sitting on the back seat. She wasn't the reason that Lucky had left in such a hurry though.

It was Dee's own fault. She'd told him that she was happy to wait until he figured himself out, and then she'd gotten greedy.

She was hoping that she hadn't run him off completely. He'd called her on Wednesday night, and he'd sounded fine – but he hadn't mentioned his hasty retreat the night before, and she hadn't wanted to seem like she was still pushing him, so she hadn't, either.

He'd told her that he had a long day out of town for work on Thursday but that he'd call her today – Friday – to see if she wanted to make any plans with him for the weekend. She'd kept herself busy writing, but she was concerned that he might not call – that he'd beaten a retreat.

She hurried back to the desk when her phone rang and smiled when she saw Pax's name on the display. She might have hoped that it was Lucky, but it was always great to talk to Pax.

"Hey, kiddo." She loved it when he called. They chatted back and forth on the computer most days, but when he rang, it wasn't usually about work – it was because he wanted to talk.

"Hi, Deedly."

She laughed. He had at least a dozen variations of her name that he rotated through. She'd come into his life when he was a teenager. He already had a mom, and she'd made sure that he understood that she respected her, and the relationship that he had with her. His dad had wanted him to call Dee *Mom* – that had been one of her early signs that she'd chosen poorly again when she got married the second time. Fortunately, she and Pax had quickly figured out their own relationship, independent of him.

"What's up?"

"I'm good. Do you have a minute?"

"I do. This is good timing. I'm just taking a break. I got an early start and I've already gotten my words for the day."

"Hmm."

"Hmm, what?"

"Does that mean that you're not sleeping again? Is everything okay?"

She loved the way he looked out for her. She'd struggled with insomnia for a while last year, and he'd tried to help by sending her articles about every home remedy and natural sleeping aid that he could find.

"I'm fine. It was just …" She was hardly going to tell him that she'd woken up from an erotic dream that she'd been having about Lucky and hadn't been able to get back to sleep afterward. "It was just one of those nights. It'll all work out. I'll get to bed early tonight to make up for it."

"I thought all that lake air was supposed to be good for you and help you sleep?"

"It is."

"And if you plan to go to bed early tonight – *Friday* night – does that mean that you haven't made any friends yet? Please tell me that you've been leaving the house?"

She laughed. "I have! You know I have. I told you the other day that I was at the bakery when you were messaging."

"Right. Yeah. As long as everything's okay?"

"Everything's fine. I'm fine. Honestly. And I know that you didn't call to check up on my sleeping habits or my social life so – go on, what *did* you call for?"

"To tell you that I talked to Max and that he can get Monday and Tuesday off in a couple of weeks. Does that work for you?"

"That'll be great. Do you want to come for the weekend – does he? And do you want to stay for the rest of the week?"

"That was what I wanted to talk to you about. I'm good to come for the weekend but normally we get a couple of days' work in after Max leaves. I …"

"If you can't stay, we can do our usual planning session over Zoom. You know that doing them in person is mostly about getting to see each other – there's no reason that we need to be in the same room. I'm more concerned about seeing you and Max together than about work anyway."

"Thanks."

"What's up? You're not happy about something, I can tell."

"I feel bad because the only reason that I can't stay for longer is because I – stupidly – agreed to go and see Dad."

"There's nothing stupid about wanting to see your dad."

Pax laughed. "Do me favor? Don't try to be polite about it – it doesn't suit you."

She laughed with him. "Sorry. I'm just trying to be supportive."

"I know. But you know that I don't *want* to see him. I'm just pissed at myself that I agreed in the first place, and now I'm even more annoyed because it'll cut into our time. But it's those specific dates because what's-her-face is throwing some kind of party."

Dee chuckled. "You know you really should call her by her name – they've been married for years now."

"Yeah. That's what the party's about –it's their anniversary party, and she's insisting that they have it on the actual date – she refuses to wait until the weekend like any reasonable human being would."

Dee smiled to herself. She'd never met the new wife, but she'd heard so much about her over the years that she almost pitied the man she used to be married to. Almost but not quite. He'd made his bed – well, the bed that Dee used to share with him – and he'd taken what's-her-face into it.

"It's not a problem, sweetheart. Honestly. When do you need to be there?"

"It's on the Wednesday, so I might need to leave you on Tuesday night. I've been checking but I can't find flights that will get me there early enough if I leave your place on Wednesday morning."

"No. That won't work. I need you and Max for as long as I can have you."

"So?"

She loved that he trusted her so much. He wasn't arguing or getting worried – he just wanted to know what she had in mind.

"So, I haven't been using my share of the plane enough lately. Max asked if I'd send it for him. I think that we should send you to your dad's place in it, too."

Pax laughed. "Ouch! But oh, yes! Yes, please! I would love that!"

Dee tried to sound innocent. "I'm only suggesting it because it'll make our schedule easier."

"Yeah, right. And I'm only so happy about it because I get to fly in a private jet." He laughed again. "Or how about we both be honest and admit that it's about time you flaunted it? You know my thoughts on the matter, Deedums. He was an asshole. The way everything went down was horrible. And the worst part about it was that he made you doubt yourself for a while there. You've more than proved him wrong. He tried to stop you from doing what you wanted to because he thought you wouldn't be able to make enough money at it. Sending the plane out there would be the best *fuck you* – and he deserves it."

Dee pursed her lips. "I don't want to be petty."

"You're not being! I am."

She had to laugh. "I just mean …"

"I know what you mean. I also know that you didn't ask for my advice, but I'm going to offer it anyway. If I was going somewhere else, would you give it a second thought or would you just send the plane?"

"I'd send it."

"Then if you don't send it because of him, you're letting him dictate what you do."

Dee narrowed her eyes – not that he could see her. "You little shit!"

Pax laughed out loud. "Thank you. I know that means that you're impressed. I learned from the best – you taught me well."

A rush of warmth filled Dee's chest. "Apparently, but I'm not sure that I like you turning it around on me."

"You know I'm only joking around – you do what you want. But everything I've said is true – and you know it."

"I do. I'm sending you in the plane."

"You should come with me."

"Oh, *hell* no! Why would I want to do that?"

"Just to rub his nose in it a bit more."

"No thank you. I'll let the plane do that for me. Shoot. Sorry, Pax. I have another call coming in. I need to go. I'll see you online in a bit."

"Okay. Later. Love you, Deederator."

She laughed. "Love you more."

She clicked over to the incoming call, hoping that this time it was Lucky.

"Hello?"

"Hi, Dee, it's Ben."

"Oh. Hi, Ben. What can I do for you?"

"It's more a case of what I can do for you. I talked to the dealer where we buy and maintain our boats. I told him about your request, and he thought it was a great idea. In fact, he liked it so much that he suggested that we set up a trial program. He sells most of his inventory in January and February – when people are starting to get excited about the upcoming boating season. Any boats that he still has in stock now may not sell until next year.

"Rather than have them sitting on his lot all summer, he'd rather be making money from them by renting them out. He's not sure that it's the smartest business move – there's a chance that it could cannibalize his sales when people catch on, they may decide that they'd rather rent than buy..." Ben chuckled. "Sorry. You don't need to know all the ins and outs. All you need to know is that he'd be happy to meet you down on the dock at the resort tomorrow morning if that works for you?"

"Oh! Yes. I mean … Sure."

"Are you? Sure? Don't worry if you've changed your mind. I know it's been a while since we talked about it. I don't want to spring this on you if you're not interested anymore."

"No. No, it's great. It's just a bit out of the blue. I really appreciate it, Ben. I do. What time tomorrow?"

"He said the earlier the better, so whatever kind of early suits you."

"We all define early differently. I can do whatever his version is. Eight, seven, six, five?"

Ben laughed. "I'd guess that Ed would say six, but I'll call him back and check."

"Do you want me to call him? I appreciate you setting this up, but I was thinking that I'd be renting from you. If you're being cut out of the middle of the deal, I don't want to put you out."

"No. It's all good. Ed's a friend. And although I won't make any money on whatever the two of you decide to do, I want to be part of the process. If things work well, Ed would want me to get involved – he'd rather give me a commission to deal with people than to have to do it himself."

"I like the sound of him already."

"He's a good guy. I'll give him a call back now, and let you know what he says."

"Okay, thanks, Ben. Actually, before you go… I feel stupid asking this, but I've never driven a boat before; he won't just expect me to ride away in it, will he?"

Ben chuckled. "No. I explained the situation to him. Don't worry, we won't abandon you. And…"

"And what?"

"Forgive me if I'm talking out of line; I'll just say that if you want to bring anyone else along with you, they'd be welcome."

Dee pursed her lips. How did he know about Lucky? That must be what he meant.

"Sorry," said Ben. "I shouldn't have said anything. I wanted to make you feel more at ease about the boat. Emma mentioned that you've been spending some time with Lucky. I thought you might feel more comfortable if he came with you."

"It's okay. You don't need to apologize. It just surprised me. I don't know if I'll see him before then, but thanks – it's good to know that it'd be okay to bring him."

The second she ended the call, the phone rang again. She made a face at it; she'd rather take a minute to wrap her mind around the fact that she was going to have to drive a boat tomorrow.

One look at the screen changed her mind.

"Hey, Lucky!" She was tempted to tell him that she'd just been thinking about him, but she decided against it. She should wait to see what he had to say, first. If he was running scared after the other night, he might be calling to say that he didn't want to see her this weekend after all.

Lucky hit send on the email that he'd been working on for the last twenty minutes. He was glad that was over with. Paperwork had never been his thing – or computer work, or whatever they called it these days. He'd always been a man of action. He'd known that there would be some desk work when he took this job, and it was okay. It was turning out to be the kind of balance that he could live with.

He spent more time out of the office than in it ... He looked up when a tap on his door interrupted his thoughts. Echo sat up; she'd been lying flat out on the floor. He had no idea why she refused to use the fluffy dog bed – the bed that it turned out that Leanne had bought for her.

"Come on in," he told Manny. "What can I do for you?"

Manny came in and went straight to Echo, squatting down in front of her to pet her. He turned to look over his shoulder at Lucky.

"Not ignoring you, but ladies first."

Lucky chuckled. "Not a problem."

Manny spent a little time with Echo before getting to his feet and coming to sit in the chair across the desk from Lucky. "What you can do for me is say that you'll come out with us when we finish."

Lucky made a face. "I was planning to go straight home and take her for a run on the beach."

"I thought you'd say that. But I had to try. Nina's getting worried about you."

Lucky shook his head. "I don't know what to make of this. Every single one of you has now asked me to come out – and has blamed your woman for it."

Manny laughed. "I'm not blaming her. I'm just telling you how it is. You did enough to keep them off your back for a while the last time you came out. But now they're getting antsy again – they want to draw you into the fold."

Lucky blew out a sigh. "I know."

"You got to him first?" Ryan appeared in the doorway and grinned at them.

"If he's threatening you with Nina, you should probably admit defeat now. She might be the sweetest of all the girls, but when she sets her mind on something, you don't stand a chance."

"He's right," said Manny. "And I can tell you now that if you don't come out for a drink with us after work, you can expect Nina to show up on your doorstep at some point over the weekend."

"And where Nina goes, Terry's not usually far behind." Cal had joined Ryan in the doorway.

"Why do I feel like this is an intervention?" asked Lucky.

"Because it almost is," said Cal.

Lucky blew out a sigh. "I don't mind coming out for a drink after work – if it's just a drink. But I know you guys, especially if the girls are meeting you there; you'll make a night of it." He looked over at Echo. "I need to get her a run. She's been in here with me all day."

He watched the looks that they exchanged, wondering what they were going to hit him with.

"We figured that you'd say that, so we were thinking that we could sit out on the deck at The Boathouse and have a drink. That way, Echo can come with us, and you can leave when you've had enough."

Lucky thought about it. It'd probably be easier to go for an hour than to try to get out of it.

"Okay."

"There's one more thing," said Dalton as Cal and Ryan moved aside to let him come in.

Lucky scowled at him as he squatted down with Echo. "What?"

The others sniggered, and Dalton shrugged. "You should bring Dee."

That caught him off guard.

"What? You should," Dalton insisted.

Lucky looked around at the others; they looked slightly more sympathetic than Dalton, and they each nodded their encouragement.

He blew out a sigh. "I don't even know if she'd want to go. You guys are talking about when we get off work at four, right? She works until she's done. She might not finish until seven or eight."

"Maybe so," said Dalton. "But you won't know unless you ask her, will you?"

Echo whined and left Dalton's side to come and sit beside him. She rested her chin on his knee and looked up at him with those big brown eyes of hers.

Dalton got back to his feet and adopted what, to Lucky, was a very familiar stance: he folded his arms across his chest and cocked his head to one side.

"Echo thinks that you should."

Lucky wanted to argue – wanted to tell his friend that he was talking out of his ass. Unfortunately, he couldn't.

As if Dalton read his mind, he laughed and said, "You hate it when I'm right, don't you?"

Lucky rested his elbows on the desk and pressed his fingertips into his temples. "Get out."

When he raised his head, the others were looking concerned, but Dalton was grinning broadly.

"You seriously want us to go?" asked Cal.

Lucky didn't know if it was a stance that came naturally to big guys like them – or if it was somehow contagious, but Cal had folded his arms across his chest, too.

Needing to lighten the mood, he smiled at Manny and Ryan. "They look like a pair of bookends, don't you think?"

The tension left the room as the two of them laughed with him, while Cal and Dalton frowned at each other.

"This end of the bookshelf wants to know if you're serious about us leaving?" said Cal.

Dalton chuckled beside him. "This end of the bookshelf can answer that question. Yes. He wants us to leave – but only so that he can call Dee, right?"

"Right," Lucky agreed.

He had to smile as they all trooped out of his office without a word. Dalton was the last one out, and he looked back over his shoulder.

"Come on, Echo. Let's get a bit of a walk in while he does his thing."

When they'd gone, Lucky took his cell phone out and scrolled to Dee's number. He'd been planning to call her this weekend. He'd said that he would.

He felt bad about the way that he left her place on Tuesday night. He felt bad, but he didn't know how he could've handled things any differently. When she'd asked him if he wanted to go inside with her, he'd been more than tempted, but he'd had to say no. He wanted to take her to bed, but no way was he ready to spend the night with her. He figured that saying no and leaving before anything happened was the lesser of two evils when the alternative was getting up and leaving afterward instead.

He hit the call button before he could talk himself out of it. This was a big deal – asking her to come out with the guys and their women was a big step in his mind. So it was better to just get it over with – it was what he wanted, so there was no point in overthinking it for hours first.

That now familiar feeling filled his chest when she answered.

"Hey, Lucky!"

Just the sound of her voice made him smile.

"Hi."

Shit. He'd grown used to her being the one to keep their conversations rolling along. Now, it seemed that she was waiting for him to take the lead.

As the silence dragged on, he knew that he had to step up. If she was being cautious, he couldn't blame her – not after the way he'd hightailed it out of her place on Tuesday night.

"How are you?" It was lame, but at least it filled the silence.

He could hear the smile in her voice when she spoke. "I'm very well, thank you. How are you?"

He chuckled. "Shit! I'm sorry. I'm not calling to ask how you are."

She laughed with him. "I'm glad to hear it."

He was surprised when she didn't ask why he *was* calling. But that was just him hoping that she'd take the lead again.

He sat up straighter. "I know it's short notice, but I was calling to ask if you'd like to come out for a drink with everyone after work."

"Oh!"

"It wasn't my idea. I... Shit! That sounds wrong. What I mean is that everyone wants you to come out – they want me to come out – they want us to come out for a drink with them after work. When I said that it wasn't my idea, I meant that... I do want to see you if you still want to see me. Just that going out with all of them wouldn't have been my first choice."

"Do you want to go?"

"No. But I don't have much choice."

"Do you want me to come?"

"I do. But I know that you might be working, and I probably disturbed you just by calling and ..."

"Hey."

He stopped short, and couldn't help smiling as he asked, "Hey, what?"

She chuckled. "Stop overthinking it. You're going. You want me to come. I'd like to go – I'd like to see you, and I'd like to meet your friends. What else is there to think about?"

He felt the tension leave his shoulders. "I've missed you."

"Aww. You mean you've missed the way I cut through all the bullshit that you get caught up in in your head?"

"No, well yeah. But not just that. I've missed *you*."

She was quiet for a few moments, and just when he started to worry, she said in a much softer voice, "I've missed you, too."

"Can I come and pick you up around four?"

"I can meet you, if you're going straight from work."

"I'd rather come get you if that's okay with you."

"It's more than okay."

"Okay, I'll see you then."

"See you later, Lucky."

He ended the call with a big smile on his face. She was right; he needed to stop overthinking it.

Chapter Seventeen

"Do you really have to put that on her?"

Dee felt bad for Echo as she watched Lucky slide the leash over her head. He was putting it on her before they even got out of the truck.

Lucky made a face. "I'm not thrilled about it, but I just feel that it's something that we need to do whenever we're around people like this."

He looked out through the windshield. They were parked in the square at the resort. Lucky had come to pick Dee up a little while ago and she'd been thrilled to see that Echo was with him. He'd explained that they were meeting up with his friends from work out on the deck behind the restaurant. Echo was fine to sit out there with them.

"I get it," said Dee. "I mean, not so long ago, I would have run screaming if I was here for a drink, and I'd seen you bringing her – even on the leash."

She turned to look at Echo, who had her front paws up on the console between them.

"But I know better now, don't I, lady?"

She had to laugh when Echo smiled at her and licked her ear.

"We all know better," said Lucky. "But we have to respect the people who don't."

They got out and he met her in front of the hood of the truck. "You don't need to worry about her; she's less concerned about the leash than either of us are. And what about you?"

Dee laughed. "What about me? You're not threatening to put me on a leash, are you? I promise, I'll be good – I won't bite anyone."

He laughed with her. "If you feel the need to bite someone, I hope it's me. I'll ..."

She burst out laughing as he squeezed his eyes shut and shook his head.

"Can we forget that I just went there?"

"Oh no! No way! Not only will I not be able to forget it – I'm going to need you to elaborate at some point. If I feel the need to bite, you'll ... You'll what?" She waggled her eyebrows. "You like the idea of me biting you?"

He chuckled. "Something like that. How about we leave it at that for now?" He jerked his chin in the direction of the deck. "They've spotted us; we should probably get over there."

Dee smiled when she saw a group of maybe a dozen people sitting out on the deck next to the railing over the water. She gave them a little wave. She wanted to laugh when Lucky gave them a chin lift, and all of the men responded in the same way.

"Is that a Navy SEAL thing?" she asked.

"What?"

"The chin lift thing – the silent acknowledgment."

Lucky chuckled. "It's not a SEAL thing. I don't think it's even a military thing. I think maybe it's just a guy thing."

He looked down when Echo whined. She was looking at the group as well, and her ears strained forward.

"She's spotted Dalton. We should get over there. Are you ready?"

Dee nodded happily. "More than ready. I'm looking forward to this."

A rush of warmth filled her chest when he held his hand out and took hold of hers. When she squeezed his fingers, his head snapped up.

"Sorry. Is this okay?" He squeezed back. "I didn't even think. I didn't... I don't ..."

She hung onto his hand when he tried to pull it back. "You should do more of that."

"Of what?"

"Acting before you think about it. Doing what feels good instead of overthinking it."

He narrowed his eyes at her but there was no missing the humor in them. "When I stop overthinking it, I promise you it'll feel good."

A little thrill ran down her spine. "I don't doubt it. And that's all I'm going to say."

His smile disappeared. "Did I mess up?"

"You did not." She tightened her grip on his hand and started walking them toward the deck. "I'm not going to say anything more because if I do, it might sound like pressure. And I'm dragging you over toward your friends because if I don't, I'm in danger of dragging you back into your truck, back to my place, and into bed."

She'd said more than she should, and she knew it. So, she was relieved when he laughed and squeezed her hand tighter. "I might be a bit messed up, Dee, but I'm not fragile. You have no idea how much it turns me on to hear that you want me."

She looked up into his eyes as they walked. "I can imagine."

He stopped dead. Echo stopped beside him as if they were of one mind. Dee, however, wasn't in on the telepathy that they shared, and she took another step before his grip on her hand stopped her, and he tugged her back to him.

When she was standing in front of him, he looked down into her eyes. "I'm sorry."

She cocked an eyebrow, not understanding.

"I really enjoy hearing that you want me. I'm a selfish bastard. It didn't occur to me that you might like to hear the same thing."

He ran his tongue over his bottom lip, sending another shiver down her spine.

"I might be acting like a nervous virgin, but you need to know that I get hard every time I'm around you. Hell, I get hard just thinking about you. I've been taking my time because … well, because I'm worried about what happens afterward – I don't sleep well. I'm scared to sleep with you."

His eyes held an intensity that turned her insides to mush when he continued.

"When I say that I'm scared to sleep with you – I mean the actual sleeping. I don't know what will happen – how it'll feel when you're in bed beside me." A small, sexy smile played on his lips when he added, "I do know what will happen – how it'll feel when you're in bed underneath me. We'll be good together, you and me, Dee. I know we will."

She gripped his hand tightly when his gaze dropped to her chest. "I cannot wait to taste you, to be inside you."

She had to press her thighs together. "Wow!" she breathed. "And after telling me this, you're going to make me sit there and talk to your friends before we can go home?"

He chuckled. "Sorry, it was a dumb move, wasn't it?" He stuck his free hand in his front pocket. "If it's any consolation, it's going to be harder for me to sit there and talk." He gave her a pained look. "It might even be too hard for me to sit down at all just yet. Maybe we should head to the bar and get our own drinks before we join them."

Dee looked down at Echo. "How about you go, and I'll take her over there to them."

"Shit. Yeah. I can't take her inside." He glanced over at his friends, some of whom were openly watching them – it amused Dee that the rest were also watching; they were just being less conspicuous about it. "I'll come with you, though – introduce you."

"You're fine. Give yourself a minute. I don't mind introducing myself."

"You sure?"

"Of course. It's not like they don't know who I am."

"Okay. Thanks." He handed Echo's leash to her – with Echo watching intently. "I know you want to see Dalton, lady, but your first priority is taking care of Dee."

Dee laughed when Echo barked – it sounded different from usual.

Lucky just rolled his eyes. "She reserves that one for when she thinks I'm being dumb. I think of it as her way of saying, *duh!*"

"She doesn't think you're dumb, she's just letting you know that she's on the same page. And I appreciate it."

Lucky surprised her when he leaned in and pressed a quick kiss to her lips. "Thanks. I'll be out in a minute. What do you want to drink?"

"I'll have a beer, thanks."

She could tell that he was surprised by her answer, but he didn't comment. She didn't see what the problem was – as far as she was concerned, there was nothing like a nice cold beer on a sunny afternoon like this.

~ ~ ~

Lucky paused on his way back outside onto the deck. The sight of Dee sitting there with the guys and their women filled his chest with that, now familiar, tingly feeling. He didn't know what it was – didn't want to examine it too closely – all he knew was that he liked it, and for now, that was all he needed to know.

He loved that she felt comfortable enough to go out there and introduce herself without him by her side. When he'd been married, Kaylee used to make a big deal about him being there for her, being right there with her as much as he could – whether that was when they were out with friends or when she went clothes shopping. She'd said that it was because he was so rarely around. He could kind of understand that – he was away on deployment so much of the time.

But it had also just been a part of her personality. She wanted someone to stand beside her – he wasn't entirely sure what her motivation was, but it seemed to him that she wanted the world to know that she belonged. He didn't even think that it was about him – not *him* in particular – more about the fact that he was a Navy SEAL. Whatever it was about, it hadn't sat well with him.

He didn't necessarily think that there was anything wrong with her being that way, just that it didn't suit him. It used to make him feel claustrophobic.

He smiled as he watched Dee laughing with Taryn about something. She didn't need anyone to stand beside her, she was more than capable of standing on her own two feet. He wasn't blind to the irony that her not needing him made him even more eager to be by her side.

He looked down at the bucket of beers in his hand. He'd been a little too eager earlier. Dee really wasn't like other women. She might have told him that it was just that she was unlike the women he'd known in the past, but there had only been a few of them, and he couldn't imagine that there were many women at all like Dee.

She brought out the best in him. He smiled – although he wasn't sure that admitting that he needed a few minutes to wait for his erection to go down or sending her off to meet his friends by herself were necessarily his best.

Just as he was about to continue outside, he sensed someone approaching, and turned to see who it was.

Ben, the guy who owned the resort had his arm around a woman, and they were both smiling as they reached him. It made Lucky wish that he'd gone out to join the others more quickly. Ben seemed like a decent enough guy, but he wasn't big on social chitchat – and he couldn't think of anything that Ben might actually need to talk to him about.

"Hi, Lucky. It's good to see you." Ben glanced out at the deck. "Oh, of course. You guys are on your Friday afternoon exodus from the office, right?"

"That's right."

"I won't keep you," said Ben. "I don't think either of us would be very popular if you don't get those beers out there while they're still cold. I just wanted to introduce you to my wife, Charlie."

Charlie smiled at him. "It's lovely to meet you."

"Likewise." He was surprised that she had an English accent.

"We won't hold you up," said Ben. "I'll see you tomorrow."

Lucky did a quick mental scan, but he couldn't think of any reason why he would see Ben tomorrow. Then it dawned on him. "Have the guys signed me up for a night out that I don't know about yet?"

Ben laughed. "Not that I know of, but that doesn't mean that they haven't. Although, to be fair, that'd be something the girls would pull rather than the guys."

"Yeah."

"What I meant was that I'll see you in the morning."

"Still not tracking."

"Oh. Sorry."

There was something weird about this exchange. From everything that he'd seen and heard, Ben was a decent, straight up kind of guy. But right now, it felt as though he was trying to lead Lucky somewhere – he just didn't know where.

"I thought that Dee would have told you already."

"Told me what?"

Ben shook his head. "I don't know which would be worse now – if I should tell you to ask her or tell you myself. No. You should ask her. It's no big deal."

"Right." Lucky didn't know what to make of this.

Charlie smiled at him. "I think we should let you get back to your friends before Ben here puts his foot in it any more than he already has. It really was nice to meet you."

"You too."

He hurried away from them. He didn't know what the hell that was all about, and he wasn't sure that he liked it. But he was more concerned about getting back to Dee. Not because he was worried about abandoning her with his friends, but because he wanted to be by her side.

~ ~ ~

Dee watched the guys greet Lucky and his bucket of beers in amusement. They all said the right things, but she could tell that they were teasing him.

"Glad you could make it." Cal gave him a pointed look.

"Finally. My beer's here." Ryan reached to pluck one of the bottles from the ice, but Lucky snatched the bucket away and came to her.

"Ladies first."

She took one with a smile and he set the bucket down to pop the top off it for her.

"Thanks."

He held her gaze for a moment before turning back to let Ryan take one.

She stroked Echo's head as she watched the guys' banter. Taryn grinned across the table at her and nodded.

Taryn's man – Dalton – was a giant. He'd come to sit next to Dee when she arrived so that he could talk to Echo. Dee could see that she was devoted to him, but she'd remained pressed against Dee's leg the whole time.

When Lucky turned back around, Dalton winked at her and murmured, "Watch this."

"You took your time, Penny. But don't worry, even if you abandoned Dee to face us by herself, I've got her back." He leaned closer and started to put his arm around her shoulders but froze when Echo growled.

Dee was stunned – and judging by the look on his face, Dalton was, too.

"It's okay, lady," said Lucky. "He's just fooling around."

Echo's whole demeanor changed, and she went back to being her usual, adorable self. She put a paw up on Dalton's knee and gave him such a sorrowful look that it hurt Dee's heart.

Dalton covered her paw with his hand.

Lucky unceremoniously shoved his way in between them and sat down next to Dee.

"What the hell was that about?" asked Terry.

Dee wasn't entirely sure that she had it right, but if she did, Terry was with Cal.

Dalton shook his head. "It was nothing. Echo's fine. She's doing exactly what she's supposed to do. I was out of line."

Lucky wrapped his arm around Dee's shoulders. "Are you okay?"

She nodded rapidly. "I'm fine. A little surprised, but she didn't scare me, if that's what you're worried about."

Dalton gave her an apologetic look. "Sorry, my mistake."

"It's not entirely your fault," said Lucky. "I should've warned you."

"I should've known. You shouldn't have needed to tell me," said Dalton.

"Any chance you want to tell me what you mean?" Dee asked.

"Before you and Echo came over here, I told her that you were her number one priority, remember?"

"Oh. Yes."

Lucky shrugged as though that explained everything, but Dee wasn't sure that it did.

"But Dalton's one of her favorite people. You guys were teammates. You might have told her to look out for me, but she knows Dalton. She knows…"

Dalton shook his head. "She knows that you follow orders. Yes, she knows me." He patted her paw, which was still resting on his knee. "If you pushed me, I might even tell you that I'm her second favorite person." He gave Lucky a rueful smile. "Or at least, I used to be. But when it comes to following an order, that comes first."

"Don't look like that," Lucky told Dee. "It's all okay. She would never hurt him; she was just ensuring that he wouldn't hurt you."

Dee looked down at Echo in wonder. "Thank you, lovely."

Echo came to her and licked her hand, before settling at Lucky's feet.

When Dee looked up again, everyone was watching the exchange.

"What?" she asked when nobody said anything.

Manny chuckled. "I think we're all just fascinated. When Dalton first came here, we thought that *he* didn't have much to say for himself. Then, Lucky arrived and made Dalton look like a chatterbox. Now, you're here, and…" he smiled at Lucky "… We're all grateful."

"And damn, girl!" said Taryn. "I thought that Echo and I were close, but it's obvious that she loves you as much as Lucky does."

Dee laughed and made light of the comment, but Taryn's words stayed with her. It was just a throwaway comment, just a turn of phrase but still… The thought of Echo loving her gave her the warm and fuzzies. Her heart was pounding as she asked herself the million-dollar question – the thought of Lucky loving her? How did that make her feel?

Leanne, who was Ryan's fiancée, and from what Dee had gathered so far, was a real firecracker, shot her a knowing look.

"And how about your dog, Star?" Leanne asked Taryn. "How's she doing?"

Taryn started to chat about the puppy that she obviously adored. Most of the group listened attentively and joined in the laughter as Taryn recounted Star's antics. Leanne caught Dee's gaze and smiled.

Dee gave her a grateful nod, hoping that Leanne had been the only one to pick up on her discomfort.

Chapter Eighteen

Lucky's heart was pounding as he pulled into the driveway at Dee's house. It had been a great evening. He'd enjoyed himself way more than he expected to. Dee had been a big hit with his friends – not that that surprised him. What surprised him was how comfortable he'd felt. He'd never been big on hanging out with a whole group of people – other than his teammates.

He hadn't thought he'd ever discover the same kind of camaraderie again. He hadn't wanted to. But there was no denying that the guys from work shared a bond, or that they were including him in it. It wasn't the same kind of bond that he and Echo shared with the team – that was something that ran way deeper – but he was still thankful to become part of something new.

He wasn't feeling comfortable now, though. Dee had been great. She'd enjoyed herself, chatting with the girls, and giving as good as she got when the guys teased them. But there had been a moment there – a moment when Taryn had said that Echo loved Dee as much as he did.

He'd felt her tense. She'd recovered quickly, but she hadn't been happy about it. He should feel relieved – he was the one who'd told his teammates that he didn't think he was cut out for love. He and Dalton were the two who had ruled out long-term relationships as an option in their lives after they retired.

He swallowed. Dalton had gone and broken that self-imposed rule. He glanced at Dee, who was making a fuss over Echo. It was tough to admit that he wouldn't mind breaking the rule himself, but judging by Dee's reaction, he wasn't sure that she'd want him to.

He brought the truck to a stop and cut the ignition. He didn't need to worry about it yet. There were other hurdles to cross before they got there. The most immediate hurdle was the one he was facing right now. They'd had a great evening out. He'd brought her home. Would she expect him to... He felt a little of his tension dissipate when he realized that if she did expect him to – if she wanted him to stick around for a while, he'd be happy to.

She surprised the hell out of him when she pressed a kiss to Echo's head and said, "I'll see you in the morning, sweet girl."

Lucky didn't know what to say. Even if she wasn't going to invite him in, he'd thought that they'd probably sit here for a little while.

Instead, she gave him a bright smile. "And I'll see you, too. Are you sure it's not too early?"

"No. It's fine."

"Well, okay then. Thanks for tonight. I really enjoyed this. Your friends are a lot of fun. And it looks like I have a whole new bunch of friends myself." She smiled. "The girls have invited me to go out for dinner with them all on Wednesday."

If his heart had been pounding before, it felt as though it might beat right out of his chest now.

"That's great."

She leaned across the console and pressed a quick kiss to his lips before reaching for the door handle. "Good night, Lucky."

He sat frozen as she climbed out of the truck. He had no clue what was going on. She could be trying to make things easy on him – since he'd fled like a damn coward the last time they'd been in this situation. On the other hand, she might be the one who was beating a hasty retreat this time. Perhaps what Taryn had said about him and Echo both loving her had been too much for her?

As he watched her trot up the steps to her front door, Echo whined.

"I know, right?" He sucked in a deep breath and let it out slowly. He could ask her tomorrow. She'd said that she'd pick him up on her way to the resort in the morning when she went to look at this boat that she was going to rent.

Echo took his finger between her teeth and shook his hand gently.

That tingly feeling filled his chest. It was stronger this time, more urgent.

"Fuck it. Come on," he told Echo as he reached for the door handle.

He got out and Echo jumped down. "Dee, wait!

She had her key in the door, and for a moment he thought that she was going to ignore him and hurry inside.

A rush of relief swept over him when she didn't. Instead, she slowly turned around.

"What's up?"

He jogged up the steps to her. "I was about to ask you the same thing."

For the first time since he'd known her, she looked nervous. She worried at her bottom lip with her teeth. That just made him want to kiss her. But he didn't feel like he should.

She gave him a weird little smile. "I asked first."

"Fair enough." And it really was fair that he should be the one to explain himself. She'd done all the running so far. It was time he stepped up. "I wanted to make sure that you're okay. I was surprised when you jumped out of the truck like that."

She slowly lifted her gaze to meet his. "It'd be so easy to lie to you right now."

His heart thudded to a halt. He hadn't expected that from her. "About what?"

She reached out and rested her hand on his arm. That made him feel better — he always felt better when she touched him.

"I could tell you that I jumped out of the truck so that we didn't have a repeat performance of last time. You know, getting carried away, and then me embarrassing myself by asking for more than you wanted to give."

He opened his mouth to speak. He wanted her to understand that it wasn't a case of him not wanting to give — just not knowing how to handle the situation afterward. The last thing he wanted to do was to hurt her by having sex with her and then going off home like it meant nothing to him.

He didn't get the chance to say anything; she cut him off before he could begin.

"That wouldn't exactly be a lie," she continued. "But it's a long way from the whole truth."

He waited for her to say more and when she didn't, he nodded slowly.

"The truth is more like you're not sure about doing this, right?"

She squeezed her eyes shut. "That sounds awful. I'm sure about you. I'm sure that I like you. I'm sure that I enjoy spending time with you and that I'd like to get to know you better. What I'm not sure about is whether that's a wise idea."

"Because of what Taryn said? Because she thinks that Echo and I are both already in love with you?"

She gave him a sad smile. "I don't think that's the case. I'm pretty sure of myself, but I don't have that kind of ego. It just made me think. I ... I'm not capable of love. Not the healthy kind, anyway. You know I've been divorced twice."

"I do."

She laughed. "And I've sworn that I will never say those two words again."

He reached up and trailed his fingers down her cheek. "I'm not asking you to."

"No, I know that. I'm just… I don't know how this will sound, but I need to say it. You obviously have your issues with women and with relationships. I would hate myself if you opened up to possibilities … and then … and then I discovered that I wasn't open to the same things."

He nodded slowly as he tried to process what she was saying. "I'm not asking you to marry me."

She let out a short laugh. "I know that."

"And even if…" He couldn't believe that he was going to say this, but he was. "Even if I do go and fall in love with you, I won't ask you to marry me."

She laughed again. "Don't look so worried. To me, that comes as a relief."

He couldn't bring himself to laugh with her. "I do want to see where we can take this. So, if you don't… Maybe it's best…"

Her eyes shone with tears as she looked up at him. "Maybe it *is* best if we call it quits now. But you know what? You told me not so long ago that we should probably call it quits before we even started, but you told me that you're a selfish bastard and so you weren't going to do that."

She nodded and straightened her shoulders, and he had to admire her strength as she pushed on. "I was relieved when you said that. So, I'm going to be selfish, too. I just don't want to disappoint you."

He closed his hand around the back of her neck and pulled her closer. He pressed a kiss to her forehead before he said, "You won't. Even if we get in deep, and then you change your mind, you won't disappoint me. As long as you do what's right for you, you'll never disappoint me."

"Aww. You may just be the sweetest guy I've ever met."

He shook his head with a short laugh. "Sweet?"

"Yes. Sweet. You might be all tough, and guarded, and look like a badass, but underneath you're just a sweetheart."

"If you say so."

Leaning against him, she rolled up on her tiptoes – he loved the way she did that, the way her body slid against his. But she cut his thoughts off from heading in that direction when she pressed a kiss to his lips and said, "Good night, Lucky. You already know how much I want to invite you in with me. But I'm not going to. I think we'll both be better off if we sleep on it instead of sleeping together."

He gave her a wry smile as she stepped back. "As much as I want to argue, I know you're right."

"Do you still want to come with me in the morning?"

"I do."

"I'll see you then, then."

He rested his hands at her hips and drew her back to him. It didn't feel right to kiss her the way that he wanted to. Instead, he brushed his lips over hers before pulling away.

"See you in the morning."

~ ~ ~

Dee rolled over and slapped the alarm clock. She hated those damned things. The sound of them set her nerves on edge – and this one was no different. She'd decided years ago when she became her own boss, that one of the luxuries she would allow herself was to wake up in her own time. She still set an alarm sometimes – if she had to be up early to catch a flight or on other rare occasions – like today. Even when she set one, she usually woke up before it went off.

She made a face as she rolled out of bed. She hadn't woken before the alarm this morning because she hadn't slept well. She sat on the edge of the bed and stretched. She was mad at herself for the way that she'd handled things with Lucky last night.

Sure, she always got a little squirrelly when the subject of love came up. Well, not *love* in general – only when it came to romantic love and involved *her* in particular. Most of the books she wrote these days were romances – and she still felt like a fraud about that. Surely, a romance novelist should at least be in a healthy and fulfilling relationship – if not married.

She'd started out writing thrillers and she'd done very well. A couple of her early books had been adapted into movies – that was how she'd met Emma. But that wasn't where her heart lay. She loved writing romance. She made a face as she got up and headed into the bathroom to get ready. She loved the *idea* of romance, of finding a happily-ever-after. But given her own track record with two divorces and a string of failed relationships behind her, she'd come to believe that perhaps that kind of thing only happened in fiction.

Once she was dressed, she went downstairs to make coffee. She needed it this morning – and not just to help her wake up after her restless night. She needed to get her act together. She needed to figure out how to handle things with Lucky. She wouldn't exactly say that she'd hurt him last night, but she'd certainly knocked him off his stride.

They'd had a great time out with his friends. He'd even started to come out of his shell. She couldn't help but smile as she remembered the way that he and Dalton had recounted stories about missions they had been on. Well, they hadn't given away any details about actual missions, but they'd had everyone rolling with laughter about the antics of their team and situations they'd faced in their days as Navy SEALS. She'd noticed that even the other guys had seemed surprised at the two of them – and she could understand why. Dalton struck her as more sullen and stoic than outgoing and jovial, and Lucky ... well Lucky was just Lucky. Sure, she'd discovered that he had a sweet side, but she imagined that even his friends would describe him as tough and guarded.

And yet, last night, the two of them could easily have been mistaken for a comedy duo. She'd loved it. She wished that she'd been able to ignore Taryn's comment about Lucky and Echo loving her. It really was just a turn of phrase.

She blew out a sigh as she put the lid on her travel mug. On one hand, she felt bad about the way that she'd handled things last night. On the other, it would be better to disappoint him now than to let things go further between them and end up hurting him.

She checked her watch; she had plenty of time. She was supposed to pick him up on her way to the resort to meet Ben and Ed. She took her coffee out onto the balcony – she should probably trot down the steps to the pool and sit down there for a little while, but then she'd only have to climb back up them. She might be trying to get more exercise, but she was never going to be the kind of woman who chose to take the stairs when she didn't have to.

She stared out at the lake as she sipped her coffee. It was a beautiful morning already. It'd no doubt be warm enough to swim in the pool this afternoon. She wondered if she should invite Lucky and Echo over to hang out and swim. She just didn't know. She'd have to see how things went between them this morning. Of course, she wanted to keep seeing him. But what she really needed to do was have a conversation with him.

She didn't relish the idea. But if she'd learned anything from all her failed relationships, it was that communication was important – probably more important than anything else.

~ ~ ~

Lucky took his coffee outside and sat on the steps that led down from the back deck into the yard. Echo followed and sat down beside him. He smiled and wrapped his arm around her when she leaned her weight against him.

"Thanks, lady. What do you think I should do?"

She whined.

"I wish you could talk. I don't know what you mean by that." He picked up one of her balls. "Want to play? We can't go for a run this morning. And I don't think I should take you while we go see Ben and this guy about the boat. I don't know how long that will take. And…" He took a sip of his coffee. "I don't know what Dee's plans are afterward. She might just want to drop me back off here."

He threw the ball, but Echo just watched it go before turning to him and whining again.

"I know! But after the way things went down last night, I'm not sure what to think. I'm even less sure what to do. Maybe I should just let it go?"

Echo barked at that.

"Yeah. I don't want to, either. But … you saw how she reacted. She was totally freaked out at the thought of me falling in love with her."

He sipped his coffee and stared out at the bushes that enclosed the yard. When he'd first arrived, they were just starting to bud. Now they were in full greenery. They blocked his view of the house behind his – Adam's house.

"You know what gets me? I'm so concerned that she's against the idea, but I'm not even worried that I like the idea."

Echo turned to look at him.

He shrugged. "What? I'm not gonna lie to you! I'm not saying that I'm there yet. But I could see myself falling for her."

Echo cocked her head to the side.

"Don't look at me like that! I'm surprised, too." He blew out a sigh. "But what does it even matter? She'll probably tell me today that we should let it go."

Echo growled.

"Sorry, lady. I know you like her, but I'm not going to push it. If she's not interested…"

Echo growled more fiercely.

"What?"

She let out three short, sharp barks.

"What are you saying?"

He wished like hell that she could actually speak. When she didn't, he made a guess at what she might mean.

"Are you saying that I shouldn't give up?"

He knew damn well that he was just saying what he wanted and blaming it on his dog. Jesus, it was a good thing he didn't have any more psych evals in his future – they'd probably lock him away in a padded cell for his own good. If he told anyone that he still couldn't sleep without a night light, and that even with that he couldn't make it through the night without nightmares, they'd think that he had issues. If he told them that he wouldn't even dare try to sleep if he didn't have Echo by his side – and that he was discussing his personal life with her – they'd probably think that he wasn't safe to be wandering the streets.

Fortunately for him, Echo was the only one who knew the full story – and she wasn't going to tell anyone. When she smiled at him, he smiled back.

"Thanks for the chat, lady. I'm going to take your advice – I'm not going to give up. I don't know all of Dee's story, but I reckon that she's doing exactly what she pointed out that I do; she's judging me by men she's known in the past." A smile spread across his face. "She's done all the running so far; we wouldn't have gotten to this point if it had been down to me. Now, it's my turn to take point, don't you think?"

Echo licked his cheek, and he laughed.

"You were just waiting for me to get there, weren't you?"

She let out a happy little yip, got up, and went to the back door.

He checked his watch and got to his feet. "You're right, she'll be here any minute."

Chapter Nineteen

As the wind whipped past her face, Dee was grateful that the last time that she'd seen Emma, she'd given her a headscarf to wear if she did decide to get herself a boat. Emma had said that she loved going out on their boat with Jack, but that the wind always left her hair looking like a bird's nest afterward.

She sat back and turned her face up to the sun. Echo nestled in close to her side, making her laugh as she kept nipping at the wind.

Her heart skipped a beat when Lucky turned to look back at them from his spot at the wheel. The way he smiled turned her insides to mush. He looked so damned happy. She was grateful to him for coming along with her this morning. She wouldn't have known what to do with the boat by herself – even though Ed had shown her everything she needed to know and had even offered to ride around with her until she felt comfortable.

If she hadn't had Lucky, she might have told Ed that she was sorry, but the whole thing was a bad idea. Instead, Lucky had chatted with him, and he had been more than happy to let Lucky take charge. That thought wiped the smile off her face. She'd been happy to let Lucky take charge, too. And she probably shouldn't do that.

Nope! She'd driven herself nuts last night *and* this morning wondering what she should do for the best. When they'd gone back to his house to collect Echo, she'd decided that she just wasn't going to overthink it. No matter what the future held for the two of them, she'd convinced herself to just enjoy it today. A heavy feeling settled in her stomach at the thought that this might be their last day.

She looked up at Lucky when the engine slowed and then stopped. She leaned forward in her seat, hoping that everything was okay. Wouldn't it be just her luck for the motor on a brand-new boat to quit on her in the middle of the lake the very first time she went out?

Lucky chuckled and came back to where she and Echo were sitting.

"Don't look so worried. I thought we might drift for a while. Is that okay with you?

"It is — especially considering that I was worried that we'd broken down."

He chuckled again. "No. It's all good. It's a great boat."

She looked around. It was bigger than she'd imagined, but she loved it. It had a little cabin in the front, a wheelhouse, that Lucky had just come down from, and this whole seating area in the back — the stern, she should probably learn to call it the stern. She liked this part the best; the seats had big comfortable cushions that could be removed and stored. There was a table that flipped up so that they could sit and have a drink — or eat if they wanted to — and there was even a swim ladder. That was something that hadn't occurred to her, but she loved it.

When she looked back at Lucky, his smile had faded. "Are you okay?"

"I am. I love the boat. And I'm so grateful to you." She frowned. "I guess if I'm looking a little unsure of myself it's because it's way bigger than I expected, and I'm a lot more nervous about driving it than I thought I would be — and I knew that I would be nervous. It's just that I was expecting something much smaller."

Lucky frowned as he sat down beside her. "You didn't choose this one?"

She let out a short laugh. "I didn't choose anything. I just asked Ben if there was a possibility of renting anything. I... I'm not complaining. Don't get me wrong. I love this thing. It's way better than what I was imagining. And to be honest, it's costing less for this than what I expected to pay for something much smaller." She made a face. "So, what am I complaining about, right?"

"I didn't hear you complain. You just don't seem as happy as I would like you to be."

She felt bad when she saw that his knuckles were turning white as he gripped the edge of the cushion beside him. She knew that he had something to say – but she'd already decided that her days of pushing him were over. It wasn't fair.

He held her gaze for a few long moments – she shouldn't be thinking it, certainly shouldn't be feeling the way she was, but she could get lost in those eyes forever.

"I wanted to talk to you about that."

Here it came. "About what?"

"About you not being happy."

"I am."

"Yeah, but like I said, not as happy as I would like you to be."

She gave him a rueful smile. "I'm sorry."

She knew that was the wrong thing to say as soon as the words left her mouth. His demeanor changed completely, and she knew that he was reading too much into those two words. So much for not pushing him; she had to explain herself.

"Don't shut down on me, Lucky, please? When I said I'm sorry, all I meant is that I'm sorry I'm not as happy as you would like me to be. I didn't mean..."

A rush of warmth filled her chest when he reached across and took hold of her hand. "You didn't mean that you're done with me?"

She shook her head slowly. "No. Part of me feels like I should be."

He surprised her when he smiled. "Then, I'm still in with a chance?"

"You are. It's not that I changed my mind about you. It's just... It's just that, Lucky, I'm fifty-five years old, and I've never had a healthy relationship. It's obvious that you have issues about opening up, let alone getting into a relationship. I reacted the way I did last night because the last thing on Earth that I'd want to do is hurt you."

"You won't."

He held her gaze as he leaned in closer. When his lips brushed over hers, she had to wonder what she was worried about. Was she crazy? He was a wonderful man; why couldn't they just...?

She lost track of the question – she lost track of all coherent thoughts when he curled his arm around her waist, drawing her closer. He claimed her mouth in a deep, demanding kiss. Her arms came up around his shoulders, and she clung to him.

This was different. This was a new side to him – a side that she liked a lot and wouldn't mind seeing more of. She moaned when he tangled his fingers in her hair and tugged her head back, allowing him to deepen the kiss.

When they finally came up for air, and he looked down into her eyes, she knew that there was no way that she could walk away from him. Whatever his issues might be – whatever her own were – he'd been right from the beginning; there was something between them.

His eyes shone as he leaned in and pressed a peck to her lips. "Give me a chance? I know that I've made you do all the running so far, but I'm going to change that if you'll let me.

You say that you don't want to hurt me, but that's not your call to make. It's a risk that I'm prepared to take."

She nodded slowly. "I just... I know that you're a big boy, and you can make your own decisions. It just doesn't seem fair to me – you told me from the beginning that you're not a good bet. Now it's my turn to tell you the same thing. I'm not. I've made a mess of every relationship I've ever had."

There was something very different about the way he smiled. He looked so much more... confident, maybe that wasn't the right word, but it was something like it.

He cupped her cheek and tilted her back, then surprised her by kissing the tip of her nose.

"There's a first time for everything, Dee. You've tried a few times and haven't got it right with relationships. I tried once and put myself off – I thought I'd put myself off for life. But now, with you, I want to try. Do you?"

How the hell could she say no to that? "I do."

He chuckled. "I'm not asking you to marry me."

She laughed with him. "That's a relief because I have no intention of ever getting married again."

~ ~ ~

Lucky could feel the tension easing in his shoulders and his chest. He'd spent most of the morning convinced that when they finally talked, she'd tell him that she was done. This was working out way better than he'd dared to hope.

"Never say never."

Her eyes grew wide. "No. I already have said never to that – and I don't just mean with you, it's a deal I made with myself a long time ago."

"Okay." She looked so worried that he let it go. It was far too early to even think about it. He could see himself wanting to settle down with her, but even if they reached that point, marriage wasn't all that important to him.

She ran her fingers down his arm, and he squeezed his eyes shut. His dick throbbed uncomfortably against his zipper, and he had to shift in his seat.

When he opened his eyes, she cocked an eyebrow at him. "I feel as though you brought me out here to the middle of the lake to have this conversation so that I couldn't run away."

He laughed. "I didn't exactly plan it that way, but you have to admit that it kind of worked out in my favor."

She laughed with him. "You might change your mind about that in a minute."

"Why?"

"Because I'm thinking that I should use this situation to my advantage, too. While I've got you here, and you can't turn tail and leave, I think it's about time that you told me why you don't want to spend the night with me."

Echo jumped down from the seat on the other side of Dee and came to rest her head on his knee.

Dee nodded at her. "She knows when you're stressed. She looks out for you. If you still don't want to tell me, that's fine. I understand, and I'll drop it." She gave him a rueful smile. "I just thought that I should ask while you can't escape me."

He chuckled, wanting to lighten things back up. "You forget my background. Echo and I could both easily slip over the side of the boat and swim home. It wouldn't be a problem for us."

"Of course! I should've thought of that." He got that strange tingly feeling in his chest when she smiled at him and said, "I know that you could do that, but I also know that you wouldn't. I don't know how, but I've known since the first time that we talked that you're a good man. And I've known since madam here scared me so much that I fell in the pool that you're…"

Lucky nodded as she searched for words. He knew exactly what she was talking about. That night when he dove into the pool after her, she'd clung to him. That had been his first sign that there was something very different about this woman. He'd had people cling to him before in rescue situations, women even, but he'd never felt the way he had when she wrapped her arms around him and hung on tight. He'd been filled with a sense of ... something. At the time, he'd thought of it as pride, but maybe it was more than that.

"I'm someone you can depend on," he provided when she still looked lost for words.

"That. Yes, exactly that. I knew that before I knew you well enough to know it."

He had to smile at the way she put it, but he knew what she meant.

"Anyway. Is this your way of getting out of it?"

"No. It's time that we talked about it. When you said that you should ask while I couldn't escape, I needed you to know that if I wanted to, I could escape." He reached up and touched her cheek. "I guess my point is that I'm not going to talk about it because I have no other choice – I *want* to talk about it because we can't move forward until I do. So, what do you want to know?"

She shifted to sit sideways so that she was facing him. When he did the same, she reached out and took hold of his hand, giving it a squeeze as she said, "I want to know everything, Lucky. I want to know as much as you want to tell me."

He liked that about her. She pushed him, but it seemed that she always gave him an out, too. Tempting as it was, this time he didn't want an out. He knew that they really wouldn't be able to move forward until he explained himself.

He sucked in a deep breath and turned to stare out at the lake for a few moments. The sun glinting on the water sparked a hundred different memories, but he pushed them all away.

This wasn't the time to get caught up in the past, this was his chance to move beyond it.

When he turned back to her, she shrugged and gave him a small smile. "You don't have to tell me anything if you don't want to."

"I do want to. I just don't know where to start."

"You don't have to tell me everything. If I got to ask whatever I wanted, I'd ask you to explain what you meant about being afraid to sleep beside me."

"Yeah." He owed her that much. "I don't sleep well." He squeezed his eyes shut, and Echo rested her paw on his knee. "Thanks lady." He turned back to Dee. "I'm just gonna dive in and get it over with. I have nightmares. Sometimes I wake up screaming, sometimes I wake up sweating, sometimes I wake up swinging, trying to fight..." He ran his hand over Echo's head. "More often than not, she wakes me up before it gets too bad."

He sucked in a deep breath and blew it out slowly before he said, "I can't sleep without a night light, and I can't sleep without Echo right there." He slowly lifted his gaze to meet hers. "I... It's... Oh for fuck's sake! I'm ashamed. There you go, that's the truth. What grown man wants to admit that he can't make it through the night because he's afraid of the dark? Saying that I can't sleep without Echo makes me sound like a little kid who can't sleep without his favorite teddy bear."

Dee linked her fingers through his, and Echo rested her chin on top of their joined hands.

"I don't imagine that any man would want to admit it, but I'm glad that you did. I'm sorry that you feel ashamed, and I know that nothing I say carries any weight – all that matters is you and how you feel about it – but I'm still going to say that I wish you didn't feel that way. I'm grateful to you, and proud of you."

He didn't try to answer; he couldn't swallow past the emotion that clogged his throat. He didn't even know what that emotion was – just that he didn't trust himself to speak.

As she so often did, Dee seemed to understand. "I'm grateful to you because not only did you go to hell holes all around the world to fight evil to keep the rest of us safe, but you're still fighting it now that you're back home, aren't you?"

He shrugged. He didn't exactly see it that way.

"I can see what you're thinking," she said. "You think that you shouldn't have to fight it; you think that you should've left it all behind. But I don't see how you could have – how anyone could have – I don't even know what you did or what happened to you, but I do know that when the mind is exposed to extremes, it can take a long time for it to recover – and it doesn't always recover." She squeezed his hand. "And if it doesn't, there's no shame in that. Would you feel ashamed if you lost a limb?"

He sat back in his seat.

"It's not so out of left field as you think; would you?"

"I can't say for sure because I didn't. But I have a feeling that no, I wouldn't."

"I don't think you would, either. So, if there's no shame in sustaining an injury that costs you a limb while serving your country, why should there be any shame in sustaining a mental injury?"

Lucky loosened his grip when he realized that he must be crushing her fingers. "I talked to a lot of therapists when I first got home – I had to." He shook his head. "Not one of them put it to me that way."

He knew that he was falling – if he'd not already fallen – for her when she swaggered her shoulders with a smile and said, "I'm not just a pretty face, you know."

He cupped her face between his hands and brushed his lips over hers. "I know that. I've known that since the very first time I saw you. There's just something about you." He chuckled – something he wouldn't have believed he'd be capable of while they were having this conversation. "Though, I will admit that first time I saw you, I gave up on you because you were scared of Echo."

Her eyes shone as she smiled back at him. "Well, I'm not going to give up on you just because you're scared of letting me in. I'm not going to batter down your door – even though that was my original plan. But I'm not giving up on you, okay?"

He pressed another kiss to her lips. "More than okay. Thank you. And if anyone's going to go battering doors down, it'll be me." He only hesitated for a second, it was time, and he knew it. "And I'm going to start with your front door if you don't invite me home with you tonight."

His heart pounded in his chest when she ran her tongue over her bottom lip. "You're invited."

He was vaguely aware of Echo moving away when Dee's lips met his. The way Dee kissed him made him not want to wait until tonight. But after all this time, he wanted their first time to be something special. Although, as her hands found their way underneath the hem of his T-shirt, and she scraped her fingernails over his abs, he promised himself that he wouldn't wait too long before they made the most of the bunk in the cabin.

Chapter Twenty

Dee set her empty wine glass down on the table. Lucky reached for the bottle to pour her another, but she covered the glass with her hand.

"I've had enough, thanks."

The way he smiled sent shivers chasing each other down her spine. "Me too, don't worry; I'm not trying to get you drunk."

She laughed. "We both know that you don't need to."

She had to press her thighs together when he let his gaze roam over her and said, "Good to know. I was starting to wonder."

"What do you mean?"

He leaned forward in his seat and rested his hand on her thigh. "Up until today, I haven't doubted that you wanted me. I don't know, maybe I'm just reading it wrong, but it feels like you're not so sure anymore – not since I told you that I plan to batter your doors down."

She had to laugh as she covered his hand with her own. "If I seem less sure of myself, it's only because I don't want to come on too strong. I don't want you to go to bed with me just because you think that I expect it of you."

There was no mistaking the lust in his eyes as he shook his head. "It's not about anyone expecting anything, Dee. It's about me wanting you."

She swallowed when he squeezed her thigh. "It's about me wanting you, too," she breathed.

He looked up at the dark sky; they were sitting out on the pool terrace where they'd eaten dinner. It had been such a wonderful day. After their ride in the boat this morning, they'd come back to the house, where Lucky had shown her how to dock it. Then, they'd spent the afternoon by the pool – and in it, all three of them had fun swimming and splashing around.

They'd been sitting here for ages after they'd eaten; night had fallen while they sat talking. As Dee followed Lucky's gaze, a meteor blazed across the sky before disappearing over the horizon.

Lucky chuckled. "I told you that I'd never forget the first time that I got to watch the stars fall with you. Now, seeing that..." He jerked his chin toward where the meteor had disappeared "... it feels like a sign that I'll never forget tonight, either."

She leaned across the space between them and pressed a peck to his lips. "I'll do my best to make sure that you don't."

He laughed. "Why does it feel like I'm trying to be romantic and you're trying to be dirty?"

She had to laugh with him. "Probably because that's exactly what's happening."

"In that case..." He got to his feet and offered her his hand. "I think it's time we went to bed."

Dee got up to join him; she couldn't agree more. As they gathered the dishes and glasses to carry them back upstairs, she noticed that Echo stuck even closer than usual to Lucky's side. It wasn't lost on her that she'd gone straight to him when he said the word bed. Perhaps she was reading too much into it, but given what he'd told her this morning, she was already wondering how Echo would feel about her being in bed with Lucky.

They left the dishes in the sink, and Dee took hold of his hand to lead him upstairs. Echo trotted on ahead of them and went straight to Dee's room.

"Sorry, I guess she feels at home," Lucky said as they followed her. "Although, how she knew to come in here, I don't know. This is your room, right?"

"It is." Dee smiled. "And as smart as she is, it's not that she just guessed. She's been here before, haven't you, lady? Remember that day when you left her here with me?"

"Oh yeah, right. I…" Lucky stopped and shook his head with a puzzled smile as he watched Echo come out of the closet.

Dee had to laugh. "You found it! Clever girl!"

Lucky cocked an eyebrow at her, and for a moment, Dee panicked. "Please don't go thinking that I bought Echo a bed as part of some devious plan to get you both to stay over. It's just that when she was up here with me that day, we had a bit of a chat. She told me that she does like a soft bed, but not a fluffy bed. So…" She was so hoping that he'd see the gesture the way she intended it. "I went online and found a dog bed with a cool cover for her. You know how they make mattresses that help you to stay cool? Well, it's a thing for dogs, too."

She looked at him, wondering what he'd make of this, but he was watching Echo with a big smile on his face. Echo had pulled the bed into the corner of the room between the dresser and the door. She climbed onto it and turned around three times before settling down.

She rested her chin on her paws and gave a contented sigh.

Lucky laughed out loud. "Thank you. She has a big fluffy bed in my office at work, but she lies on the floor next to it. I couldn't figure out what her deal was." He met her gaze. "I love that the two of you understand each other like that."

Dee felt a rush of relief wash over her. "I do, too. She's amazing. I love her –" she stopped short when she realized what she'd said.

Lucky came to her and rested his hands on her hips – it was hard to concentrate whenever he did that, but she managed to focus enough on his words that they put her at ease.

"It's okay. You don't need to be afraid of that word. I'm not. We both know that she's not. If we're being honest, then I have to tell you that I'm already more than half way in love with you."

Dee's heart pounded even harder at his words – and it was already hammering from the feel of his hands on her.

"Hey." He tilted her chin up so that she had to look into his eyes. His gorgeous, brown eyes, that right now felt as though they were staring right into her soul. "I heard you when you told me – that you're no good at love. I just hope that you heard me when I told you that however I feel isn't your responsibility – that I'm prepared to take the risk of loving you, no matter how it might work out."

All she could do was nod; she had no words.

He brushed his lips over hers, and she felt goosebumps break out on her arms when he added, "Right now, I think that we're past the time for words. I think you need to let me show you – let me love you."

She couldn't help it, she let out a short laugh. "Damn, Lucky! Coming out with shit like that, I should let you help me write my books." As soon as the words were out, she was afraid that she'd blown the moment.

She hadn't. Lucky threw back his head and laughed with her. "I'm just telling you the truth, Dee, that's all. And the truth is that the time for talking is over."

He reached down to grab the hem of his T-shirt and pulled it off over his head. Dee's breath caught in her chest at the sight of all those muscles. Sure, she'd seen him dressed in only swim shorts a few times now – and it had been as sexy as hell then – but there was something very different about it when she knew that in a few moments, they'd both be naked together.

And it turned out that she'd overestimated the time it would take. By the time she gathered her senses, she was lying, naked, face-to-face with him on the bed, and their clothes were in a pile on the floor.

He tucked his fingers under her chin and pressed a kiss to her lips. "You okay?"

"More than okay," she said as she curled her arm around his waist and drew him closer. "And I have to tell you that I'm impressed."

He closed his hand around her ass and held her against his thick, hard erection. "Why, thank you."

She chuckled. "That wasn't actually what I meant – I would have used a … bigger word for that. I meant that I'm impressed at how quickly we got here."

He leaned in and spoke against her lips. "Don't worry, I don't have any plans to rush what comes next. But it took me so long to get here that I just didn't want to waste any more time."

"As far as I'm concerned, it was time invested – not wasted."

Her breath caught in her chest when he rolled her onto her back. His eyes shone with amusement as he smiled down at her.

"Well, I hope you don't mind me investing a little more time. Now that we're here, I'm in no hurry."

She shook her head, eager to discover what exactly it was that he was planning to take his time over.

He lowered his head to hers, and in the moment before their lips met, she noticed that Echo had turned around in her bed – she now had her back to them.

But when Lucky nipped her lips, and then kissed her, coaxing her tongue out to play with his, she forgot all about Echo.

She'd been with enough men in her years, but not one of them had affected her the way that he did. Just his kiss made her feel as if she was melting underneath him. When he brought his hand up and cupped her breast, she moaned into his mouth.

She moaned again in disappointment when he lifted his head, but he gave her the sexiest smile and winked. "Don't worry, I'll be back."

He didn't give her any time to wonder where he was going; he kissed his way across her jaw and then down her neck. When he closed both hands around her breasts, and rolled her nipples between his fingers and thumbs, she tried to press her thighs together, but he was nestled between them.

He ducked his head, and all she could do was lie back and enjoy as he lavished attention on first one breast then the other with his lips and tongue. When he kissed his way down over her stomach, she grasped the sheet beneath her.

Spreading her thighs wider and holding them open with both hands, he made her gasp when he trailed his tongue over her entrance in one long lick.

"Oh my God, Lucky!"

He lifted his head and gave her a very satisfied-looking smile. "Yeah?"

Her heart felt as though it melted in her chest – he looked so damn happy, and this felt so damn right. She chuckled as she shook her head. "Not a thing. Back to work."

Feeling him laugh against her — his body shaking between her legs, and his breath warming the wetness between them — made goosebumps break out over her whole body.

"Yes, ma'am."

She opened her mouth to answer, but all that came out was a moan when his tongue entered her, and his thumb found her clit.

She let her head fall back and gave herself up to him. She was completely at his mercy, and when he closed his mouth over her clit and sank two fingers inside her, there was nothing she could do but go where he took her.

Her hips rocked in time with him as the pressure built low in her belly. He carried her higher and higher until she shouted his name when he pushed her over the edge, sending her flying away on the best orgasm that she'd had in years.

When she finally regained her senses, she opened her eyes to find his staring back into them.

"Hi."

"Hmph," she mumbled.

He cocked an eyebrow, and she pushed at his shoulder.

"Is that a smirk on your face, Evan Penny? It is; you're smirking at me, aren't you?"

He chuckled. "Yeah. Can you tell me that I don't have reason to?"

"No, I can't," she said with a smile. "In fact, I can tell you that you have every reason to smirk. Wow!"

She put her hand to his shoulder again and pushed harder. He looked a little puzzled, but he let her turn him onto his back — there was no way she could manage that if he didn't want her to — and smiled up at her when she straddled him.

He rested his hands at her hips and pushed up into the heat between her legs. "Are you saying that you're ready for me?"

She shook her head and ran her tongue across her bottom lip. "No, I'm saying that you'd better get ready for me."

He gave her a puzzled look.

"I want something to smirk about, too."

She kissed him but didn't linger there for too long. Instead, she worked her way down his body, running her fingers over the planes and ridges of his chest and abs. She followed her hands with her mouth, licking and nipping, loving the little sounds that he made, and the way he tangled his fingers in her hair.

When she was face to face with his cock, she curled her fingers around him, and traced circles over the tip with her tongue.

She had to smile when she heard him breathe, "Jesus, Dee!"

She closed her lips around him and slowly lowered her head, swirling her tongue as she went. He was thick, and so hard, she cupped his balls with one hand, keeping the other wrapped around the base of him.

Just as she started to bob her head faster, his hands came under her armpits, and he pulled her up and off him. The next thing she knew, she was on her back again, looking up into his eyes.

His cock was now throbbing between her legs, and he hooked his arm behind one knee, lifting it and opening her up to him.

"You don't like that?" she asked incredulously.

"Oh, I like it. I like it a lot. But I've waited and wanted to be inside you for so long now. If I let you finish what you were doing, it'd be a while longer."

She loved that all his hesitation seemed to have disappeared. He wasn't letting her take the lead anymore – and she loved that. She loved it even more, when he thrust his hips and entered her in one swift move.

She gasped and let her head fall back against the pillow. "Lucky!" she breathed.

He nuzzled his face into her neck and made her skin tingle when he whispered into her ear. "Yeah, I am – lucky. And I've never felt as lucky as I do right now."

She brought both legs up and wrapped them around his waist. "You feel so damned good! I don't mind telling you that I feel lucky right now." She smiled. "In every sense."

He nodded, but as he started to move, there was no need for more words — their bodies were expressing themselves far more eloquently without them.

He drove deeper with every thrust, and she lifted her hips to meet him. They fit together perfectly, and they soon found a rhythm. She dug her fingers into his ass as he braced himself over her and let go.

There was nothing hesitant about this. He was giving her all that he had – fast and hard. She was gladly taking him. When she scraped her nails down his back, he pounded even harder and gasped her name.

All she could do was cling to him. The world seemed to spin away until they were lost in a place where nothing but the two of them existed. She felt him tense and knew what was coming. She'd hoped that they might go there together but...

He slid his hand between them, and the second that his thumb brushed over her clit, every muscle in her body tensed and she gasped, "Lucky!"

"Come for me, Dee. Come with me!"

He thrust deep and hard, and as if in response to his command, her orgasm washed over her, hitting her like a tidal wave that swept her away. She felt him tense and grow impossibly harder for one, two, three more thrusts, and then he held deep and let go.

Wave after wave of pleasure swept through her, all emanating from and returning to the place where they joined. If she'd thought that her first orgasm was the best that she'd had in years, this one might just be the best ever.

As they slowly returned to earth, he slid one arm underneath her and held her tight as he buried his face in her neck. For a moment, she was worried; she didn't know how he was going to react.

Then, he lifted his head, and when she saw the look in his eyes, she knew that she didn't stand a chance – even before he spoke. And when he did, he sealed her fate.

"I told you that I was half way there." He dropped a kiss on her lips. "Now, I have to tell you that I just fell the rest of the way."

~ ~ ~

Lucky couldn't have stopped himself from telling her that if he wanted to – and he didn't want to. He'd known that she was special, but now? Now, he knew that she was everything. No matter what demons he had to fight, he wasn't going to let them stand between him and this woman.

He didn't know if it was good or bad that it had taken making love to her before he completely understood it. There was no denying that he did understand now – it had hit him like a ton of bricks. She was it for him. He wanted to spend his future with her. More than that, he didn't want to imagine the future without her.

The way her eyes shone when she reached up and ran her fingers over his cheek reassured him.

"Did we just have a religious experience?" she asked with a little laugh.

He raised his eyebrows and waited, hoping that she wasn't going to make a joke out of it. He'd roll with it if she did – he'd have to. But he desperately wanted her to have felt it in the same way that he had.

All the humor left her face, and she cupped his cheek in her hand. "Don't look so worried. I'm trying to make light of it, because I don't know what else to do with it. All I'm saying is that… What just happened here – what we just shared?" She pressed her lips together. "It's made a believer out of me."

He wanted to relax – wanted to think that she meant what he hoped she did, but he waited.

"I might not be any good at love, but I don't think that I'm going to be able to stop myself falling for you anyway."

His whole body relaxed, and he collapsed on top of her before rolling to the side, taking her with him.

"I want to say that we'll be able to work it out, no matter what. I need you to know that's what I want." He blew out a sigh. "But I guess I'll have to let you decide that in the morning."

She leaned in and spoke against his lips. "It'll be fine. You told me that no matter what happens, I should just let Echo be in charge, right?"

"Yeah. I have the feeling that I might not sleep at all – I don't think I'll be able to relax that much. But if I do fall asleep, and I wake you by struggling or shouting or … anything, Echo knows what to do. She'll come right to me. I hate to say this, I'm not trying to push you out, but the best thing for you to do will be to stay out of the way."

She proved once again that she wasn't like other women he'd known when she smiled and said, "Don't worry. I'm not going to get upset or feel ousted by her." He loved that she glanced over at Echo and smiled before she continued. "I don't mind telling you that if I didn't know her and didn't know what a special relationship the two of you have, I might have felt a little left out. But honestly, I'm grateful that she's here. I'm grateful that you have her, and that I can rely on her to take charge."

"Okay then."

She smiled and pressed a kiss to his lips. "It is. It's all okay, isn't it?"

Lucky lay there staring up at the ceiling long after Dee had drifted off to sleep. They'd chatted for a while, and when she'd burrowed down beneath the sheets and taken him in her mouth again, she'd proved him wrong – he was still capable of going twice in one night. He grinned to himself. And he'd be happy to let her remind him of that as often as she liked.

He glanced over at Echo, who was curled up on the bed that Dee had bought for her. He felt bad that she'd had to turn her back a couple of times, but now that Dee was sleeping, she was watching over him again.

He'd brought his night light with him, but Dee already had one plugged into the socket by the dresser. It cast a golden glow over Echo, and that seemed fitting. She felt like his guardian angel, and tonight, he needed her perhaps more than ever.

He held his hand out and she came and licked it. "I'm getting tired, lady. I might sleep. I hate that I need to ask you but…"

She whined and put her paw up on the bed, letting him know that he didn't need to ask – she'd have his back, just like she always had.

Chapter Twenty-One

The darkness was heavy and oppressive, even more so than usual. Lucky tried to curl into a ball. He couldn't hear the footsteps yet, but he knew that they would come. He needed to protect himself, he'd learned to use one arm to cover his head and to wrap the other around his middle. He was pretty sure that both arms had been broken in the time that he'd been held here. But at least they'd protected his ribs and organs from the kicks and blows that would have caused even more damage.

Something was wrong. He couldn't curl into a ball. He felt as though he was shrouded in something, and there was a hot, heavy weight on either side of him. Had he died? He didn't understand. He could hear distant sounds – but it wasn't the usual sound of footsteps coming toward him.

No, it was murmuring. Someone was speaking. The warm weights on either side of him were moving. He didn't know what was going on. Were those weights bodies? Shit! Had they captured his team? He'd been here for so long that he'd clung to the hope that the rest of his team had made it out of that canyon. He had to hold onto that hope. If they were dead…

He tried to reach out, but whatever he was covered in was wrapped tightly around him. The sounds grew louder, drew closer. The heavy weights were moving. They weren't just weights, they were bodies – living, breathing bodies.

He wasn't alone! He didn't know how long he'd been here, but if he had to guess, it must have been months. He hadn't felt the warmth of another human presence in all that time.

He froze when the sounds started to become clearer. One of them wasn't a human sound.

It was a whine. Could it … could it be…?

He turned toward the sound, and wet warmth spread across his cheek. It was similar to the feeling of blood pouring down his face – warm, sticky; a feeling that he was all too familiar with after the beatings. But it couldn't be that – there was no pain. There'd been no blows.

The wetness spread across his face again, and then again. Then he heard another whine. It really was!

He opened his eyes to find Echo's nose an inch from his own. She licked him again and then let out a happy little yip.

He wrapped his arm around her and buried his face in her fur. "Jesus, lady! We did it! It's morning, isn't it? I made it through the night."

Echo surprised him by lifting her head and instead of licking him as she usually would, she looked over his shoulder. And then it hit him. There were two bodies in this bed beside himself.

He slowly started to turn over, but Dee's voice greeted him before he could, and he could hear the smile in it.

"Good morning. You were sleeping so soundly that I didn't like to wake you."

He pushed himself up into a sitting position, leaning back against the headboard. When he held his arm out, she came to sit beside him he loved the feel of her leaning against him – especially the weight of her heavy breasts against his chest.

"I didn't give you any trouble in the night?"

She looked up at him with a gentle smile. "Not a peep. I slept pretty well myself. I did look over and check on you a few times, but it seemed to me that you were resting peacefully."

He shook his head in wonder. "It took me a long time to get to sleep, but once I did… That's the best night I've had since I came to Summer Lake."

She wrapped her arm around his middle and smiled up at him. "Well, just know that you're welcome to sleep over here whenever you like. If you need me to wear you out so that you can sleep, I can do that."

She waggled her eyebrows, making him laugh.

"I think I'll have to take you up on that offer. Thank you. But… I don't think it's just because you wore me out."

She laughed. "Okay, I can try harder."

He laughed with her. "That's not what I mean; but if you want to try, I won't stop you. What I meant was that I don't think that I slept so well because you wore me out – I think it's because I finally relaxed." He met her gaze and held it. "I think that you… me… *us* …" He waved two fingers in between them. "Whatever *this* is, whatever we share, is good for me."

She reached up and pressed a kiss to his lips. "I'm glad. And I have to tell you that I think it's good for me, too."

~ ~ ~

"You caught some sun," said Lucky. "We'll have to get you some better sunscreen."

Dee went to check herself in the mirror in the hallway. He was right, she did look a little pink. "Oh well," she shrugged. "I'm lucky, I don't stay red, I tan quickly. Unless you're embarrassed for your friends to see you out with a lobster, I'll be fine."

He came to her and rested his hands on her hips. "There's so much wrong with what you just said. For starters, I could never be embarrassed for my friends or anyone else to see me with you." He pressed a kiss to the tip of her nose. "I know that they'll all agree with me that I'm living up to my name –

I'm Lucky, remember? And don't you dare go calling my beautiful woman a lobster. You're just a little pink. I didn't know if you'd want to put some cream or something on before we go. That's all."

She wrapped her arms around his waist and smiled up at him. "That's sweet of you, but I'm fine, thanks. I bet by the time we get over there, I'll look sun kissed instead of medium rare."

He rolled his eyes at her – she'd already learned that he wouldn't engage with her if she spoke about herself in a less than complimentary way. "Are you ready to go, then?"

She went to the island in the kitchen to fetch her purse. "I am. Should we stop at your place on the way there, or on the way back?"

They'd had another wonderful day. Last night had been amazing. Yes, the sex had to be the best that she'd ever had, but that wasn't even the best thing about it as far as she was concerned. She'd been nervous about how Lucky would cope with spending the night with her, but it had turned out way better than she hoped.

When she woke up this morning, she'd been convinced that he'd be up already – if she was honest, she'd been half expecting that he might have left. Instead, he'd been sleeping peacefully beside her. That had made her happy, and when Echo had come to her and smiled – there was no doubt in Dee's mind at all, Echo really did smile – she'd believed that everything was going to be okay.

She'd been a little concerned at the way he struggled before he woke, but just as Lucky had assured her that she would, Echo had been right there, licking his face until he awoke.

They'd had a leisurely breakfast out by the pool. Then, they'd sat on the loungers relaxing. They'd talked some, but Dee loved that they didn't need to chat all the time. Lucky was naturally taciturn, and it seemed that with him, she didn't feel the usual need to run her mouth, either. She liked to think that she was a naturally laid-back kind of person, and sitting out in the sun with Lucky she'd realized that she was truly content.

He leaned in and pressed a kiss to her forehead. "We should maybe stop on the way back." His big, brown eyes bored into hers. "Are you sure that you want us to stay again tonight?"

She nodded rapidly. "I'm absolutely sure. The only doubt that I have is whether you're comfortable with it. I know that you have to go to work in the morning – and I don't know if two nights in a row might be too much."

"Nope." He smiled and pecked her lips. "There's nothing for you to doubt about that. Although… Given the way I slept last night, you might want to decide if you want to set any limits on how often we stay over. I got more sleep last night than I have in the last three nights put together."

She bit down on her bottom lip as she looked up into his eyes. "It kind of scares me a little bit, but I don't feel the need to set any limit." Her heart pounded as she said that. Surely, it would be sensible to be more cautious. One amazing night didn't mean that they should throw caution to the wind and dive in head first.

"We can play it by ear," Lucky said. "I think as long as we keep being honest with each other, it'll be fine if one of us feels the need to pull back at some point."

"I think you're right." She checked her watch. "I also think that we'd better get a move on if we're going to get over to the other side of the lake on time."

"Yeah. We'd best get going."

Dee had thought that they'd spend the entire day relaxing by the pool; Lucky had seemed fine with that idea, too. But he'd received a phone call about an hour ago that had changed their plans.

His friend, Dalton, had called to invite them over to Taryn's restaurant for a drink. Well, he'd invited them over for dinner, but Lucky had declined that invitation. It made Dee smile that he was obviously irritated at his friend for intruding on their day – but when Dalton had pushed, and she'd assured him that she wouldn't mind going over there for a drink, he'd gotten quite enthusiastic about the idea.

As they rode around the lake to Four Mile Creek, she was grateful that he'd suggested he should bring his Hummer. It had been a long time since she'd ridden around as a passenger. It gave her the chance to just relax and take in the scenery in a way that she couldn't do when she was driving.

She was staring up at the mountains when he reached across and took hold of her hand. "Are you okay?" he asked. "You're quiet over there."

She chuckled. "I don't talk *all* the time."

He laughed with her. "That's not what I meant." He turned and shot her a quick wink before turning his attention back to the road. "Although, you do talk at least half the time."

That took her by surprise so much that she actually spluttered. Lucky laughed out loud and squeezed her hand.

"What?" he asked. "We both know it's true."

She dug her nails into the palm of his hand and tried to glare at him, but she couldn't stop smiling. "We do. I just didn't expect you to say so."

He lifted a shoulder. "I don't see anything wrong with saying it. I'm not criticizing. I like it. You know I do – at least, I hope you know."

"I do. It's all good. I like you teasing."

"Good. But back to the question. You're quiet, and looking thoughtful, and what I really wanted to do was check that you're okay with this. Are you okay with Taryn?"

"Yes. You've got no worries there. I like all your friends. Taryn's… Outspoken. I'm not sure that's the right word, but you know what I mean."

"I do. That's why I was asking if you're okay with this."

"I'm fine. Honestly. What I was going to say is that Taryn's the kind of person who says what's on her mind. I'm the kind of person who appreciates that. I like her. Oh, and I don't think I told you that I ran into her in the bakery in town one day, and we had a bit of a chat. We're on our way to becoming friends in our own right." She squeezed his hand. "It's not like you and Dalton have to watch over us and just hope that we'll get along."

"So, I can relax, then?"

"You can. And if it makes you feel any better, I was quiet and looking thoughtful because I was enjoying the scenery, and I realized that it's been a long time since I've been a passenger. I've driven through some beautiful places over the last few years, but I never really got to take them in because I had to focus on the road."

"Happy I can do that for you." He looked as though he had something else to say, so she waited. It was a few minutes before he glanced over at her again. "My first instinct was to say that I'll be happy to drive wherever we go, so that you can enjoy the view. But that's not right. How about we take turns driving?"

"I like the sound of that." And she did – especially because she knew that they were talking about more than just trips in the car.

~ ~ ~

Lucky grinned at Damon when he set a beer down on the bar in front of him.

"And you thought that Taryn had summoned you over here so that the four of you could hang out together, didn't you?"

He laughed. "I should have known better. Dee did tell me that she and Taryn had a budding friendship of their own going. I just didn't expect Taryn to kidnap her and Echo."

"You know what she's like," said Damon.

"I don't know her all that well, yet. But I'm learning fast."

He jumped when a hand came down on his shoulder, and he turned to see Dalton grinning at him. "I'll give you a tip, then. Take it from one who knows – if you want to survive around Taryn, you're going to need to learn damned fast. That woman's enough to keep anyone on their toes."

"She keeps you in line."

Dalton laughed. "I don't know about *in line,* that'd be no fun for either of us, but she definitely keeps me on my toes. I should warn you that she's taken a shine to Dee. So, whatever the two of you have going on, Taryn's planning to draw her into the fold."

"It's okay. I'm good with that." Lucky could tell that although his friend was hiding it well, Dalton was concerned. "I can see why you'd think that I might not like that idea. But it's all good – I do like it. Instead of wanting to hold back and feeling uncomfortable that she might be part of our social circle, meaning that I'd still have to face her if things don't work out between us, I'm grateful to Taryn for giving her an in that's not dependent on me."

Dalton pulled up a seat next to him and cocked his head to the side. "Explain."

Lucky had to laugh. "I'm not going to ask if Taryn likes it when you get that bossy attitude and start coming out with one-word commands." He shuddered. "I really don't want to know."

Dalton laughed. "And I'm not telling either way. But with you, I know it works. So, go ahead, explain."

Lucky blew out a sigh. "You know I'm not much of a talker."

"So, keep it brief."

Lucky narrowed his eyes at his friend. "I'm glad that she's making friends with Taryn. I hope that she'll make friends with the other women, too. Yes, I like it for her sake – she's new in town and it'll be good for her to have friends. But... Don't look at me like that; I'm getting there. Mostly, I hope that she and Taryn will become friends, because I'm thinking that she and I will become more than friends."

Dalton tried to hide a grin but didn't manage it. "You're hoping ... or you already are more than friends?"

Lucky took a slug of his beer while he decided how he wanted to answer that. He wasn't the kind of person to go around bragging that he'd slept with a woman. Then again, Dalton already knew that – and he wasn't that kind, either.

"You know what I mean," said Dalton. "I'm not prying."

"I know. Put it this way ..." He knew that his next words would probably be more surprising to Dalton than anything else he could say. "I stayed at her place last night."

Dalton sat back in his seat. "And...? Again, you know what I mean. I'm guessing you did okay since you're here together now." He rolled his eyes. "At least, you came over here together. You're not together *right* now because Taryn stole her."

Lucky laughed. "Like I said, I'm not worried about that, I'm happy that they're doing it. I know Taryn wanted to get some time with Echo. And I know that Echo will keep an eye on Dee no matter what. And... Yeah." He shook his head. He was still surprised at how well he'd slept. "Echo stayed in the room."

Dalton folded his arms across his chest. "And?"

"And I didn't think that I was going to be able to sleep." He glanced at Damon, who was hovering nearby. He didn't think he was trying to eavesdrop. It was more that he had a feeling that Damon would be able to understand – better even than Dalton could.

Damon caught his eye and started to move away, but Lucky shook his head. He had a feeling that the two of them might become friends, given time.

"You need anything?" Damon asked.

"No. I'm good. Just letting you know that we're good."

Damon held his gaze for a moment. "Thanks. I didn't mean to listen in."

"It's not a problem. I reckon that one of these nights we should take each other out for a beer."

Dalton nodded. "I reckon that might do the pair of you good." He turned back to Lucky. "But tell me the rest."

"Like I said, I didn't think that I'd be able to sleep, but I did." He smiled. "Both my ladies were awake before me this morning, and I got a kiss on the cheek from each of them."

Dalton grinned and grasped his shoulder, giving him a shake. "That's awesome! I told you, Echo picked Dee out for you, just like she picked Taryn for me."

Lucky nodded slowly. The first time Dalton had said something like that, it hadn't sat well with him. Now, he was starting to think that his friend was right. Echo had always had his back; he trusted her instincts. And when it came to Dee, it seemed that she'd come through in a big way for him.

"Do you think you could have a word with her for me?" Damon asked.

Lucky gave him a puzzled look, wondering what he might want with Dee.

Dalton laughed. "You should see the look on your face, Penny! I think Damon's talking about asking Echo for some help with the ladies."

Damon nodded. "I am. I haven't had much luck in that department, but I don't mind telling you that seeing all of you guys makes me think it might be time for me to try again."

Lucky shrugged. "I'll ask her if she feels like playing matchmaker for you – if Taryn ever brings her and Dee back."

Dalton looked down at his phone. "She just texted. They're on their way back now. She wanted some Echo time, and she wanted Echo and Star to play together. I think she was just killing a few birds with the same stone by asking Dee to run over to the house with her."

"Yeah. I'm not complaining. Not really."

All three of them turned at the sound of raised voices coming from the end of the bar. Two women, one who looked to be in her twenties and the other in her fifties were getting into an argument.

Lucky guessed that they might be mother and daughter, and it was confirmed when the younger woman shouted, "Why do you have to be so stubborn, Mom? This is no place for you! You should come home."

The older woman glanced over at them, and Lucky felt bad for her when she looked embarrassed.

She answered her daughter in a much quieter – but no less vehement – voice. Lucky guessed that she was trying to shut her up and calm her down.

Dalton turned back to him and made a face. "I'm glad I don't have kids."

Lucky nodded. Becoming a father had never felt like an option to him. He didn't feel as though he'd missed out. Especially not if the younger woman at the other end of the bar was anything to go by.

"Hey guys, we'll meet you out on the terrace."

Lucky and Dalton turned to see Taryn waving from the entrance to the restaurant. He smiled when he saw Dee standing beside her, holding onto Echo's leash. They all knew that Echo didn't need it, but he'd thought it best that she should wear it.

He gave Dee a chin lift and started to get to his feet. As much as Taryn loved them, she didn't allow Echo or Star into the restaurant – and he could understand that. She did have an amazing doggy area set up on the terrace outside, though. She'd even had landscapers come in and install a patch of turf.

He and Dalton started toward them, but stopped in their tracks when the mother and daughter at the end of the bar raised their voices again. Lucky's heart thudded to a stop when Echo let out a short, sharp bark and lunged forward.

Dee didn't stand a chance; the leash slipped through her hands. Echo bounded through the restaurant toward the two women. He, Dalton, and Damon all hurried toward them as well.

In her usual fashion, Echo skidded to a halt just shy of the two women. Lucky found it interesting that the mom didn't seem too fazed, while the daughter screamed and ran.

"Echo! Return."

She turned and looked over her shoulder at him and damn him if she didn't smile. What the hell was she up to now?

Having been closer, Damon got there before he and Dalton did. Lucky was impressed with the way he vaulted over the bar. He positioned himself between Echo and the older woman as he reassured her.

"Sorry about that. I promise you, she's safe. She won't harm you."

Lucky loved hearing the absolute confidence in Damon's voice as he reassured the woman. He hadn't known Echo for long – he'd only met her a few times – but it seemed that he already knew her well.

Lucky was there just a few steps behind Damon. He caught his fingers inside Echo's collar and spoke in a low voice. "What are you up to, lady?"

She let out one of her happy little yips and turned to look at Damon. She barked once, and then set out toward the door that led onto the terrace. Lucky let her lead him, knowing that Dee and the others would follow.

Once they were safely out on the terrace, he apologized to Dalton. He knew that he'd have to apologize to Taryn when she came out – after she dealt with the hysterical younger woman.

Dalton just gave him a rueful smile. "You don't get it, do you?"

"No. Get what?"

"Think about it. What was Damon saying two seconds before the girls appeared?"

Lucky had to think about it. "Oh shit! No. No way."

"No way, what?" asked Dee who had just joined them. "What's wrong?"

Dalton chuckled. "It seems that Echo's found herself a new purpose in life."

When Dee just gave him a puzzled look, he continued, "First, she brokered a peace treaty between Taryn and me. Then, she set her sights on you for Lucky."

Lucky relaxed when Dee smiled.

Dalton grinned. "Now, she seems to think that she's got the two of you on the right track, so she's looking for her next couple to match up."

Lucky glanced back in through the doors. When he saw Damon talking to the mom who'd just been arguing with her daughter, he had a feeling that Dalton was right.

He looked down at Echo, and she smiled. When he looked back up, Dee was smiling at him, too. "I was going to apologize for letting her go. But there was really nothing I could do to stop her." She looked in through the doors at Damon and the woman. "And seeing *that*, I'm glad that I couldn't stop her." She reached down and patted Echo's head.

"You're smarter than the rest of us put together, aren't you, lady?"

They all laughed when Echo barked happily.

Chapter Twenty-Two

Dee looked down when Echo pressed her wet nose into her hand. "It's okay, I trust you. You can run around if you like. I know you won't go off."

She pursed her lips. "Or I don't *think* you will. Tell me…" She laughed "… I wish you *could* tell me. Do you just matchmake one couple at a time? And if you do…" She looked at Echo more intently. "Does that mean that you think that Lucky and I are good?"

Echo barked one of her happy barks.

"Good. Because I think so, too." Dee's smile faded as they continued walking along the water's edge. "Things are going really well, aren't they? I can't believe that you guys have stayed here every night. I mean, don't get me wrong, I love it. I just wish you could tell me how he's doing. He seems to be sleeping well. I don't know how long it takes him to get to sleep…"

She shook her head as her words trailed off. Lucky had hardly been back to his place since Saturday morning. It was Wednesday now. They'd already established a bit of a routine;

when he went to work in the morning, Echo stayed home with her.

This morning was the second time that Dee and Echo had ventured down to the beach. The irony wasn't lost on her that not so long ago, she'd been terrified of dogs like Echo and hadn't wanted to be on the beach. Yet, here she was, not just walking at the water's edge with her, but talking to her as if she understood every word.

"I guess I just have to trust that it's all okay, don't I? I don't mind telling you that I'm enjoying it. But I don't know what to do about this weekend. I wish you could tell me what you think. I think you'll love my boys – and I think that they'll love you, too. But it's probably not the best idea to have you all staying at the house at the same time, is it?"

Echo looked up at her and whined. Dee decided she should probably take that as agreement.

"I do want you to meet them, though. We can all take the boat out. And we can hang out by the pool, too."

She checked her watch. She should probably turn around soon; they were getting close to the more populated part of the beach. She could see people up ahead and some dogs as well.

"It's not that I don't trust you," she told Echo. "Although, I won't lie to you, I am a bit nervous. But I need to get to work, as well. I'm on the last stretch with this book now. I'd love to be able to get it finished before the boys arrive. So, come on, let's turn around and go back."

She turned around, hoping that Echo would follow. Her heart sank when she didn't.

"Please, Echo. Come on. I don't want to insult you by putting the leash on you. And we both know that I couldn't drag you anyway, even if I did. So, please can we go home now?"

Echo seemed to lean forward as she sniffed the wind. Dee knew what was going on when her ears strained forward, even while Echo remained still.

"Oh no. What have you spotted? Is Dalton up there? Someone else you know?"

Echo whined and her whole body seemed to quiver in anticipation. Dee followed her gaze, but she couldn't see anyone she recognized.

"Oh. Oh no! It's that dog, isn't it? I never thought to ask. Lucky's never said anything about how you do with other dogs. I know you love Star, but Star's different. Star's... family."

She slipped the leash over Echo's head, knowing that it would be a pointless gesture if Echo decided to take off but needing to feel as though she'd at least tried. They both watched the dog farther up the beach. It was running along the water's edge, in much the same way that Echo liked to. There was someone with it, but it wasn't on a leash. Dee didn't recognize the man walking behind it. She just hoped that he was someone understanding.

"Can we *please* go home?"

She'd swear that the look on Echo's face was apologetic in the moment before she took off. Dee let go of the leash. She'd learned the hard way on Sunday that there was no point in trying to hold her back, and that leash hurt when it was ripped through her hands.

She set off at a jog after her, halfheartedly calling, "Echo, return!" When Echo got something into her head, she didn't even return to Lucky. Dee didn't expect her to listen to her.

She held her breath when the other dog spotted Echo and started running to meet her. She pressed her hand to her chest, trying not to let the memories flood her mind. If Echo got into a fight … If she got hurt … If she …

Dee squeezed her eyes shut. If the worst was going to happen, she'd rather hear it than see it. After a few moments, with no growls or snarls, she dared to take a peek. Relief washed over her when she saw Echo and the other dog circling each other. Echo's tail was wagging. The other dog didn't have one but its whole body was wiggling in what looked like excitement. Dee wasn't sure what breed it was, she'd guess a shepherd of some kind.

As she hurried toward them, she heard the man call, "Ollie! Come back, mate!"

The other dog – Ollie, apparently – ignored his human, just as Echo ignored Dee.

As they got closer, the man looked at Dee. "He won't cause any trouble, what about your dog?"

"I don't think so." She jerked her chin toward the dogs. "I don't mind telling you that I was a little worried at first, she's not actually my dog. But she's very well trained. And look." She had to smile.

Echo and Ollie seemed to have reached a conclusion from their mutual sniffing that all was well, and even that they could be friends by the look of it.

Ollie barked twice, and Echo tilted her head to the side as if she was listening intently. When Ollie barked again, Echo barked back. Ollie seemed to bow down before her, before turning and bounding away. Echo gave chase, and they both raced away down the beach. Dee was grateful that they were headed toward the house – away from people.

The man gave her a rueful smile. "Sorry about that. Ollie's a good boy, but he doesn't get much company. Looks to me like he just made a friend."

Dee nodded. "I'm just glad that they took a liking to each other and didn't get into a fight."

"I wouldn't fancy Ollie's chances against her. What's her name?"

"Echo." Dee didn't look at him as she spoke, she was too busy watching the dogs run down the beach. "I don't know if I can get her to come back."

The man chuckled. "I wouldn't worry too much. They'll run out of beach soon and have no choice but to come back." He held his hand out. "I'm Michael, nice to meet you."

She shook hands with him. "You too, I'm Dee."

"Oh! Are you Emma's friend?"

"That's me."

"I'm an old friend of Emma's. We grew up here together."

Dee took a better look at him. She wouldn't have taken him for a local. He had a trace of an accent – Australian, maybe?

He smiled. "Honest, I am. I know you met most of the gang over the years. You know Missy and Ben and Pete, don't you?"

She nodded.

"I was one of the gang when we were kids, but I moved to Oz. I'm a doctor. I moved back home a few years ago."

It rang a bell with Dee, but she was more concerned about Echo than in getting to know exactly who he was. She was a little less panicked than she had been, though. She even smiled as she watched Echo and Ollie play.

"Ollie! Come on, mate! We've got to go. I'm going to be late for work."

Ollie looked from Echo to Michael and back again. Dee could tell that he was torn between doing what he was told and hanging out with his new friend.

Michael chuckled. "Is there any chance that you'd be interested in setting up a play date for the two of them? I haven't seen that guy look so happy in ages."

Dee had to agree. Both Ollie and Echo had what looked like huge smiles on their faces as they trotted back up the beach toward them. "Like I said, she's not my dog. But I have a feeling that Lucky would be happy for the two of them to hang out sometime."

"That's right! When you said that her name was Echo, I knew there was something there. Lucky works with Dan and the guys, doesn't he?"

"He does."

"Well, I'm sure that I'll see you around." Michael took his wallet from his back pocket and handed her a card. "If you want to give me a call – or if Lucky does – I'd love to get these two together again sometime."

"I'll tell him." Dee had to laugh. The dogs had reached them now, and Echo flopped down on the sand. Ollie flopped down beside her, nestled in as close to her side as he could get. Echo turned and licked his cheek just like she did with Lucky – in fact she did it with Dee and Dalton, too. Now that she thought about it, Echo had also licked Taryn's cheek on Sunday. Perhaps it was something that she did with all her favorite people.

"Uh-oh!"

"What's wrong?" asked Dee.

"I know that look on Ollie's face. He's not just made a new friend. He's gone and fallen in love with her. He got that same look in his eyes when he first met my son, Ethan. And the first day we brought baby Billy home." Michael shook his head with a rueful smile. "It looks like it's mutual, too. I swear that Echo just batted her eyelashes at him."

Dee laughed. She didn't think that dogs could bat their eyelashes, but when she double checked on Echo, there was no missing the starry look in her eyes. "I'll tell Lucky that she'd appreciate it if we can get them together again as soon as possible."

Michael chuckled. "I'd like that – but not as much as Ollie will. Come on, mate! We need to get a wriggle on."

Ollie pushed to his feet with a reluctant huff, and Echo followed him. Dee snatched for the end of the leash.

"I'm sorry, Echo. But we really need to go home now, too. Don't worry, we'll make sure that you get to see Ollie again."

Echo looked up at her and whined. Ollie turned around and came back. Dee's heart melted as she watched the two dogs stare into each other's eyes for a moment before Michael whistled and Ollie ran back to him.

She didn't have the heart to ask Echo to come back up to the house. Not while she was sitting there watching her new friend leave. Dee sat down in the sand beside her and didn't know whether to laugh or cry when Echo sat up on her hind legs. When Ollie looked back, she waved one paw at him.

"Damn, girl! You're breaking my heart here! We'll find a way for you to see him again, I promise. Okay?"

Echo let out one of her happy barks and got up, turning to head back to the house.

Dee shook her head as she trailed after her. She didn't know what Lucky would make of this.

~ ~ ~

"Hey, sugar! Are you here to pick up a takeout order? I didn't see one come in. Kallen must've taken it. I'm glad you're here; I had the guys in the kitchen save a big bone for Echo today."

Lucky eyed the girl behind the bar – Kenzie. He'd forgotten about her. If he'd remembered, he would have taken his time and arrived at The Boathouse a little later. As it was, he was here early to meet the guys.

She winked at him and rested her elbows on the bar. "You can give me all the death stares you like. If you want your dinner, you're going to have to talk to me. And I know you love that dog of yours, and you won't deny her a bone just because you're a grouchy bastard."

Lucky threw his head back and laughed.

"There you go. See! Doesn't it feel better to laugh?"

She was only joking around with him, but her words hit Lucky right in the chest. She was right; it did feel better to laugh, and he realized that since he'd been with Dee, he'd been laughing a lot.

"It does. I don't mind admitting that you're right." He smiled through pursed lips. "Right that it feels good to laugh – and right that I'm a grouchy bastard."

She grinned at him. "Maybe you used to be, but grouchy bastards don't laugh much and now that you've got the hang of laughing, I don't see you giving it up anytime soon. I don't see how you could with Dee around. She's awesome. I really like her." She narrowed her eyes at him. "You better be good to her, you hear me?"

"I hear you. And I intend to be. And not just because you told me to."

"Good." She looked down the bar to where a couple had just arrived. "Do you have a few minutes? I don't know where Kallen is – but I'll see about your order."

"It's fine. I'm not here for takeout. You go see to them. I'm meeting the guys for a drink. I'm early; I can wait."

She raised her eyebrows at him. "What, so now that you're with Dee you're suddenly deciding to get sociable with the guys?"

He couldn't help but smile at the hint of an accusation in her tone. "Take it easy! You don't need to go getting mad at me on her behalf. She's out with the girls tonight. If she were home, I'd be right there with her. I'm only out with the guys because she encouraged me to come. Although, if you keep giving me shit, I can always go home and…"

"Oh no! Don't you dare!" Kenzie scowled at him even as she backed away to go and serve the couple, who were starting to look impatient. "No way do you get to blame me. You keep your ass on that stool, or I'll tell Dee that you cost Echo her bone, you hear me?"

Lucky had to laugh as he watched her go. She was right – it really did feel better to laugh.

He turned when he heard voices behind him. "You never told me that Lucky had a twin brother." That was Manny.

"He doesn't, but I can see why you'd think it," said Dalton.

"What do you think's up with him?" Ryan asked.

"I can't say for sure, but my guess is that he's drunk," Dalton answered.

Lucky scowled at him, but Dalton just laughed. "Come on, Lucky. Seeing you sitting at the bar by yourself, laughing, what other conclusion am I supposed to draw?"

"I don't know, but drunk? How long have we known each other?"

Dalton smirked at him. "I don't mean that you've had too much to drink. More like you're intoxicated – you know, high on life… and love."

Lucky held his gaze for a long moment. His initial reaction was to tell his friend that he was full of it; to try to defend himself against the accusation. But as the moment drew out, he realized that what Dalton had said wasn't an accusation; it was an observation. And more than that, it was an accurate one.

A slow smile spread over his face as he nodded and held his hands up in a gesture of surrender. "What can I say? You got me. I'm not going to deny it."

Manny and Ryan grinned at him, but Dalton folded his arms across his chest and cocked his head to the side.

"What? I thought you'd be happy."

Dalton laughed. "I am happy! I was just taking a moment to let it sink in. I don't mind telling you that I've been worried about you – the rest of the team has, too. I have a deal with Tiny that if I couldn't find a way to get you to settle here, it's his turn next."

Lucky sucked in a deep breath. The team looked out for each other – they always had. It might be different these days in that they were scattered across the country, each living their own lives, but there was still a bond there that most would never understand.

Ryan gripped Manny's shoulder and steered him farther down the bar. "Come on, old man. We'll get the drinks in and let these two have a moment."

Even when they'd gone, Lucky still didn't know what to say. Dalton came and slapped him on the back before climbing up onto the stool next to him. "Opening and closing your mouth like that – like a fish out of water – doesn't suit you, bud. I don't know what you're so shocked about, anyway."

Lucky shrugged. "I don't, either. We all have each other's backs."

"As much as we can," said Dalton. "It's not been as easy with you. You closed us all out. And you're the one we all worry about the most."

Lucky shook his head. "There's nothing for anyone to feel guilty about."

"Who mentioned guilt?"

Lucky glared at him. "I did. Because I know how you all feel. I think what the rest of you guys suffered while I was held captive was just as bad as what I went through."

Dalton glowered right back at him. "That is bullshit, and you know it. Yes, it was a fucking nightmare not knowing if you were dead or alive, not being able to get back there to extract you. And yes, every single one of us lived with – and still lives with – the guilt that you were taken, and we weren't. But no way does any of that compare to being kept in a fucking cave for eight months and having the shit beaten out of you every single day."

Lucky was surprised that Dalton was speaking so openly. They rarely talked about what had happened. He hadn't thought that there was anything left to say.

He blew out a sigh. "Well, you can tell Tiny… In fact, no. I'll call him myself. I'll call the rest of the guys, too."

"And say what?" Dalton asked.

Lucky smiled. "The same thing as I'm telling you right now. That I appreciate it, but I wish you'd all get over it. If you guys want to go on feeling guilty, I can't stop you. But if you do, it's your choice, and I'm not taking any of the blame. I'm moving on. I'm happy. You were right when you said that I'm kind of drunk… High on life… It's all down to Dee, I'll even say it out loud – I'm in love with her." His smile faded. "I might not have exorcised all my demons yet; it's still going to take me some time and it won't be all plain sailing. But with her by my side I know I can take those fuckers down one by one."

Dalton grinned at him. "You do realize that when you tell the guys that, they're going to want to meet her?"

Lucky laughed. "I'll look forward to it. She'll blow their socks off. She's amazing."

"Oh my God!" They both turned to see Kenzie leaning on the bar listening to them. "I feel like I should be taking notes here. This is awesome!" She grinned at Lucky. "I would never have guessed that you had it in you!"

Lucky exchanged a puzzled look with Dalton, who asked, "Had what in him?"

Kenzie laughed. "I'm not sure that you'll understand it, big fella. Romance. This guy," she pointed at Lucky, "he's like a woman's favorite chocolate."

Lucky and Dalton exchanged another look.

Kenzie laughed. "Dark and bitter on the outside, and filled with sweet, gooey goodness on the inside."

Dalton burst out laughing and slapped him on the back. "Damn! Now, I'm the one who wishes I was taking notes."

Lucky just rolled his eyes at him. He had a nasty feeling that Dalton would remember and recount that one without any need for notes.

Chapter Twenty-Three

Dee groaned as she rolled over. She'd had a great time with the girls last night. She liked every single one of them. Taryn was probably her favorite – she was a hoot! But her friend, Evie, was great, too. And Izzy – Dee had spent a long while chatting with her and her friend, Audrey. She really liked the two of them.

And the sisters – what were their names? She hadn't had as much time with them, but she was hoping to get to know them better. Marianne, and Chris, that was it. And Marianne was a big reader; she knew and loved all of Dee's books – the thrillers and the romances. Sometimes, it could get awkward when she met people who'd read her books – whether they enjoyed them or not – but she'd really enjoyed talking to Marianne. She was one of her favorite kind of readers – she discussed the characters with Dee as if they were mutual friends.

She forced her eyes open but closed them again quickly with another groan when the morning light hit them. She knew she shouldn't have had that last drink – who was she kidding?

She probably shouldn't have had the last two. But it had been such a fun night, and she couldn't wait to do it again.

She cracked one eye open to check on Lucky. He was still sleeping. He seemed to have had a good night with the guys at The Boathouse. She'd ridden back over to this side of the lake in a cab with Izzy, Evie, and Ria, and they'd gone into The Boathouse to meet up with the guys to go home.

Lucky – and she imagined the rest of the guys, although she hadn't been paying that much attention to them – obviously hadn't drunk as much as she and the girls had. Fortunately, he'd been amused rather than annoyed that she was more than a little tipsy.

He'd brought her back here to the house, helped her to undress – since the buttons on her blouse had refused to cooperate. And when they'd climbed into bed, he'd wrapped her up in his arms. She smiled and opened both eyes to look over at him. She'd loved feeling so safe and cherished. She hadn't lasted long before she drifted off to sleep, but she hadn't missed the way that he'd murmured sweet things to her as he held her. Her heart started to pound; he'd even told her that he loved her.

She closed her eyes again and let a rush of warmth wash over her. She might have her hang-ups about relationships, but she wasn't an idiot. She wasn't going to deny that even though she hadn't wanted to, she'd gone and fallen in love with him, too.

Echo jumped up onto the bed and settled in between them. She rested a paw on top of Dee's hand and licked her cheek. Dee scratched her ears with a smile. Between the two of them, Echo and Lucky had helped her get past a whole bunch of fears and hang-ups that she'd been carrying around for far too long.

As she lay there with the early morning sun streaming in through the windows, she made up her mind. She was going to stay here in Summer Lake. She'd have to see what Lucky thought, but she might even put in an offer on this house; Austin had told her that it would be going on the market at the end of the season. Looking at it from the outside, it wasn't what she would choose. But like everything – it wasn't external appearances that mattered, it was what was on the inside. And inside this house, she'd figured out a way to be happy.

She looked over at Lucky again – she'd also discovered that her life wasn't over in the way that she thought it was when it came to love. She was going to give her all to see what she and Lucky could build together. It might not work out – she was old enough and wise enough to know that. But she was going to give it her best shot.

She was no fool – there would be plenty of bumps in the road ahead for them. One, or no, make that two, bumps were coming to visit this weekend. She didn't know how Max and Pax would feel about Lucky, but she did know that neither of them would just accept him with open arms before putting him through something of a test, at first.

She blew out a sigh. They wouldn't give him a hard time just for the fun of it, but she wished that they could fast-forward through this initial meeting and get to a place where they all knew and were comfortable with each other.

The sound of a horn blaring outside brought her back to the moment. Echo jumped down from the bed and went to the window. Resting her paws on the windowsill, she looked out. Seeing her so alert and prepared to guard them, Dee just hoped that she wouldn't feel the need to defend Lucky against any hostility she might sense from the boys.

She started to sit up, but at the same moment Lucky yelled. She turned to see if he was okay just as he yelled again.

"No!"

It all seemed to happen at once. Dee tried to duck, but she didn't manage to dodge Lucky's fist as it flew through the air.

He caught her temple, knocking her back onto the bed. Echo jumped up, landing between them. Dee cowered back when she heard her growl, but she was growling at Lucky. She flung all of her weight against him, knocking him back as his arms flailed, punching wildly at nothing.

He shouted again, a stream of curses. Dee's blood ran cold as she listened. He was equal parts furious and terrified. She'd never heard anything like it in her life. Her first instinct was to try to comfort him, but her survival instincts were stronger than that.

She brought her hand up to the side of her head. If it had been pounding before, it was ten times worse now. As she watched, Lucky was struggling against Echo. The way Echo snarled, took Dee back to that day on the beach when she was a kid. And yet, she wasn't afraid. She believed with all her heart that Echo would never hurt either of them.

Lucky's struggles grew weaker. Echo leapt on him, with both paws in the middle of his chest, she knocked him back down onto the bed. Tears streamed down Dee's face as she watched. She didn't know what battle Lucky was fighting, but the expression on his face made it clear that he felt like he was losing.

He didn't give in, though. Desperation mixed with defeat as he fought his beloved dog, and she overpowered him. Dee was sobbing as she watched Echo pin him to the bed with all her weight. She'd stopped snarling; she was whining as she licked the tears from his face.

His struggles grew weaker. Then he stilled. After a few moments, his hand reached up, and he sank his fingers into Echo's fur. "Jesus, lady! I'm so sorry!"

Echo was lying on top of him, she was still whining as she licked his cheek over and over.

Dee held her breath; she could tell that he had no idea where he was and even less that she was there. She didn't know much about what he went through, but she knew from experience that it took a little while to transition from the horrors of a nightmare back into the real world.

She could see the moment that realization hit him. His hand dropped away from Echo, and he slowly turned his head to look at her.

He was still panting from the exertion of fighting Echo, and fighting whatever was going on in his head, but he inhaled sharply when his gaze landed on her.

"Oh fuck! Dee! Are you okay? I'm sorry! I'm so fucking sorry! What did I do?"

She started to shake her head, then thought better of it – it hurt like hell. "It's okay, Lucky. I'm fine. Honestly. You didn't do anything wrong."

He hesitantly reached out across the space between them but let his hand fall to the bed before it reached her. "Don't lie to me, sweetheart. You're holding your head. Let me see. Please."

"I'm fine. I promise. You didn't do anything wrong. I just... I got in the way."

She'd never seen him move as fast as he did when he let out a tortured sounding cry and leapt from the bed.

"I'm so fucking sorry! I should've known better. I shouldn't have done this. I should never have..."

"Lucky! Stop!" It hurt her head to say it so forcefully, but she had to get through to him. She knew in her heart that if she didn't get through to him right now, he'd leave... and might never come back.

He was visibly trembling as he stood beside the bed, running his hand through his hair. "I'm so sorry! I didn't mean ... I would never!"

"It's okay. I know that," she said in her most soothing tone. "Calm down. Sit down. Please. Lucky, take a deep breath, and listen to me."

She could tell that he was torn between doing as she said and turning on his heel and leaving. She held her breath. There was no point trying to cajole him further. It was his decision to make, and if his nightmares still had such a tight hold on him that they could make him walk away, it broke her heart to face it, but she knew she'd have to let him go.

As the silence between them dragged on, Echo broke it with a low whine. Dee wanted to kiss her when she gently took Lucky's finger between her teeth and led him around the bed to Dee's side.

Dee scrambled to sit up and make room for him. Some of the pressure in her chest eased when he sat down beside her.

She tentatively stroked his back. His muscles were taut, and she could feel the tension coming off him in waves.

"I promise you that I'm okay."

He slowly turned to face her, and this time when he reached out, he gently brushed her hair away from her temple where his fist had caught her. It seemed like all the light went out in his eyes.

"I hurt you," he whispered.

She could feel the tears streaming down her face, but she couldn't stop them.

"You didn't mean to. I just got in the way."

He closed his eyes and dropped his chin to his chest. "I can't do this, Dee. It's not safe for you."

Echo growled at him, and Dee wished that she could do the same.

She wanted nothing more than to hold him and reassure him, but she knew that she wouldn't get through to him that way. Instead, she lifted her chin and squared her shoulders.

"If that's what you want, then I can't stop you." It might be the truth, but her heart felt as if it was breaking as she said it. "I'm not going to beg you, Lucky. I want to – but I know there's no point. If you believe that you can't do this, then don't. But don't you go blaming it on me. I'm not at risk, and I know it."

The way he looked at the side of her head, which was throbbing, made his opinion clear.

She scowled at him. "I could've walked into a door and done that."

"Jesus, Dee! That sounds like you're a battered wife – making excuses for the bastard who hit you."

She rolled her eyes. "I didn't mean it like that. I meant that this …" she pointed at her head "… could've happened to me in any number of ways – accidental ways. And if it had, you wouldn't be thinking about throwing in the towel with me, would you? And this is the same, Lucky. It was an accident."

He hung his head. "I did it to you."

She closed her eyes. "Not on purpose."

"But who's to say that I won't do it again? Who's to say that I won't…" A pained look crossed his face. "I could hurt you even worse than I already did."

"No. You couldn't. I know it; and when you come back to your senses, you'll know it, too. Echo would never let you hurt me. Not for my sake, or for yours. The only reason that you caught me this time was because she was looking out the window, and I didn't react quickly enough to move out of the way. It was an accident, Lucky. A freak accident." She swallowed. "If you want to use that as a reason to end this, there's nothing that I can do to stop you." She reached up and touched his cheek, "but I hope that you won't."

The lines around his gorgeous, brown eyes were etched with pain when he met her gaze. "I don't want to end this. I love you."

She had to swallow around the lump in her throat. "Then don't. And I wasn't going to tell you yet, but you should know – I love you, too."

He curled his arm around her waist and held her close, but ever so gently. "I want to take care of you, Dee, not hurt you."

She finally felt as though she could relax. She smiled up into his eyes. "Why don't you make me a cup of coffee, then?"

Under other circumstances, the confusion that crossed his face would have made her laugh. Instead, she held her breath until he figured out that she was joking. When he did, he was the one to laugh – it was short and almost humorless, but it gave her hope.

~ ~ ~

"It's not like you to be in the office all day, let alone in the office and slacking."

Lucky slowly turned his chair around to face Dalton; he'd been staring out the window.

"Don't fold your arms at me," he said when his friend struck his familiar pose and leaned in the doorway. "Come in. Sit down."

Dalton's eyebrows drew together as he pulled up the chair across the desk from Lucky.

"What's up? I thought you were good. I thought you'd turned over a new leaf and decided to be Happy-go-Lucky. You were good last night. Things seemed great with Dee when you left. What happened?"

Lucky blew out a sigh and leaned back in his chair. "I hurt her."

Dalton gripped the arms of the chair. "Explain."

"This morning. I ... I ... it happened again."

"The nightmares?"

"Yeah."

"Shit. And?"

"It started out the same as usual. They came for me. I was trying to fight them off. And ... I don't know exactly what happened. I just remember I was fighting them. I landed a blow. Then someone was pinning me down – that someone was Echo, and she eventually got through to me."

He stopped and swallowed when he realized how hoarse his voice sounded. "When I was properly awake, I saw Dee sitting there – holding her head."

"Is she okay?"

"She says she is." He shook his head. She's going to be bruised. More than likely have a black eye."

"Tell me that you talked to her?"

He nodded slowly. "She already knows the deal. It's not the first time it's happened. Usually, Echo's right there. But she was at the window. I ... when I realized what I'd done, I wanted to leave. I fucking hurt her Dalton. I *hit* her."

Dalton held his gaze for a long moment. "How did she react?"

"The same way that she always does; she took it in stride. Told me that it was an accident – a freak accident at that."

"And you? How did you react?"

"Like you'd expect. I wanted to cut my hands off so that I could never do that again. My first thought was that I needed to end things. I... I want a future with her, you know that, but I won't put her in danger to have it."

Dalton pursed his lips. "Do you honestly think that you would – that you could – hurt her? I mean, I'm inclined to agree with her – it was an accident. Do you really think that Echo wouldn't be able to stop you if you actually tried to harm her?"

Lucky closed his eyes. "No. I know that she can stop me. I'm ninety percent sure that I wouldn't be able to hurt her. I think there's something inside me that would stop me." He met his friend's gaze. "But is that enough? What if...?" He shook his head.

"You can't go there. You can't live your life – or *not* live your life – trying to avoid *what if's*. In this case, I'd say that it's not even your call to make. What does Dee say?"

"Like I said – that it was a freak accident. You know me, you know damn well that I was ready to walk out of there and never look back."

"Did you tell her that?"

"I didn't need to. She knew it. For one thing, it was obvious. And for another… She knows me."

Dalton frowned. "And she persuaded you to stay?"

He gave his friend a rueful smile. "We both know that she wouldn't have been able to."

"What then?"

Lucky gave him a rueful smile. "She said that if I want to use it as a reason to end things, there's nothing that she can do to stop me. But she hopes I won't."

"I knew I liked her. So, why are you still sitting here at six o'clock, staring out the window instead of on your way home to her?"

Lucky shrugged. "She's working, and I just wanted to get straight in my head."

"Then, let me help you. If you're going to be in a real relationship with her, there's going to be stuff that comes up. Stuff that you both need to deal with – stuff that will make you both question whether being together is the right thing to do. It's not easy; ask me how I know." He smirked. "Taryn and I have had more than our fair share of bumps in the road. There's a reason that I call her a piece of work and she calls me a pain in the ass. But it's worth it – we both believe that. It's like anything – if you want it for the long term, you've got to be prepared to deal with the shitty side – and there's always a shitty side.

"For what it's worth, my money is on this being the one and only time that you hurt Dee. It sucks, I'm not trying to make light of it, I can't imagine how I would feel in your shoes, but unfortunately, it goes with the territory of you being who you are. Do you want to spend the rest of your life alone just so that you can be sure that you'll never do anything like that again? Or are you prepared to take the risk?"

Lucky shrugged.

"Well, you need to decide. And I'd say that you need to decide fast. Dee's made her mind up – she's prepared to take the risk. The only question you need to answer is – are you?"

Lucky shrugged again. "I want to. But I just can't stand the thought…"

"Look at it this way," said Dalton. "How did we used to work? We made our plans, but we always knew that the shit could hit the fan at any moment. So, what did we do?"

Lucky rolled his eyes at him. "We had contingencies for our contingencies."

"So, what's the worst that could happen?"

Lucky didn't even want to think about it. "I could hurt her – worse than I already did." His blood ran cold.

"Don't look at me like that. I don't want to think about it either. But you have to face it. Is that something you can live with?"

Lucky really didn't think that he could.

"Let me rephrase that, then. Would you rather spend the rest of your life without her, just to eliminate what's maybe a ten percent chance? And bear in mind that if you say yes, you're also saying that you have no faith in Echo."

Lucky stared at him. "I do have faith in her."

Dalton raised his eyebrows. "Then, maybe you need to sit here a while longer and really let that settle in. I have faith in Echo – and in Dee for that matter. And she's already told you how she feels."

"I know all the logic. I know what you're telling me. It's just… I hate it, Dalton. I thought – hoped, if I'm honest – that it'd get better. I thought that maybe the nightmares would stop."

"And maybe they will," said Dalton. "You're not telling me that you expected it to be *easy*, are you? Because we both know how that one goes."

Lucky gave him a rueful smile. "The only easy day was yesterday."

"You've felt as though you were finding your feet, since you met Dee. What happened this morning felt like you fell down, right?"

"Right."

Dalton raised his eyebrows. "And if you fall seven times?"

"Rise eight."

Dalton pushed to his feet. "I hope you will."

"Yeah. I think I've already decided. I don't want to walk away – there's too much good between us."

"I think so. And her kids are coming this weekend?"

"Yeah." He'd been starting to feel a little better, but the thought of meeting Dee's sons while she was sporting a bruise that he'd given her made his heart sink.

Dalton gave him a rueful smile. "Maybe you should take them out on that boat of hers – get them in a place where they can't walk away from you while you explain yourself."

"Yeah." He and Dee hadn't found time to take the boat out again. It might yet earn its keep – even if it was only as the setting for uncomfortable conversations.

Chapter Twenty-Four

When Dee pulled up in the parking lot at the airport on Saturday morning, she cut the engine and checked herself out in the mirror on the visor. She wasn't a pretty sight. She'd done what she could to cover up the bruising with makeup, but there was no disguising the fact that she had a black eye.

She really wasn't bothered by what had happened. In her mind, it was just an accident. Lucky could have caught her with an elbow, turning over in his sleep and done the same kind of damage, she was sure. He was still a little leery, but she was hopeful that she was winning him over to her way of thinking.

She was looking forward to seeing the boys, nothing could take away from that, but the timing could've been better. She wanted them to get to know Lucky, and him to get to know them. But she knew however she explained this, her bruises weren't going to endear him to them.

She made a face to herself as she climbed out of the car. She'd just have to do her best to keep things upbeat over the weekend. She'd asked Lucky if he wanted to come with her to meet them, but he'd said that it was probably best if she came by herself.

He had a point; she could use the time alone with them to try to explain things in a way that they might understand. She also knew that they might be angry at him. If that were the case, she'd rather try to talk them down herself than have things blow up in her face immediately.

She knew that if they got mad at Lucky, he'd only agree with them, and Echo wouldn't take too kindly to them showing any kind of hostility toward her beloved human.

She hurried toward the door when she spotted a guy holding it open for her.

"Thanks," she said.

"No problem." He was tall and built, with gray hair – although, he didn't look that old, not to her. "You're Emma's friend, Dee, aren't you?"

"That's me."

The guy smiled. "Sorry, by the look on your face, I'm not the first to greet you that way, and you have no idea who I am." He held his hand out. "I'm Smoke. Smoke Hamilton. I'm a friend of Emma's, and I run this place. It's your Falcon that's on final approach, isn't it?"

Dee checked her watch before shaking hands with him. "It is?" They were early. She chuckled. "I mean, it is mine. I'm surprised that they're ahead of schedule."

"They got an earlier departure than expected out of Tucson."

"I'm glad I came early, then."

She looked around and nodded. "This place is great. I wasn't sure that we'd be able to land here."

Smoke smiled. "You'd be surprised, not many people know about the place but there's a hell of a lot more jet traffic than you'd expect in a town of this size."

Dee chuckled. "I might not have expected it before I came here, but now that I've been here a while, I get it. There are a lot of jet type people in town, aren't there?" Her smile faded as she looked at him more closely. "Oh! And you're one of them, aren't you? Hamilton. I knew I recognized the name. You're from the Hamilton Groves family, aren't you?"

He smiled. "Originally, I am. I'm nothing to do with the business, though."

"No. I remember now. Emma told me. You don't just run this place, you own it, don't you? And you run a charter service, right?"

He smiled. "I'm in partnership in this place. I manage a couple of jets for folks who live here, and yes, I run a charter service. Mind if I ask how much you use the Falcon? I haven't seen you out here since you arrived."

Dee smiled through pursed lips. "I know. I keep thinking that I should probably get rid of it. It's a ridiculous expense. There was a time when it made sense – I was traveling a lot. But these days…" She shrugged. "I could probably sign up for one of those companies… You know, like NetJets or something?"

Smoke chuckled. "You could. But I hope you don't. If you're planning on staying in town, we could give you a better deal than they ever would." He looked thoughtful. "And if you're not decided about getting rid of the Falcon just yet, I wouldn't mind having a chat with you sometime about maybe putting it into our program."

Dee gave him a puzzled look. "Oh! You mean like you could rent it from me when you need an extra plane?"

"Something like that," said Smoke. "It would come in handy to have access to it when we get busy – we have three jets in the program, but it's pretty much guaranteed that when all three are flying, someone calls wanting another. It'd be great to have access to a fourth - and it'd offset some of your costs."

Dee took a card out of her purse. "That sounds like it's something that might benefit both of us. I really don't want to give it up, so if you can help me justify keeping it, I'll be grateful to you."

Smoke took the card. "How long is your family here visiting?"

"They're leaving on Wednesday morning."

"Okay. I'll give you a call later next week, then, shall I?"

"Please do. I'll look forward to it."

Smoke turned to look out through the windows, the jet had just touched down and was thundering down the runway toward the building.

"I hope you have a good visit. And hopefully we'll see you around — you moved here, right? You're not just here for the summer?"

Dee smiled. Her decision on that was made. "I'm staying," she said.

"Okay, then. I'll talk to you soon."

Dee watched him walk away before turning back to the windows. A big smile spread across her face when she saw the boys coming down the steps. It was always so good to see them. As she watched them chat as they walked across the tarmac, she realized that she needed to stop calling them boys. They were young men in their own right, now. She needed to remember that.

Her hand came up to touch the side of her face; she hoped that this would go better than she feared.

She hurried to the door to meet them when they came in and was soon wrapped up in a hug from Pax — that was his way. Max on the other hand, hung back until they were done. When Pax let go of her, he stepped forward and pressed a quick kiss to her cheek.

"It's good to see you, Mom. I —" he looked at her face more closely. "What happened?"

Her heart sank. She'd been hoping that she might be able to get them home before she had to explain. "What do you mean?" she asked, but she couldn't do it. She'd always been honest with both of them. "Sorry," she continued. "I know exactly what you mean."

He narrowed his eyes at her. "I know you do. So, what aren't you telling us?"

Crap! She'd gone and made it worse. "I *am* telling you. I was just hoping to be able to say hello first." She looked down and was glad to see that they both had their own bags. In most of the airports that they flew into, there was usually someone around to carry the luggage, but Dee didn't see why healthy young men like them shouldn't carry their own.

"Come on, I'll tell you on the way. I want you to see the house."

Pax frowned at her. "Why don't you tell us now."

She rolled her eyes. "I'm fine! I promise you, guys. It was an accident."

She knew that was the wrong thing to say even before she saw the expressions on their faces. They reacted the same way that Lucky had.

"Please tell me that *he* didn't do that? The guy that you're seeing?" Max's hands were curled into fists at his sides.

"Calm down, sunshine."

"You can forget that," said Pax. "Max might be as mild-mannered as it gets, but no way can he let that go – and I can't either. What's going on, Deedly?"

She blew out a sigh and looked around. "Can we at least start walking while I explain?" She didn't wait for an answer and was grateful when they followed her outside.

"Okay. The honest answer is yes, Lucky caught me with his hand, but it was an accident." She scowled right back at them. "I'd like to think that you know me better than that! Do either of you seriously think that I would let a man hit me and then make excuses for him?"

They exchanged a glance before shaking their heads. Part of her wanted to laugh, the scene reminded her of when they were kids and she'd caught them out in something. Instead, she knew that she needed to push her advantage.

"Well, thank you for that, at least. This is probably too much information about your mother, but since you pushed, I'll tell you. Lucky was a prisoner of war. He still struggles with some PTSD issues. The only way that really manifests is in nightmares. In his dreams, he's back in the cave where he was held, and when the … evil … I'm going to say it, bastards who took him, come for him in his dreams, he tries to fight them off. The other night, he was trying to fight them, and I got in the way."

They'd reached the car now, but none of them got in.

Max shook his head. "How often does it happen? How often does he have these nightmares? You're right, it isn't really something I want to think about with my mom, but should you really be sleeping in the same bed as him?"

She had to hide a smile at the way his cheeks colored up when he said that. "I appreciate your concern, I really do. But another thing that I should have told you is, you know his dog? I told you about her?"

They both nodded.

"You said that she's called Echo?" Pax asked.

"That's right. Well, she's a former Navy SEAL just like him. She served with him. They've been through hell together. She looks out for him. She wakes him up whenever he's having a nightmare. The only reason that she didn't get to him in time was because she was looking out the window because she'd heard something out there. Normally, she gets to him and wakes him up before he even starts to struggle. This was just a one-off – a freak accident. I promise you."

Max was looking thoughtful. "And what does *he* think?"

She understood where he was coming from, and she also knew that this was the time to come clean – to be completely honest and not hide *anything*. "It freaked him out. He was devastated when he realized that he'd hurt me. In fact, he wanted to call it quits with me – he'd rather do that than ever hurt me."

She looked at them both in the eye before she continued. "I had to persuade him that it'll be okay. And to be honest… I'm not sure that I've totally convinced him yet. So…" She blew out a sigh. "What I really want to ask you both is to please not push him too hard about this – for my sake. But I'm not going to do that. I understand that you need to figure him out for yourselves before you'll be happy. So, all I will do is ask you to approach this with an open mind. You both know that I wasn't looking to get involved with anyone ever again. Please bear that in mind as you get to know Lucky. There's a reason that I've fallen for him."

"You've *fallen* for him?" asked Pax.

"I have. Now, can we please get in the car and go home? I'm excited for you to see the house. I want to show you the pool – and the boat!"

As she pulled out of the parking lot at the airport, she had no idea if they were prepared to give Lucky a chance or if they'd both go on the offensive as soon as they met him.

"When is he coming over?" Max asked.

"I told him that I'd play it by ear."

"Sooner would probably be better than later," said Pax.

Dee just nodded. She could tell that they were both going to stew on it until they got the chance to interrogate him.

"How about you guys tell me, then?"

Max looked over at her from the passenger seat. "You should call him when we get to the house. Ask him to come over."

She blew out a sigh. "Okay. We can do that. Just remember, guys. Open minds, please?"

She felt herself relax when Pax laughed. "We'll do our best, Deedums, but cut us some slack, would you? You have to remember that we know better than most just how bad your taste in men is. Our dads prove it."

Dee rolled her eyes at him in the rearview mirror. "Okay, okay! You have a point. But I'm telling you, Lucky's different. In fact, when I drive you guys back to the airport on Wednesday morning, I'm going to ask you if I was wrong." She chuckled. "And I'll expect you to be honest."

"Don't worry, we will." Max's tone said that he fully expected to tell her that she was wrong.

~ ~ ~

When they reached the bottom of the steps that led up to Dee's gate, Lucky looked down at Echo, and she whined.

"I don't know how this is going to go, lady, but I need to ask you a favor."

She sat down in the sand and looked up at him, her head cocked to the side.

"When we go up there, I think those boys are going to give me a hard time. And I need you to get this – they are boys. I know that they'll look like men to you, and you'll want to protect me, but please don't. Even though I expect that they'll look like men, and I'll treat them as such, given the situation, we both need to remember that they're boys, boys who just want to look after their mom. They both deserve our respect, just as much as she does. You want to protect Dee, right?"

Echo barked.

"Then, you need to understand that you and those boys are on the same side." He blew out a sigh. "And I am, too. I want to protect her – even if it is from me."

He looked up the steps. For a moment, he considered turning around and going back to the house. But it was only a moment. He'd spent the last couple of days thinking about it, and he was committed to this – committed to Dee. This morning, he'd done something that he'd sworn he'd never do. He'd called his contact at the VA and asked him for some recommendations. He was still shocked at himself, but he was going to go through with it – he'd booked himself an appointment with a hypnotherapist in Salt Lake City. There were others much closer, but Brad at the VA had told him that this guy was the best in the country. Lucky felt like he needed the best – and he was hoping that better meant faster.

"Come on," he told Echo. "Let's get up there and meet these guys. Hopefully, if they'll let us in, they're about to become a part of our lives."

Echo ran up the steps ahead of him, when she reached the gate, she sat and waited. When Lucky caught up with her, the smile on her face made him feel as though this might just turn out okay.

Half an hour later, he was starting to think that his optimism had been unfounded. Max and Pax had stayed close to Dee the whole time. He'd managed to peck her cheek when he first arrived, but beyond that, they'd made sure that he couldn't get anywhere near her.

Dee was doing her best to keep things light. She kept steering the conversation toward her work, and how her book, that was almost finished, was coming along. Whenever Max opened his mouth, she spouted something about *his* work. She'd already told him about how she and Lucky had watched the meteor shower together.

Lucky appreciated what she was trying to do, but the longer it dragged out, the more tense he felt. He wasn't one to tiptoe around anything. And he could sense – and appreciated – that the boys wanted to get things out in the open, too.

Echo had done better than he'd expected. She'd been friendly with Max and Pax. It seemed to Lucky that she was doing her best to lighten things up, just as Dee was. She'd gone to each of the boys and rested her paw on their leg – as if she were trying to reassure them.

Now, they were all sitting around the table by the pool, and Echo had come to sit beside him. She'd done what she could to ease the tension, but it felt that since she hadn't made much progress, she was falling back to her default – prepared to defend him.

He patted the back of her neck, and she looked up at him. He wanted to ask her to help him out, but he could hardly say anything with everyone listening. Fortunately for him, the two of them didn't need words.

She let out one of her happy sounding little yips and went to Dee. Taking her finger between her teeth, she gently tugged.

Dee laughed. "What's the matter, lady? What do you want?"

Echo took three steps toward the house before turning around and coming back to Dee.

Dee looked around at them and shrugged. "I guess she wants some girl talk. I'll be back." Her expression sobered. "We all know that I've been trying to delay this moment. Just do me a favor, please, and give him a chance?"

She directed that last part to the boys, and Lucky was surprised when she came to him and kissed his cheek before following Echo. When she reached the bottom of the steps, she looked back over her shoulder and added, "He's important to me. You've both said for years that you want to see me happy – Lucky makes me happy."

No one spoke as they watched her and Echo walk back up the steps to the house. When they disappeared inside, Lucky tried to force himself to relax as he faced the boys.

"How do you want to handle this? Do you want me to explain myself first? Or would you rather launch right in with your questions?"

They exchanged a glance. He had Pax down as the leader of the two – he was a little older, and way more outgoing. So, he was surprised when Max spoke first.

"I have questions."

"Fire away."

"How do you know that it won't happen again?"

"I don't." He could tell that they were both surprised by that answer. "I'm not going to bullshit you, guys. I'm fucking terrified that it might happen again. At first, I was prepared to walk away from your mom to ensure that it won't."

Pax scowled. "So, she doesn't mean that much to you? You could walk away that easily?"

He shook his head slowly. "No. It's because she means the world to me that I thought I should walk away. And that's also the reason that I can't."

"Having met Echo," said Max. "Having seen the way that she is with both of you, I can see how she would be able to help." He met Lucky's gaze. "I'm not going to bullshit you, either. I didn't want to like you, but I do. What matters to me is that Mom should be happy – and safe. Even before she said it, I could see that she was happy. And I can also see that you wouldn't hurt her intentionally." His shoulders slumped. "But that doesn't mean that you won't, does it?"

"No. It doesn't. And that tears me apart."

"Dee said that it's PTSD," said Pax. "Have you had treatment for that?"

Lucky blew out a sigh. "No. I never wanted to. If you want to know the truth, after the first few sessions that I went to after… after I came home, I swore that I would never go back. My verdict was that it was pointless. Pointless because it didn't matter – I had Echo, and it didn't affect anyone else. Now…"

He looked each of them in the eye before he continued. "I still don't think that the kind of talk therapy that's generally offered would be any use to me. But... Yesterday... I made an appointment to see a specialist."

"What kind of specialist?" Pax asked.

He'd been hoping that they wouldn't ask that. A lot of people thought that hypnotherapy wasn't real. He wasn't entirely convinced that it would work himself, but he was prepared to give it a try.

When he looked up, Max's pale blue eyes were boring into his. He looked... Hopeful.

"I'm going to see a hypnotherapist. Apparently, there's been a lot of research done in the last couple of years and..."

A rush of relief hit him when Max smiled. "That's good. I got really interested in hypnosis a couple of years back. I read a bunch of research out of Harvard." He turned to Pax. "That shit works."

Pax looked less convinced. "But how do we know that it'll make a difference?"

"We don't," Lucky told them honestly. "I'm not sure that I'm entirely convinced myself, but..."

Max turned back to him. "You need to figure out how to convince yourself before you start." He already had his phone out. "What's your email address? I'll send you some articles that should help you understand a bit more."

Lucky had to hide a smile as he told Max his email address. They still had a long way to go, but the fact that the kid wanted to help him had to be a good sign. While Max tapped away at his phone, Lucky met Pax's gaze, and was relieved to see him nod.

"I'll say the same as Max. I didn't want to like you – but I do. And since what Dee wants is what matters most, I'm on board to help. If she wants to be with you, we all know that it's not our place to stand in her way. All we can do is everything we can to make sure that she's safe."

"Thanks guys."

Max nodded, but Pax shook his head. "We're not doing it for you."

"I get that. I'm thanking you for being on the same team as I am. We're all only trying to do what we think is best for Dee."

Chapter Twenty-Five

When they landed in Tucson, Max wrapped his arm around Dee's shoulders as they walked across the tarmac to the FBO building. He'd said goodbye to Lucky and Pax before they left the plane, but she'd wanted a minute alone with him.

Once they were inside the building, she gave him a hug.

"Thanks so much for coming, sunshine. I can't believe how fast the time went."

"It always flies when we get together." He smiled. "And this time we already have our next visit set up – and it's not too far away."

She gave him a rueful smile. "I wish I could believe that it's just because you're so eager to come back and see me…" She cocked an eyebrow at him.

He laughed. "We want to know that you're okay. That's all." He glanced out through the windows to where the jet was waiting for her. "I don't mind telling you that I'm hopeful. I don't even mind telling you that I was wrong, and you were right. You said you were going to ask if I thought that Lucky was different – he is. I like him, Mom. I like him a lot. I can see that you're good together. I just hope that this guy that he's going to see in Salt Lake will be able to help him."

"I do, too. Although, it's like I told you before, I honestly don't believe that it's going to be a problem. You've seen how Echo is with me. Even if Lucky were deep in the grip of his nightmares, she wouldn't let him hurt me."

"I think you're right." He smiled. "I love that dog! She's awesome."

"She is, and there was no mistaking that she went and fell in love with you and Pax, too."

Max laughed. "You know we're not just coming back so soon to check on you, don't you? We had so much fun in the pool with her, and on the boat with Lucky. He's not just different for you, you know? Pax was right when he said that both our dads are proof of your terrible taste in men. Lucky's proof that your taste has improved. He did more dad stuff with us over the last few days than either of our deadbeats ever did."

Dee closed her eyes. "I'm sorry…"

"Don't, Mom. You can't say that. You can't be sorry that you chose the assholes you did in the past. If you hadn't chosen my dad, I wouldn't exist. And if you hadn't chosen Pax's dad, we wouldn't have Pax in our lives. You can't have any regrets." He smiled. "In fact, looking at it that way makes me feel even better about Lucky."

"How's that?" she asked.

"Because when you think about it, it might seem that you've chosen poorly in the past, but you can't deny that your choices worked out well. Which hopefully means that even though Lucky might not seem like the best choice, this might also work out way better than we think."

She wrapped him in a hug and spoke next to his ear. "Thanks, Max."

He gave her a quick squeeze before stepping away – he wasn't big on expressing physical affection, especially not in public.

"Yeah. Anyway. I should get going. I'll give you a call before the end of the week and let you know if there's going to be a chance that you might be able to see the Eta Aquarids this weekend."

She grinned at him. "Thanks. I hope so."

She watched him walk away before turning to go back out to the plane. She couldn't be prouder of him.

Lucky caught Pax's eye as the plane turned onto its final approach at Denver. "It was good to meet you. I appreciate you giving me a chance. Like I said, I'll let you know how I get on this week."

Pax's sly smile took him by surprise. "Don't say goodbye yet, I want you to come in with us."

Lucky gave him a puzzled look. "I thought your dad was meeting you."

Pax grinned. "He is."

"Pax." There was a stern note in Dee's voice. "I told you, I'm not coming in. There's no need. And I have no desire to see him."

Pax chuckled. "Please?"

"Why?" Dee asked.

Instead of answering her, he turned to Lucky. "My dad's an asshole. Actually, that might not be fair. He's not all bad, but there's no way that even Dee can deny that he was an asshole to her. He used to put her down all the time. She would have started her writing career five years sooner if it wasn't for him. He used to tell her that she was a dreamer – and he tried to shoot down all her dreams."

Lucky glanced over at her. Dee shrugged, looking embarrassed.

"My dad bought himself a little two-seater plane, and because of the payments on that, he didn't want Dee to give up her steady job so that she could write full-time." Lucky knew exactly where the kid was coming from when he said, "I know I shouldn't, but I just want him to understand how things really are. I want him to see the plane – and to understand how stupid he was. And more than that, I want him to see the two of you together – because there's no way he'll be able to miss how happy she is now."

Lucky nodded. "It's up to your mom, but I'm good with that."

Dee looked from Pax to him and back again. "That sounds to me an awful lot like rubbing his nose in it."

Pax laughed. "Exactly."

Dee rolled her eyes. "There's no need. I don't care what he thinks. Maybe he even helped me. Him being so convinced that I couldn't make it only made me more determined to prove that I could."

"I know," said Pax. "But can you honestly tell me that there isn't even a tiny little part of you that would love to see the expression on his face?"

Lucky chuckled when Dee shrugged. He could see the answer written all over her face, even if she didn't want to admit it. He didn't see any harm in trying to push her in that direction.

"You know," he said. "I wouldn't mind going inside to use the bathroom."

She smiled at him through pursed lips and pointed toward the back of the plane. "There's a perfectly good bathroom back there."

He chuckled. "Maybe I'm shy about going in there."

She laughed. "Yeah, like I believe that."

He winked at Pax. "I think I need to go inside the airport with you."

Pax grinned back at him. "I think you do, and we can't leave Dee out here by herself."

A golf cart was waiting to pick them up when they landed. Lucky sat in the back with Dee, his arm wrapped around her shoulders.

She looked up at him. "I'm not sure this is a great idea, you know."

He chuckled. "Neither am I, but Pax seems to think it is, and I trust him."

Pax turned around from the front seat. "Thanks, Lucky. I told you when I first met you on Saturday, that I didn't want to like you. Now, I can tell you that not only do I like you, but I trust you, too."

Lucky just nodded. There wasn't anything he could say – but damn, it felt good.

When the golf cart came to a halt outside the building, Pax peered in through the windows as he grabbed his bag.

"There they are."

"*They?*" Dee asked.

Rather than answering her, Pax looked at Lucky. "Deedly probably hasn't told you about what's-her-face, has she?"

"Nope."

"Yeah. She's not much older than I am. Dad made Dee feel as though she was too old and…" He looked at Dee. "Somehow not as good as what's-her-face. That couldn't be further from the truth. I knew that if I told you that she'd be here as well, there was no way that you'd come inside."

He turned back to Lucky. "I figured that since you're going to be around for a while – and I'll say it, hopefully a long while – you should probably know the whole story. I've never been able to convince Dee that none of the shit my dad fed her is true. So, I'm asking you for your help."

Lucky wrapped his arm around Dee's waist and drew her into his side. "I'll be more than happy to help."

Dee looked up at him as they followed Pax inside the building. "I don't need any help. I'm over him – I have been for years – and I'd rather not have to see him, or her!" she told him in a very loud whisper.

Lucky chuckled. "We won't stay long, I promise."

As Pax led the way, Lucky eyed the man who Dee had been married to. He didn't look like an asshole – he didn't look like Lucky's kind of person, either.

Both he and the younger woman standing with him looked more than a little surprised when they spotted Dee.

"Hey guys," Pax greeted them. "Lucky and Dee brought me back, and they had to come inside while the plane's being refueled."

The plane wasn't being refueled. The pilot had told Lucky that they'd do that on the return leg, in Salt Lake when they dropped him off. He was relieved to see that Pax's ears and neck turned red as he said it – it was good to know that lying didn't come too easily to him.

"Dee," her ex – Ken, Pax had said his name was – stepped forward. "It's good to see you. You're looking well."

She nodded. "Thanks."

Lucky already knew that lying didn't come easily to her. It amused him that she wouldn't even go with the fake nicety of saying that it was good to see him, too.

Ken looked him up and down. "Lucky, was it? You have a plane?"

Lucky frowned. Surely, he knew that Dee was the one who owned the plane. "I don't. The Falcon belongs to Dee."

Ken's face turned white as he spun back to look at Dee. "A Falcon! You own a Falcon jet?"

Lucky was so proud of her as she stood a little straighter and nodded. "I do."

"What the...?" Ken spluttered for a few moments before visibly pulling himself together. "Did you sell another book for a movie?"

Pax laughed. "I told you that Dee's a big author, these days. She doesn't need a movie deal."

Ken shook his head. "I had no idea. You must be making a fortune..." He looked at Dee more closely. "I had no idea."

Lucky waited for Dee to speak; he wanted her to tell Ken that he *should* have an idea – that she'd tried to tell him in the past that she could make it big. But she was a better person than Lucky. She just nodded.

The younger woman standing beside Ken caught Lucky's gaze and smiled. It sent a shiver down his spine – a shiver of revulsion. She reminded him of his ex-wife. She was looking at him in that same way, as if she was weighing up whether he could be of any use to her.

He drew Dee closer into his side and turned to press a kiss into her hair. "We should probably get going. We don't want to hold you guys up."

"Where are you going from here?" the wife asked.

When Dee didn't seem inclined to answer, Lucky said, "We just came from Tucson and our next stop is Salt Lake City. I'm dropping in to see a former colleague" – it wasn't the whole truth, but it wasn't a lie, either.

"What line of work are you in?" Ken asked. Lucky started to understand why Pax thought he was such an asshole when he looked Lucky over again and added, "You look like you're in the fitness business." He chuckled and looked at Dee. "Is he your personal trainer?"

Lucky forced himself to laugh along, even though he'd rather land his fist in the middle of the asshole's face. "I can see why you'd think that I was in the fitness business. But I'm in security – always have been, one way or another. And after a career as a Navy SEAL, staying in shape is just part of who I am."

He couldn't resist looking Ken over in a way that made clear that he didn't expect the other man to understand. He wasn't in horrible shape, but middle age was showing on him in a way that it wasn't on Lucky.

"You were a Navy SEAL?" the wife asked with a gleam in her eye.

Lucky had to laugh when Pax rolled his eyes at him. "He was, and he's already started teaching Max and me some stuff out on the water. We can do more, next time, right?"

"You know it, bud."

Ken frowned. "On the water? Like, diving?"

Pax laughed. "No. In Dee's boat. But come on, we should let these guys get going." He came and wrapped Dee in a hug, and then surprised Lucky by giving him a quick hug, too.

Back on the plane, Lucky reached for Dee's hand as they rose into the sky above Denver.

"Are you okay?"

She chuckled. "I am. I'm a little surprised at you. I'm not surprised at Pax – he's been wanting to engineer a situation like that for years. But I am surprised at you for aiding and abetting him."

He leaned across and pressed a kiss to her lips. "You shouldn't be surprised. He asked for my help in building you up and putting the asshole who used to drag you down in his place. I'm never going to pass up an opportunity to do that."

She smiled through pursed lips. "Thank you."

He unfastened his seatbelt and wrapped his arm around her, drawing her closer. "You never have to thank me, Dee. Not for a damn thing." He ducked his head to kiss her again. "I'm the one who owes you thanks. And if I get my way, I'll be thanking you every day for the rest of my life."

She smiled up at him. "Are we there, then? Because if that's what you want – it's what I want, too."

"I want us to be there – I think you know how much I want that. But before I say it, I want to see what this guy in Salt Lake says."

She chuckled. "You mean your former colleague?"

He had to laugh. "I do. I might not know him personally, but he is another Special Forces guy – he got into hypnotherapy when he was trying to work through his own issues."

Her expression sobered. "Are you sure you don't want me to stick around?"

"Want?" He nodded. He was glad that things had worked out the way that they had – that he'd been able to come along with her to take the boys home, and that she was dropping him in Salt Lake to meet with this hypnotherapist – Eli. She'd already offered to stick around for the rest of the week with him, but he knew that she needed to get back to work herself, and he had no idea how this whole deal was going to go. If it put him in a bad place, he'd rather work through it by himself before subjecting her to it.

"Of course, I want you with me. But like we talked about, it's for the best if you go on home. You have things to do. And besides," he smiled, "Echo's waiting for you. You told her that you'd be home tonight."

She smiled. "I did. I guess us girls will just have to keep each other company until you come home to us."

"Saturday. I have the three days of sessions, but I'll leave there as early as I can on Saturday morning and be home to you early evening."

The way she looked up into his eyes, he had to say it; "I love you, Dee."

"I love you, too." Her hand came up around the back of his head, and she pulled him down into a deep, lingering kiss that

made him wish that she could at least stay with him for the
night.

Chapter Twenty-Six

By Friday afternoon, Dee was done. She was done with her book, and she'd sent it off to her long suffering-editor – who had been more than a little shocked that she was ahead of schedule. She was usually late.

As she sat beside the pool, staring out at the lake, she realized that she was also done with Lucky being gone. It had only been a few days, but she missed him.

She looked down when Echo rested her chin on her lap and whined.

"I know. You miss him, too, don't you, lady?"

Echo barked.

"He'll be back tomorrow. And from what he said last night, it sounds as though this hypnotherapy is going to be good for him."

Echo's tail swished across the ground behind her.

"There's something I've been meaning to ask you."

As those big brown eyes stared up at her, Dee would swear that Echo understood every word.

"I know that you enjoy hanging out here. I know that you were the one who brought us together in the first place – and

I'll be forever grateful to you for that. But…" She blew out a sigh. Not only was she talking to a dog, but she was about to ask her for permission.

She ran her hand over Echo's silky head. "I don't care what anyone would think if they could hear me right now. They can't. And besides, what you think is what matters most. I know that he's been your man for a lot of years. And you've made it plain that you don't mind sharing him with me. But what do you think if we make it a permanent deal?"

She had to laugh when Echo yipped and got to her feet. She put both paws up on Dee's knees and barked happily before she took off. She raced three times around the pool before coming back and wiggling excitedly in front of Dee.

"I take it that's a yes, then?"

Echo barked again.

When her phone started to ring Dee made a face and decided to ignore it. She knew that it wouldn't be Lucky – he had his final session with the hypnotherapist this afternoon. At least, it was his final session for this visit. He'd told her that he felt that it was doing him so much good that he wanted to go back – that this was something he wanted to keep up with. But apparently, the hypnotist – therapist? She wasn't really sure what to call the guy, but she'd go with miracle worker if Lucky continued to feel and sound as good as he had over the last few days – had told him that they could conduct their sessions online.

Dee had gotten a good feeling about the guy on Wednesday night when Lucky had called her after his session. She'd thought that this might be an ongoing – as in a lifetime – kind of deal, where Lucky would have to keep seeing someone. Instead, the therapist had told Lucky that the long-term plan was for him to be able to learn to manage himself. She liked that a whole lot better for him.

She looked down at her phone when it beeped with an incoming message.

Emma: Come out tonight! No excuses. I know Lucky's out of town. If you don't come out, I'll think that you prefer sitting home alone to spending time with me and the girls.

Dee: Echo's one of the girls, too. I don't want to leave her home alone.

Emma: Then don't! Bring her with you. It'll be fine. We're only having an early night of it. We're going to sit out on the deck at The Boathouse – we'll call it a night before it gets busy.

Dee looked down at Echo. "How do you fancy a night out with the girls?"

Echo barked happily.

Dee: Okay. What time?

Emma: Yay! Want me to pick you up on my way into town?

Dee: That's okay. We can walk.

~ ~ ~

"Are you headed home tonight?" Eli asked Lucky as he walked him out of his office.

"No. I had no idea what these sessions were going to be like. I figured I'd give myself tonight to decompress and then head home in the morning."

Eli smiled. "Let me guess, this wasn't as harrowing as you expected, was it?"

Lucky had to smile back at him. "There was nothing harrowing about it. I wish I'd come to see you years ago."

Eli shook his head. "Don't even go there. There's no saying that it would have worked this well for you before now. Being with Dee is what gave you the motivation to finally try to get through this."

"It is."

"You were determined. You came here with a much more open mind than most of the guys I see. You had a definite purpose – that makes a difference."

"All I know is that I've made way more progress than I thought I would. And I'm grateful. If there's ever anything I can do for you…"

"Thanks. The only thing I'll ask of you is that if you ever run into someone who you think I could help, you tell them about me." He chuckled. "And tell them that hypnosis isn't a bunch of bullshit."

Lucky laughed with him. "You know I kind of thought it might be when I came here."

"Almost everyone does. But you didn't let that stand in your way."

"As a matter of fact, I might know someone who could use your help – do you have a card I can pass on to him?"

Eli handed over a few cards. "Dish them out at will. I'd appreciate it."

When they reached the door, Eli shook Lucky's hand. "I'll talk to you next week – but like I said, if you work with what I've given you on the self-hypnosis, I think you'll be fine without me in a month or two."

Lucky held his gaze. "I'd like to think that might be the case, but if you don't mind, I'll still want to check in with you at least once a month for a while."

Eli smiled. "That's up to you. I'll be happy to work with you as often as you want to – but I have to be honest; I'm looking forward to seeing the day when you trust yourself enough to know that you've got this."

"Yeah. Me too."

"What are you going to do with yourself this evening?"

"I'm going to take it easy. I'll pick up something to eat on my way back to the hotel. When I get there, I'll call Dee. After that, I think I'll get an early night so that I can hit the road early in the morning."

"It's good to see you looking relaxed as you say that."

"It's good to feel relaxed. I've slept through the night like a baby since our first session."

"And long may that continue, but you have the tools to deal with it if it doesn't."

"All thanks to you."

Eli grasped his shoulder. "I'm just a guide, you're the one who has to walk the path."

After he'd eaten the takeout he'd brought back to his hotel room, Lucky reached for his phone. He'd waited until now because he knew that Dee was supposed to be finishing her book today. He didn't want to interrupt her if she was still working.

But he didn't want to wait any longer. He called her number, put the phone on speaker, and threw it down on the bed.

"Hey, you. How are you?" she answered.

"I'm good. All done here, and I can't wait to come home to you."

He could hear the smile in her voice when she answered. "Good. Because I feel the same way. I just want you back now. How did today go? Was it another good session?"

"It was. I really feel like this has helped, Dee."

"I'm glad."

"And what about you? How did you get on with your book? I'm not disturbing you, am I?"

She chuckled. "You are not. I finished it this afternoon. I've even been out for a while this evening with the girls."

He was happy to hear that. "Only for a while? I'm surprised that Taryn doesn't have you out drinking all night again."

She laughed. "No. Tonight was a lot tamer – it was with the younger girls, Emma and her friends."

"And how did that go? Did you enjoy it?"

"I did. I wish that I hadn't put off going out with them for so long. They're a lot of fun, and I didn't feel like the odd one out – the only oldie."

He chuckled. "You're not old. You're younger than I am."

She laughed with him. "You know what I mean – compared to them I am."

"Who went? Did Emma pick you up and give you a ride?"

"No. They wanted to get together early, and to get home before The Boathouse got busy. So, Echo and I walked there."

"Down the beach?"

"Yes, down the beach. You're not the only one who's getting over things that have lived in your head for years."

"Good. I'm glad to hear it. Have you heard from the boys?"

She laughed. "I talked to Pax this morning – he was back at the airport, headed home. He was bitching about his dad. That's the first time that he's spent more than a couple of hours with him in years. He did ask me to tell you thank you for the other day."

"Next time you talk to him, you can tell him that it was my pleasure." It might be petty, but Lucky couldn't deny that he had enjoyed their little encounter with Dee's ex. "And talking about things that have lived in our heads for years, I hate thinking of that man bringing you down."

She laughed. "I'm over that, too. I promise. And it's funny, you know, before the boys met you, they weren't optimistic. They told me that I have terrible taste in men – and they weren't wrong. Neither of them has much time for their own father. But we both know that you did more than win them over. They're both looking forward to seeing you again."

That made Lucky smile. "I'm looking forward to seeing them, too."

"I don't know if I should tell you this, but Max even said that you did more with them last weekend than either of their deadbeats did with them in years."

Lucky sucked in a deep breath. "Wow."

"Yeah, that's what I thought when he said it. I hope that doesn't feel like any kind of pressure."

"Hell no! It feels damn good, Dee. I promise you that I will do my best with them. I know that you have two ex-husbands, and I'm the third guy to come along in your life but –"

He stopped abruptly when she laughed out loud.

"Sorry! I'm not laughing at you, I promise. It's just something that Charlotte said tonight."

He frowned, not understanding.

"You can imagine that the girls were grilling me about you. I don't know if you've noticed, but it seems that everyone who comes here to Summer Lake ends up meeting the love of their life and getting married."

His heart started to pound. "But you don't want to get married again."

"That's what I said, isn't it? I don't know, Lucky. But that wasn't the point anyway. You know who Charlotte is?"

"Yeah, she's married to Ben, isn't she? She's English?"

She laughed. "She is. And when Emma tried to get the rest of them to give me a break by telling them that I'm not looking to get married again because I've already been married twice Charlotte came out with something that…"

"What? What did she say? Why did you stop?"

"I stopped because I don't mean anything by it."

"Okay. What did she say?"

Dee let out a short laugh. "When Emma said that I've already been married twice, Charlotte thought it was really funny because you know how we say the third time's the charm? Well, she said that in England they don't say that – instead, they say that it's third time lucky."

He sat there on the bed in his hotel room, staring out at the Wasatch Mountains with a big smile on his face. "And you like that? You didn't set her straight?"

"Umm, yes, I liked it. And no, I didn't."

"I know that you said you didn't mean anything by it, but how would you feel if I wanted to read something into it?"

His heart started to pound as he waited for her to answer. He hadn't thought that marriage was that big of a deal to him either way. But now, he was hoping that it might be a possibility.

"Let's just say that I'm a writer, I like readers. So, if you want to read something into it …"

He felt himself relax. "Okay."

"Okay," she agreed.

"Are you and Echo settled in for the night?"

"We are. Do you have any idea what time you'll be back tomorrow?"

He was relieved that she seemed as eager to change the subject as he was. He just hoped it was for the same reasons.

"I might need to leave a little later than I first thought. There's a couple of things I'd like to do while I'm here. It won't take me long; I should be back before dark. I'll keep you posted on the way. Is that okay with you? Are you and Echo good?"

She laughed. "You don't even need to ask. We'll be hanging by the pool, waiting for you to come home to us."

Damn, he loved the way that sounded.

"Okay. I'll get back to you as soon as I can. I love you, Dee. Good night."

"I love you, too, Lucky. Good night. Oh, wait! Echo, come here, lady. It's Lucky; say good night."

Echo barked and then he could hear her panting down the phone.

He closed his eyes and let the happiness wash over him as he listened to his woman and his dog bid him good night.

Chapter Twenty-Seven

Dee set Echo's dinner bowl down in front of her and had to laugh when Echo gave her a sad look.

"I know! I'm sorry. I told you that he'd be back by dinner time, but he got a later start than he expected. I'm sad, too. But the last time that he called, he said that he won't be too late – he should be back by dark."

As far as she was concerned, dark was later than she wished. She wasn't mad at him, just disappointed that they wouldn't get more of the evening together. She smiled – although, the plus side was that by the time he got back it would be almost bedtime.

She wasn't worried about how he might sleep. For one thing, he'd been amazed at how well he'd been sleeping since he started working with Eli. And for another, she intended to wear him out when she got him into bed – after she was done with him, he'd need his sleep.

She hurried to the counter when her phone rang.

"Hey," she answered. "Are you nearly here yet?" She laughed. "I know I sound like an impatient little kid, sorry. I can't help it. We just want you back now."

He chuckled. "I'm on my way. I just wanted to check in again. I'll be there by dark."

"What time does it go dark anyway?"

"It should be full dark by nine."

She laughed. "You sound like Max. He likes to be precise about the difference between sunset and dusk and dark. Did you know that there are three different kinds of dusk?"

She could hear the smile in his voice when he answered. "I did."

"Did you know that because it's a military thing? Or… Why do I get the feeling that you've spoken to Max?"

He chuckled. "Because I have."

"Oh! How come? Is everything okay?"

"Everything's great. I just wanted to check in with him."

He sounded a bit strange, but she chose to let it go. She'd rather be excited that he and her son were talking, than get concerned about why.

"Don't worry. It's all good stuff. And we did talk about what we're going to do the next time he and Pax come."

That made her forget any concerns she'd had – she just loved that the boys had taken to him – and that he had taken to them, too.

"I love that. And you really do like them, don't you? You're not just putting up with them because they're mine?"

"No. I wouldn't do that. I think you know me better than that."

"You're right, sorry. I do."

"There's no need to apologize, Dee. I just want you to understand that I like them for the people that they are. I was about to say that they're good kids, but they're not. They're fine young men."

A rush of warmth filled her chest. "Thank you. That means a lot coming from you."

"It means a lot to me that they were prepared to give me a chance."

Dee looked down when Echo came to sit beside her and leaned against her legs.

"Echo's telling me that she needs you to hurry up home, too."

"Tell her that I'll see you both soon. I'll let you go now."

"Okay. Drive safe."

"I will. And I'll let you know when I'm about half an hour out."

"Thanks. Oh, and Max told me that we might be able to see some meteors tonight."

For some reason, he sounded a little tense when he answered. "Okay. That'll be good. I love you, Dee. I'll see you later."

"Love you, too." She gave Echo a puzzled look as she ended the call. "Maybe he's just tired, but I feel like there's something going on with him."

Echo didn't seem too concerned, so Dee decided that she shouldn't be, either.

~ ~ ~

Lucky smiled through pursed lips as he ended the call. He needed to relax. There was no way that she could know what he'd been talking to Max about. Just because she'd figured out that he'd spoken to him and she'd mentioned meteors, it didn't mean anything. He was just... Nervous? Was that it? Was he nervous? He hadn't thought that he was given to nerves.

Whatever it was, he didn't need to worry about it anymore. The next time he spoke to her, she'd know what the surprise that he had in store for her was.

He glanced over at the passenger seat − at the pale blue-green bag that he'd picked up in that fancy jewelry store this morning. He wasn't at all sure that Dee would want what was inside it. But that didn't stop him from being one hundred percent sure that he wanted to give it to her. If she just wanted to wear it as a piece of jewelry, he could live with that. But he was hoping that she might accept it in the spirit he wanted to give it.

His phone startled him out of his thoughts. He hit the button on the steering wheel to answer the call.

"This is Lucky."

The sound of Dalton's voice filled the rental car. "How did it go?"

"It went well. Really well. Way better than I expected."

"Are you back yet?"

"Nope."

"Do you want to bring Dee over to the restaurant tonight?"

"Nope."

"I see this hypnotherapist guy didn't manage to make you any more talkative, then?"

Lucky laughed. "No, but that wasn't what I was there for."

"I know."

"He did do a lot of good in helping me to manage the shit inside my head."

"You think?"

He knew that Dalton had been skeptical about hypnotherapy, but to his friend's credit, he'd still encouraged Lucky to go.

"I don't just think. I know. I've slept like a baby the last couple of nights."

"That's good. I get the feeling that you don't want to say much. So, I won't push. I thought you might be back by now; I was calling to see if you guys wanted to come out tonight. Since that's a no, do you want to bring Dee and Echo over to hang out with Taryn and Star and me tomorrow?"

Lucky thought about it for a moment before he smiled to himself. "Can I let you know in the morning?"

"Sure. Do you want to ask Dee first?"

"I do. I want to ask her..." Was he really going to tell Dalton?

"You still there?"

"Yeah."

"Talk to me, Penny. What's going on? I know you; you're hiding something."

Lucky chuckled. "I'm not hiding. I'm just deciding if I want to tell you."

Dalton laughed with him. "Decision made. You do. Spit it out."

He glanced over at the bag on the passenger seat again. "I'm going to ask her if she wants to marry me."

He heard Dalton sucked in a deep breath, but he didn't say anything.

"What?" Lucky asked when he couldn't take the silence any longer.

"Do you think that's a good idea?"

"Why wouldn't it be?"

"For starters, you've always said that you don't want to get married again. And you should probably know that Dee told Taryn that she was done with marriage. That was one of the things they bonded over. All the other women seem to be up for another trip down the aisle."

Lucky blew out a sigh. "That's why I said that I'm going to ask her if she wants to marry me. I'm not going to ask her to marry me."

"That's just semantics, buddy. I'm not sure they make much of a difference in this case. You can get as picky as you like over the meaning of the words, but the end result is still the same. Either she wants to marry you, or she doesn't. And since I have insider information that the whole concept of marriage isn't something that she wants to go anywhere near again, I don't want to see you get knocked off your feet. You're doing so well. I'd hate to see you take a fall like that. It might set you back."

Lucky scowled. "Fall seven times; rise eight. Remember?"

"Yeah."

"And besides. It's not as though I'm going in blind and hopeful. I know that when it comes to marriage she's already said never again. But…"

"But you're still prepared to set yourself up for a fall like that?"

He had to laugh. "I appreciate the way you look out for me – even against myself. I really do. But it's okay Dalton. If she says no, that'll be fine. It's just … I never thought I'd want this, but since I do, I won't forgive myself if I don't ask. And hell, even if it's a no, I don't think she'll be too mad at me – I'm still going to give her the ring, and it's a pretty damn good ring, even if I do say so myself."

Dalton laughed. "Okay. As long as you know what you're doing, I've got your back."

"Thanks."

"Wait a minute, so you're going to ask her tonight?"

"Yeah."

"Good luck. And given that, I want to see you tomorrow one way or the other. If she says yes, we'll get everyone together, and she can show off the ring. If she says no, either I take you out for a beer if things are bad, or the two of you can come and hang out with Taryn and me and the dogs. After a couple of hours, Taryn will have convinced you of all the reasons why marriage is a terrible idea anyway."

Lucky chuckled. "Thanks, bud. That sounds like a plan to me."

The evening had dragged by, and Dee and Echo had gone back up to the house after the sun had set. She grabbed her phone off the table when it beeped with a text.

Lucky: Do you want to come out?

Dee: Out? Where to?

She wasn't thrilled at the idea. She'd been looking forward to getting him home and having him to herself. But if he wanted to go out, she'd go.

Lucky: Meet Me Where the Stars Fall.

She stared at her phone with a puzzled smile on her face. He had to mean that spot up on the way out of town where they'd watched the meteor shower. Her heart felt as though it melted in her chest. He was so sweet! That must have been what he was talking to Max about. He knew about the meteor shower tonight.

Dee: I'm on my way.

Lucky: Thank you, sweetheart. I'm already there. See you soon.

Dee grabbed her keys from the hook and looked around for a sweatshirt.

"Come on, Echo. He's back. We're going to go meet him."

Echo barked and went to sit by the front door.

"You know what? Give me a minute," said Dee.

Five minutes later, they were backing out of the garage. Echo sat proudly in the passenger seat, and a cooler with a couple of beers and some bags of chips and snacks sat on the backseat.

Dee grinned over at Echo as they headed out of town. "Isn't this great?"

Echo whined and pawed at the window. Dee laughed and let the window down for her.

"Go on, then."

Echo looked as happy as Dee felt. She stuck her head out the window and sniffed the wind with a big smile on her face.

It was fully dark by the time they reached the pullout. She smiled when she saw Lucky's truck parked way down at the end. He flashed his headlights twice.

By the time she pulled up next to him, he was out of his vehicle and waiting when she opened her door.

His arms wrapped around her before her feet even touched the ground, and he claimed her mouth in a kiss that took her breath away and made her want to drag him straight home and forget about the meteor shower.

When they finally came up for air, she looked up into his eyes, and the smile on his face took her breath away all over again.

"Wow! You look… Great! You look happy, Lucky. Really happy."

He ducked his head for another quick kiss before he answered. "That's because I am happy. I love you, Dee."

She wrapped her arms around his neck. "I love you, too."

They both looked down when Echo leaned her weight against their legs. "Sorry, lady. I missed you, too." Lucky told her.

"What do you think, do the two of you want to climb up in the back?" He jerked his chin toward the bed of his truck.

"Just give me a minute," said Dee. "I brought a cooler."

He grinned at her. "I like the way you think. But we think the same way. I have goodies stashed up there already."

"What do you have? I brought beer and chips."

He chuckled. "You can leave those in your car. I went a little more up market."

"Ooh! I like the sound of this."

He closed his hands around her waist and lifted her up onto the tailgate. Once she was seated, he stepped between her legs and claimed her mouth in another kiss that let her know just how much he'd missed her, too.

When he finally broke away, she ran her fingers down his cheek. "I hope we're not planning to stay too late? I'm excited to watch the stars fall with you, but I'm more excited to get you home… to bed."

He nipped at her lips, and the twinkle in his eyes confirmed his words. "I'm excited to get you home, too. But I really want to do this first. Okay?"

"It's more than okay, Lucky. It's wonderful. Thank you so much."

When they were settled under the blanket, leaning back against the pillows that he'd propped up against the cab, Dee curled her arm around his waist and hugged him tight.

"I love you, Lucky. And I've tried really hard to avoid the play on words, but I feel like I'm the lucky one."

He tucked his fingers under her chin and made her look up at him. "No. It's not just my name, it's my nature." His smile faded. "The guys were all worried that my luck had run out when I was captured. But it turned out that even in that situation, I was luckier than the rest. A total of twelve men were taken that week that they captured me. They had me for eight months – but I was the only one who came out alive."

Dee hugged him tighter. "You amaze me. You amaze me that you survived it, and you amaze me even more that you can see that as being lucky."

He pressed a kiss to her forehead. "I don't mind telling you – it's not as though you don't already know – I haven't always felt lucky since then. But I do now. You make everything that I lived through worthwhile. If I'd died in that hole, I never would have met you."

A tear ran down her face as she shook her head. "Well, you have me now. And if I get my way, I'm never letting you go."

~ ~ ~

Hearing her say that gave him hope – if she never planned to let him go then maybe there was a chance that she'd want to marry him. He stared into her eyes, wondering if he should just come right out and ask her.

He let the moment drag on too long and she started to look uncomfortable.

"I mean, if you don't want …"

He pressed a finger to her lips. "Don't, sweetheart. Don't think even for a second that I don't want to spend the rest of my days on this earth with you. I do."

He bent his head and claimed her mouth in a kiss that he hoped could tell her how much he loved her.

"I love you, Dee. I want to …" He almost chickened out, but he had to do it. "Fuck it! I'm going to ask you. I want you to marry me."

He hurried on when her eyes grew wide.

"I know that's not a great proposal, but it's not really a proposal." Damn, he was messing this up. "What I mean is. I'm saying that I want to marry you. But I'm not asking you to marry me – I'm asking you if you want to marry me?"

He held his breath, and Echo whined beside him as they both waited for her to speak.

His heart sank when she reached up and touched his cheek. "I told you that I never wanted to get married again –"

"I know. I'm sorry. I shouldn't –"

"Lucky, stop."

He bit down on his bottom lip and waited.

She smiled. "Slow down. Let me finish. What I was about to say was that … When I told you that … I was wrong."

"You were? You mean …?"

His heart felt like it exploded in his chest when she met his gaze and nodded. "I mean ... Yes. Well, I know you didn't ask me, so ..."

He scrabbled behind him for the bag that he'd stashed with the ring and held it out to her. "I'm asking now."

She looked at the bag and then back up at him.

Shit! He tore it open and pulled out the box inside. Flipping it open, he showed her the ring. "I got this. Just in case." He pressed a kiss to her forehead. "I was going to give it to you anyway. It's beautiful – just like you are. And I wanted you to have it. And ..."

He realized that he'd run out of words, and tears were streaming down her cheeks. He took the ring out of the box and slid it onto her finger. "Marry me?"

She nodded and half laughed, half sobbed as she said, "Yes." It took her a few moments before she recovered. When she did, she looked down at the ring.

"It's perfect."

"It had to be – to match you. I told you a while back that you're perfect – and you are, perfect for me."

Echo barked and came to sit between them.

Dee smiled at her. "I told her that I had something to ask you tonight, too."

"What's that?"

"I hope that you've already answered the question by giving me this, but do you want to move in with me?"

He nodded happily. "I'd love to."

"I want to buy that house."

He shrugged. "Want to buy it together?"

"I'd love to."

As they sat there, drinking the champagne that he'd packed into a cooler, looking up at the stars, with Echo nestled between their legs, Lucky knew that he was finally living up to his name in a way that he'd always wanted to. He wasn't claiming to be lucky because he'd gotten off lightly compared to others. No, he was Lucky because he'd finally found the best thing to ever happen to him.

Dee sucked in a sharp breath and pointed as a meteor shot across the sky before disappearing over the horizon.

He nodded. "I told you I'd never forget getting to see the stars fall with you."

She chuckled. "I should probably train you to not say that whenever Max is around – he won't be impressed."

He tightened his arm around her. "It's okay. That's what I called it when I spoke to him earlier. I told him that I wanted to bring you out to watch the stars fall when I asked you to marry me."

"You did?"

He nodded happily. "I had to ask him and Pax if it'd be okay with them. I couldn't put you in a situation like that – have them not happy with you."

"You are the sweetest man."

He laughed. "If you say so."

"I say so, and you should probably get used to hearing that because the girls will no doubt call you sweet when they hear about how you proposed."

He felt that strange pride feeling sweep over him. "You want to tell them?"

She nodded eagerly. "I can't wait. If that's okay with you?"

"It's okay with me, and if you like, you don't have to wait any longer than tomorrow, Dalton said he'd get our friends together to celebrate if you said yes."

"Aww. I'd like that. I'd like to get Emma and the other girls there, too."

Echo barked and they laughed as they followed her gaze. Three meteors shot across the sky in close succession.

Dee leaned in to kiss him. "Maybe we should invite Michael and his wife to come. They might bring Ollie."

Echo's ears pricked up at that. She let out three sharp barks and ended on a long howl at the moon.

Lucky laughed. "Anything to make the two ladies I love happy."

As he watched Dee make a fuss over Echo, it sank in – he wasn't just making them happy. He was happy, too. Happier than he'd ever been – and this was just the beginning;

;

A Note from SJ

I hope you enjoyed Lucky and Dee's story. There was a time, not so long ago, when I didn't know how many more Summer Lake Silver stories I'd have to tell you. I should have known better than to doubt! Davin and Tino still want to wait a while, but Echo was happy to volunteer her services to help me set up the next one.

She took a shine to Damon – you saw her do her best to introduce him to Jo. I don't know yet how much of a role she'll play in getting them together – but I'm eager to find out! Their story will be Summer Lake Silver, Book Eleven, Walking on Sunshine - and if you want a little sneak peek, keep turning the pages.

In the meantime, I'm still rotating through series. So, the next book to release will be the next MacFarlands book, which is Kolby and Callie's story.

You might think that his whole life had been preparing him for a role as bodyguard to a beautiful country singer. He was raised a cowboy, had a career as a Navy SEAL, and he's spent the last few years working private security contracts. But when Kolby MacFarland is assigned to protect Calypso Rayne, he couldn't be less prepared for the way she makes him feel.

The working title I've had in my head for this story has always been When Kolby Met Callie, but in keeping with the series – and with the way story unfolds, the official title is The Cowboy's Undeniable Love.

After that, we're going back to The Hamiltons in Napa for Xander and Tori in Vodka and Violets.

We've seen glimpses of them in earlier books in the Hamiltons series - they've known each other since they were kids growing up in Napa. They might come from big name wine families, and be considered 'wine-country royalty', but neither of them was comfortable in that world.

Even though they've barely seen each other in decades, Xander made it his mission to keep Tori safe when danger crept into her world. And when her life in Nashville dissolves around her, he's determined to stay by her side for whatever comes next – even if neither of them know what that might be.

Check out the "Also By" page to see if any of my other series appeal to you – I have the occasional ebook freebie series starters, too, so you can take them for a test drive.

There are a few options to keep up with me and my imaginary friends:

The best way is to Sign up for my Newsletter at my website www.SJMcCoy.com. Don't worry I won't bombard you! I'll let you know about upcoming releases, share a sneak peek or two and keep you in the loop for a couple of fun giveaways I have coming up :0)

You can join my readers group to chat about the books or like my Facebook Page www.facebook.com/authorsjmccoy

I love to hear from readers, so feel free to email me at SJ@SJMcCoy.com if you'd like. I'm better at that! :0)

I hope our paths will cross again soon. Until then, take care, and thanks for your support—you are the reason I write!

Love

SJ

Walking on Sunshine Sneak Peek

When Jo got back to her room in the lodge, she closed her eyes and threw her phone down on the bed. She really didn't need this. She was supposed to be here to enjoy a break. Okay, so, retirement was way more than a break – but retirement felt like too big of a deal to face it all in one go. So, she kept telling herself that this trip to Summer Lake was just a break.

She scowled at her phone when it beeped with another text. What she really needed was a break from her daughter. Why she'd thought that bringing Mallory out here for the weekend was a good idea was beyond her. She knew better.

She snatched her phone up. It was Sunday afternoon, and Mallory would have to leave in a little while. As much as she wanted to, she really shouldn't just ignore her until she left.

Mallory: Meet me in the bar? We should talk before I leave.

Jo: I'll be down there in a few minutes.

Of course, when she got down there, there was no sign of Mallory. Jo pulled up a seat at the bar. All she needed to do was get through the next hour or so. Then, her daughter would go back to her life in Orange County, and tomorrow, Jo would be able to make a start on settling into her new life here in Summer Lake.

"Hello again. What can I get you? Is it one for the road before you leave us?"

She felt a touch of heat in her cheeks when the bartender, Damon, came to her with a big smile on his face. He'd been so friendly every time she came into the bar. She needed to get over it. It was just that he was good at his job – and she'd been starved of attention for so long, that a flirty bartender made her feel special.

"I'll take a G&T, heavy on the G." She smiled. "Don't worry. It isn't for the road."

He braced his hands on the edge of the bar and cocked his head to the side. He was a big man – huge. Even with the bar between them, he towered over her.

His eyes twinkled as he said, "Are you about to make my day and tell me that you're not leaving us? You're sticking around? That's the best news I've had all weekend."

She smiled through pursed lips. "I bet you say that to all the girls."

"Nope. Just you." He looked all around as if checking to see if anyone was listening before he leaned closer.

Jo automatically leaned in to hear what he had to say.

"Truth be told, I'm glad to see the back of some of them."

She laughed. She wasn't about to tell him – she felt awful even admitting it to herself – but she knew how he felt, she'd be glad to see the back of Mallory when she left.

He glanced over her shoulder and his smile disappeared. "I'll get you that G&T – and if you want to come back to see me tonight, after the crowds have departed, it'd be my pleasure to get you another."

She nodded happily. If he wanted to drum up some business – and fill his tip jar on a quiet night, she'd be happy to oblige. It'd beat sitting stewing in her hotel room over whatever parting shots Mallory left her with.

"Mom."

"Mallory." She plastered a smile on her face as she turned to greet her daughter.

"I'll need to get on the road shortly, but I wanted to see you before I go."

"I'm glad. I know you're not thrilled about me staying here, but I don't want to leave things on a sour note between us.

Let's just enjoy half an hour together before you leave, can we?"

Mallory's lips pressed into a thin line. "I can't enjoy anything about this place. It's …" she looked around "… it's ridiculous to think that you might move here."

As Jo sucked in a deep breath to steady herself, she noticed Damon slide her G&T across the bar. She shot him a grateful smile and took a drink before facing her daughter.

"I already have moved here, sweetheart. I'm going to look at the house tomorrow."

"But you can still back out! You haven't signed anything yet! Please, don't do it! Come home!"

Jo took another slug of her drink – grateful that Damon had done as she'd asked and gone heavy on the gin.

"Where exactly are you calling home?"

"You know damn well where I mean! I mean our home! The home where I grew up! The home that dad's hoping that you'll return to. And I'll tell you something, you should take this chance – he's not going to wait forever!"

Jo closed her eyes. "You mean the house that I moved out of more than a year ago? The house that he moved his secretary into two days after I left? I don't know how many ways I can say this, sweetheart. I really don't. I have no intention of going back to your father – *ever*. I'm not going to say anything else on the subject. I'm glad for you that you have a good relationship with him still – but I don't, and I have no desire to."

"Why won't you get it through your head? He's sorry. It's over with Juliette. He wants you home. Coming out here to a little town in the boonies like this is ridiculous!"

"I don't care if he's sorry! I don't care if his affair is over. All that matters to me is that the marriage is over. That's what you need to get through *your* head – and your father does, too."

"Why do you have to be so stubborn, Mom? This is no place for you! You should come home." Mallory wasn't exactly shouting, but her voice was raised.

Jo managed to rein herself in. This was pointless. She wasn't going to convince Mallory of anything, and she had no desire to get into a screaming match with her – especially not here.

She glanced around, feeling embarrassed. Damon was chatting with two men sitting farther down the bar – they were the only ones who'd been disturbed by Mallory's outburst. He gave her a reassuring smile, which she appreciated.

Even if all he was doing was earning his tips, she didn't care. He was the most supportive presence she'd had in her life for a long time.

He and the two guys he was with turned when a woman called from the entrance, "Hey guys, we'll meet you out on the terrace."

The woman had a friend with her, and they each had a dog on a leash. Jo had always wanted a dog. Just as she was wondering if getting a dog was finally going to be possible for her, Mallory interrupted her thoughts.

"You're not even listening to me, are you? I can see why Dad –"

No. That was too much. Jo had taken as much as she was going to. "Why he what, Mallory?" she snapped. "Why he started sleeping with his secretary? Why he threw away thirty years of marriage? Tell me what exactly it is that you can see – and then, maybe you can explain it to me."

Mallory opened her mouth to reply, but she didn't get the chance. One of the dogs barked and then, it was running through the restaurant – coming straight for them. Mallory screamed and fled. Jo watched in disbelief as Damon vaulted over the bar – just … vaulted, as if it was nothing. At the same time, the dog skidded to a halt in front of her. Jo somehow knew that it meant her no harm.

She felt even more assured of that when Damon positioned himself between her and the dog and said, "Sorry about that. I promise you, she's safe. She won't harm you."

He said it with such absolute confidence that she believed him. Still, she was a little stunned as she watched one of his friends lead the dog away.

"Hey."

She turned back to him when she realized that he was still standing beside her – in fact, he'd taken a step closer. She had to tip her head back to look up at him. This was the first time that they'd been on the same side of the bar, and he was even taller than she'd realized.

"Are you okay?"

"I am. Thanks. I'm fine. I will be." She looked around, wondering where Mallory had gotten to. "I need to check on my daughter."

He met her gaze and held it. "Can I still get you that drink later? Say, seven thirty?"

She nodded. It seemed strange to make an appointment to come down to the bar, but she owed him even more after he'd leapt in to protect her just now. And she already knew that she'd want another drink later. Her gaze landed on Mallory, who was complaining loudly about the dog to the woman who, Jo believed, owned the place.

"I'll be back later. I need to go and sort that out."

"Good luck."

"Thanks." She blew out a sigh – she was going to need it!

"What are you doing back here on your night off?"

Damon smiled at Taryn through pursed lips. "Just here for a drink."

She narrowed her eyes at him, and Dalton laughed beside her. "You mean that you're here to follow up on what Echo tried to help you with earlier?"

He grinned. "I guess I do."

Taryn gave them both a puzzled look, but Dalton wrapped his arm around her and pulled her against him. He ducked his head as if to kiss her but swerved away at the last moment and grinned at Damon.

"Make a break for it while I distract her."

Damon laughed at the way Taryn batted at Dalton to get off her, but he did as he'd told him and walked out to the front of the restaurant. It'd be better to meet Jo out there and avoid Taryn subjecting them to twenty questions.

He was still surprised at himself for asking Jo to meet him for a drink like this. He hadn't been on a date in years. He'd been joking with Lucky and Dalton earlier – asking if they'd ask Echo to do some matchmaking for him – and not five minutes later, Echo had come flying into the bar and stopped at Jo's feet. Damon didn't know what to make of that – but he did know that he wasn't going to waste the opportunity.

Jo had caught his attention the first time she came into the bar on Friday afternoon. There was just something about her. She was warm and funny and … he didn't know how to describe it, but he felt drawn to her.

After he'd met her daughter, he felt protective of her, too. He'd assumed that Jo would be leaving tonight, as most of the guests did, but when he discovered that she wasn't, he'd decided to take a chance and ask her out.

He smiled when he saw her hurrying down the hallway from the hotel lobby. Her stride faltered when she spotted him.

"Oh! I … is this right? Are you leaving?" She checked her watch, looking flustered.

He strode to meet her. "No. I'm not going anywhere – not without you, anyway."

She gave him a puzzled look. "Are you just starting your shift? Am I making you late? We'd better get in there."

He cocked his head to the side not understanding. "My shift?"

"Yes." Now, she looked confused. "I'm sorry. I think I have this wrong. You look like you're ready to leave. I thought you were working."

"I'm not working. Sunday is my night off. And I am ready to leave – I thought we could go over to the wine bar – have you been there?"

Her cheeks turned bright red. "I don't understand."

He chuckled. "Help me out – what don't you understand?"

"I thought I was coming to see you while you were working."

He stared at her. Shit. She thought he'd invited her back for a drink as a customer?

"Is that the only reason that you said yes?"

She met his gaze and held it. "I ... uh ..."

She looked so uncomfortable that he let her off the hook. "Okay. So, we had a bit of a misunderstanding. But here we are, so ... would you like to go for a drink with me? It's my night off, you see."

She still looked confused, but after a few moments, she smiled. "I would, thank you. I'd like that a lot."

He chuckled and offered her his arm. "Then come, let me introduce you to life in Summer Lake."

A sense of ease crept over him when she slipped her arm through his and smiled up at him.

"I haven't been here for long myself, but I can tell you that it's way more than just some small town in the boonies."

Her cheeks flushed. "You heard what Mallory said?"

"I did." He squeezed her arm. "Yeah, sorry about that but it was hard not to. I just want to say one thing, then I'll let it go."

"What's that?"

He smiled. "I'm proud of you. I don't really know you, and it's none of my business, but from what I heard, you're standing your ground, and starting a new life – that takes guts." He gave her a rueful smile. "I know because I've been there, too. I admire your strength."

"Thanks."

He couldn't read the look on her face, so he let it go. They were through the lobby and out in the plaza now.

"Anyway, let's go get that drink."

When she smiled at him, he felt something settle inside him. He didn't know what it was about her that made him feel so … at ease, but he was hoping that he might get the chance to find out;

;

PS Project Semicolon

You may have noticed that the final sentence of the story closed with a semi-colon. It isn't a typo. Project Semi Colon is a non-profit movement dedicated to presenting hope and love to those who are struggling with depression, suicide, addiction and self-injury. Project Semicolon exists to encourage, love and inspire. It's a movement I support with all my heart.

"A semicolon represents a sentence the author could have ended, but chose not to. The sentence is your life and the author is you." - Project Semicolon

This author started writing after her son was killed in a car crash. At the time I wanted my own story to be over, instead I chose to honour a promise to my son to write my 'silly stories' someday. I chose to escape into my fictional world. I know for many who struggle with depression, suicide can appear to be the only escape. The semicolon has become a symbol of support, and hopefully a reminder – Your story isn't over yet

Also by SJ McCoy

Summer Lake Silver
This series features couples in their fifties and older. Just because a few decades—or more—have skipped by since you were in your twenties it doesn't mean you can't find love, does it? Summer Lake Silver stories find happily-ever-afters for those who remember being thirty-something—vaguely.

Marianne and Clay in Like Some Old Country Song
Seymour and Chris in A Dream Too Far
Ted and Audrey in A Little Rain Must Fall
Diego and Izzy in Where the Rainbow Ends
Manny and Nina in Silhouettes Shadows and Sunsets
Teresa and Cal in More Than Sometimes
Russ and Ria in Like a Soft Sweet Breeze
Adam and Evelyn in When Words Are Not Enough
Dalton and Taryn in Can't Fight The Moonlight
Lucky and Dee in Meet Me Where the Stars Fall
Coming Next
Damon and Jo in Walking on Sunshine

Summer Lake Seasons
Angel and Luke in Take These Broken Wings
Zack and Maria in Too Much Love to Hide
Logan and Roxy in Sunshine Over Snow
Ivan and Abbie in Chase the Blues Away
Colt and Cassie in Forever Takes a While
Austin and Amber in Tell the Stars to Shine
Donovan and Elle in Please Don't Say Goodbye
Coming Next

Tiffany and Brayden in What's A Guy To Do?

Summer Lake Series
Emma and Jack in Love Like You've Never Been Hurt
Holly and Pete in Work Like You Don't Need the Money
Missy and Dan in Dance Like Nobody's Watching
Smoke and Laura in Fly Like You've Never Been Grounded
Michael and Megan in Laugh Like You've Never Cried
Kenzie and Chase in Sing Like Nobody's Listening
Gabe and Renée in Smile Like You Mean It
Missy and Dan's wedding in The Wedding Dance
Ben's backstory in Chasing Tomorrow
April and Eddie in Dream Like Nothing's Impossible
Nate and Lily in Ride Like You've Never Fallen
Ben's Story in Live Like There's No Tomorrow
Smoke and Laura's wedding in The Wedding Flight
Leanne and Ryan in Fight Like You've Never Lost

The Hamiltons
Cameron and Piper in Red Wine and Roses
Chelsea and Grant in Champagne and Daisies
Mary Ellen and Antonio in Marsala and Magnolias
Marcos and Molly in Prosecco and Peonies
Grady and Hannah in Milkshakes and Mistletoe
Jacob and Becca in Cognac and Cornflowers
Bentley and Alyssa in Bourbon and Bluebells
Slade and Willow in Whiskey and Willow
Coming Next
Xander and Tori in Vodka and Violets

Remington Ranch Series

Mason

Shane

Carter

Beau

Four Weddings and a Vendetta

A Chance and a Hope Trilogy
Chance Encounter

Finding Hope

Give Hope a Chance

MacFarland Ranch Series
Wade and Sierra in The Cowboy's Unexpected Love

Janey and Rocket in The Cowgirl's Unmistakable Love

Deacon and Candy in The Sheriff's Irresistible Love

Laney and Luke in The Cowgirl's Inevitable Love

Coming Next

Kolby and Callie in The Cowboy's Undeniable Love

Ace and Ari in The Rancher's Inescapable Love

The Davenports
Oscar

TJ

Reid

Spider

Love in Nashville
Autumn and Matt in Bring on the Night

Standalone Novella
Sully and Jess in If I Fall

About the Author

I'm SJ, a coffee addict, lover of chocolate and drinker of good red wines. I'm a lost soul and a hopeless romantic. Reading and writing are necessary parts of who I am. Though perhaps not as necessary as coffee! I can drink coffee without writing, but I can't write without coffee.

I grew up loving romance novels, my first boyfriends were book boyfriends, but life intervened, as it tends to do, and I wandered down the paths of non-fiction for many years. My life changed completely a few years ago and I returned to Romance to find my escape.

I write 'Sweet n Steamy' stories because to me there is enough angst and darkness in real life. My favorite romances are happy escapes with a focus on fun, friendships and happily-ever-afters, just like the ones I write.

These days I live in beautiful Montana, the last best place. If I'm not reading or writing, you'll find me just down the road in the park - Yellowstone. I have deer, eagles and the occasional bear for company, and I like it that way :0)

Made in United States
Orlando, FL
07 September 2023

36804472R10212